T0278427

IF
WE
TELL
YOU

FOR AURELIA, AND ZARA, AND JONAH

Published in Canada and the U.S. by Kids Can Press Ltd.
25 Dockside Drive, Toronto, ON M5A 0B5

Kids Can Press is a Corus Entertainment Inc. company

www.kidscanpress.com

The text is set in Minion Pro.

Edited by Patricia Ocampo and Tanya Trafford
Cover design and typsetting by Andrew Dupuis

Printed and bound in Canada in 6/2024 by Friesens

CM 24 0 9 8 7 6 5 4 3 2 1

FSC
www.fsc.org
MIX
Paper | Supporting
responsible forestry
FSC® C016245

Library and Archives Canada Cataloguing in Publication

Title: If we tell you / Nicola Dahlin.
Names: Dahlin, Nicola, author.
Identifiers: Canadiana (print) 20230569188 | Canadiana (ebook) 20240294513 | ISBN 9781525311475 (hardcover) | ISBN 9781525313578 (EPUB)
Subjects: LCGFT: Detective and mystery fiction. | LCGFT: Novels.
Classification: LCC PS8607.A2995 I33 2024 | DDC jC813/.6 — dc23

Kids Can Press gratefully acknowledges that the land on which our office is located is the traditional territory of many nations, including the Mississaugas of the Credit, the Anishnabeg, the Chippewa, the Haudenosaunee and the Wendat peoples, and is now home to many diverse First Nations, Inuit and Métis peoples.

We thank the Government of Ontario, through Ontario Creates and the Ontario Arts Council; the Canada Council for the Arts; and the Government of Canada for their financial support of our publishing activity.

IF
WE
TELL
YOU

NICOLA DAHLIN

Kids Can Press

CHAPTER
1

LEWIS

The pickup we stole had a crack right across the middle of the windshield. If you focused on it, the world split in two. I hunched down in the passenger seat, my eyes fixed on the stretch of road below the crack. Cameron jacked up the driver's seat and sat tall.

"You don't have a learner's permit," I said. "What if we get pulled over?"

My brother glanced my way. "Are you kidding me right now? *That's* what you're worried about?"

He was right. Ranking today's events on a scale of temporary disaster to life-threatening catastrophe, illegal driving would be a two at most. Car theft maybe a three.

What we'd left behind was a solid ten.

I hoped things couldn't get any worse, but the plan was sketchy. A lot could go wrong.

As we passed our town's boundary, I twisted around and watched the welcome sign disappear behind the bend in the road — *Longview, population 307.* Would they change it to *303*? Mom and Dad were gone, too. My stomach twisted, and I thought I might throw up the burger I'd wolfed at the barbecue. I wound down the window. The hot, dry wind funneled off the mountains, whipping my hair. *Mom and Dad will find us*, I told myself over and over.

As soon as the road straightened out, a motorbike tore past. Then it was just us and the highway and the sunshine-yellow canola fields on either side.

I closed the window against the buffeting wind and took a breath. I needed to calm down and work through solutions to the most obvious worst-case scenarios. So far, this day had been like a math problem — a random collection of constants and variables that were somehow connected. We'd almost died today. If I didn't work out why, it could happen again.

Cameron swore. His hands gripped the wheel.

Before I could ask what was going on, I saw it — a blue flashing light in the distance.

I searched the fields on either side of the highway, already knowing there were no gaps in the fences on this section of road, but hoping one would appear. Our closest escape route was the Wagner Ranch road, but the police would reach us long before we got there.

The patrol car roared toward us, and we rattled to meet it in a stolen truck. I concentrated on breathing. *Suck in a lungful of air. Whoosh it out. In and out. In and out.*

I breathed until I was calm enough to care that I was inhaling mold and dog hair, then I checked on Cameron. The only parts of him that weren't rigid were his eyes, which darted between the approaching cop car and the speedometer.

"You're going too slow," I said.

"You're supposed to slow down when their lights are flashing."

"Only if they're stopped at the side of the road."

He glared at me. "Do you want to drive?"

No way. We'd been driving since we were twelve, but Dad taught us on dirt roads, which have their own set of challenges like potholes and cattle drives and getting sucked into ditches when you edge past a combine. But dirt roads don't have stoplights or lane markings, or patrol cars zooming toward you with blue flashing lights.

"Cameron." I gripped the edge of my seat.

He turned on the radio — a cheery country song about being sixteen, wild and free, which made everything seem worse. What I needed was for Cameron to tell me that everything would be okay and that he had a plan. But he was belting out the chorus, eyes fixed on the road, his lanky body jamming to the beat. How could he sing about being sixteen, when we might not live long enough to know what being sixteen was like?

As the siren's wail filled the car, drowning out the music, I forced myself to seat-dance. I was a carefree fifteen-year-old who was *not* racing away from a crime scene in a stolen pickup truck. I didn't need a mirror to know I looked ridiculous. I had my twin.

I snuck a look into the patrol car as it screamed past — two grim-looking officers. Neither had the full beard of our local sheriff, or the thick glasses of his deputy. Strangers, thank goodness, who hopefully wouldn't remember seeing us.

Cameron glanced in the rearview mirror, then smacked the steering wheel. "Yes!"

A giddy excitement bubbled in my stomach. We'd done it.

But what would happen when they arrived at the barbecue

and discovered we'd run?

"Drive faster," I said.

Cameron glanced at the dashboard. "Right. Sorry, still in stealth mode."

He pressed his foot on the gas, revving the engine until the truck got the message and accelerated.

I checked the map on my phone — fifty-one minutes until our destination. I switched off the radio.

Cameron turned it back on.

I lowered the volume. He increased it, glanced at me for a reaction, then turned it back to a fraction above where I'd set it.

Cameron's dedication to country music was one of the many things about him I didn't understand. Why he'd given himself a buzz cut last week was another. Our ears were too big for short hair, and to make matters worse, he had a tan line in the middle of his forehead. I'd never shave my head. Which, come to think of it, was probably why Cameron had shaved his.

Two songs later, the yellow canola fields morphed to green ranch land. Wagner's chestnut cows wandered aimlessly in the fields. Munching grass, the sun on their hides, no decisions other than which of their buddies to follow around, no worries other than swishing their tails to get rid of flies. No idea they were beef cattle, or that they'd be dead by next spring.

"Why are we running away?" Cameron asked.

"Because we're not cows."

Cameron smacked my arm. "Lewis, focus."

"Ow!" I stopped staring at cows and turned my attention to my brother. His eyebrows were pulled together. His lips tight.

"I can't work this out alone," he said.

"You're driving. I'm navigating. How is that alone?" I checked my phone. "Forty-three minutes. Traffic looks good."

He glanced at me. "What happened back there — it wasn't our fault."

He was right, it wasn't. But it didn't change anything.

Cameron rubbed his head. Looked out his window. Then eyes back to the road. "We shouldn't have to run and leave everything behind."

He meant Molly — he didn't want to leave Molly behind. She was my best friend, too, but this wasn't the time to worry about things we couldn't change.

"I'm not talking about this." I turned up the radio.

Country music hurt my ears, but it was better than having a pointless conversation. We couldn't go home, not now, maybe not ever.

Cameron plucked a bag of sunflower seeds off the dashboard, then held them out to me. They reminded me of road trips with Mom and Dad — stopping for gas-station ice cream and chewing on seeds in between. Mom was the champion. She could work the sunflower kernels out of the husk faster than any of us.

I dug out a pinch of seeds, popped them in my mouth. Cameron did the same. My tongue worked at a husk, but before I could free the kernel, Cameron opened his window and spat. We chewed and spat until our jaws ached and the scratch of the husks made our tongues raw.

Two lanes became four as we merged onto the highway.

"Does your route take us past the track?" Cameron asked.

"Probably." The go-karting track was next to the airport, between the Amazon warehouses and rental-car storage lots. It was Mom and Dad's go-to treat for our birthday, and always a big deal. We hardly ever came into the city because Dad didn't like crowds and Mom hated the noise.

Cameron turned off the radio, then rested his arm on the center console. Whatever he was about to say, I wasn't going to like it.

He cleared his throat. "There's a police station a block from there."

My hands shook as I zoomed the map on my phone. "I'll find a different route."

"I think we should go," he said. "To the police."

"Not funny." This was so not the time for messing around.

I zoomed the map too far and got a bunch of meaningless lines.

Cameron hit the brakes. My seat belt locked.

"Sorry, didn't see the lights change," he said.

I closed the map app, then opened it up again and typed in the airport.

Cameron tapped the steering wheel.

"Got it," I said. "We can make a right turn a few blocks before the police station."

"I'm not leaving Canada."

What? Was he serious?

I stared at him. "Mom and Dad gave us a plan. And it does *not* include staying in Canada or going to police stations, regardless of their proximity to recreational facilities. You heard Dad. *Calgary airport. Trust no one.*"

The backpack Mom had thrust into my arms as I'd tried to hug her was between my feet. *It contains everything you'll need,* she'd said. She was wrong. It didn't contain my parents, for a start, and I was pretty sure it wasn't harboring a spare brain for my brother.

I glared at Cameron. "The only reason we're driving to the city is so we can leave it. Immediately. On a plane."

"And fly across the ocean to meet some woman Mom's never mentioned before?" He made his you're-so-naive face. "Maybe we should save a seat on the plane for whoever's trying to kill us. We could all check in together. Share snacks."

He was trying to be a smart-ass, but his hand went to his stubbled head. He always dragged his hand through his hair when he was nervous or scared, and right now, he was probably both. We both were. Which was why, for once in his life, he needed to do what he was told.

After a long pause, he added, "We've done nothing wrong. The police will help us. They protect the innocent. Trust me."

Whenever Cameron said "trust me," it usually ended badly. It wasn't that he didn't think things through, he just always focused on the problem directly in front of him and was overly optimistic about the outcome. If this *had* been a math problem, he would've flipped to the back of the textbook by now. And copied down the wrong answer.

"And what about Mom and Dad?" I said.

"Wherever we go, they'll find us; you know they will."

"We're following the plan." I leaned as far away from him as I could get. My seat belt jammed. I huffed. Undid it. Shifted and reclipped.

We drove in silence past the big houses on the outskirts of the city, the ones owned by rich city people who wanted to be ranchers, but without the hard work. Four lanes became six, and the fake ranches were replaced by houses crammed so close together they looked like they were sheltering from a snowstorm.

The traffic got denser. Cameron's grip on the wheel got tighter. A semi thundered past us, shaking our truck. Sweat beads formed on Cameron's forehead as he steered against the back draft.

"You've got this," I said.

I kept my eyes on the traffic and alerted Cameron whenever I saw brake lights or stoplights or lanes blocked by roadwork.

As downtown's glass skyscrapers rose above the sprawl, signs for the airport appeared. My heart rate slowed down. Cameron's knuckles relaxed.

I counted down the exits for Cameron, who stayed in the slow lane even when we got stuck behind a horse trailer.

Three more exits to the airport.

Two.

"Next exit," I said.

Cameron nodded.

I recognized the street where the highway spat us out. It had a pattern to it — park zone, two blocks of stucco bungalows, strip mall, stoplight, repeating over and over for miles. This one city street held more houses than our village and the neighboring two towns combined.

A plane passed overhead, its jet engines rumbling through my chest. I watched it streak across the blue sky and leave a trail of white. Two hours from now, we'd be up there and on our way to Edinburgh.

"The right turn's coming up," I said. "At the next set of lights."

Cameron sailed through the stoplights without turning.

I looked at my phone as it recalculated the route to the airport. "Don't worry, we can take the next right."

He turned left. And left again.

Into a parking lot.

Without a word of explanation, he slid into a spot. Pulled on the hand brake. Unclipped his seat belt.

I peered out the window at a redbrick and glass building, *Calgary Police Service* emblazoned across it in blue lettering. Was he serious? He'd actually brought us here?

I grabbed my brother's arm. "Mom said no police."

"Mom's not here. She left us, remember?" He jerked out of my hold, reached into the back seat to grab his backpack, then swung open his door. "You don't have to come with me."

He jumped out. Slammed the door.

And I was alone.

Then I was slinging my backpack over one shoulder, racing after him, my sneakers slapping hot pavement.

Cameron had made it to the entrance before I managed to catch hold of his backpack. He spun around, forcing me to let go.

The doors whooshed open, and my brother turned and stepped inside.

Mom said no police.

But Dad had said to stay together — *stick together but stay apart; identical twins are memorable.*

My heart was thumping in my ears — stay-or-go, stay-or-go, stay-or-go.

Traffic rumbled. Above my head, the Canadian flag fluttered merrily in the breeze.

Going in there would be like climbing to the top of a roller coaster with no idea what was on the other side. It could be another climb, a loop-de-loop, or we could run out of track and plummet to our deaths. Mom would tell me to breathe. I sucked in a lungful of air, then puffed it all out. It didn't work. My heart was still racing. My stomach twisted in knots.

I pulled out my phone. Hit Mom's number.

It went straight to voice mail.

The doors whooshed open again.

Cameron stood in the doorway, determination on his face. "Hurry up."

My shoulder brushed the flagpole as I raced inside.

CHAPTER
2

CAMERON

The police station was all glass and chrome, and if it wasn't for the cops striding across the white tile, I'd think we'd stepped into a fancy downtown office.

Lewis stood behind me, breathing. And every breath was telling me this was the worst idea ever. But I wasn't going to run away without trying the obvious first. Lewis might be smarter than me, and Mom and Dad more capable, but I was the only one who wasn't panicking. Yes, my heart was thumping as if I'd just sprinted ten laps of the Baxters' field, and yes, my muscles were urging me to keep running, but at least I was thinking straight.

Lewis squeezed my arm. "We're going to miss our plane."

I marched up to the reception desk, closed in with glass. A sign taped to the window told us we were all *working together for a safer city*. My mouth went dry.

The officer on duty was typing, her fingers flying over the keys. Her eyes darted back and forth between a handwritten form and her computer screen. I cleared my throat.

Without looking up, she slid a form under the window.

"We're here to report a serious crime," I said.

Lewis appeared beside me. "A serious *event*. Not a crime."

I glared at him. He needed to let me do the talking. "I'm Cameron Larsen, and this is my brother, Lewis. We're from Longview. We'll be in your system by now."

The officer let out an impatient breath, then looked up. She glanced at me, then Lewis, then me again. The usual reaction. Really? I'd sacrificed my hair, and we still looked the same?

"Take a ticket. Fill out the form." She pointed to a red ticket machine on the counter, then to people waiting on rows of gray plastic chairs off to the side. They all looked like ordinary, law-abiding citizens, but what did I know? I thought my parents were, too.

Lewis tore off a ticket, his eyes wide with a silent *what are we doing here?*

I snatched the form off the counter and sat in the first row of seats. My backpack clunked against the backrest.

Lewis hovered. "We should leave. They don't seem interested."

"They will be," I said without looking up from the form. Once they realized who we were.

I squished both our first names into the box at the top of the form. Everything else was the same — family name, address, date of birth. I checked my phone for today's date — August 2, halfway through summer vacation. Giving a statement wouldn't be easy, but by the time school started up, the police would have everything sorted, Mom and Dad would be off the hook and life would be back to normal.

Lewis sat down beside me. I could hear him breathing again as he read over my shoulder. It was killing him that I was filling out the form, but he was left-handed and he'd smudge the ink.

And if Lewis hated anything more than insufficient detail, it was messiness.

My hand shook as I filled in the *Summary of the Incident* box. I stuck to the basics. It only took two sentences. Seeing it on the page made me doubt myself — had it really happened? I made a tight fist, then relaxed, hoping it would steady my hand. *Stay calm, don't freak out Lewis any more than he already is.*

"You should say they were white, and the woman was blond, and the man was bald," Lewis said. "And you didn't fill in eye color. The man's were coffee-bean brown, the woman's hazel-ish."

The only time I'd seen their eyes was when they were empty and staring at the sky. But I'd been distracted by the bullet hole and the blood, and screaming for my parents.

"Analyzing the exact shade of their irises wasn't my top priority." I scribbled *brown eyes.* "Happy?"

"He was about six-two, she was five-eight-ish."

"You're kidding, right?" Did he really not get it? "They're lying dead on our patio, Lewis. The sheriff will know their shoe size by now."

A woman with a little kid curled up beside her glared at us, then covered the kid's ears. I tried to smile. Lewis did his goofy wave. I wanted to tell her they'd tried to kill us first. I wanted to stand on the chair and scream, *This is not our fault!*

"Number 560," the officer behind the desk called. "Please approach."

A round man wearing a flannel shirt and a baseball cap jumped up. I followed him to the counter and slid our form under the window.

When I got back to the chairs, Lewis was unfolding our ticket, which now looked more like a spitball. "We're 571 — eleven people ahead of us. We'll never make our flight."

I shrugged out of my backpack and sat back down. I'd give a statement, convince the police Mom and Dad were innocent, then we'd go home. Mom and Dad would figure out where we were and come back. The more I thought about it, the more I realized how simple it was. The pressure in my chest faded. My legs didn't feel hollow anymore.

Beside me, Lewis opened his backpack, pulled out a hoodie, then dug around inside. I'd never seen the packs before this afternoon. Mom had rushed off to retrieve them, while Dad told us the plan. The fact that they'd had them packed and ready meant this afternoon hadn't been a complete surprise. Why hadn't they warned us? Lewis I could understand, but me? I was the oldest. They should've told me.

Lewis opened a passport, flicked through the pages, then zipped it away in an inside pocket of his pack and kept rummaging.

A group of cops clomped by on their way to the coffee machine.

A bag of chips crinkled behind us.

The woman beside us told her son it wouldn't be much longer.

The AC continued to hiss out fake air.

I closed my eyes, but saw the knife sticking out of torn flesh and the bullet wound. Mom looking fierce. Our neighbors screaming. Dad holding a gun. Blood pooling.

I snapped my eyes open and focused on the floor. The chair legs were bolted to the white tiles. A candy wrapper lay scrunched and forgotten. *Trust no one. Calgary airport, then Edinburgh.*

A cop strode into the waiting area and cleared his throat. The guy had a mullet and his neck muscles were so jacked that blue veins stood out against his pasty white skin. He looked more like a hockey player than a cop.

"Cameron and Lewis Larsen." He pointed to a door marked *No Entry.* "Follow me."

I felt a sudden urge to run away.

Instead, I ignored my racing heart and the panic on Lewis's face, swung my backpack over my shoulder and approached the cop. With every step, I willed my brother to do the same.

The cop held the door. "Both of you."

I looked back at Lewis, who was perched on the edge of his seat, his mouth hanging open.

Time stretched.

Eventually, Lewis stood, glanced at the exit, then stumbled toward us.

The cop led us through an open area — desks half occupied by uniforms, phone conversations, tapping of computer keys. Past a vending machine. Into a corridor lined with doors. At the far end, an exit sign glowed red. *Identify your escape routes.* It's what Dad always told us. *Emergencies by definition are unexpected.*

Halfway down the corridor, the cop opened a door. "In here."

Lewis nudged me inside, then followed. The tiny room had no windows, just a white plastic table and four wooden chairs. The ceiling was the same gray as the walls, which made it feel like it was pressing down on me, the walls closing in.

"Stay put." The cop banged the door shut.

I spun around, shoved Lewis out of the way and yanked the door open again.

"Will you be okay in here?" Lewis said.

"I'm good. We won't be here long." If I repeated it enough times, maybe I wouldn't feel so claustrophobic. Maybe the pressure in my chest would ease off. Maybe the smell of stale sweat and confinement would fade. I tried to ignore that I was trapped in a box-like room and concentrated on Mom's trick of counting backward from twenty, eyes closed, pretending I was in the back field.

Lewis dragged a chair over to prop open the door.

Seventeen, sixteen, fifteen.

"Do you think they'll believe us?" he said.

Twelve, eleven, ten.

I took a deep breath and opened my eyes. "I'll do the talking."

Lewis probably remembered every detail and had analyzed the heck out of each one, but a story can be told different ways, and if I was better than Lewis at anything, it was knowing how to tell the right story. This was up to me. I had to keep it together. I'd give a statement, and we'd get out of this room and go home.

Lewis drummed his fingers on the table.

"Stop doing that," I said. "And the leg thing."

He put his hands on his knees to stop them jiggling. "Should I go and get us something from the vending machine? It had chips."

My phone buzzed in my pocket. Molly. A rambling text with question marks and exclamations. The cops were still in our yard. Everyone had been interviewed, and they were now searching our house. I should never have left. Did Molly think I was a coward for running away? I texted back we were at the police station sorting it out and that I'd be home soon.

Footsteps approached, and then a Black lady wearing a pink blouse dragged the chair from the door back to the table. The door swung shut, and the room shrunk.

It's just a room. I can leave any time I want.

The detective sat, laid our form on the table and assessed us — Lewis's shaggy hair and his crumpled *Math? Easy as pi* T-shirt, then my shorn head and soccer top.

"You're a long way from home. Two fifteen-year-old boys with a morbidly spectacular story to tell." She motioned for me to sit.

The table was pitted with cigarette burns, and there was a gross, sticky patch right in front of me. I leaned back in my chair and folded my arms.

The detective clicked a pen. "I'm Detective Abdo," she said. "How about we start at the beginning?"

The beginning, I decided, was the point in the day when nothing had happened, but everything changed. "Someone stashed a bag of guns in our garage."

"What?" Lewis spun in his chair and stared at me.

"It was you who told me to look in there." Which was true.

"For beer." Lewis looked at Detective Abdo. "I told him to look in the garage for alcohol, not firearms."

I glanced at the clock above the door — it was later than I thought. Our friends would be heading to the creek soon. Everyone would be there. Except us. And the beer.

"Did your parents have permits for these weapons?" Detective Abdo looked from Lewis to me, her face unreadable.

I shook my head. The bag was hidden in the pile of camping gear. I assumed someone, maybe one of Dad's logging crew, had decided our overstuffed garage was the perfect place to hide illegal guns. I expected Mom and Dad to be shocked when I told them. Turns out they weren't.

The detective sat back in her chair and waited for me to continue.

"They weren't normal guns." I wiped sweaty palms on my shorts and tried to keep my voice strong. "Two had silencers screwed on the ends. I think the other two were automatic." I'd seen hunting rifles before. Half of our neighbors had them. The ones I found didn't belong to farmers. They were for snipers on rooftops or soldiers in battle.

The bag also contained a knife, silver-handled and double-edged, which could've been for skinning deer. I'd been wrong about that, too.

"Had *you* ever seen these guns before?" the detective asked Lewis.

Lewis was glaring at me, his mouth open. I nudged him.

He jumped out of whatever worry was spiraling through his brain and looked at Abdo, eyes wide. "No! Mom hates guns. We weren't even allowed cap guns. She hates knives, too. In fact, anything scary. She's against all forms of violence. Especially gun related. And knife related. The throwing kind as well as the stabbing ones."

An image of Mom throwing the knife — *thwack*— into the woman's chest flew through my mind.

Abdo tapped her pen on the table.

Sweat trickled down my back. *Crap, this room is hot.*

"Tell me about your parents." Abdo's pen hovered above a pad of paper.

What did she want to know? That Mom closed her eyes when she laughed and drove our truck like a race car? That she loved sitting in the back field painting the mountains as the sun set? That she still tucked me in at night, even though I was three inches taller than her? Would the police care that Dad smelled of pine trees and engine oil and wore a beanie, even though I'd told him it wasn't cool? That he whistled while he cooked, chewed his bottom lip when he helped me with homework and cried when he heard songs from the eighties? That our neighbors called him "Davey"?

I thought I knew my parents.

Turns out, I didn't.

I shrugged. "Not much to tell."

Lewis shifted his chair closer to the table. "Our parents are nice people. Our mom drives Mrs. Baxter to the supermarket every week because she doesn't see so well anymore. And our dad's always the one who goes out in snowstorms to help people when they drive off the road and get stuck. Ask anyone in Longview. Or Turner Valley. They'll tell you the same." He sank back. "Everyone loves them."

Abdo wrote something in her notepad, then glanced at our form. "And what can you tell me about the victims? Other than the color of their eyes."

Lewis was sitting too close. I shifted away from him.

"No one noticed them at first," Lewis said. "We were having a barbecue, and our yard was full of people."

"We'll need a list of witnesses," Abdo said, making it sound like a challenge.

I leaned forward. "The RCMP already have everyone's names. And their statements."

"And the corpses," Lewis added. "They'll have them, too."

I'd left Molly to explain two dead bodies to the police. My last text had said we'd be home soon. Could I keep that promise?

I rubbed my head. "Can you skip to the bit where you tell us what the heck's going on and that you have everything under control?"

Abdo sat back in her chair. "Why did you run from the scene of a double murder?"

I jerked forward in my chair. "It wasn't murder."

"It was definitely self-defense," Lewis added.

"What made you think your lives were in danger?"

"Getting shot in the head tends to be fatal." I rubbed my temple, remembering the feel of the cold, hard barrel of the gun digging in. Remembered the panic in my bones, as if my entire body had been scooped out and I was watching and hearing everything from a distance. Someone had screamed. Our neighbors were huddled in one dark blur.

"The man grabbed Cameron," Lewis said. "Put him in a neck hold and shoved a gun against his head. Then the woman pointed a gun at me. They were serious. If our parents hadn't killed them, we'd be dead."

"It was a hostage-type situation?" The detective clicked her pen.

"Exactly," Lewis said. "That's exactly what it was."

"What did they demand? Money? Jewelry?"

"Probably," Lewis said.

Abdo raised her eyebrows.

"They weren't speaking English," I said.

"And did your parents reply? In any language?"

Lewis shook his head. I stared over Abdo's shoulder at the door.

Mom had been crouched on the roof of our shed. One second, she was holding the knife, the next, it thudded into the woman's chest.

The arm around my neck tightening.

A pop of a gun.

The ground rushing toward me.

I thought I'd been shot. And all I could think was, *Will Lewis be okay without me?*

And then my brother was dragging me to my feet, and Dad was sprinting toward us, a gun in his hand. Blood seeped from a bullet hole between the eyes of the man who'd grabbed me.

My stomach twisted at the memory. I glanced at Lewis. He was alive. We were both still alive.

"Where are your parents now?" Abdo asked.

Lewis looked down at his hands. "We don't know."

Mom and Dad had driven in the opposite direction, the hay bale they'd offered to drop off for Molly's horse still in the bed of the truck. I thought they'd change their minds and come back for us. They didn't.

"Could you repeat that?" Abdo said.

I sat up straight. "My brother said we don't know. They left. We don't know where they are now."

"So, it was your decision to leave Longview?" Her eyes narrowed. "How exactly *did* you get here?"

Crap.

The original cop, the wannabe hockey star, burst in, chest puffed. "Can I have a minute?"

Abdo scraped back her chair. "Excuse me for a moment."

As soon as the door clicked shut, I texted Molly to ask which officers had turned up. I should never have left.

Lewis shifted to face me. "Why didn't you tell me about the guns?"

I watched the dots blink on my phone — she was typing back.

Lewis punched my arm. "Cameron."

"I thought you'd panic." Because he always did.

"Why would you care if I panicked? As you constantly keep telling me, you're not my babysitter."

I ran my hand through my hair, but there wasn't enough to pull on. I'd cut it too short, but it was a small price to pay. Nobody had confused me for Lewis in the last couple of days, and our soccer coach had finally shouted my name rather than the number on the back of my shirt.

My phone pinged, and I dipped my head to read Molly's reply.

I don't recognize them. They didn't tell us their names. What's happening? Are you both OK?

What the heck? Turner Valley had four RCMP officers, and we knew them all. They drank coffee in the Lazy Horse Café and visited our school every semester to read out gruesome statistics about drugs. If Molly didn't recognize them, they weren't local.

I turned the phone to show Lewis.

He read the text, then jumped up. "Why did they send out-of-town police? I told you we should've gone straight to the airport."

"You're panicking," I said. "Just like Mom and Dad were panicking when they told us to run."

He looked at me. "Have you even looked in your backpack? Mom and Dad gave us passports and plane tickets and rolls of cash. And burner phones. They thought this through."

My stomach dropped. What kind of people kept rolls of cash and burner phones at the ready?

"Mom and Dad killed two people," I said. "On purpose. Without hesitating."

The words were out before I could stop them. But the Mom and Dad I knew weren't murderers. So, which version of them was true?

"What are you saying?" Lewis looked at me as if he didn't know me. "You don't trust them? They don't love us anymore? We should stop being a family?"

Of course Mom and Dad loved us. They'd killed two people to keep us safe. And I loved them. But maybe not as much as Lewis did? Was that it? I didn't love Mom and Dad enough to do what they'd told me to do? I dropped my forehead into my hands. This was too difficult.

The door dragged over the carpet again as it opened. Lewis scuttled back into the chair beside me. I raised my head. My vision blurred for a second, and then Abdo and her sidekick were sitting opposite us.

Sidekick looked pissed. Abdo disappointed.

"Do you have any ID?" Abdo said.

"Passports." I picked my backpack off the floor.

Lewis squeezed my arm. "We didn't bring them, remember?"

I dug in my backpack for the passport. Lewis kicked me in the shin, then trod on my foot, applying pressure until I got the message and dropped my bag.

"Jennifer and David Larsen do not reside at the address you gave," Abdo said. "There's a David Larsen in Calgary, but he's ninety-three. No Jennifer Larsens anywhere in the entire province."

"You're wrong. Check again." What the heck was going on?

"Just to confirm," Lewis said. "You did type in *Longview*?"

Sidekick banged his fist on the table. "Okay kids, fun's over."

"Fun?" Anger shot through my veins. "You think we made up watching people die for fun? You think our parents abandoned us for a laugh?"

"Our mom's an artist," Lewis said. "She works in the Longview gallery. You could search up their website."

There were no photos of her, but her name was on the webpage and so were her paintings. I looked Abdo in the eyes. "And our dad works for the Western Forest logging company. Call them. They'll tell you."

"There's no record of Lewis and Cameron Larsen either," Sidekick said. "Not with your date of birth. Not twins anyway. Which you two obviously are."

Lewis hugged his backpack.

A lump formed in my throat. "What does that mean?"

"It means either you're lying to us, or you don't exist." Abdo stood. "So, which is it?"

CHAPTER 3

LEWIS

I'd expected this to be a roller-coaster ride, but we'd been thrown clear off the track into an alternate reality where our whole family didn't exist. It had to be a mistake. How could we not exist?

"We're not lying," Cameron said. "And obviously we exist, we're right here in front of you. So, what's the third option?"

"There isn't one," Detective Abdo said.

Cameron's chair toppled as he stood. "Yes. There is."

My heart rate had been too high for too long. Did that mean my blood was getting too much oxygen or too little? I tried to remember what we'd learned in science class. Tried to imagine the textbook. The diagram of the heart's chambers and valves. It didn't work. My heart continued to race. Panic still buzzed inside my head like a swarm of bees.

"I need you to calm down, son," the deputy said, his eyes focused on Cameron.

Cameron hunched as if he was about to lunge at the man. "I am *not* your son."

According to Detective Abdo, we were nobody's sons.

My head started to spin along with the bees inside of it. A racing heart must lead to insufficient oxygen — I now had real-life data to prove it. I gripped the corner of the table. *I am Jennifer and David Larsen's son. I have parents. I have a brother.*

Detective Abdo righted Cameron's chair. "Let's all take a breath."

Her deputy grunted. Cameron shifted his chair farther back from the table before slumping back into it.

The detective clasped her hands on the table. "You seem like good kids."

I nodded. We were. Everything would be fine. They might not believe us, but they'd help us because, like Cameron said, the police helped the innocent.

"Have you taken drugs?" the deputy said.

"No!" I looked at Cameron to back me up, but he was looking at the ceiling, shaking his head.

"One of your friends offered you a pill." Detective Abdo took over in a friendlier tone. "And you took it, just to try."

"That's your answer to all of this?" Cameron said. "We took drugs and made it up?"

I glanced at the clock above the door — only forty minutes until our plane took off. I'd never been on a plane before, but how difficult could it be? The airport terminal was five minutes away. We could still make it.

My brother would get us out of this. He always had a plan. Like the time we went snowmobiling with Molly on Widows Peak and got caught in a snowstorm. Cameron was the only one who held it together and found us shelter. Or when we snuck out to Hunter's party and drove the truck into a ditch. It was Cameron who figured out how to get us out.

"Schenk," Cameron said. "The man who grabbed me was called Schenk."

I glared at Cameron. What kind of plan was that? We needed to shut this down, apologize, then run.

Cameron's eyes urged me to help him out. "When Dad crouched over the guy's body, remember?"

Of course I remembered. Dad had closed the dead man's eyelids, then said, *I can't believe they sent Schenk.* But instead of answering Cameron, I tipped my head in the direction of the door. If we had any hope of catching the plane, we needed to leave *now*.

Detective Abdo clicked on her pen. "And how would you spell *Schenk*?"

Cameron threw up his hands. "How the heck should we know? We never met him before, and he was too dead to introduce himself."

The minute hand on the clock snapped forward.

"Was it a dare?" the deputy said.

"What? You think our dad shot someone for a dare?" Cameron said.

My muscles twitched with the urge to sprint out of there.

"I think maybe *you're* here on a dare," the deputy replied. "Wasting police time is an offense, so maybe you could meet us halfway and explain why you decided to spend a sunny Saturday afternoon dreaming up fake names and reporting a crime that never happened."

"What about the two dead bodies?" Cameron said. "What more proof do you need?"

Twenty-five minutes until the plane took off. I kicked Cameron under the table. He kicked me back.

"We called the RCMP," Detective Abdo said. "And they confirmed what the system already told us. No one called 911. No emergency vehicles were dispatched. No crimes were committed today. In fact, in Longview's long and distinguished history, no one has ever been shot. Your sheriff was quite smug about that."

What?

"No!" Cameron jumped out of his chair.

"All of our neighbors called 911," I said. "Molly, the Baxters, everyone at the barbecue; we saw them all calling."

"There must've been at least *twenty* 911 calls." Cameron threw up his hands. "How could you miss that?"

Detective Abdo stood, then picked up her notepad. "It's the holiday weekend, and it's thirty-five degrees outside. Half my team's rescuing drunk teenagers from drowning in the river, and the other half are responding to domestics. And I'd like to get home in time to take my children for ice cream, so please, talk it over and decide whether you want to be driven home with a caution or spend the night in a cell before we ship you off to juvie."

She slid our statement and a pen across the table, then followed her deputy to the door, where she paused. "If you don't feel safe going home, there are better options than a police record. The city has lots of good youth programs."

"Our parents will look after us." As soon as we found them, they'd look after us.

The second the door clicked shut behind her, I snatched my backpack from the back of the chair and Cameron's from the floor. "We need to go."

"Why don't the police know about the bodies?" Cameron

looked lost.

"Remember the last thing Mom told us?" I clutched his shoulders. *"A truth relies on what came before it."*

Cameron frowned.

I hadn't understood what Mom meant either. I mean, something's either true, or it isn't. But now that I was no longer me, I understood. People believed I was Lewis Larsen because that's what Mom and Dad had told everyone. The truth of me being Lewis was built on fifteen years of lies.

"If we want to know what's true and what isn't," I said, "we need to find out what happened before today, maybe even before we were born, and we can't do that if we're locked up."

I could see my brother thinking. His eyebrows pulling together while he tried to figure out a new plan. But we already had one, and it started with catching a plane, which was about to take off.

"Cameron, we need to leave." I shoved his backpack into his stomach. "Before the police come back."

Finally, he nodded an okay.

I let out a breath, then opened the door a notch. Detective Abdo was on the phone. Everyone else looked busy and completely uninterested in us.

"Go left," Cameron said. "There's an exit at the end of the hall."

We crept toward the gloomy end of the corridor, where an exit sign glowed red. I hesitated — would the door be alarmed? Cameron pushed on the bar. My body tensed, waiting for a siren that never came.

CHAPTER
4

C A M E R O N

Lewis's eyes were blank and staring at the sky, a bullet hole between them. Blood pooled. Molly screamed.

I woke with a jolt, gasping. My phone clattered to the floor. It took me a few breaths to remember where I was, to get my heart rate under control. I was in the airport. Lying across hard plastic seats, waiting for a flight because it turned out you couldn't just sprint onto the runway and hop on a plane.

We'd made it through check-in and security, and into the departures hall in time to watch our plane soar into the sky. Lewis and I had checked in at separate desks and both been told the same thing — we'd arrived too late. The next flight to Edinburgh was in two days' time. The only way to get to Britain now was to catch the London flight, which left in five hours.

I glugged the rest of the water I'd bought, then scooped my phone off the floor and read Molly's last text for the hundredth time.

The police told me not to contact you. For your own safety.

I messaged her again. Another version of my last twenty unanswered texts: I'll come home soon. Please let me know you're OK.

The departure hall gradually emptied until the waiting area for the flight to London was the only one with any people left in it. I was sitting at the other end of the terminal in an empty waiting area, surrounded by other empty waiting areas. It was now dark outside. Planes no longer taxied past the window. There were no last calls for flights to Frankfurt or Amsterdam, or requests for missing passengers to make their way to gates 72 or 83 or 87. No rushed footsteps accompanied by the rumble of wheels. Just the odd bang of a bucket from the cleaning crews.

I went to find Lewis.

I wished I could be like him — trust that Mom and Dad were waiting for us in Britain armed with nothing but a reasonable explanation. Maybe my brother's big brain had managed to dream up a scenario where our parents were retired superheroes or victims of amnesia. But I didn't want them to be anyone else, because if they were, then who was I?

The passport in my back pocket said I was Daniel Johnston from Vancouver. Nobody was looking for him. Not even his friends. He had none. But I was still me. Brown eyes, brown hair, caterpillar eyebrows, legs incapable of building muscle, a crooked pinky finger from when Lewis slammed it in the truck door when we were five. A new name didn't change that.

And I still had a brother, who was sitting five gates away.

Turned out Daniel Johnston from Vancouver *didn't* have a brother.

Lewis held out his passport. "See?" Under Lewis's photo was the name *Thomas Walker*.

Lewis looked like crap. His thick hair stuck out, and dark rings circled his eyes. His new white *caution, moose-crossing* shirt, bought at the airport's gift shop, was already crumpled, half tucked. I probably didn't look much better. Other than my hair, which wasn't long enough to stick up. I smoothed down my blue *don't feed the bear* shirt.

I glanced from his passport to mine. "We don't even have the same birthday."

"I'm already sixteen." Lewis took both passports and compared them. "I'm older than you. Awesome."

Not awesome. This was about as far from awesome as you could get. I was the oldest. Born three minutes before him. On the fourteenth of June. No one was allowed to take that away.

I snatched my passport back. "I need food."

After ordering, we sat at a table next to the window. I focused on how the frothed milk of my hot chocolate tasted like chocolate ice cream and how chocolate had always been my favorite. I knew that about myself. I was still me.

"Do you think the hot dogs were ever eaten?" Lewis stared at his sandwich. "The ones on the barbecue."

I imagined our backyard, empty of us, covered in blood and police tape.

"Are you going to eat that?" I picked up his sandwich and took a bite.

"You're a savage, you know that?" He scraped back his chair and strode back to the counter to order another one.

Two airport security officers strolled by. My heart kicked in. It had been silent for the last few hours, but now it was back, thrumming in my ears. The officers joined Lewis at the counter, one a head shorter than him, the other a head taller. Lewis did a double take, then his shoulders tensed. The barista asked for his order a second time. When Lewis hesitated, the taller officer glanced his way. I put my hands under the table and pretended to be absorbed by an invisible screen on my lap. We should've kept our distance, that had been the plan. Lewis was supposed to wait at the departure gate, and I'd stay away until the last call for boarding. But I'd wanted to convince Lewis not to get on the plane. We had enough cash for a few months, enough for a motel in a remote mountain town. After everything died down, I'd contact Molly, and slowly, piece by piece, Lewis and I would put our lives back together.

Lewis had paid and was now hovering at the end of the counter, waiting for his sandwich to be heated. His hands twitched by his sides. I willed him to wait there. The barista poured two coffees, no frills, and handed them to the security officers. I wiped clammy palms on my new sweatpants and kept my head down.

Their stiff shoes clicked against the concrete floor as they passed.

Breathe.

I couldn't let them see my face. Identical twins are memorable. It was why Dad had told us to stay together, but avoid being seen. And why Lewis was Thomas Walker, and I was Daniel Johnston. It was why, if we stayed here, we couldn't be brothers. I'd spent the last few months wishing I hadn't been born a twin, but I'd never wished away Lewis.

Lewis thanked the barista as she handed over his sandwich — panicking, but still polite.

As he approached the table, I stood. "Board early. I'll see you on the plane."

CHAPTER 5

CAMERON

My ears ached from having the airline earbuds squeezed into them for the last four hours, the volume cranked high to drown out the jet engines. I was now watching my second movie on the tiny seatback screen and kept expecting aliens from the first movie to leap onto the speeding train in this one.

I couldn't see Lewis — he was about fifty rows in front of me, on the other side of a curtain. Turns out open plane tickets get you into business class, unless the last business class seat is filled by your brother. Then they get you any seat left.

I pulled out the earbuds and looked out the window. We were still flying over Canada's forests and lakes. Why hadn't Mom and Dad arranged to meet us in an isolated cabin in the Rockies, or the arctic tundra of the Northwest Territories, rather than flying to another continent?

A baby cried. I knew the feeling — I couldn't sleep either. The man beside me was snoring, his shoulders pressed against mine, his knee in my space. I snuggled into the hoodie that Mom had packed for me, closed my eyes and tried to convince my brain the drone of the engines was our truck. Lewis was beside me, with

Mom and Dad up front. Cool boxes and camping gear in the bed. We were heading out of town to a creek Dad's team had found while cutting firebreaks up by Deadman's Pass. The hiss of air in my face was our AC, which never did run cold.

The overhead lights flickered to life. Passengers were raising their seats, folding trays. Fastening seat belts. I must've finally fallen asleep, because my neck was stiff, my mouth dry. I rested my forehead against the cold window. The plane's shadow was gliding over ocean rather than land, and up ahead was a jagged coastline that must be Britain.

My snoring neighbor jerked awake and started a rapid-fire conversation with me about airplane food. I didn't catch half of what he said, but when he finished complaining, I asked him what happens after we land.

"Luggage carousels." He dug out a packet of mints from his pocket. "Then grow old waiting for the baggage handlers to do their job."

"What if I don't have bags?"

"Then you're lucky. All you're left with after passport control is customs. And with no bags, you'll have nothing to declare. Free as a bird after that." He popped a mint in his mouth, then offered me the packet.

Suddenly feeling sick, I shook my head. Our passports had to be checked again?

I looked out the window, my stomach in knots. The plane dropped through the clouds, and Britain appeared — a patchwork of fields and small scattered towns. As we got closer to London, the fields shrunk, the towns grew and roads with lines of traffic became visible.

The landing was bumpy. Rain pelted the windows. The second the seat belt sign pinged off, passengers leaped out of their seats. Overhead compartments sprang open, bags were dragged out. The man beside me tried to squeeze into the already-crowded aisle. *Good luck with that.*

Lewis was waiting in the terminal building looking like he'd just woken up from a very deep sleep. Next time, I'd take the business class seat.

"We need to go through passport control," Lewis said, frowning.

"Yeah, I heard."

Together, we followed the herd of passengers from our plane. Posters of bubbly bus drivers and astronauts and nurses welcomed us to Britain from the walls of the tunnels.

"They'll look at our passports more carefully than they did in Canada, seeing as we're entering rather than leaving," Lewis said. "Do you think they'll be able to tell they're fake?"

I stopped. Tired people flowed round me, making their irritation known through huffs and tuts. Lewis took a few more steps, realized I was no longer by his side, then turned.

"What?" His hair was sticking up, and he had a blob of dried grossness in the corner of his mouth.

"Do you ever engage that massive brain of yours?" I pushed past him and rejoined the march of the wheelie bags.

He caught up, hitching his backpack higher. "No one heard me."

"Maybe announce it over the loudspeakers next time."

When we reached the moving walkway, I veered right, stepped on and kept walking. Lewis stayed on solid ground. I could see him out of the corner of my eye, striding to keep up.

I switched on my phone and was welcomed to the United Kingdom, *roaming charges apply*. Molly still hadn't texted. No messages from our parents. I took a photo of a plane taxiing outside the rain-drenched window and sent it to Mom and Dad. They'd figure it out.

As the walkway ended, I took a deep breath, then merged with Lewis. "What's your full name and date of birth?" I asked him.

He rolled them off, but didn't sound convincing.

"Repeat it a few times in your head. Lying takes confidence. If you don't believe it, no one else will." I knew how to pretend to be what everyone expected me to be. The cool twin to Lewis's nerd, the laid-back one to his constant anxious mess. The capable one.

"Where were you born?" I said.

"Toronto."

"Make eye contact, otherwise you'll look guilty. Why are you here?"

He opened his mouth, but nothing came out.

I tugged him to the side. "Go to the washroom, wipe the drool off your face and keep repeating over and over in your head that you're here on vacation. The less details you give, the better. Don't ramble."

"Got it. No rambling."

"And dream up a reason why you chose London over Paris or Rome." I pointed to the washroom sign. "And do something with your hair."

Lewis had to make it through passport control. If he didn't, I couldn't go back for him. His identical twin showing up with a different date and place of birth wouldn't help his case any. We could argue adoption for the different second names, but the rest screamed fake passports, and we'd be back on a plane to Canada before we'd left the airport.

I checked my phone — just after 4:00 p.m. We'd skipped forward in time — over nine hours in the air, but sixteen hours had passed.

Lewis reappeared, looking sharper. "I want to see Buckingham Palace."

I gave him a hug.

"What was that for?"

I gripped his shoulders and pushed him back, so I could look him in the eye. "I'll see you on the other side of customs."

"What if I screw this up?"

"You won't." I tugged him back into the flow of people, drifting left when an arrow pointed the way to customs and a set of escalators that sunk to the level below.

"You go first." I squeezed his arm. "I'll follow in a few minutes."

I nudged him toward the top step, then watched him descend. When he stepped off at the bottom, he froze. *Come on, Lewis. Get it together.*

"Excuse me."

I turned to see a lady with a baby strapped to her chest, a folded stroller in one hand, a toddler clinging to the other and a heavy bag dragging one shoulder down.

"Could you help us?" She tilted her head down at the little girl. "She's scared of escalators. I need to carry her."

She sounded English — every word had distinct edges.

"Yeah, sure." I took the stroller. "I can take the bag, too, if that helps."

She dropped her shoulder, and the bag began to slide. "Thank you."

I caught it before it hit the floor, swung it over my shoulder and smiled down at the girl, who was wearing pajamas and red rubber boots.

I stepped onto the escalator first, holding the collapsed stroller over my shoulder like a shovel. As the hall below came into view, I searched for Lewis among the hundreds of people winding their way back and forth through a maze of taped-off channels. He was easy to spot in his white T-shirt, head raised, looking toward a row of imposing desks at the far end of the hall.

As I stepped off the escalator onto solid ground, I moved to the side, ready to return the stroller. The girl clung to her mother, her face turned inward. The lump that was the baby squirmed.

"Could you unfold it for me?" the lady asked, one arm around her daughter, the other rubbing the baby's bum. "Red lever. Give it a yank."

I rotated the stroller. Turned it upside down.

"Here …" She handed me the girl, who clung to me like a monkey.

"That easy?" I said as the frame shot open like an umbrella.

I knelt, peeled tiny fingers off my arms and set the girl in the stroller. The baby let out a sound halfway between a creak and a scream. The lady bobbed up and down, rubbing the baby's back. I clutched the strap of the diaper bag, sagging and heavy, and began to slide it from my shoulder. The baby wailed. The mother bounced. The girl stretched her arms up and asked for her blankie.

"I could line up with you," I said.

The woman nodded, bounced, pointed to the stroller, and together we joined the end of the line, which snaked back and forth across the width of the hall. When the baby calmed down, the woman pulled a blanket from the bag on my shoulder and gave it to her daughter.

The line moved, and as we shuffled forward in the confines of the roped-off channel, a different group of people shuffled past in the opposite direction. No white T-shirts.

"I'm Padma Collingwood." She held out her hand.

Collingwood, the same name as my second-grade teacher, who smelled of licorice and gave out bouncy balls for good work.

We shook hands. "Daniel Johnston."

"Are you here to visit family, Daniel Johnston?"

"Vacation. I want to see Buckingham Palace."

"The Tower of London's better," she said. "More intrigue and betrayal."

We shuffled forward again. We were at the first bend now, the one where I'd seen Lewis.

"Are you looking for someone?" Padma said.

"No!" *Crap, that sounded weird.*

I cleared my throat. "Are you on holiday, too?"

"God no, wouldn't be much of a holiday with this lot." She patted the baby's bum. "I live here, just back from a quick trip to introduce this one to his grandparents."

I stiffened as two policemen in black body armor strode down the length of the hall, automatic weapons slung across their chests.

"Don't worry about them," Padma said. "They're here for terrorists."

The gun against my head. Lewis yelling for Mom and Dad. A bullet hole between blank, staring eyes. Blood.

"Daniel." Padma touched my arm. "If there was any real threat, there'd be more than two of them, believe me. I work for the police."

My breath caught. She was police. I searched the customs hall for an excuse to walk away, but there were no washrooms or water fountains, only solid walls with dazzling images of palaces and soldiers wearing tall furry hats.

Padma's daughter held out her hand and asked for a drink, and Padma crouched to root underneath the stroller.

Two rows ahead, Lewis came into view. As I caught his eye, my heart rate lowered.

"Aren't you a bit young to be going on holiday alone?" Padma stood and handed her daughter a sippy cup. "Kids your age usually travel in packs or trudge behind their parents listening to angsty music."

"I'm older than I look." Not that I knew how old I was. Yesterday, I'd been fifteen, but maybe Lewis's passport was nearer the truth, and we were already sixteen.

She tilted her head, as if she was trying to guess my age. "What are you planning on doing while you're here? Other than taking pictures of the palace?"

Why was she asking all these questions? I should never have lined up with her. I scrambled for ideas of what I'd want to do if I really was on holiday.

"A Chelsea soccer game." It was the team Dad and I always cheered for, even though he secretly preferred the European Champions League over English Premiership. He pretended he didn't, but the only time he'd ever teared up over a soccer game was when Ajax lost 6–1 to Napoli.

"We call it football," she said. "But if you want an egg-shaped ball and grown men tackling one another, then I'd suggest rugby."

I nodded. "Right. Soccer is football."

The line surged forward, and we rounded another bend.

"Not much of a partier, then?" she said.

Cameron Larsen was a partier. Was Daniel Johnston?

"If you were a partier," Padma continued, "you would've run away to, I don't know, Spain or Greece." She waved her hand in the air. "Or Thailand."

"I'm not running away." Lewis would have a fit if he knew I'd walked into an interrogation with a British policewoman.

"Sorry, none of my business," she said. "Habit of the job."

I spotted Lewis again. When he saw me talking to Padma, he spun to face the front of the hall.

Padma pulled her phone from her back pocket. "I need to text my partner that we're almost through."

She typed more words than you'd think were needed. Or did she mean her police partner, and she was notifying them that she'd met an underage runaway?

"They must've opened up another desk." Padma put her phone away, looked to the front of the hall. "We're moving."

The crowd felt it, too. People dug out passports, zipped away phones. I pulled out Daniel Johnston's passport from the top pocket of my backpack. Resisted opening it to check his birthdate. September 14. Vancouver.

As we rounded the last bend into the final stretch, Lewis stepped out of the crowd and approached a counter. The female customs officer looked at him as if she was about to pass a death sentence.

"They won't bite," Padma said. "The only reason they look grumpy is because they have tedious jobs. Unless you have a banana hidden in your rucksack, you'll be fine."

I dragged my eyes away from Lewis. "Banana?"

"They're scared of foreign fruit flies. Cunning little buggers — can bring countries to their knees." She nudged the stroller forward. "Had a banana in my bag when she was a baby, almost got arrested."

Lewis was gone. An old couple stood where he'd been. The glass exit doors slid closed behind someone, but I couldn't see who.

Padma pointed at the diaper bag. "Hang it on the pram handles."

The line in front of us thinned as people dispersed to the row of counters.

"Thank you, Daniel Johnston. You are a gentleman."

I had a sudden urge to grab Padma's hand and beg for help.

"If you need anything while you're here," she said. "A friendly face, decent cup of tea, you can leave a message for me at Scotland Yard. I'm on maternity leave, but they'll pass it on."

Worried my voice would crack if I said anything, I nodded.

She touched my arm. "Stay safe, Daniel Johnston."

Then she left me.

Her daughter twisted around in her stroller and waved goodbye. Someone nudged me from behind, pointed to a counter at the far end. I took a deep breath, squared my shoulders and stepped into the void.

The customs officer didn't look up, just held up his hand in a "go-no-further" gesture. I was in no-man's-land. My heart raced.

Time slowed. I took a step back, wanting to melt into the safety of the herd. Without looking up, the officer waved me forward.

"Next time, stay behind the line, sir."

I nodded. Clutched Daniel Johnston's passport. Did I wait until he asked for it or offer it up?

He held out his hand. I placed Daniel Johnston's passport, and my future, in his palm. My heart thumped so loudly I worried he could hear it. He ran the passport through the scanner, watched the screen, frowned. Scanned it again.

"Date of birth," he said still looking at the screen.

"June 14."

He looked at me for the first time. What had I said? I'd said September, hadn't I?

"September 14," I said.

If I'd said June I should explain why — my brother's birthday, which was true, or the date I was returning.

Don't ramble.

"September 14. Sorry, I thought you asked me something else."

He peered at me over wire-framed glasses. "What's the purpose of your visit?"

Make eye contact. "Vacation, short vacation."

"Traveling alone?"

Keep your answers short unless asked for more detail. "Yes."

Make eye contact. Too much. Look away. Back. *Crap.*

He cleared his throat. Looked down at the passport, flicked pages. Then *bang* — stamped it. Handed it back.

Resisting the urge to run, I headed for the doors, which spat me out in the baggage hall.

Padma was at one of the moving belts, her little girl out of the stroller and jumping up and down on a baggage cart. No sign of Lewis.

Hugging the perimeter, I headed for the "nothing to declare" exit.

The glass doors whooshed open, and I stepped into the crowded airport. I wove past an old lady hugging two little boys and taxi drivers displaying their customers' names on pieces of paper. Then Lewis was on me, his arms around my shoulders pulling me in. I hugged him hard, so happy to have him back.

"You stink," I said.

He let me go. "That was intense. Even my sweat is sweating."

"Where do we go now?" I searched for signs, not knowing what I was looking for. How far *was* Edinburgh from London?

Someone jostled me from behind. I whipped round. A man with a white beard and a turban was struggling with a bulging suitcase. When I turned back around, Lewis had his phone out.

"We can either fly to Edinburgh or take a train," he said.

"No way am I going through another passport check." Even thinking about it made me nauseous. "How do we find a train to Edinburgh?"

He scrolled through his phone. "Looks like we need to get to King's Cross Station. And according to the woman next to me on the plane, it's pronounced *Edinbrrra*."

"Probably best not to tell total strangers where we're heading," I said.

"Right, good point." Lewis shoved his phone in his back pocket and looked up at an overhead sign with arrows to taxis, buses and trains. "We need to get to the city center first. What do you think? Bus or train?"

"Train." I'd never been on a train before, but it seemed the obvious way to reach a railway station.

As I led the way, it hit me we weren't in Canada anymore. We'd flown across the Atlantic Ocean and were on a whole different continent. We didn't belong here. Knew no one.

I took a deep breath. We'd made it this far. The hard part was behind us. All we had to do now was catch a couple of trains. We'd be with Mom and Dad again soon. I'd know the truth. Have a name. A birthday. Be the oldest again.

CHAPTER 6

L E W I S

The train into London arrived at Paddington Station, like the bear with the marmalade and the hat. I wondered which was named after which. Mom would know. For some reason, she loved that book. From here we had to catch the subway to King's Cross — five stops, nine minutes. Easy.

According to the internet, nine million people lived in London, and it looked like half of them were here waiting for trains. We weaved our way through rolling suitcases and shopping bags. I dodged a little boy with flashing Spider-Man sneakers, then almost squished a pigeon that refused to move. By the time I looked up, Cameron was three strides ahead. He was the same size as me, but somehow managed to take up more space. I tried to catch up, but it was like navigating a corn maze — I'd spot a way through only to find it blocked by a food stall or a barrier or a double stroller. The mass of people was so dense, we would be easy targets. No one would notice if someone pulled a knife. A sniper could be perched on one of the metal beams above us, their crosshairs following my head. It would be a clean shot. Unless, of course, I was trampled by the crowds before they could pull the trigger. Or shoved under a moving train. Or arrested.

A coffee cart wheezed steam, and I dove in the opposite direction, crashing into a man carrying a tray of sandwiches. I spluttered an apology, then scuttled after Cameron.

Once we were through the ticket check, the crowd spread out like water flowing from the end of a hose, and the station opened up into a vast space with a curved glass roof.

Cameron appeared at my side. "Focus. Look for signs for the subway."

An announcement for platform changes boomed over the clamor of people and the chug and squeal of the trains. As it crackled into silence, a woman in a wheelchair hummed past, zooming in the direction of a tour group gathered around a raised umbrella. I tugged Cameron toward them, hoping the red-circle symbol of the London Underground would leap out at us.

And then I saw him. The guy with the goatee and the ponytail.

He'd been in the airport.

And now he was at Paddington Station, leaning against a bookstore window. Panic bubbled in my stomach.

"Why did you stop?" Cameron said. "Did you see the subway?"

I grabbed my brother's shoulders. "Someone's following us."

"How do you know?"

"He was in the airport."

Cameron frowned.

"Nine *million* people live in London," I said. "Plus *another* million tourists a day. No way I see the same guy twice. Never trust coincidences, remember?"

It was what Mom always said, before we went on school trips or to soccer games in other towns — *Be aware of your surroundings, trust your gut, but never coincidences. They're like shooting stars, rare and not worth wishing on.*

"Where is he?" Cameron started to twist around.

"*Don't* look." I tightened my grip on his shoulders. "He's outside the bookstore."

Cameron knocked my hands away and turned. "The one reading the newspaper, or the one with the high-vis vest?"

"To the right of the newspaper guy," I said. "Pale skin. Goatee, ponytail, squinty eyes. Navy tee, jeans. Black high-tops."

"Holding a leather jacket?"

I grabbed Cameron's arm to steady myself. "That's him."

"Crap." Cameron's head whipped back around, his eyes wide. "He saw me. And he's got something folded in his jacket."

I forgot to breathe, then gulped down too much air.

We took off toward a brick wall that curved to reveal an escalator to the subway. As we sank past billboards for stage shows and blockbuster movies, my neck prickled. This could not be happening. But some part of my brain had already decided it could because my heart sped up, and my muscles urged me to run.

"Follow me." Cameron edged past the person on the step below, then the next one and again.

I did the same — *sorry, excuse me, thank you,* all the way to the bottom. Then we squeezed past suits and sweaty shirt backs and arms of tattoos until turnstiles barred our way.

"Don't overthink it," Cameron said, then leaped over the metal bar.

Was ticket evasion a crime? Someone shoved me. I half-jumped, half-straddled the turnstile, stumbled, then raced through musty tunnels, following signs for the yellow Circle line.

Eventually, we burst through the tunnels onto a platform and straight onto a waiting train. Cameron jabbed the button over and over, but the door refused to close. More people boarded. We shuffled farther inside to let them in. I willed the doors to shut, the train to move. *Please move.* The platform refilled, and people continued to shove their way onboard. Finally, the doors beeped. As the train shuddered into motion, I grabbed the overhead bar.

"Did you see him?" Cameron asked. "Did he make it?"

I scanned the passengers, their ears plugged with music, scrolling through their phones, reading magazines. "I can't see him, but maybe. Probably."

Were the compartments connected? If Goatee Guy had made it onboard, could he search the whole train?

At every stop, the subway car rearranged itself. People shuffled off, more squeezed their way onboard, and empty seats refilled before the tube rattled into the next stretch of tunnel. I checked every new face.

Cameron had his head down. His breath came in short bursts. Was he counting?

We were in a metal box, underground, the pitch-black tunnels grazing the side of the train. He must be losing his mind. I slid my hand along the bar until my pinkie touched his clammy fingers.

How much longer? I'd forgotten to count stops. Was it five stops and nine minutes or nine stops and five minutes? Either way, we still hadn't reached King's Cross. A route map was pasted above the window — a yellow line, each dot a station. I counted the dots — Gloucester Road was the fifth stop. And after that South Kensington, Sloane Square, Victoria, St. James's Park, Westminster. A string of stations that didn't include King's Cross.

Panic pulsed through me. We were on the wrong train!

As we came out of the tunnel, the brakes squealed. The doors beeped.

"Get off." I shoved Cameron. "We need to get off."

As soon as our feet hit concrete, I was off through the tunnels, Cameron on my heels.

When we reached the escalator, Cameron clung on to the handrail. I tugged him off at the top, and as soon as we reached the sidewalk outside, he slumped into a crouch, his back against the station wall, his head in his hands.

The sidewalks were packed — girls in a chain of linked arms, a family with bare-legged toddlers on their shoulders, a cute teenaged boy, sunglasses flipped up on his head. He reminded me of Hunter, the same stocky build. I couldn't believe I'd finally asked someone out, then missed our first official date. At least I had a reasonable excuse. Not that your parents killing two uninvited guests at a neighborhood barbecue was reasonable, but at least Hunter wouldn't feel stood up.

I crouched down next to Cameron. "You good to go?"

We had to keep moving. Just because I couldn't see Goatee Guy, didn't mean he wasn't watching us from behind a newspaper stand or a telephone box.

Cameron took another deep breath, then raised his head. "I'm good."

We took off at a run. Our feet slapping the sidewalk, arms swinging. My heart beating blood and oxygen and fear. Cameron kept my pace, his strides mirroring mine, his footfalls synchronized. He was my perfect shadow.

We ran alongside a wide river. A red-and-white city tour boat chugged past in the opposite direction, its top deck crammed with passengers. On the other side of the river, clear pods rotated on a massive Ferris wheel.

Cameron shoved me from behind. "Go over the bridge."

The bridge was bustling with tourists and traffic, but we could hide in the crowd.

We darted into the road. The green walking man of the pedestrian lights turned red. Engines revved, horns beeped. A church bell chimed. We kept running.

The bridge was crammed with tourists all facing the direction of the clanging bell, their phones out.

"Cycle lane!" Cameron shouted.

Angry bike bells trilled. Someone yelled. We kept running. Caught up with the next group of bikes and overtook them. In the lane beside us, red double-decker buses and black taxis rumbled over the bridge. A car horn blared.

A solid mass of bikes was up ahead. We leaped back onto the sidewalk, nudging through tiny gaps, calling out apologies.

"Slow down." Cameron grabbed the back of my shirt.

People crushed in on us — elbows and bags, and phones raised over heads taking photos. Cameron squeezed past me, then edged to the left of every person until there were no more gaps and the wall of the bridge was in front of us.

I leaned against the stone, breathing hard. When I'd caught

my breath, I searched for the bell that continued to mesmerize everyone on the bridge.

A stone tower, with a giant, white clock face — Big Ben. It had to be. I was looking at Big Ben. And the giant Ferris wheel must be the London Eye. I should be excited. We were in Britain — the land of castles and kings and queens and great battles. All around us, people were smiling. A couple next to us kissed for a selfie, and on our other side three little kids waved down at a boat as it emerged from under the bridge.

I wanted to be on holiday, too. I wanted Mom and Dad to appear, waving tickets for the Science Museum or the Tower of London. They'd hug us and say it had all been part of the surprise and ask if we wanted to go to Buckingham Palace for tea and cucumber sandwiches before we set off.

Big Ben's chimes vibrated into silence — five o'clock.

I checked my phone — King's Cross Station was two miles away, but there was no way I'd get Cameron underground again. We needed to walk. Or flag down a taxi.

Cameron was scrolling through photos on his phone — Molly hugging her knees next to a campfire, Molly riding her horse, laughing.

He should've asked her out months ago. I'd told him to do it ... I wouldn't feel left out. What did he have to lose? Fifteen years of friendship wouldn't disappear because of one awkward date.

"Hurry up and text her," I said. "We need to go."

"Give me your phone." Cameron held out his hand.

"Why?" Actually, I didn't care. I just wanted him to start moving again. I slapped my phone into Cameron's waiting palm.

He closed his fingers around it, then stretched his arms beyond the bridge's wall, a phone in each hand. He rotated his wrists. One small movement. Gravity did the rest.

"What are you doing?!" I jerked forward just in time to watch our phones plop below the surface of the water. Cameron and Lewis Larsen's friends and memories and documented lives sinking into the murky water of the Thames.

"Phones are traceable. It's probably how he found us." Cameron pushed away from the wall into the flow of pedestrians, which was moving again.

I followed. "They won't believe we're down there when no one saw us jump."

"All that matters is they can't use them to track us."

We had burner phones, I reminded myself. We might've lost contact with everyone else, but Mom and Dad could still reach us.

Cameron looked past me, his eyes wide. I spun around. People were parting to let someone through — goatee, tied-back hair, navy tee.

We jumped back into the bike lane and ran.

CHAPTER
7

CAMERON

For our twelfth birthday, the only thing Lewis asked for was for
us all to be together. Forest-fire season had started early, and
Dad had been on back-to-back shifts since early May, cutting
firebreaks in the trees to starve the fires. The weeks slipped
by, and every morning white ash covered our black truck and
smoke smothered the sun. But on the day of our birthday, when
it seemed hopeless, Mom arrived at school, the truck loaded
with camping gear. The three of us drove into the mountains,
to the edge of Dad's camp. Campfires were banned, of course,
so we roasted marshmallows on aluminum foil on the roof of
the truck. Looking back, it was a crazy thing to do, but Mom
had promised Lewis we'd be together, and she never broke
promises.

We'd arrived in Edinburgh, and Mom would be here.

The train journey had been four hours of fields and brick
towns with church steeples whizzing past the window, then
stretches of ocean. Four hours of the rumble of the train and
of checking the aisle for Goatee Guy and of clutching the flip
phone, waiting for it to ring.

We were now in a black cab crawling through Edinburgh's stop-start traffic. It was still daylight, but the sun was low, bouncing off the golden stone buildings. Lewis had his head stuck out the window, rambling excitedly about cathedrals and castles. The breeze was cool and damp, and smelled like a mixture of horse feed and gravy. What kind of city was this?

I checked the flip phone again. Lewis had called them burner phones, which made them sound exciting. They weren't. I knew flip phones existed — our homeroom teacher had one clipped to her belt that she never used because they're basically useless. No apps, no internet, no games. They make phone calls, and if you have abnormally tiny thumbs and an unnatural amount of patience, you can send a text.

I'd worked out how to take a photo and snapped one of the inside of the train car — plaid seats, overhead luggage racks, the ticker-tape screen announcing *Edinburgh Waverley* as the final stop. Then I'd texted it to the only contact stored, Chelsea, as in the soccer team. It had to be Dad's number.

"Glencairn Crescent's coming up, lads. Which end do you want?" The taxi driver rolled his *R*'s and sounded out the *T*'s.

I leaned forward to reply through the glass divider. "Drop us here."

He pulled out of the flow of buses and cars, and squealed to a stop at the side of the road.

Lewis had a roll of cash out and was frantically searching for the right note. Eventually, he handed one over, and the driver started digging for change.

"It's okay, we're good," I said.

The driver pointed across the street. "You want to go up

there, then take the second right."

I decided I liked Scottish accents. They reminded me of country music — bubbly and soothing. I couldn't live here though. The streets were packed with people, and the place really did stink.

I swung open the door and stumbled stiff-legged onto the sidewalk.

Lewis shuffled out after me, then thanked the driver and slammed the door.

Three buses rumbled past going to Glasgow, Falkirk and Drum Brae, followed by a burst of cars, including our taxi, then a tram, its brakes screeching. When the stoplights changed, we jogged across the tram tracks, then the road, dodging people who were running to catch the tram.

Once we were on the opposite sidewalk, I held out my hand. "Show me the address again."

Lewis handed over Mom's sticky note — *Margaret Ross, 20 Glencairn Crescent, Haymarket, Edinburgh.*

"Do you think he followed us?" Lewis glanced over his shoulder.

"Don't worry, we lost him in London." I wasn't convinced, but the last thing I needed was Lewis panicking.

"Good," he said. "That's good. He can't track us now."

We should've ditched our phones as soon as we left the Calgary police station. How many times had Dad tracked us through our phones? How many times had Mom warned us electronic footprints were easier to follow than real ones?

We turned down the street the taxi driver had pointed out. Parked cars lined the cobbled road bumper to bumper, each one small enough to fit in the bed of our truck.

"That smell's everywhere." Lewis sniffed the air. "What d'you think it is?"

"Horse feed and gravy?"

He laughed, then started running. "Come on, we can ask Mom."

I took off after Lewis, my backpack slapping my back. Excitement flushed away my worries about still being followed. I couldn't wait for Dad to wrap me in a hug, while Mom explained everything. Lewis was right, they'd have a good reason for leaving us.

We turned right onto Glencairn Crescent, which was two semicircles of houses with a mass of trees in the middle. The stone houses were all joined together, and the only way to tell where one house ended and the next one began were sets of steps leading to shiny front doors. As we strode down the street, Lewis read out the house numbers — "27, 26, 25 …."

We stopped in front of number 20. *Drummond House* was printed in gold paint on the glass panel above the door.

Lewis leaned over spiky railings and looked down. "There's a basement, too."

I peered over the railings at a set of worn stone steps leading down to another front door. Mom and Dad didn't rush out of either door to meet us.

It shouldn't have been a shock. What with no texts and them having lied about everything else. But my chest tightened, and I could feel the pressure of tears behind my eyes because I really had expected them to be here. Mom had promised.

———

L E W I S

Instead of climbing up the six stone steps to the navy-blue front door, Cameron leaned against the railings, dropped his backpack on the ground between his feet and pulled out his burner phone. I recognized his expression. It was the one that said, *I'm done caring, now it's your turn.* I could argue I'd contributed as much as him to our escape, more if you factored in his detour to the police, but I was too exhausted to argue.

I checked the house number again against the address. My heart clenched at the sight of Mom's curly handwriting, her round-topped *M*'s and the dot in the middle of the zero. Would she be here? Would Dad? What if they weren't? What if Margaret Ross had moved or died or was a psychopathic serial killer?

I trudged up the steps. The house was the same as all the others on this street: wheat-colored stone, two floors of tall windows and a third story of small, peaked windows.

I searched for the doorbell, gave up and knocked.

No answer.

I knocked again, harder this time.

A dog barked from deep inside. An excited bark that grew weary.

A bell tinkled above my head as the front door opened. My heart sped up at the thought of Mom being on the other side.

"Was the play as riveting as you expected …" The woman took off her glasses, letting them dangle from a chain around her neck. "Well, you're not Nora Bidwell."

She was old. Not walking-stick old, but definitely grandmother old. Her hair was a gray bob, her white skin wrinkled. She wore a red zip-up fleece with baggy jeans. And her singsong Scottish accent evaporated any hope that she was a transplanted Canadian who was somehow related to Mom.

She pulled the edges of her fleece closed. "If you're one of Aisha's pals, it's too late to be calling, even if you had the right house."

"Are you Margaret Ross?" *Please let this be her.*

"I am, indeed."

My whole body relaxed. Even though Margaret Ross couldn't be family, she was still the woman Mom had wanted us to find. We'd finally made it to safety. To a shower and a bed and someone who didn't want us dead, or locked up, and might actually care that we hadn't eaten a vegetable for two days.

"My mom sent us here," I said. "Jennifer Larsen."

"You're an American? Why on earth didn't you say? Come in, come in." She opened the door wide and waved me inside.

I looked back at Cameron, then stepped into the hallway.

"Did the MacLeans send you?" she said. "They fair enjoyed their stay. Gave me four stars."

A wooden desk took up most of the hallway. Behind the desk was a staircase to the second floor. Were Mom and Dad up there?

A black dog the size of a coffee table nudged its way through the door to my right, trotted over, then jumped up on me, its front paws reaching my chest.

"Haggis! Come here, you wee scoundrel." Margaret Ross reached over and tugged at its collar.

The dog looked up at me with pleading eyes. But Cameron was the dog person.

"You arrived on the London train, I expect." She told the dog to sit, then stepped behind the desk and opened a black, leather-bound book. "Now, let's have a look at what we have."

I watched the stairs, expecting Dad to thump down them, his arms outstretched and ready to give me one of his bear hugs.

"How many nights are you after?" Margaret ran her finger down the page.

"I don't know," I said. "Have my parents checked in yet?"

I strained my ears for Mom's voice.

"The only guests I have are the Fisbys and Nora Bidwell." She looked up at me. "Are you a Fisby?"

I wanted to sink to the floor and refuse to move until Mom and Dad arrived.

"They're from Blackpool," she said as if it would jog my memory.

"I'm sure they're very nice people," I said. "But I don't know the MacLeans or Nora or the Frisbees."

"Fisbys," Margaret said.

Why would Mom send us to a complete stranger?

"My name is Lewis Larsen. My mom and dad are Jennifer and David Larsen." I scrambled for Mom's maiden name. "Reid — you might know her as Jennifer Reid."

Margaret Ross showed no signs of recognition — no *aha* moment, no *silly me, of course your mother's here.*

"Can you check the book again?" My voice wobbled.

The bell above the door jangled. I didn't need to turn around to know it was Cameron. His footsteps have a signature tune of their own.

As he came to stand beside me, my heart rate lowered.

Margaret looked at my brother, then at me, then back to Cameron again. "There's two of you?"

"Are they here?" Cameron asked me.

"You're twins." Margaret Ross's hand went to her chest. "I know exactly who you are."

So, not a complete stranger, but clearly not someone who was expecting us.

She blustered round the desk, strode to the door with amazing speed and held it open. "I'm going to have to ask the both of you to leave."

Cameron swore, then slid his backpack off his shoulder and dumped it on the floor. "We're staying. This is a hotel, isn't it? And we have money."

"I've no rooms for you. Or your mother. You tell her that from me." Margaret straightened her shoulders. "And, while you're at it, you can tell her I don't appreciate her underhanded way of asking an old friend for a favor. Jennifer Larsen, indeed."

I looked at the three keys dangling from the edge of the desk. We'd been so close to finding Mom and Dad, and having a place to stay. My body had started to relax and now it was a struggle to stay upright.

"Where the heck are they?" Cameron looked exhausted.

"They'll be here," I said. "They're on a train."

The photo was fuzzy, but it had definitely been a train.

Cameron's eyes sparked with hope. "How do you know?"

I fumbled in my pocket for the burner phone, then handed it to him. "Just a photo. No message."

It hadn't needed a message. They were on a train. They were on their way.

Cameron shoved the phone back at me. "*I* sent you that."

"No, it's from Dad." The text had come from the only contact stored — Ajax, the Dutch soccer team Dad supported. Ajax couldn't be Cameron.

"It's from Dad," I said. "It has to be."

Cameron pulled out his burner phone and typed. My phone pinged. Ajax is me.

Margaret Ross looked at me, then Cameron, and tutted. "What a fine mess your mother's made."

Cameron rubbed his cheeks like he used to when he was little to stop himself from crying. I slid to the floor and hugged my shins. Where were Mom and Dad? I needed them to tell us everything would be okay. And I needed them.

I hadn't realized I was crying until my body shuddered, and then I gave up trying to hold it in and sobbed until I was too exhausted to keep going. My head pounded, and my throat was raw. And I was slumped in the hallway of a guesthouse with a stranger watching me. I wiped my eyes with the back of my hand, took a shaky breath, then raised my head. Cameron sat against the wall, knees bent, the dog curled up against him.

"You done?" he asked me.

"Shut up." I wiped my eyes again.

He stood and held out his hand.

The dog bounced between us, but Margaret yanked it back.

Cameron pulled me to my feet, then handed me my backpack. "We'll find another hotel."

"Nonsense," Margaret said. "You're in no fit state to traipse about the city. I've an attic bedroom. Too many stairs for my regular guests." She rummaged through the desk drawer, then held out a key. "There'll be time enough tomorrow to explain why you're here. Until then, stay out of sight. Mind you, check the coast is clear before you come hurtling downstairs."

"We don't need your help." Cameron swung his backpack over his shoulder.

"Yes, we do." I took the key from her.

Mom and Dad would come.

CHAPTER
8

LEWIS

The attic stairs creaked. I hadn't noticed last night, but after fifteen hours of sleep, my brain had emerged from survival mode and was registering non-life-threatening details. Like the fact that the brown and cream carpet running the length of the second-floor landing looked like chocolate-chip cookie dough. And as cars passed on the cobbled street outside, their wheels made a *thub-thub-thub* sound.

We walked past the closed doors of the guest rooms, each one of them silent. Given it was mid-afternoon, it seemed more likely that tourists would be out exploring the city than tucked up in their beds.

Cameron stopped at the top of the stairs that led to the main floor. "I think someone's down there."

I strained to hear. "Is it Mom and Dad?"

Cameron looked at me. "If Mom and Dad were here, they would've woken us."

"Not necessarily," I said. "They might've decided to let us sleep because ..."

"Shh." Cameron crept halfway down the staircase.

Mom would've let us sleep, but Cameron was right. Dad would've crashed upstairs and shaken us awake. On his weekends off, he always bounded into our bedrooms and announced it was a fresh-powder ski day or a blue-sky lake day or simply that the world was waiting for us to get up.

"It's just the radio." Cameron started moving again.

The cookie-dough carpet continued down this set of stairs and into the main floor.

Cameron opened one of the doors behind the reception desk. "Washroom." Then rattled the handle of the door opposite. "Locked."

The room to the right of the front door smelled of woodsmoke. It was a living room, with armchairs and knitted cushions and patchwork blankets. Framed embroideries of Highland cows and Loch Ness monsters cluttered the walls.

Cameron joined me in the doorway. "It looks like a craft store threw up in here."

The dog barked. We heard Margaret Ross telling it to calm down.

"Do you think she'll let us stay?" I said.

"She made it pretty clear we're not welcome. Mom was wrong about her helping us." Cameron shoved his hands in his pockets. "And if Mom was wrong about that, then maybe she was wrong about …"

"Don't even say it. They'll be here soon." But worst-case scenarios flew around my brain. I refused to let any of them land.

The dog barked again, then bounded into the hallway. Cameron crouched to fuss with it, leaving me to face Margaret Ross.

"I heard the pipes knock," she said. "That shower's finicky."

If finicky meant it only had two settings — light mist or skin-stripping, laser-beam strong — then it was finicky. But if she'd let us stay, I'd learn to love the shower.

"I'm sorry for last night," she continued. "You took me by surprise. Please, call me Maggs — everyone does."

I grinned. "I'm Lewis, and that's my brother, Cameron."

Cameron stood. "How much do we owe you?"

"Away." Maggs waved off Cameron's question. "As if I'd charge Katrina's boys."

"Katrina?" I said at the same time as Cameron said, "I thought you didn't want us here."

The front door rattled.

"Quick march." She herded us across the hallway into the room to the left of the front door. "Don't mind the dog, she's harmless. Use those long legs of yours. Straight through the dining room and all the way to the back of the house. Not a peep until I give you the all clear."

The dog barked at our heels as we strode through a room with three round tables covered in lacy tablecloths and a large embroidered cow watching from the wall.

"Nora," we heard Maggs say from the hallway, "did you have a pleasant meander?"

The dog overtook us and bounded through a doorway at the far end of the room.

The back of the house was one big room. A gleaming white kitchen at one end flowed into a living area at the other. The floors weren't the painted floorboards of the attic or the chocolate-chip carpet of the rest of the house, but polished wood. The table at the window was glass-topped on a sleek silver pedestal, the chairs around it, modern white plastic. No tassels or patchwork or rainbow knitted cushions. Or needlework livestock.

The white walls were bare, apart from a single giant painting that Cameron was staring at.

"That's one of Mom's," he said.

"What?" I stood beside him shoulder to shoulder and tried to see what he was seeing.

It was painted from a great height, looking down on a city, maybe Edinburgh, with the ocean beyond.

"You can tell by the sky," he said.

My heart sped up. He was right. Mom always painted the sky at sunrise or sunset with red cotton-candy clouds.

I moved closer. Traced the artist's signature with my thumb. "Katrina Murray. Do you think that's Mom's real name?"

"Not Jennifer?" Cameron turned away from the painting. "Or Larsen. Or Reid."

"Right you are, Nora," we heard Maggs say. "Put your feet up while I put the kettle on."

Maggs bustled into the room, closing the door behind her.

She turned on the tap and filled the kettle, then said, "It's one of your mother's."

Cameron sent me a *told-you-so* look.

"It sat in its packing tube for a decade before I could bear to have it framed. It took me another couple of years before I hung it. It didn't seem right after all the heartache and mayhem she caused."

"What do you mean?" Cameron asked.

"Why was she in Scotland?" Cameron's question was better — heartache and mayhem sounded important, but I wanted to know why Mom had sent us here. Why Scotland? Why Margaret Ross?

"As opposed to where?"

"Home," Cameron said. "Canada."

"Canada, indeed. Your mother's as Scottish as I am."

"No," I said. "She's Canadian."

"Do you have a photo of her?" Cameron said.

Good idea. Maybe we'd got the wrong guesthouse, and two doors down, another Margaret Ross was baking us a welcome cake and fluffing up the spare beds.

The kettle whistled. The dog barked.

"I've a photo of her in my bedroom." She poured the water into a teapot. "I've one of the two of you as well. You're no taller than Haggis. I'll take this through, then fetch them."

She placed the teapot on a tray, along with a mug and a milk jug and a plate of cookies. "Put the kettle back on, would you, and make us some tea."

Cameron held the door for her. "We don't drink tea."

"It's about time you started," she said. "There aren't many problems a good cup of tea can't solve."

As soon as Cameron closed the door, I said, "Why would she say Mom's Scottish?"

Cameron gave me the look that said, *Let me explain the way the world works.*

"Mom and Dad lied," he said. "About our names. Our birthday. What makes you think they wouldn't lie about where they were born? The question is *why*. That's what we need to find out."

I nodded at Mom's painting. "Mom never lied about being an artist."

"Wow, we managed to find one thing she didn't lie about." He slumped onto the couch. "For all we know, Maggs is our grandmother."

"Who died twenty years ago in a car crash?" I said.

He shrugged. "How do you know that wasn't another lie?"

Cameron was being ridiculous.

The dog scratched at the door. Cameron lunged to open it.

Maggs followed after the dog, holding the empty tray in one hand and photos in the other. "It's all go out there. The Fisbys are back, too."

Cameron was fussing with the dog again, so Maggs offered me the photos. The top one was of Cameron and me aged about five, running in our backyard, superhero capes flying behind us. The second one was of Mom, but much younger than I ever remember her, wearing skin-tight jeans and a baggy shirt. She was sitting in a deck chair, cradling a mug, smiling at the camera. We were in the right place. The right Margaret Ross. So, where were Mom and Dad?

"The one of Katrina was taken here, in the back garden," Maggs said. "I'd ordered some wool from the craft shop. Or was it embroidery thread? I must've forgotten to pick it up because she brought it over. She often dropped in after that, on a weekend after she'd closed up the shop. It's a café now. As if we don't have enough."

"You didn't know our mom when she was little?" I said.

"No, she was a student by the time we met."

She wasn't our dead grandmother, then. I shot a smug look

at Cameron that was wasted because he was crouched down, rubbing the dog's belly.

"Is it Mom?" Cameron said without looking up.

"One of Mom, and one of us."

Cameron stood. "Was she born here?"

"No, she's a west coast girl, your mum. If you cut her open, she'd have it written in her core like a stick of rock." She waved at the painting. "The painting's proof of it."

I peered at the painting. "So, it's not of Edinburgh?"

"Oh, it's Edinburgh, all right," she said.

"Which is on the *east* coast," Cameron said. "We saw the ocean from the train."

"It is." She marched across the room to the painting, then pointed to the islands in turn. "This island's Cramond, and this one's Inchcolm, which are right enough, but this one, see how it looks like a sleeping warrior?"

I screwed up my eyes until the island blurred. "Is it holding a shield?"

"What's wrong with the island?" Cameron said.

"Well, it's Arran." Maggs took a step back and folded her arms.

I looked at Cameron. Cameron looked at me. Which one of us was going to ask the obvious question?

"What's wrong with Arran?" I said.

"Nothing's wrong with Arran." She headed back to the kitchen. "It's a lovely place. Plenty of walking, and Brodick Castle's worth seeing. And if you ever go, there's a restaurant in Lamlash …"

"What's wrong with Mom *painting* Arran?" Cameron said.

"Well, it's not on the east coast, it doesn't belong," she said. "Arran's on the west coast, spitting distance from the island where Katrina grew up."

"Why did she move to Edinburgh if she loved home so much?" Cameron said.

"University. She studied politics or economics, I never could remember. She wanted to go to art school, but your grandparents wouldn't have it, and your mother was a pleaser. There wasn't a rebellious bone in her body. It's what I told the police, and I stand by it."

My brain sifted through the information — west coast, politics, art school …

"Police?" I said.

Cameron, who was still staring at the painting, spun around. "Mom's a criminal?"

I stared at my brother. "Why would you even ask that?"

What was it with him? There *were* other logical explanations for the last two days. I'd made a mental list — Mom and Dad were undercover cops or super spies or had been placed in witness protection.

"Was she?" Cameron asked again.

Maggs looked from Cameron to me. "Why don't you help me with the dinner, and after the rush, we can each tell our stories. How does that sound?"

It sounded like delay tactics.

"Now, stretch those arms of yours and reach up there." Maggs pointed at an overhead cupboard. "Fetch me a chopping board."

"If it was good news, you'd tell us," Cameron said.

"Which one are you again?" she asked him.

"Cameron."

"Well, then, Cameron, you can stir the mince. Lewis, you're in charge of veggies. Slices, cubes, whatever you fancy."

I retrieved the chopping board, slid a knife from the block and got to work. With my hands busy, my brain quieted down.

"You can cook," Maggs said.

I shrugged. "Mom and Dad made us learn."

When we were little, Dad would place his hands over ours while we sliced, angling the blade away from our fingers. I pretended his hands were covering mine now. He cut vegetables into thick, randomly shaped chunks, whereas Mom always sliced neat, identical strips, her knife barley clipping the chopping board.

I chopped, Cameron stirred and Maggs alternated between checking on her guests and checking on us.

"Why are you being so hard on Mom and Dad?" I asked Cameron.

"Why are you not? You heard Maggs — heartache, mayhem, police. Even if you're willing to overlook the lies, they killed two people. In front of us. In front of Molly and all our neighbors."

"They were protecting us," I said.

"They were pros, Lewis. You saw them. Mom threw the knife all the way from the shed, and Dad's bullet didn't miss either." He stirred faster, the spoon clanking the sides of the pot. "Mom changed her name. And her nationality. She said she studied art, but she never did. Why would she do that?"

"Witness protection," I said. "Undercover cop."

"An undercover cop in Longview. What was she investigating? Cow tipping?" He stopped stirring and looked at me. "Just because you don't want it to be true, the simplest explanation is always the right one."

"That's not exactly how it goes," I said. Mom said it better.

"Whatever words Mom used, it's what she meant," he said. "No matter how much you want a different answer, you can't ignore the bits you don't like. You're the one who's always going on about facts and constants and solutions."

The facts were Mom and Dad loved us and would always protect us. The constants were we were a family. And the solution was to find them.

"No way Mom and Dad are criminals," I said.

"And you think I want them to be? But it's not going to be good, is it? Maggs is hardly bursting to tell us."

"You're wrong." But something in the pit of my stomach disagreed.

I dumped a heap of diced tomatoes into the pot, splattering red sauce over Cameron's shirt.

He looked down at the stains. "Dude, really?"

After we'd cooked, Maggs served her guests, and then it was our turn to eat.

Maggs asked for our story first, and Cameron gave a factual account of the previous two days, skipping over the painful bits — him hugging Molly as Dad dragged him away, and me clinging to Mom as she promised to find us.

Maggs didn't seem shocked that two people had tried to kill us and were now dead.

"Did you ever meet our dad?" I asked between forkfuls.

"I don't think so. But maybe if I saw his face. Do you have

a photograph?"

We had plenty, but they were on our phones at the bottom of the Thames.

"He has a beard," Cameron said. "And a big laugh and massive hands."

"Mom would've met him after she left Scotland," I said. "He's Canadian."

Maggs nodded. "That would make sense. Someone who didn't know her past."

I dropped my fork in my bowl. "What past? What did she do?"

I looked to Cameron for support, but he was bent down stroking the dog.

"It's easier to show you." She stood, cleared away our plates. "Don't move, I'll fetch my computer."

She took her time. The tap whooshed on. Dishes clattered. When she called the dog to come for its dinner, it licked Cameron's face, then trotted to the kitchen.

Cameron looked at Mom's painting rather than me. I wiped a drop of sauce off the glass table, then rubbed away the smear.

Maggs finally came back carrying a laptop, the dog at her heels. She sat and started to type, then scrolled, her lips tight, her shoulders tense.

"Whatever happened to unbiased reporting? Why do people want all this drama?" She continued to scroll, tutted, clicked, then scrolled some more. "The BBC's the best of a bad lot. It'll have to do."

She slid the computer over to me. "This should've come from your mother. Don't shoot the messenger."

My hands shook as I tilted the screen. "Cameron, do you want to read it with me?"

Cameron was now sitting on the floor, the dog's head in his lap. "Give me the summary."

At the top of the screen were two photographs. In the first, Mom wore a black graduation gown with a red lining. She had one of those flat, square hats on her head, her dark curls springing out from underneath. She looked happy and excited. The other photo was of Dad. His blond hair was cut short, and his face was leaner and clean-shaven. His was a posed photograph, too, but it looked more like a passport picture.

I read the headline below their photos — *The Faces of Evil.*

It felt as if an icicle had pierced my chest. And as I carried on reading, the ice spread to my lungs and my belly.

I slammed the laptop shut.

"What?" Cameron's head shot up. "What did they do? Lewis, just tell me."

My hands were shaking. My whole body was shaking.

Cameron pried the laptop out of my grip and opened it.

The reporters were lying. The police were lying. And the whole country was crazy enough to believe them.

Cameron turned the laptop to face Maggs. "This is our dad."

Maggs's face paled. "Dear Lord."

CHAPTER
9

CAMERON

I woke up to Lewis's heavy breathing and wondered why he was sleeping in my room. Then I remembered we were in the attic of a guesthouse, and Mom and Dad were terrorists.

Everything we'd learned last night crashed over me all over again. Seventeen years ago, Mom and Dad had masterminded the deadliest riot in the United Kingdom's history, and to this day they remained at the top of Britain's most-wanted list. And not only was Mom Scottish, but it turned out that Dad was Dutch — Katrina Murray and Koen van der Berg. Terrorists with a bounty on their heads. A big one. They'd lied to us about everything. But did their lies make them guilty, or was it their innocence that had forced them to lie? And if my parents *were* terrorists, what did that make me?

I burrowed farther under the quilt, but the questions kept going round and round in my head. I needed to do something. Move. Make progress. Eat.

I slipped out of bed, pulled on my sweatpants and grabbed my backpack. A neatly folded pile of clothes sat outside our door. Maggs had gone from trying to throw us out to washing our clothes, and even though I wanted to believe she wouldn't switch back, we had to be ready. I found my soccer jersey in the pile, then crept downstairs.

Haggis was asleep, curled up in her dog bed in the kitchen. The fridge hummed. I turned on the lights, squinted at the brightness, walked into the island, swore. The oven clock shone out the time — 4:37 a.m.

Lewis wouldn't be up for hours. He'd stayed up all night with Maggs's laptop balanced on his knees, the fan whirring, searching for proof that Mom and Dad were innocent. I wished I had his certainty. The knot in my chest might loosen and let me breathe. I might be able to think straight and figure out what we should do next — stay here or move on.

I searched through the pantry, but the closest thing resembling breakfast was porridge oats, which, according to the instructions, needed cooking, and I was too tired to fight with the stovetop. The same for the fridge food — raw bacon, eggs and a bulging black sausage that I wouldn't eat even if it *was* cooked.

Dad always made pancakes for us on Monday mornings. According to him, they made everything better. Is that something a terrorist would do? Make pancakes dribbled with a syrupy smiley face?

I settled for a jam sandwich and a glug of milk from the carton, then turned my attention to my backpack.

Mom had packed everything we needed to run away, but had she packed for what came next? I tipped the bag upside down, the contents rattling onto the floor. The roll of cash, Daniel Johnston's passport, and the flip phone with only one number saved — which I now knew was for Lewis. The toothbrush was in a tartan cup next to the sink upstairs. The hoodie was on the floor next to my bed.

I breathed in the smell of my newly washed soccer jersey. No trace of home left.

As I pulled it over my head, I thought of the last time I'd put it on — Saturday morning before going to meet Molly down by the creek. She'd just fed her horse and had pieces of straw in her hair. As I picked them out for her, I'd rehearsed in my head what I wanted to say. In the end I chickened out — we had a month left of summer. I had plenty of time to tell her how I felt. Truth is, if Lewis was interested in girls, Molly would have chosen him — he was the one who made her laugh.

Haggis trotted over from her basket and licked my arm. I ruffled her ears, then picked up the backpack again. The outside pockets were empty except for what I'd put in them — airline headphones, boarding pass and a train ticket. An internal pocket was empty, too. I dug my hand in to make sure and felt the edge of something, not in the pocket, but behind it, in the lining.

Cutlery rattled as I opened and closed drawers. Haggis barked.

"Shush." I stroked her head. "Don't suppose you know where the scissors are?"

After I'd exhausted all options, I took a knife from the block and sliced open the lining.

An envelope.

I turned it over in my hands — blank and sealed. No weight to it. A letter, then.

Mom would've written everything down — why they'd lied, how to find them, what we needed to do to make this right and go home. And this time I'd ask Molly out. And Lewis would go on his date with Hunter, and everything would be as it should be. My hands shook as I tore it open.

Not a letter.

It was an official-looking form with a red coat of arms at the top — a British birth certificate for Willem Murray van der Berg, born May 20. Another name. Another birthday. Was this who I really was — a British boy named Willem?

But it wasn't Mom's name on the birth certificate, and there was no way Mom and Dad had stayed in Britain with the whole country hunting them. It had to be fake. Another lie.

I paced the kitchen. They must've known Maggs would tell us everything. Is that why they sent us here? To find out the truth? For Maggs to look after us when we did?

I needed fresh air.

As I unlocked the back door, Haggis bounced with excitement.

I grabbed her leash and clipped it on. "You're in charge of directions."

It wasn't light outside, but it wasn't dark either. Mom would say the sky held the promise of the sunrise. Dad would say unless you were a moose or a chipmunk, it was too damn early to be awake.

Haggis bounded down the stone steps to the grass, pulling me behind her. The yard backed onto an alley, which backed onto other backyards. Light shone from a handful of windows.

Haggis sniffed the grass, tugged at the leash, sniffed some more.

"Come on, girl." It was too cold to stand still. I needed a jacket. I needed more clothes, period. And if I could persuade Lewis to move on, then we'd need a decent phone with internet.

I'd told Lewis we'd take one day at a time, one decision at a time, but what was our next move? If we went home now, what would I tell Molly? My parents are terrorists, and I'm not Cameron Larsen, but don't worry. I'm exactly who I've always been? I'm still me.

Haggis raised her head and barked. Then dragged me toward the house next door and barked again.

"What's up, girl?" But I could already see what had caught her attention — a shadow on the wall of the house.

My skin tingled. What the heck was it?

As Haggis tugged me closer, I realized it wasn't a shadow at all, but a real person breaking into the house next door. They were holding on to a window ledge about to hoist themselves inside.

My heart skipped a beat. Was it Goatee Guy?

Should I hide until he was through the window or race back inside and wake Lewis? Would we have time to escape before he realized he'd got the wrong house?

His shoe scraped against the stone.

I dropped into a crouch, my breath coming fast.

He lost his footing and yelped. A high-pitched sound that didn't match my impression of Goatee Guy. Whoever it was, they were now dangling from the window, their feet scrambling to find a foothold.

I let Haggis drag me closer. And closer. Until I could see that the person hanging from the window ledge wasn't as stocky as I'd thought. They had a bulky backpack and were wearing a dress. Definitely not Goatee Guy.

I took a deep breath and told my heart to stand down. We were still safe.

It would be easy to walk away and pretend I hadn't witnessed the next-door neighbor being robbed. But as I turned for the back gate, I heard Dad's voice in my head — *doing the right thing isn't always easy, but it's always worth the effort.* Which was rich coming from a man who'd run away and hidden for the last seventeen years. But I wasn't him. I wasn't a coward.

I launched myself at the house, wrapping my arms around the thief's waist.

Dad had play-wrestled with us enough times that I knew what to do. The trick was to fire your elbow into their gut, then use the thick part of your skull on their nose or, better still, their windpipe.

As we tumbled onto the grass, my knee slammed the corner of the bottom step. Pain shot up my thigh. I curled into a fetal position, waiting for a kick or a punch. When none came, I leaped up, fists raised, my breath coming fast.

Another spike of adrenaline pulsed through my body.

The thief was almost as tall as me. Her dress looked like something from an old movie, with flared sleeves and a swingy skirt, the colors muted in the half-light. A scarf made from the same material as her dress was wrapped around her head like she'd just stepped out of a convertible. Instead of attacking, she struggled out of her backpack, her headscarf tangling in the straps.

"I'm calling the police," I said to buy time while I figured out what to do next.

She freed her scarf, then dumped her backpack on the ground. "Brilliant idea."

I lowered my fists. "Just go. And don't come back."

She adjusted her headscarf. "One teeny, wee flaw in your plan, Einstein. I live here."

Crap. I just tackled Maggs's neighbor?

"You're not a fan of doors?" I nodded at the back door. "Your house has two of them."

"Which chime like Big bloody Ben when they open. They forgot the windows though." She looked up at a second-floor window. "Not so clever now, are you, Mum?"

Breaking curfew. I knew what that felt like. "I can show you how to bypass the alarm."

She bent down to stroke Haggis, who was nuzzling her. "Would that be in return for not charging you with assault?"

Assault? What the heck had I done? If she reported me, we'd have no choice but to run again.

"Don't have a heart attack, I'm only joking. Maggs would kill me if I got one of her guests arrested. Wouldn't she, Haggis?"

She ruffled Haggis behind her ears, then held out her hand. "I'm Aisha."

I scrambled for a name.

When the answer came, it was obvious. I even had a birth certificate to prove it.

"Willem." And just like that, I became someone else.

She tilted her head. "Why are you taking Haggis for a walk in the dark?"

"Couldn't sleep."

"Guilt or jetlag?"

"Jetlag." And the general fear that comes with being in a country that thinks your parents are terrorists and having so many questions racing through your brain that sleep is impossible.

"You just flew in, then?" she said. "Where from?"

Lewis would know what answer to give. He'd have worked through the pros and cons of every country in the northern hemisphere.

"It's not a trick question." She dusted down her dress.

"Why can't your mom know you've been out?" I said.

She looked down at Haggis. "If he tries to dognap you, girlie, you have my permission to bite."

Way to go, Cameron. Make enemies with the neighbors, why don't you?

She picked up her backpack — blue, with *Lothian Swim Club* embroidered in white letters. It looked heavy.

"You want me to throw that up once you're inside?" I asked.

"My guess is American," she said. "The accent, of course. And you're polite, yet dodgy."

"Or you could carry it yourself."

She glared at me, then heaved the backpack onto her back.

"You have yourself a wonderful day," I said.

"Ha ha." She looked up at the houses opposite where lights were flickering on, and then up at the sky, which was now tinged with orange.

Her face fell. "Chuffing hell. Mum'll be up soon."

A light came on inside her house.

"Quick," she said. "Help me up."

I dropped into a crouch, interlacing my fingers to make a platform.

She stepped onto my hands and reached for the window ledge. "Thanks, dodgy neighbor."

I catapulted her through the window. Heard a bump and

a groan, then the window slid shut, and she was gone. Haggis barked a goodbye, then tugged me on.

We walked through the neighborhood until the sky turned pink and the sun rose. Until people started trudging down their front steps with briefcases and coffees in their hands. Until my throbbing knee threatened to give out.

Maggs was awake when we got back. She was dressed in denim overalls and fluffy socks.

"Where on earth have you been?" she said as I closed the back door.

"Around the neighborhood." I hung the leash on the hook by the door. "Haggis took me for a walk."

"Good grief, child." She shook her head. "Did you learn nothing from our conversation last night? No one can know you're here. Please tell me Nora didn't see you. She's up with the larks, that one, and nothing gets by her."

"She doesn't know who I am," I said. "You're my mom's friend and *you* didn't recognize us until you saw Lewis and me together."

Okay, wandering the streets was probably a bad idea until we knew if Goatee Guy had followed us, but hiding from Maggs's guests was overkill.

Maggs poured water into the teapot. "Nora's a journalist."
Oh.

I hobbled over to the island and pulled out a stool. "What kind of journalist?"

"The curious kind. She writes a column on arts and culture now, but in her day, she was quite the investigative journalist. She reported on the riots, but, then again, what journalist didn't? The

March of the Illegal Dead, they called it." Maggs poured milk into two mugs. "Those poor people; the refugees and immigrant workers and all those families who turned up to show their support. It was meant to be a peaceful demonstration and also a celebration of people's cultures. There were musical bands, and food stalls, and dancing, you know."

I'd only read that first article Maggs had shown us, but Lewis would know. He'd kept digging, trawling through every website he could find. I'd fallen asleep feeling the tension radiating off him.

"Do you think my mom did what everyone says she did? Do you think she's a … terrorist?"

The word stuck in my throat.

"If I did, I'd hardly be letting you stay," Maggs said. "But if Nora gets so much as a whiff of a story, she won't stop until she's uncovered every detail, and where would you and your brother be then? The media would have a field day. The whole world would know where to find you."

I wrapped my arms around my stomach and focused on the flecks of color in the countertop. If the whole world knew where to find us, Mom and Dad would have to stay away. And who would protect us then?

Maggs took a breath and patted my hand. "But no one saw you, so we're fine."

My stomach twisted.

"I met Aisha from next door." And tackled her to the ground. "Do you think she'll tell anyone?"

Please say no.

"Aisha won't give you away," Maggs said. "That girl would leap in front of a lorry to save a rabid cat."

My body went loose with relief.

Maggs frowned. "I suppose she was on her way to the pool?"

"She had a swim bag with her, but she was on her way back." Although, considering she felt the need to hoist herself through a window, I doubted she'd come from the swimming pool.

Maggs checked the time on the oven, then tutted. "It's too early for her to be back from training. She must've stayed out all night with her swim friends."

Maggs fetched a can of dog food from the pantry and opened it, all the while muttering about how Aisha knew better than to traipse around the city in the wee hours, and her parents would eventually allow her some freedom again, but it would take time, and Aisha was many things, but patient she was not.

As she bent down to fill Haggis's bowl, I crept toward the dining room door.

"I've made tea," Maggs said.

She poured two cups, then slid one across the island. "Sit yourself down."

I shuffled back, curled my hands around the warm mug and hung my head. "I'm sorry about being seen, but I needed to be outside."

"Next time open a window." She took a sip of tea.

"I wanted to walk."

"Which is all well and good," she said. "Until you're recognized, and I lose my business, and my neighbors never speak to me again."

I felt a stab of guilt, then frustration replaced it. "We didn't ask for any of this."

Maggs put her cup down. "And I did?"

"We weren't even alive when the riots happened," I said. "My mom was your friend. You could've done something."

What would I have done if it had been Molly? Anything. Because I'd have known she was innocent. But maybe deep down, Maggs knew Mom must've done the things the papers said she did.

"People died," Maggs said. "*Children* died. The entire country was out for blood, but not Katrina's, no, because she upped and disappeared."

I peeked up at her. "They came after you?"

She shook her head. "Why would anyone be interested in a landlady who happened to frequent a craft shop? No one knew we were friends. Katrina kept her life in tidy, wee compartments. Her family. Her studies. Her weekends in the shop and visiting me. She kept us all separate. I think she played different parts in each. I like to think I knew the real Katrina, but who knows?"

I pulled my hand through my nonexistent hair. "But you still think she's innocent?"

Maggs, tipping the teapot over her mug, hesitated mid-pour. "I do."

"But?" I said.

Maggs finished pouring her tea, then topped up my mug even though I hadn't touched it yet. "As I said before, Katrina never wanted to disappoint anyone, especially the people she loved. And I never met this man, your father, but maybe ..."

"No! No way." I jumped up, sloshing tea over the side of my mug. "Dad would never make Mom do something she didn't want to. Just. No."

"There you go, then," she said. "You've got your answer."

How was that an answer?

"Don't give me that look," she said. "If the jumper doesn't fit, then unravel the wool and knit yourself a scarf."

I had no idea what she was talking about.

She sighed. "If the story makes no sense, you need to unpick the facts all the way back to the beginning, then rearrange them."

"If I unpicked everything, I'd be at the barbecue with a gun against my head." I rubbed my temple, remembering the pressure of the barrel.

This was such a mess. I wanted everything back to the way it was. Riding my bike over to Molly's, swimming in the creek, going for ice cream. Dropping in to see Mom at the gallery. Listening to Dad's stories. On his last shift, he rescued a wolf pup from a trap. Would a terrorist do that?

"And what do you know about the people who pointed the guns?" Maggs took another sip of tea.

"A man and a woman." I shrugged. "They spoke what I thought was German, but could've been Dutch. Dad recognized the man. Called him Schenk."

"There you go," she said. "You have your first stitch."

How did that help? Maggs tilted her head as if she was waiting for me to catch up.

"Dad *knew* Schenk," I said.

Maggs nodded.

"Schenk and his partner wanted something, I think." But what did Mom and Dad have that was worth killing for?

I looked at Maggs. "Schenk's the first stitch!"

"Good lad," she said. "Now you need to work out the second stitch. Then the third and keep knitting until something takes shape."

I started to pace as energy pulsed through my body. My knee ached. I ignored it. Haggis barked and ran around me in circles, so I crouched down and stroked her in long, calming strokes. If we could find out who Schenk was, we'd know what Mom and Dad were running from. And if we knew that, we'd know who they'd been before they were our parents.

I needed to tell Lewis to stop wasting time researching the riots and start looking for Schenk.

The ceiling above our heads creaked, and we both looked up.

"The Fisbys are up." Maggs said. "Best get on with breakfast. Lay the tables, would you? Then make yourself scarce. And for pity's sake, stay inside."

CHAPTER
10

LEWIS

Half my brain was unconscious, and the other half felt like it was recovering from amnesia. And my brother was about to get himself shot.

"So you're just going to wander into town?" I said to Cameron, who was standing with his hands on his hips looking like he was about to go save the world.

"I need to get out," Cameron said. "You do realize you slept half the day."

I wished I was still asleep rather than slouched at the kitchen island staring at a bowl of gloopy papier-mâché, trying to muster the energy to eat. I prodded it with my spoon.

"It's porridge," Cameron said.

"Knowing what it is doesn't make it any more appealing." I let go of the spoon, and it stood upright like a flag planted at the North Pole.

"I'll be back in an hour with a real phone with an actual screen and internet."

He had a point. Maggs's laptop had run out of battery last night, and by the time I woke up, she'd claimed it back to check her website for new bookings. And now she was out, and there was no sign of the computer anywhere, and I needed to keep digging for information. I had to find something that proved Mom and Dad weren't terrorists. Some detail that even if no one else had noticed, I would.

Cameron leaned down to pet the dog. "Once we've got a phone, we can call Molly and find out what's going on back home — the sheriff must know something about Schenk by now."

My blood rushed to my feet as I jumped up. "You can't text or message her. Or log into any of your accounts. There's a reason Mom gave us burner phones. No electronic footprints."

He sighed. "I'll buy a prepaid SIM card. I'm not a complete rookie."

Maybe not, but he was taking way too many risks, like always.

"Risk is a combination of probability and consequence," I said. "You can minimize the probability of being traced all you like, but it's the consequence you should be worried about."

"Will you stop quoting Mom?" Cameron gave the dog one last pat, then straightened. "She isn't here and even if she was, I'm not sure we should believe anything she said."

I waved my spoon at him. "Be angry with her all you want, but she managed to stay hidden for seventeen years, so I think she knows what she's talking about."

Cameron's shoulders dropped. "Fine. You win. I'll buy a decent phone, and then we'll figure out how to use it."

He opened the back door, shoved the dog back inside when it tried to escape, then turned to go.

"And deodorant," I called after him. "Roll on. No scent."

I gave up on breakfast, scraped the contents of my bowl into the trash and washed the few dishes that were in the sink. The house was quiet. The guests were out at the Fringe Festival, which Maggs had described as a "cornucopia of performing arts." Maggs was also out and wouldn't be back until teatime. Considering she drank tea all day, I had no idea what time that was.

The dog went to sleep.

With nothing to distract me, images from last night flashed through my brain. I'd read so much about the riots, they'd followed me into my dreams. It was the children I'd seen while I'd slept, in fancy dress and painted faces, dancing, waving flags, then being carried on shoulders and laughing at the sky. And then they were falling. A boy, his face painted with a spider's web, blond hair matted with blood, reaching out from the crush of bodies, screaming to be pulled free. A little girl in a pink princess dress being carried, her dark head lolling, her feet swaying.

Two children had died in the riot. I'd read the list of victims' names. In my nightmare, they were dressed as Spider-Man and a Disney princess.

I slumped on the couch and put my head in my hands.

Mom and Dad had been at the march. Grainy photographs captured on traffic cameras, but it was them. Mom's hair was short, the curls from her graduation photo cut out. Dad had looked like the photo from the website Maggs had shown us — thinner face, short-cropped hair. But it was them. And there was more evidence — tapped phones in hotel rooms, a rental car abandoned with a nail bomb in the trunk, witnesses who placed them at the core of the first violent act, a map with their known movements plotted in red. And then a photo of a fair-haired man bringing a baseball bat down on the head of a fallen policewoman. It could've been Dad. It could've been a hundred other men. And even though the name Schenk didn't appear in any of my searches, it could have been him, the man Dad shot on our patio. But according to the police, it wasn't Schenk, or one of a hundred other men. They'd confirmed the bat-wielding cop-killer was Dad — by tracking his progress, a trail of photos and witness statements, a baseball bat found in an alley with his fingerprints on the handle. It was enough. All that was needed.

My head pounded. I'd slept too long or hadn't slept enough, or maybe this was what jetlag felt like. Mom would tell me to hydrate.

The glasses were in the fourth cupboard I tried. Instead of taking out only one, I emptied both shelves and lined wine glasses and tumblers and beer mugs on the island. Then I emptied the cupboard next to the fridge and put all those coffee bags and tea boxes and chocolate mixes on the floor. Shoved the dog, now awake and prancing through the packages, into the dining room and closed it in. All the glasses went into their logical home next to the fridge, then I took out a tall, straight tumbler and, not moving my feet, opened the fridge, grabbed the milk and poured myself a perfect glass.

I drank, refilled, drank again, then picked up an armful of tea boxes and opened the cupboard above the kettle. Full of tins. Maggs was worse than Mom.

It took two hours to bring order to the kitchen. Then only two minutes for the images of the riot to barge back into my head.

The guest lounge had some storage — a sideboard filled with board games stacked haphazardly and shelves of disorganized books. The dog followed me, then immediately fell asleep in a patch of sunlight in front of the window. How many hours of sleep did dogs need? And where was Cameron?

If I could show him the photo of the man with the baseball bat, maybe he'd spot something. A missing finger or a mole or something that would prove it wasn't Dad.

I was halfway through organizing the board games when the dog leaped onto the armchair and barked at the window.

I stepped over Monopoly cards and Scrabble tiles on my way to the window. The dog looked at me, then back outside.

A group of people were coming up the front steps.

I ducked, then raced to the kitchen, still clutching a Monopoly card.

The bell above the front door tinkled.

I shut the kitchen door, then leaned against it, my heart pounding.

Footsteps.

Scratching at the kitchen door, followed by a bark.

Then a knock.

"Maggs?" a female voice said. "Are you home?"

I needed Cameron.

I looked out the back window. Could I hide behind the garbage bin? In that bush?

The dog barked.

The woman knocked.

I needed to breathe. Suck in air, puff it out. Then I needed to open the door and tell the guest in a calm voice that Maggs would be back soon, smile, promise to pass on a message, then retreat.

I cracked open the door. The dog shoved itself though the gap.

The woman put her hands on her hips. "And who in heaven's name might you be? Does Maggs know you're back there?"

"Yes, she does." I waved the Monopoly card as if it proved I was allowed to be here. "She left me in charge until teatime. I'm tidying. Kitchen's done. Lounge is in progress. Everything's good. Better than good. Do you need anything in particular?"

I should've stayed in the attic.

The woman held out her hand for me to shake. "I'm Nora Bidwell. I didn't quite catch your name."

Nora? This was the woman Cameron had told me to avoid at all costs because she was a journalist. My heart rate flipped into fight-or-flight mode, which seemed to be its new default setting.

She narrowed her eyes as if she was trying to place me.

"I'm Will." I reluctantly shook her hand. "Short name. Easy to remember. Only one of me."

Please don't come home now, Cameron.

I stepped out of the kitchen and closed the door behind me, just in case he came bursting through the back door.

Nora Bidwell was a tall Black lady, her brown, chin length hair held behind her ears with gold clips. She was wearing a flowery summer dress and sneakers.

"New guests have arrived," she said. "And I'm not qualified to hand over keys."

"Maggs isn't here."

"I am aware, but that does not make the guests' presence any less real."

She drummed her fingers against the guidebook she was holding. "As the only official person present, I believe it is your responsibility to hold the fort, as it were."

Maggs had told us to stay hidden.

Cameron had made me promise not to talk to anyone at all, Nora-the-journalist in particular.

I'd already broken both of those rules. Checking in a guest wouldn't break any more.

The woman's eyebrows questioned my next move.

"I should see to the new guests."

"Marvelous idea. Clever boy." Nora Bidwell turned and led the way through the dining room into the front hall.

"This young man will help you," she said to the two people waiting in the hallway, then she climbed halfway up the stairs, stopped and watched from above.

I strode behind the desk, trying to look competent, and fixed my eyes on the reservation book. Today's date was blank.

"We don't have a booking," the man said.

He wore glasses. White skin, silvery hair. Button-down shirt. His details were old, but he stood straight, as if he was holding in energy, like he might start jogging on the spot or drop down for a few push-ups any minute. Beside him was a teenaged girl. Short and compact, like a gymnast. Blue hair. Really blue, like cotton candy. That's all I could see of her because she was looking down at the cookie-dough carpet.

"I think we might have a room." I used my most formal voice.

"We need two." The girl looked up. Her eyes were blue, too. Her skin paper-white, which made the pimple on her cheek stand out even more. Like a flashing neon light demanding to be noticed. She looked back at the carpet.

"My granddaughter and I would like two rooms. Next to each other if possible."

Did I have the authority to give away rooms? I ran through the guests. Two sets — the Fisbys and Nora Bidwell. Two guest rooms occupied out of five. I turned the page, scanned the dates. It was a week until the next guests arrived.

"We'll take however many days you have," the man said. "We're on a road trip and can be flexible. Once we're settled, maybe you can recommend some shows."

"I think we might have space, but the owner will be back very soon." *Please, Maggs, come back.*

"I wouldn't refuse a cup of tea while we wait." The man tipped his head toward the dining room. "And a biscuit would be nice if there's any going spare."

"Tea. I can do that." And hide in the kitchen until Maggs came back.

The man patted his jacket pockets, found a car key, then turned for the door. "Ruby, why don't you help the boy whip up some tea and biscuits while I bring in the bags."

"I don't need help," I said.

"Ruby, run along and help."

The girl, Ruby, looked at her grandfather, then at me.

The bell above the front door jangled, and we all turned to see who it was. *Please, don't let it be Cameron. Not now.*

Maggs stood in the doorway, a grocery bag in each hand.

I let out a breath.

"Fortuitous timing." The man took one of the bags from her. "Please, allow me."

The stairs creaked. Was Nora Bidwell going up or coming down?

I rushed to take the other bag from Maggs. "We have two new guests."

"So I see." Maggs took the bag from the man and handed it to me. "Take the shopping to the kitchen, dear."

I retreated to the kitchen before Ruby could follow. Before her grandfather suggested she help unload the shopping. Before Nora Bidwell swooped downstairs and started asking questions.

———

CAMERON

I'd unboxed the smartphone in the shopping mall and inserted the prepaid SIM card. All I had to do now was figure out how to contact Molly without being traced. News traveled fast in Longview — if the sheriff knew who Schenk and his partner were, Molly would, too.

As I opened the back door, Lewis piled into me and gave me a hug.

"For the love of God," Maggs said from behind him. "Do the two of you share half a brain? Which part of 'stay inside' did you not understand?"

I unpeeled myself from Lewis. "I got the phone."

"Took you long enough," he said.

I chucked deodorant at him.

Maggs scraped out two chairs from the table, then glared at us.

We sat. Lewis and me on one side of the table, Maggs on the other. I held the new phone that would connect us to the world. Lewis clutched the deodorant that would help him smell better.

"Where on earth have you been?" Maggs said.

"You said you'd be out until teatime." Whenever that was.

"I didn't ask why you thought you could get away with it."

I showed her the phone. "I went to buy this."

"A phone?" She raised her eyebrows. "You risked exposing your whereabouts, your brother's whereabouts, not to mention my part in sheltering the two of you, for a mobile phone?"

"Yes" was the answer, but from the look on her face, it wasn't the right one. I *knew* it would only be a matter of time until she threw us out. I looked down at the phone. We'd find somewhere else to stay, then we'd contact Molly. And after that, I'd figure out the rest.

Lewis sat up straight. "We needed to keep searching things up, and you hid the laptop."

She pushed herself up from the table, ambled to the couch and opened a drawer in the coffee table.

"Oh," Lewis said. "I didn't know there was a drawer there. Sorry."

She slid the laptop onto the table, then folded her arms.

Lewis shouldn't be apologizing. I was sick of running and hiding and being made to feel guilty when we'd done nothing wrong.

"We'll collect our things and go," I said.

Lewis looked at me. "What? Why?"

"This was never going to work," I said.

Lewis looked from me to Maggs.

I stood. "Come on, Lewis. We can't find Mom and Dad from here."

"We don't *need* to find them." He stood and looked at me. "They said they'd come here. We have to stay."

Then he looked at Maggs. "I know you're taking a risk helping us, which is very kind, but we were almost shot. We watched people die. There was blood. Lots of blood. And we had to leave everything behind. Our house, our friends and our parents."

Maggs sank back into her chair. "The both of you will stay here. I'll not have you galivanting around the country on your own."

Lewis shrugged me a "why not stay?"

Of course he wanted to stay. He still believed Mom and Dad would come for us.

"Put the kettle on, would you?" Maggs said. "I think we could all do with a cup of tea."

Tea? Again?

I stomped to the sink, turned the tap full blast.

"I'll do whatever's in my capacity to help you find your mother," Maggs said.

"Why?" I asked over the whoosh of water.

Lewis glared at me.

"What?" I said. "She can't keep flip-flopping between wanting to chuck us out and wanting to help."

"I apologize for that," she said. "But I saw how your grandparents suffered, and I didn't want the same fate to befall me. But I'll not abandon two youngsters."

"What happened to them?" Lewis asked.

Maggs eased herself out of the chair and joined me at the island.

"The press hounded your grandparents. Printed all sorts of rubbish about them." She popped the lid of the cookie tin and pulled out a packet of cookies. "None of it was true, of course, but people needed someone to blame and, in the absence of the real culprits, they blamed your grandparents for bringing a monster such as your mother into this world."

My whole body tensed at the word *monster*. Mom was not a monster. I was not the son of a monster.

"What happened to them?" Lewis said.

"It got so bad they couldn't leave their house. They had to close their business. The final straw was their cat. Someone killed the poor wee creature. Posted it back though their letter box in pieces."

I glanced at Haggis sleeping in her dog bed, and a shiver ran down my spine. "So, their car crash might not have been an accident? You think someone killed them?"

"Killed them?" Maggs paused in the middle of unwrapping the cookies. "No child, they're not dead. They moved to the Highlands, which some may say is as good as. But they were alive and kicking last I heard."

"We have grandparents?" Lewis said.

Grandparents who'd never sent us a birthday card or a Christmas present or stuck our embarrassing school photos to their fridge.

"Do they know we exist?" My chest tightened.

"I expect your mother told them." Maggs opened a cupboard, then closed it. Opened another. And another. "Where on earth did the mugs go?"

"Above the kettle," Lewis said. "And the glasses are next to the fridge. The pots and pans next to the oven. It makes more sense that way."

"Well, I never," Maggs said, beaming. "You can stay as long as you like."

"We can't. We need to leave." I glared at Lewis. "And before you ask, no, we can't go and live with our grandparents."

"Why not?" Lewis asked.

"Because someone's after us," I said. "And living with grand-parents is too obvious."

Plus, they didn't want us. If our grandparents had loved us at all, Mom wouldn't have told us they were dead.

"Your brother's right. It'll be why your mother sent you to me. No one outside of the family knew we were friends. We have no connection that anyone could possibly trace." Maggs dribbled milk into three mugs. "This is the safest place for you."

"I'm not staying indoors," I said.

What I should've said was thank you, but there was no way I was going to be locked away in the attic.

"We can't be seen," Lewis said to me. "Stick together, but stay apart, remember?"

I was sick of Mom and Dad's advice.

"I agree," Maggs said. "One of you might go unnoticed, but identical twins would be commented on by the entire street. Nora's already asking questions. No surprise there."

"The journalist?" I said. "Why? She hasn't seen us. She has no idea we're here."

Lewis fiddled with the deodorant. "She saw me and wanted to know who I was."

Crap. "What did you say?" *Please, not the truth.*

"I said I was you," he said. "I mean Will. Because you said that's what you told the neighbor, because of the birth certificate, so I thought it best to stick to the same story."

"Good thinking." I snatched a cookie off the plate. "She won't get suspicious if she only saw one of us, will she?"

Lewis jumped up. "You're a genius."

Not often Lewis called me smart. I bit into a cookie. Sweet chocolate and tangy orange. Yum.

"We pretend there's only one of us," Lewis said.

"Wait, what?" I choked on cookie crumbs.

Maggs slapped my back. "It's a fine idea."

"You *are* aware there's actually two of us," I said when I recovered. "We might look the same, but we can't physically morph into one person."

Looking like Lewis was bad enough. No way was I going to pretend to *be* him.

"You can if one of you stays hidden," Maggs said.

Becomes a prisoner more like. "I'm not doing it."

"I'll hide," Lewis said. "I can stay in the attic and keep researching. You'll be down here being Will. People already know you exist."

"They know *Will* exists," I said. "I'm not Will."

Lewis threw up his hands. "Any better ideas?"

Maggs nodded. "You'll be the son of an old friend earning his board while you experience the city. It's close enough to the truth. You'll help in the kitchen, serve breakfasts and dinners, and clean the rooms. As long as my guests only see one of you, no one will be any the wiser."

"Let me get this straight," I said. "I slave away all day, while Lewis lazes around in his bed?"

"You get to wander about outside as well," Lewis said. "And I'll be able to research the riots some more."

"Forget the riots. We need to work out how to contact Molly and find out what the sheriff knows about Schenk. And we could ask her to search the house and the shed and the garage. Maybe Mom and Dad left us a paper message."

"That would be called a letter," he said.

"Thanks. Helpful. Really."

The dog bounded to the closed door leading to the dining room and barked.

"Oh, dear Lord," Maggs whispered. "Someone's there."

We all looked at one another. Lewis's eyes were wide. Maggs frantically waved us into the pantry, then went to check who it was.

CHAPTER
11

LEWIS

I backed through the door into the dining room cradling the teapot, my heart racing, palms sweating. So much for staying hidden in the attic.

Scalding hot teapots are tricky to carry. Clutching the handle with one hand and resting the spout on the back of the other, I shuffled to Nora Bidwell's table. Would she blame the rattling lid on incompetence, or would she guess it was nerves?

Nora finished spreading butter on her toast, then looked up. I avoided her gaze and focused on the Fisbys' abandoned plates — porridge half-eaten, orange juice untouched.

"Don't clear them," Nora said. "They're coming back."

I slid the teapot onto the table, a spurt of brown tea splodging the white tablecloth. "Maggs said your cooked breakfast will be out in a few minutes."

She'd actually said "in a jiffy," but I was too stressed to use alien words. And too tired. The alarm had gone off at 6:30 this morning, seven hours earlier than I'd woken up yesterday.

"May I ask you something?" Nora said while cutting her toast into four neat pieces, her gold bangle clanking against the plate.

Maggs had warned me not to entertain any questions from Nora. One question would turn into three, and from there it was a slippery slope. She was a bloodhound.

Someone grunted. Not Nora, because she was smiling expectantly at me.

The window table, which had been vacant five minutes ago when I'd delivered Nora's toast, was now occupied by a man hidden behind a newspaper. All I could see was his knobbly knuckled fingers holding the paper. And his legs — business-man pants and brown leather shoes. The grandfather from yesterday?

"Whatever possessed you to cut off your hair?" Nora said to me.

I glanced at the kitchen door. Cameron was on the other side, helping Maggs break eggs and make tea and stir porridge. It should've been him serving out here, but dinner last night had been a zoo, and Cameron had cooked and served and washed up afterwards, all while I was "messing around with pointless internet searches." Not pointless. I was trying to find Schenk and figuring out how to contact Molly without being traced, just like Cameron had asked me to. I'd reminded him we were a team, which he interpreted as an offer to help, and before I could list all the reasons why it was a terrible idea, I was standing in front of the bathroom mirror, Cameron shaving my head. The buzz cut looked as catastrophic on me as it did on him. But it was comforting to look the same again.

I rubbed the fuzz on my head. It was itchy.

"Did you shave it for a girl?" Nora poured her tea. "Or perhaps a boy?"

I didn't know which was more improbable; my shaved head improving my chances of dating, or the chance of stumbling across a possible date while locked up in Maggs's guesthouse.

"Leave the lad alone," said the man from behind his newspaper. "Let him keep his secrets."

He had a Scottish accent, so not the grandfather I'd checked in yesterday who'd sounded like the people in London. Or Mr. Fisby, who emphasized his *O*'s and dropped every *T*.

"I don't have secrets." I glanced at the kitchen door again. I didn't know how Cameron managed to avoid conversation. I wished he could teach me.

"The boy doth protest too much." Nora smiled. "I'll keep digging until I find out."

Another grunt from newspaper man.

Nora tilted her head, waiting for my confession.

Sweat ran down my back. Could she see I was panicking? Would it make her more suspicious? Of course it would.

I was saved by the Fisbys bursting into the dining room, arms wide in a ta-da stance. They were wearing matching bright-green pants and shiny orange shirts. The outfit made Mr. Fisby, who had a ring of brown hair around his bald head, look like a caterpillar. The fuzzy kind that Mom liked because they ate the weeds.

Nora clapped. "Marvelous."

Mrs. Fisby scanned the room, then looked at me. "We'll need some cups, Will."

"But mum's the word." Mr. Fisby zipped his lips closed. "Maggs banned us from rehearsing our act in the dining room after an incident last year."

"Condiments," the man muttered from behind his newspaper.

Mrs. Fisby, who was wiping her spectacles with a napkin, added, "Midair collision of a saltshaker and a vinegar bottle. Nasty mess."

"Smelled like a fish and chip shop for a week," newspaper man mumbled.

Mr. Fisby stacked the glasses and teacups from the vacant table. "These'll do."

Nora patted the chair beside her. "Front row seat, Will. No need to battle the festival crowds to witness the Fantastical Fisbys. Sit yourself down."

"I'll check on your breakfast." I took a step toward the kitchen just as Mr. Fisby threw a glass to his wife. I jerked back to avoid it.

Mrs. Fisby caught the glass, and as she sent it up into the air, Mr. Fisby tossed her a teacup. My escape route became blocked by Mr. Fisby feeding glasses and cups to his wife.

He stopped at five.

I waited for two juggling rotations just to be sure, then edged around the Ferris wheel of crockery.

I was almost at the kitchen door.

Two more steps.

"Will," Mr. Fisby called me back.

He'd stacked the saucers from around the room. "Feed me one at a time, would you, mate?"

Nora watched me.

Newspaper man remained silent behind his newspaper.

I took the stack off Mr. Fisby, then picked up the top saucer and held it up.

"Attaboy," Mr. Fisby said. "Aim for my tummy button."

I threw him the saucer, which he caught and tossed in the air.

"Keep 'em coming," he said.

I fed him saucers until he was juggling six.

Nora clapped as the Fisbys spun glasses and mugs and saucers in the air.

Now was my chance.

"Is there room for two more spectators?" The grandfather from yesterday stood in the doorway.

He nodded a hello to me, said good morning to the room in general, then strode to the table under the embroidered Highland cow. His collared shirt and front-creased shorts were at odds with his footwear — white athletic socks with canvas sandals. His blue-haired granddaughter shuffled in behind him, her hands in the front pocket of her gray hoodie, her eyes on the floor.

The grandfather patted the tablecloth as if to make sure his eyes weren't deceiving him. "We seem to be short on crockery."

He chuckled, glanced at the Fisbys, then focused his attention on me. "Bet you don't have jugglers entertaining the guests over breakfast in Canada."

His granddaughter rolled her eyes. "It's not normal here either."

My heart, which was already beating too fast, did a weird flutter. How did he know I was Canadian?

"I'll get you some cups." I skirted round the flying mugs and saucers and glasses, then dove into the sanctuary of the kitchen.

Cameron looked up from the sink, where he was washing dishes. Maggs stood at the stove turning an omelet. The radio was singing a song from the eighties. The dog was sprawled across the couch sleeping.

"How's it going out there?" Maggs asked.

I leaned against the island. "I can't do this."

"Maybe you should swap," she said. "Your brother's been whinging about washing up."

"What happened to one of us staying in the attic at all times?" I said.

"*Tch.*" Maggs sprinkled shredded cheese on the omelet. "As long as one of you hides back here until everyone's gone for the day, no one will be any the wiser."

"They ask too many questions," I said.

Cameron glanced over his shoulder. "The trick is to avoid eye contact and not engage in conversation."

"Good grief, child. Is that why my guests didn't ask for seconds last night? Of course you engage in conversation."

"See," Cameron said to Maggs. "Told you he'd be better at it than me."

"Nora Bidwell's a journalist," I said. "How do we know she isn't here to investigate us? And retired circus performers? The Fisbys look more like accountants. How do we know it's not just a cover?"

"Please tell me they're not juggling my crockery," Maggs said.

I threw up my hands. "And neither of you thought to warn me about random newspaper guy? When did he check in?"

Cameron spun around, soap suds dripping from his hands, and looked at me as if to say, *What the heck?*

"It's only Angus," Maggs said. "Always turns up for breakfast — cheese omelet and a pot of tea."

Cameron dried his hands. "And who is Angus, exactly?"

"He lives downstairs, and, mind you, address him as 'Professor Pham.' He still deserves respect, even if he is retired."

He was a neighbor, then, which made his presence a little less scary.

"Why does he come here if he has his own place?" I asked.

"Because he likes my cooking." Maggs pressed down on the omelet with a spatula, making it squeak. "And I expect he's lonely."

Cameron shrugged and turned back to the sink.

"He's good company on the days I have no guests," Maggs said. "But I'll admit there are times I regret selling him the flat."

"Why did you sell it then?" Cameron asked.

"It was after the riots." Maggs turned off the gas.

The riots? "What did the riots have to do with it?"

She slid the omelet onto a plate. "Well, for starters, I didn't know if the press would make the connection between your mother and me, and ruin my business. And then there was the worry of your mother and whether she'd need money for lawyers. So, when Angus knocked on my door asking if I'd consider selling the basement flat, well, it seemed the sensible course of action. And the back bedroom up here suits me fine."

"You didn't think the timing was suspicious?" I asked.

"Why did he choose *your* door?" Cameron said at the same time.

"You're fretting about Angus Pham? The man can't even make an omelet." She held out the plate and teapot. "Stop wittering and take the man his breakfast before it goes cold, and then come back for Nora's sausages. Have the Ratcliffs come down yet?"

I stared at Professor Pham's omelet. Was it a coincidence he'd chosen Maggs's door? *Coincidences are like shooting stars, rare and not worth wishing on.*

"Lewis, dear. Brian Ratcliff and his granddaughter Ruby. Have you seen them?"

I looked up. "They just arrived."

"Coffee or tea? Poached or fried? Bacon, sausage, black pudding, or a combination thereof?"

"I'll ask them." I put the plate and teapot on a tray and trudged to the door.

"Don't make eye contact," Cameron said. "Especially with Pham."

I nodded, then pushed the door open with my shoulder.

The Fantastical Fisbys show was over, and the two of them were chatting with Nora about their street performance this afternoon. I kept my eyes down when I passed.

As I slid Professor Pham's plate and teapot onto his table, he lowered his newspaper, then folded it.

He was Asian with a mop of white hair and half-moon spectacles, dressed in a white shirt, tie and navy cardigan.

"Have I seen you here before?" he said.

I felt my cheeks flush. Did Cameron say to make eye contact or avoid it?

"I'm helping out," I said.

He grunted, shook salt over his omelet. "I hope you're doing a good job."

"Will." Brian Ratcliff waved me over.

Thank goodness.

I scuttled over to Brian's table. "Would you like sausage or bacon?"

He looked at his granddaughter, who was curling the corner of the tablecloth. "Ruby, why don't you ask Will your question."

Her shoulders stiffened.

"Wi-Fi." She looked up. "What's the password?"

She looked less ghost-like than yesterday. Her cheeks were pink, and the bags under her eyes had faded.

"My granddaughter's a computer buff," Brian said.

"I code," she mumbled. "It's not that difficult."

"The password's 'Haggis,' like the dog," I said.

"Haggis is offal and oats cooked in a sheep's stomach," Brian said. "Not dog. God forbid."

"The dog, Gramps. Mrs. Ross's dog. She's called Haggis."

"There's a dog?"

"So, you know about computers?" I asked. Maybe Ruby would know how we could contact Molly without being traced.

She shrugged, then fiddled with the corner of the tablecloth some more.

"Will, dear," Nora said. "We're discussing what shows you might enjoy. Come, tell us what attracts teenagers to the Fringe Festival these days."

The professor rattled his cup on its saucer. "Leave the lad alone, Nora. Not everyone wants to be featured in one of your articles."

I looked from the professor who'd moved in downstairs right after the riots, to the journalist who'd reported on them, to the granddad who somehow knew I was Canadian, to the retired circus performers who looked more like accountants. If this was a game of Clue, I'd be suspicious of every single one of them.

CHAPTER 12

CAMERON

After breakfast, the Fisbys left for their street performance up near the castle. The other guests, including the professor, loitered, drank tea and generally prevented us from wandering freely.

"He's just a professor." Lewis sat at the kitchen island scrolling through websites while I washed dishes. "It says here that he taught history at the University of Edinburgh. Retired seventeen years ago after a distinguished career that included twenty-three published papers and a book on the Reformation that's still used in schools today."

"So, his random appearance at Maggs's door after the riots was just that — random." I didn't call it a coincidence because if I had, Lewis would doubt himself and race down another rabbit hole of research.

I dried the last breakfast plate. "Thanks for helping, by the way."

"I've had a tough morning," he said. "Serving guests is stressful."

"I know, I did it last night. Remember?"

I hadn't thought through that Lewis sharing Will's chores meant he'd also share Will. That I'd become one half of a fake person.

"I spent last night searching up Schenk because you asked me to," Lewis said.

"Which was a waste of time." I popped off the cookie-tin lid. The chocolate ones with the orange jelly inside were the best.

Lewis carried on. "I've made a list of every British newspaper. If I read each one, starting a month before the riots, I might find him."

No matter what Lewis was called, he'd always be Lewis — nerdy, obsessive, organized, anxious.

I rummaged in the tin until I found two of the orange-jelly biscuits, bit into one and put the other in front of Lewis. "Or we could contact Molly and find out what stories are leaking from the sheriff's office about Schenk."

"It's not that easy. The only way to cloak our location is to register with a special server, which seems like the opposite of hiding who we are."

"And the blue-haired computer girl?"

"Ruby?" Lewis frowned.

"I thought you were going to ask if she knows another way." I popped the rest of the biscuit in my mouth. Cookie, not biscuit. I was Canadian and I was eating a cookie.

"I said it might be worth *one* of us asking her," Lewis said.

"Now would be a great time." I leaned over and shut the laptop. "I'm going for a walk."

At the mention of a walk, Haggis launched herself off the couch and skittered across the polished wooden floor toward me. Before Lewis could dream up a million reasons why I shouldn't go, I unhooked the leash and opened the back door.

And came face to face with Aisha. *Crap.*

She startled at my sudden appearance, her eyes wide. Green eyes, which I hadn't noticed in the half-light of our first meeting, and her skin was light brown. She was now dressed in a white sweatshirt, a kilt and a matching tartan headscarf.

Haggis squeezed past me and bounded down the steps into the yard. I slammed the door behind me before Aisha spotted Lewis.

"How's the neighborhood-watch thing going?" She looked round me at the closed door. "Did you clobber an unsuspecting guest over the head by mistake?"

"Ha ha."

"Is Maggs in?"

"She went to the bakery."

"Does she know you're lurking in her kitchen? She's not fond of guests in her personal space."

"Not a guest."

She tilted her head. "What are you, then?"

"A kitchen hand." What the heck was that?

She raised her eyebrows. "Didn't they stop being a thing with the advent of electricity?"

"I'm helping out. Cleaning and serving and stuff. A kind of summer job."

"Okay, then. Not dodgy at all," she said. "Anyway, I only came to bring these for Maggs. Entry tickets for the castle — she gives them to her guests."

A clatter sounded through the open kitchen window. I cringed. What was Lewis doing?

Aisha looked up at the window. "If Maggs isn't home, who's in the kitchen?"

I plucked the tickets from her fingers. "Aren't tickets electronic now? You know, with the invention of QR codes and cell phones."

Aisha turned her attention back to me. "A comedian as well as a chimney sweep."

"Kitchen hand."

"When you're done scrubbing floors and shoveling coal, you should use one," she said. "And if you see me in the gift shop, I'm not shoplifting. I work there. No need to tackle me to the ground."

"Castles aren't really my thing," I said.

"And yet, you strike me as someone who might enjoy skulking in dungeons." She glanced at the kitchen window again before heading for the gate, stopping to give Haggis a pat on the way.

Once she'd disappeared down the alleyway, I slumped against the door. That was close. How long before we got found out? It had been four days since we left Canada. Four days since Mom and Dad told us to run, then never followed. We needed to talk to Molly. It wasn't only about finding out about Schenk, I also needed to know she was safe, and that she didn't hate me.

I left Haggis sniffing the grass and marched back into the kitchen. "Haggis is outside. I'm going to find Rosie."

"Ruby," Lewis said without taking his eyes off the laptop screen.

The dining room was empty, but voices drifted from the lounge.

The journalist was sitting in one of the armchairs opposite a man who must have been the professor. The granddad, Brian, sat between them on a dining room chair. The professor's forehead was scrunched, like he was trying to search for an answer to a question. All three watched me cross the room to the blue-haired girl, sitting by the fireplace, a computer on her lap.

Her grandfather jumped up. "Have you come to join us, Will?"

The man was wearing socks with sandals. Who did that?

"I wanted to ask your granddaughter something," I said.

How to fix the Wi-Fi? How to get rid of a virus on Maggs's laptop? How did you start a request that ended with *can you help me be invisible?*

"And what have you there?" Brian snatched the tickets out of my hand. "The castle? What a fabulous idea. Ruby would be delighted to go with you."

"No," I said. "I mean, yes, you can have the tickets but that's not ..."

"Ruby, sweetheart," Brian said. "Up you get. Will's taking you to the castle."

Ruby looked more shocked than I was. She glanced at her laptop as if she was searching for an excuse to say no.

"It's fine," I said. "You're busy; maybe next time."

She shut the laptop. "I'm not busy."

I should send Lewis. He'd be more excited about seeing the castle than I was, and he was far better at charming people. Everybody liked Lewis.

"Are you ready?" Ruby stood.

The hairs on the back of my neck rose as I realized the professor, Nora and Brian were all staring at me.

"I'll meet you outside in ten minutes," I said, then ran from the room.

Lewis's reply was a decisive *not a chance.* He was still recovering from the breakfast inquisition. What if Ruby asked questions, and he let slip that Mom and Dad were the suspected terrorists behind the London riots? I wasn't sure how something like that slipped out, but when Lewis sank into worst-case-scenario territory, logic rarely changed his mind.

Ruby was waiting for me outside, music plugged into one ear. We walked in silence to the station and caught the tram to the city center. Before we'd even made it to the first stop, Lewis texted to ask if he should go back to the attic, or if it was safer to stay in the kitchen. I didn't reply.

We got off at Princes Street, a road with more buses than cars and more pedestrians than sidewalk, and joined a mass of people waiting at a crossing, a blockade of stores at our backs. It felt like London all over again — people pressing in on me, stealing all the air. Even though the stoplights hadn't changed, people took advantage of a gap in the traffic and sprinted across the street. We shuffled forward into the void they'd left.

More people arrived, crowding the edge of the sidewalk, trapping us. The phone buzzed in my pocket.

The instant the lights changed, we surged forward.

At the other side of the street, concrete and stone gave way to grass and trees. The park fell away, then climbed up and up and up until it collided with a mountain of black rock. And perched on top of the rock, the castle.

"It looks like it's watching over the city," Ruby said.

"Are you talking to *me*?"

She shrugged. "My playlist ended."

As we walked down the grass slope into the valley of the park, I checked the phone. Lewis had almost bumped into Nora on his way back to the attic and was now hiding in the downstairs washroom. How long did I think he should wait? I resisted typing back that if he'd come to the castle, he wouldn't be trapped in a washroom. And he'd already be chatting to Ruby about contacting Molly.

"If your phone's more exciting than the castle, you could go back," Ruby said.

"How much do you know about phones?" I asked. "I mean, if, for example, I texted you right now, could you trace it back and find my location?"

"You're standing right in front of me."

"But if I wasn't?"

"Yes," she said.

I grinned. This was awesome.

Ruby stopped walking and looked up at the castle looming above us. "Did you know the Stone of Destiny's kept at the castle? For twelve hundred years all true kings and queens of Scotland have been crowned on it."

"How could I stop you from tracing the text back to me?" I was going to be able to message Molly, maybe even talk to her.

Ruby looked at me and frowned. "If you give me the ticket, I'll go by myself."

"I want to come," I said.

"You want to, or you have to?" she said. "I'll tell Mrs. Ross you came with me, and we had a brilliant time. I'm assuming you're here because my granddad asked her to tell you to keep me company."

"That's not why I'm here." I looked up at the black cliffs. "I've never been to a castle before."

Ruby huffed and continued walking.

We left the park and followed a cobbled street that curved up and around the jagged rock. When we finally made it to the top, the castle was how I imagined a castle would be — turrets either side of a stone arch guarded by iron knights with swords.

We lined up, flashed our tickets, then wove through an outer courtyard full of tourists snapping photos. Once we were through the arch, the cobbled path narrowed, stone walls towering above us on either side. I felt like I'd been transported back in time a thousand years.

And then a plastic sign came into view, advertising half-price T-shirts.

The gift shop was dug into the wall and looked like it should store gunpowder rather than souvenirs, and standing in the doorway, restocking a rack of postcards, was Aisha. *Crap.*

"Hello, dodgy neighbor," she said. "The dungeons tempted you after all?"

I nodded at Ruby. "I'm here with a guest. Ruby's staying at Maggs's."

"Hiya." Aisha held out her hand. "I'm Aisha, and if you want a tour from someone who actually has a clue, let me know."

Ruby hesitated, then shook Aisha's hand. "Where's the Stone of Destiny?"

"You know where the Great Hall is?" Aisha asked.

"No."

"Have you ever visited the castle before?"

Ruby shook her head.

Aisha turned to the back of the store, yelled she was taking her break, then strode into the alley. "Are you coming?"

"Don't waste your break on us." I ran to catch up with her. "We'll find it."

How could I quiz Ruby about being untraceable with Aisha hovering? She already thought I was dodgy.

"I like giving tours," Aisha said. "And I need a break from Americans asking me to recommend a clan tartan that would suit their distant and tenuous Scottish heritage. So, please don't ask me about yours."

"I'm Canadian," I said, even though I was half-Scottish, half-Dutch. And, as it turned out, maybe not Canadian at all.

Ruby and I followed Aisha through another archway, deeper into the castle. Eventually, the wall to our right fell away, and the sky appeared.

We threaded our way between real-life cannons and tourists taking selfies to a low outer wall. The city spread out below us — stone buildings and church spires and turrets. And beyond the city was the ocean, flat, calm and reflecting the sun.

It was the view from Mom's painting. She'd been here, standing exactly where I stood, and she'd never mentioned it. It was small in comparison to everything else she'd failed to mention, but for some reason it stabbed at me.

I could see the blobby islands Maggs had named, but where the sleeping-warrior island had been in Mom's painting, the ocean was empty. Had Mom really added it as a reminder of home?

"I didn't know the sea was this close," Ruby said.

Aisha leaned on the wall. "You came for the festival, then?"

"I didn't know about the festival either. My granddad got it into his head he wanted to come to Edinburgh." Ruby shrugged. "And it has a castle, so not the worst place I've been. Except for the smell."

"Yeah," I said. "What is it?"

"Breweries. Beer and whisky have been the backbone of Scotland's economy for centuries." Aisha's voice took on the authoritative tone of a tourist guide.

So, not gravy and horse feed. At least I'd managed to uncover one mystery.

"It used to be distilled and smuggled out of the city using the tunnels, but now the breweries are all out in the open, clogging up the air."

"Edinburgh has underground tunnels?" Ruby said.

If I could think of anything worse than being in a dark, dingy tunnel, it would be a dark, dingy tunnel that stank of breweries.

"Only a few stretches are still accessible, and no one knows how far they extend," Aisha continued. "But by piecing together stories of whisky smuggling and prisoner escapes, we think they linked the beach with the castle and the castle with Holyrood Palace and from there all the way into one of the country estates. It's how they smuggled Mary, Queen of Scots out of the castle. Or so the stories go."

Ruby's eyes went wide.

"Come on, you can see her crown," Aisha said. "It's in the same building as the Stone."

We followed Aisha up a curved cobblestone path, through another archway and into a courtyard. A line of tourists snaked back and forth outside one of the buildings.

"That's the queue to see the Stone of Destiny," Aisha said. "I'll give you a tour of the Great Hall while it dies down."

"I don't mind lining up," I said. "So, if you'd rather get back to work …"

"What's the Great Hall?" Ruby asked.

"Exactly what it says on the tin." Aisha linked her arm with Ruby's. "A great big hall."

"You're not selling it," I said.

Aisha and Ruby marched into the long, stone building arm in arm. I followed.

The Great Hall was like a church — a high ceiling of arched wooden beams, stained glass windows and a worn stone floor. Swords and breastplates hung on the paneled walls, and suits of armor stood guard on either side of a massive fireplace. A handful of tourists were reading information plaques and snapping photos.

Ruby stood in the center of the hall and looked around in awe.

"Mary, Queen of Scots threw a banquet here in 1561, when she returned from France," Aisha said.

Aisha and Ruby continued to talk about Mary, Queen of Scots, how she gave birth to her son in the castle, then was imprisoned and had her head chopped off. Then they moved on to other kings and queens, and battles between siblings and cousins. The castle was nine hundred years old. Thousands of people died here. I left them to it. I didn't need any more depressing facts.

I wandered over to one of the stained glass windows and looked out at the ocean. Why did tourists cram themselves into the city when they could be on the beach? If I didn't need Ruby's help, I'd head there now. Longview was six hundred miles from the ocean, but it had the same wide-open sky, the same feeling of being free.

Ruby and Aisha stood side by side, their heads bent together. How had they become friends already? How did people do that? I'd met Aisha three times now, and she hadn't so much as smiled at me. *I* should be the one staying hidden, not Lewis. He'd be over there chatting, asking Ruby to help him contact Molly and making sure Aisha liked him enough that she'd protect our secret if she found out.

I left the view of the ocean and went to try to make friends.

"… the London riots?" Ruby said.

My blood ran cold. How had the conversation moved from sixteenth-century executions to the riot? Or maybe she was talking about an ancient riot protesting the cost of candle wax?

"Shh," Aisha said. "He'll hear you."

If they were talking about me, then it was game over. Forget contacting Molly, forget waiting for Mom and Dad. We'd need to leave the city.

"What will I hear?" I shoved my hands in my pockets and waited for the accusations to fly.

"Not you." Aisha tilted her head at a boy who was standing with his back to us, staring at the empty wall above the fireplace.

He was bulky enough to be a couple of years older than us, seventeen, maybe eighteen. The back of his T-shirt was dark with sweat, his blond hair plastered to his neck, and he was wearing athletic shorts and running shoes. He looked more like a runner taking a breather than a tourist.

"Why are we talking about him?"

Aisha shushed me, then shepherded us into an alcove.

"Because of the Mary painting." Aisha pointed to the empty wall the boy was staring at. "Mary, Queen of Scots was on loan to a gallery in London. The whole exhibition was stolen during the riot. Keep up."

Okay, so we were back to the riot.

"Which riot, exactly?" I asked. "Are we talking ancient history?"

"And they never found any of the paintings?" Ruby asked over my question.

Aisha glanced at me, but answered Ruby. "One turned up in a South American dictator's house when he was daft enough to give an interview in front of it on national television."

This century, then.

"And another was rescued from a tech billionaire, who swore he didn't know it was stolen. And there's a rumor the Wallace family has the Mary painting."

"And now he's here." Ruby looked toward the boy at the fireplace.

"Who is he?" I asked.

"Jamie Wallace," Aisha whispered.

"Are you sure it's him?" Ruby said.

Aisha nodded. "He swims on a different team, but I've seen him and his sister at swim meets often enough that we'd say hi if we bumped into each other somewhere outside of the pool."

"Like Edinburgh Castle?" I said cheerily.

Now the conversation was clearly about a boy called Jamie and an art theft, rather than the riot, I felt a bit giddy.

"Exactly like in Edinburgh Castle," Aisha said. "So, keep your voice down."

Ruby looked back at Aisha. "Have you ever asked him about

the Mary painting?"

"What's the point?" Aisha said. "His family denies having the painting, and because they're from some ancient clan descended from royalty, everyone believes them."

The tour group we'd dodged earlier streamed inside, taking over the space and swallowing Jamie Wallace.

"Everyone lies," Ruby said.

"That's cheery," I said, even though I agreed. "Why don't they hang up another painting? There must be some gruesome battle scene collecting dust somewhere."

Chatting wasn't so difficult. Maybe I *could* make friends with Ruby and Aisha.

"Nothing will hang there until the painting is returned," Aisha said. "It's bad luck to give up hope."

Ruby twisted a bracelet round and round on her wrist. "Optimism's overrated."

"And hope doesn't have a sell-by date," Aisha said.

"It does eventually," I said. "If you're realistic about people."

They both looked at me. I shrugged.

"Is that why you assumed I was a criminal?" Aisha folded her arms. "Because you're *realistic* about people?"

"You were *climbing through a window at 5:00 a.m.*," I said. "What was I meant to do?"

"Not leap to conclusions," she said.

"History isn't the only place where horrible people do evil things," I said. "But next time I see someone breaking into your house, I'll cheer them on."

"It would be better than innocent people having their lives ruined." Aisha's face flushed.

My skin prickled. Had the conversation swung back to the riots? Was she accusing me, or were we still talking about Jamie Wallace?

Aisha continued to glare at me. Then her phone pinged, and she was scrambling in her fluffy kilt bag.

She read her phone, then looked at Ruby. "Sorry, I need to go. Two coachloads of tourists descended on the shop. It was lovely to meet you."

She didn't say anything to me, just sprinted out of the hall, her tartan scarf floating behind her.

"Do you think Aisha's headscarf's part of the uniform?" I turned to look at Ruby, who was looking at me as if I'd just asked if the earth was flat.

"It's a hijab," she said.

"Oh, that makes way more sense."

"How can you not know what a hijab looks like?" she asked, her eyes still wide.

Because three hundred people live in Longview, and the nearest mosque is in the city. I shrugged. "I thought she just liked wearing scarves. They do look good. But, you know, it's pretty hot today, so I did wonder."

Ruby tilted her head, then slowly shook it. "I'm going to see the Stone of Destiny."

So much for making friends.

I watched Ruby march outside, wondering if I should follow or give up on this plan and get back to Lewis. I checked my phone — Lewis was safely back in the attic and wanted to know if Ruby would help us or not.

I shoved my phone in my pocket and went after her.

She was at the end of the lineup, which had shrunk to two families and an elderly couple wearing matching tartan rubber boots.

"Mind if I join you?"

"Why?" Ruby said. "You don't seem excited about any of it."

"Murder and betrayal aren't my thing." I held out my hands. "You've got to admit some of it's pretty grim. The story of the teenaged brothers being beheaded at a dinner party?"

She nodded. "Okay, I'll give you that."

The family ahead of us were waved inside. Ruby and I shuffled forward.

"The Stone sounds cool though," I said. "And crowns are always ... sparkly."

"Again with the sarcasm." She turned her back on me.

Here goes nothing. "I need your help," I said.

Ruby turned back to face me. "Finally, he speaks the truth."

I crossed then uncrossed my arms, then shoved them in my pockets. "I need to contact someone without being traced. Will you help me?"

"Why should I?"

"Because I gave you a free ticket."

"Which Aisha gave you."

"Because I came with you to the castle, then."

"To manipulate me into helping you."

A man in a waterproof kilt and a red windbreaker waved us into the crown room.

"Go home," Ruby said, then walked inside.

I wished I could.

CHAPTER
13

L E W I S

Cameron told me to stop researching the past and focus on the here and now, but it was a gigantic black hole of nothingness. It took ten minutes to scan news headlines and social media and find out there was nothing to find out — no double homicides within a thousand miles of Longview, no mention of Schenk. No secret message posted on social media by Mom and Dad, or Molly or Hunter or any of our other friends. We'd been gone four days. A single post showing a smidgen of concern would've been nice.

Every time the bell above the front door jangled, I jumped up and peered through the attic window. Ruby's grandfather and Maggs left first. Then Professor Pham, and five minutes after that, Nora clomped down the front steps with a long-lens camera around her neck. Once the house was empty, I took up tidying where I'd left off. The bookshelf in the guest lounge was packed with books arranged in no logical order.

I arranged the books alphabetically by author. Then emptied them out again and started stacking them by category — guide books on the top shelf, fiction on the second, then craft books on the remaining three shelves.

The house creaked and groaned.

I called out a hello, thinking maybe Cameron and Ruby were back from the castle. The only reply I got was a half-hearted bark from the dog.

Halfway through arranging the craft books by height, with the laptop balanced on a dogeared copy of *Knit without Knots*, I refreshed the open tabs. The Longview art gallery had removed Mom's name from their website with no explanation. Dad's logging company's social media feed remained a steady stream of campers reporting wildfires. No pleas for help to find one of their missing team leads. How was no one missing us? Where did they all think we'd gone?

I went to check on the dog. Stretched out on the couch in the back room, she raised her head, gave me an unimpressed look, then went back to sleep.

I looked at Mom's painting. Underneath her signature, I noticed a date — eighteen years ago, a year before the riots. Had she any idea what was about to happen to her?

The sideboard under Mom's painting was stuffed with shoe-boxes, handwritten dates on the lids. I sorted through them until I found one dated eighteen years ago, then opened it. It was filled with photographs. A few were of ocean views, but most were of people at the guesthouse — Maggs posed with an array of guests on the front steps and in the backyard.

My breath caught when I finally found one of Mom. She was clinking wine glasses with a woman who looked a lot like her. Same shaped face. Same curly brown hair. Same smile. I flipped over the photo, and on the back, written in Mom's curly handwriting, was a note: *Me and Clare toasting your knitting trophy. See you soon.*

Who was Clare?

Mom told us she didn't have any family other than us. She'd lied about her parents being alive, but she'd never lie about having a sister. Would she?

I slipped the photo into my pocket to show Cameron when he got back, then boxed up the others.

After checking the websites again, I vacuumed dog hairs off the couch, then tried vacuuming the dog. She wasn't happy.

Cameron still wasn't back, and the only new thing on social media was a photo of a tomato on Mrs. Baxter's Facebook page. This was pointless. I closed all the social media tabs, then searched up London during the year of the riot. The dog was still avoiding me, so I had the couch to myself. I settled in and worked my way through the data.

Other than the riot, not much happened in London that year — some excitement over a cricket match, a sprinkling of murders and more rain than usual. And an art theft that was interesting only because it happened on the same day as the riot. Oh, and the queen's hat caused a stir at some horse race. No idea why.

Mom had been living in London. She'd read these headlines as they were happening. Had she worried about the murders? Been sick of the rain? Watched the cricket match?

When the dog leaped up from her bed in the kitchen and barked at the dining room door, I scrambled off the couch and dove into the pantry.

"Lewis?" It was Cameron.

I let out my breath, grabbed a random box and causally stepped out of the pantry.

Cameron tilted his head to read the front of the box, then frowned. "What the heck is *suet*?"

I shoved the box back on the shelf. "I've had a terrible time, thanks for asking. No one's posted anything. The house makes strange noises. And the dog hates me."

Cameron held out a brown paper bag. "And you forgot to eat."

Grease seeped through the paper, and the smell made my stomach rumble. "Fries?"

"Chips," he said. "There's a difference. Chunkier. Shaped like slugs."

I wrinkled my nose.

"If you don't want them ..."

I snatched the bag from him. "Did you ask Ruby about contacting Molly?"

"Ruby won't help," he said. "We need to find another way."

He bent down to wrestle the dog, who had been nudging him with her nose since he came in. What did Cameron have that I didn't?

"I found something." I dug the photo of Mom out of my pocket.

Cameron ruffled the dog's neck one more time, then stood and peered at the photo. "You've got to be kidding. Another relative Mom forgot to mention?"

"It says on the back that her name's Clare."

Cameron snatched the photo off me and flipped it over. "No way."

"What?"

He took off running, the dog at his heels.

"Cameron?"

I didn't have the energy to follow. I sunk onto a kitchen stool and unwrapped the brown paper bag. Fat, golden slugs, just like Cameron said. I bit into one. Crispy on the outside and fluffy in the middle. *Mmmm.*

The *bang, bang, bang* of Cameron running up two flights of stairs stopped, and two chips later, it started up again as he raced back down.

"Can't be a coincidence," he said as he strode back into the kitchen.

He held out his fake birth certificate for me to take. I had one, too. The envelope was now under my mattress, along with the passport. It was just another prop in case we needed to run again, and I had no intention of going anywhere. Mom and Dad would eventually come here.

"Look at the name on it," he said.

"Willem Murray van der Berg. You already told me."

"Look at the mother's name."

Clare Murray, where mine had said Katrina.

"Who the heck is Clare?" Cameron took back the certificate, then smoothed it out on the island. "And look at the place of birth."

I stood next to him and read the whole thing. "Rothesay. Isn't that …"

"Mom's hometown." Cameron pulled out the phone. "At last, something to go on."

I looked over his shoulder while he texted Maggs.

Does Mom have a sister?

The dots blinked as she typed her reply.

The dots vanished.

"We should phone her," Cameron said. "It'd be quicker."

"Tempting, but she joined Ruby's granddad on a bus tour. He might overhear."

Maggs was typing again.

When her text finally flashed up, I read it out loud.

Delayed due to roadwork on the M8. Please make a start on dinner. Potatoes need peeling. Quite big, six or seven should do the trick. Haggis will need to be walked. Loch Lomond was glorious. Brian quite impressed.

More dots.

I assumed you knew about your aunt.

Aunt. We had an aunt. Clare Murray.

"We need to go to Rothesay," Cameron said.

What? No! We couldn't leave. "She probably doesn't even live there anymore. And Rothesay could be hundreds of miles away. We can't be away for that long. What if Mom and Dad turn up?"

"Mom put Clare's name and Rothesay on the birth certificate for a reason. What if that's where Mom is? With her sister, waiting for us?" He opened the laptop and searched up a map of Scotland. "It's the only lead we have. Do you want to find Mom and Dad or not?"

CHAPTER
14

LEWIS

We left the guesthouse at dawn, Cameron out the front door, me out the back armed with the photo of Mom and Clare, and a bag of cheese sandwiches, which Maggs had left out for us with a note saying *good luck and mind the jellyfish*. We changed trains in Glasgow and were now in a town I couldn't pronounce.

Cameron and I met up outside the railway station before setting off for the ferry. The town was only three blocks deep, with squat, white houses lining the narrow streets. We couldn't see the ocean yet, but based on the smell of seaweed and the cry of seagulls, we were close.

"Did anyone on your train car seem familiar?" I asked.

Unlike the one-hour train ride from Edinburgh to Glasgow, which had been packed, the second train was quiet.

"No." Cameron looked back at the railway station. "Most had kids with them. One guy was alone, but he got off two stops before us. How about yours?"

I nodded at the family walking ahead of us, the two little kids swinging sandcastle pails. "Just them, and another family."

Cameron checked the map on the phone. "Next right." He looked up. "At the church."

As we turned right, the world opened up, sea and sky filling the view.

Cameron stopped and stared. "It's like one of Mom's paintings."

I got that spinny feeling in my stomach that I get whenever I stand at the top of a mountain — like I'm about to be swallowed.

Cameron tugged me across the road onto the pier, where we sat, legs dangling over the edge.

A rowboat made its way across the bay, a man in a yellow raincoat and a little girl in an orange life jacket, oars dipping in and out of the water. Farther out, seagulls circled a fishing boat, squawking in excitement, and beyond that a white ferry glided toward us, flags flying.

Its horn blasted, long and low. "Does that mean it's about to dock or sink?" I asked.

Cameron pointed at the nearest island. "Assuming that's Rothesay, we could swim from here if we had to."

"You look like you want to," I said. "First time I've seen a smile on your face since ..."

"Since we became stateless fugitives with multiple fake identities?" he said.

"I was going to say since we lost Mom and Dad."

He looked out to sea.

"Do you really think Mom and Dad will be there?" I asked.

"If they aren't, Clare must have some idea of where they could be. Why else would Mom send us here?"

I hoped Cameron was right, but Mom could've put Clare's name on the birth certificate for other reasons: backup in case Maggs threw us out, or as a blood donor in case we got shot, or maybe Mom simply wanted us to know Clare existed. But for the first time since the barbecue, Cameron looked happy, so I kept quiet.

When the ferry docked ten minutes later, the front of the ferry lowered like a drawbridge, then clattered onto the concrete slip. Cars trundled off, their tires clonking over the edge of the ferry's tailgate. Foot passengers followed. As soon as the last car turned onto the road, a man in a high-vis orange jacket waved the waiting cars onboard. We followed with the rest of the foot passengers — hikers with backpacks, the family from the train and a couple pushing bicycles.

As the ferry rumbled from the dock, we made our way to the front, then leaned on the side, the salty wind in our faces. Waves slapped the hull.

I peered into the water. "Can you see any jellyfish?"

"Forget the jellyfish. Do you think this is where we were born?"

"I thought Maggs told you Rothesay was crawling with press after the riot," I said. "No way Mom would've risked coming back here to have us. It would've been impossible for her to hide with two babies and journalists asking questions."

"If not here, then where?"

"Does it matter?"

He shrugged and continued looking out to sea, toward the island.

We chugged past fishing boats and clusters of seagulls bobbing on the water. A windsurfer crossed the ferry's path, its red sail full of wind, the woman leaning so far back she was almost touching the water. She zipped over the waves, past the island toward a much bigger island.

I nudged Cameron. "Look, that's the sleeping-warrior island from Mom's painting."

He straightened. "Holy crap."

Cloud shadows drifted over the island's peaks, making it look like the warrior was stirring. Is that where Mom had hidden before we were born? Right next to her home, protected by the sleeping warrior?

"Do *you* think Mom painted it because she was homesick?" Cameron asked.

"No."

He raised his eyebrows.

"First off," I said, "if Mom were homesick, she would've painted *this* view of her actual home. And, second, she painted it when she was still living in Edinburgh. She could've jumped on the train and come back whenever she wanted."

"How do you know when she painted it?"

"There was a date under Mom's signature, eighteen years ago. According to Maggs, Mom didn't leave for London until the following year."

He kept his eyes on the warrior island. "What was it Mom said about paintings?"

I imagined Mom in her overalls, her hair in a loose braid, her fingers splodged with a rainbow of colors. *"They capture an emotional truth of a moment in time."*

Her favorite thing to paint was the mountains from our backyard — green in the summer, peaceful and sprinkled with golden larches in the fall or swallowed by raging winter storms. The mood of them changed, but she never, not once, inserted a random peak that didn't belong. So, why had she done it in the Edinburgh painting?

As we approached the island, the town of Rothesay took shape. Red stone buildings, a church spire. Sailing boats moored in the bay. My chest fluttered with excitement. Were Mom and Dad here?

On our way down the gangplank, I tripped over a bike. The man wheeling it apologized, then noticed Cameron, and his eyes darted back to me. I felt Cameron tense up beside me.

Cameron grabbed my arm, and we jumped off the ferry slip onto the beach.

"We should've caught separate ferries," I said as we marched along the shoreline, stones rattling under our feet.

"We won't be here long," Cameron said. "We find Clare. She tells us where Mom and Dad are hiding. Then we find them and leave."

I wanted to tell him not to get his hopes up. This town was small. Mom would've been recognized if she'd come back.

I checked over my shoulder. The family from the ferry were behind us, the little kids already racing for the water. I searched for the couple with the bicycles and finally spotted them cycling down the pier in the opposite direction.

I stopped. "Are we even going the right way?"

Cameron took out the phone and checked the map, then pointed to the row of stone houses along the seafront. "It's one of those."

Maggs had given us the address of Mom's childhood home. The one her parents sold after their cat had been posted through the mailbox in pieces.

"Only one of us should go," I said.

"Good call." Cameron sat down on the beach. "Come get me when you're done. If they don't recognize Clare's name, show them the photo."

"Thanks a lot."

He stretched his legs and tilted his face to the sunshine. "Use your charming voice."

CAMERON

I watched Lewis trudge up the beach, seagulls flying out of his way. He hopped up on the pier, crossed the road, then stood on the sidewalk debating between a yellow front door and a red one. Mom had grown up in one of those houses. With a sister.

A squeal made me turn back to the ocean. Farther up the beach, three little kids paddled, while a dog ran in and out, splashing them.

I took off my sneakers, then tiptoed down the beach, avoiding clumps of slimy, purple seaweed and sharp rocks. The waves frothed as they collided with the shore, then rattled back through the stones. When the next wave slapped my feet, ice cold spiked through my bones.

I stretched my arms and breathed in the salty air. The tightness in my chest evaporated. If things had been different, we might've lived here.

A man called out and held up popsicles for the paddling kids. An ice-cream van, plastered with pictures of popsicles and cones, was parked on the pier; a group of teenagers stood next to it waiting to be served. Were any of them related to me?

I checked on Lewis. A middle-aged white man was standing in the doorway talking to him. When I looked back out to sea, the peaks of the warrior island were shrouded in cloud. Mom would've been able to see it from her bedroom window. When she was my age, she looked out at this view, paddled along this shore.

I worked my way up the beach, then sat on the edge of the pier and dusted grit and sand off the soles of my feet. I'd just finished tying up my sneakers when Lewis arrived.

"Well?" Hope fluttered in my belly.

"I've got directions." He grinned and waved a scrap of paper. "Clare still lives here."

The flutter in my stomach became a full-blown churn. Even if Mom and Dad weren't here, Clare would know where to find them.

CHAPTER
15

L E W I S

Clare worked in a car mechanic shop tucked behind the fishing tackle store just off the main street. The man who lived in our grandparents' old house said it wasn't far. Rothesay isn't big. We were about to meet our aunt. Excitement fizzed in my stomach.

We jogged along the pier, past an ice-cream van and a bench crammed with teenagers and a woman being pulled by a yappy dog. Past a squabble of seagulls flapping and squawking their annoyance at being disturbed.

Cameron pretended to be calm, but every time we passed someone, he glanced at them.

When we reached the statue of the man with the massive moustache, we left the pier and crossed the road onto the main street. The stores had their doors propped open — a fishmonger with trays of fish laid out on beds of ice, a butcher with a window full of sausages and slabs of meat, and tourist shops spilling onto the sidewalk with racks of postcards and plastic beach toys.

And then the fishing tackle store.

And an alley.

And then we were standing in front of *Argyll & Bute Motors, all makes and models.*

The roll-door was open, the smell of engine oil drifting out to meet us. A black car was parked inside.

Cameron and I looked at each other.

Music blared from a radio on a cluttered workbench, but there was no sign of anyone.

Cameron stepped into the workshop and shouted hello.

When we'd turned up at Maggs's door, we had no idea what to expect. But this was different — we were Clare's nephews. If Cameron was right about her hiding Mom and Dad, then she'd be expecting us. Even if she wasn't, she'd be happy to see us. Wouldn't she?

I followed Cameron around to the front of the car. Steep, metal steps led down into a pit, a caged light bulb dangling over the edge.

The sound of metal clanking against metal came from under the car.

Cameron crouched next to the steps and peered into the pit. "Hello? We're looking for Clare Murray."

"We're fully booked today," called up a female voice. "If you book an appointment online, I'll get back to you."

"What now?" Cameron stood and dragged a hand through his stubbly hair. "We can't say any more until we know it's her."

Another clang of metal followed by whoever was under the car swearing.

"We really need to speak to Clare," I shouted into the pit. "It's a matter of life and death."

"We're not in a movie," Cameron hissed.

I held out my hands, inviting him to do better.

A sigh from under the car, then, "Move away from the pit."

We took a step back.

"Farther," she said. "Back where I can see you."

We shuffled backward until our backs hit the workbench.

Footsteps on the ladder.

A flash of a red baseball cap.

The woman was wearing safety goggles, a smudge of grease on the corner of one lens. She wore dark-blue coveralls, safety boots, and was clutching a wrench. She was shorter than Mom, and her braided hair looked a lighter shade of brown, but she had the same pointy chin.

Cameron took a step forward. "Are you Clare Murray?"

Her fist tightened on the wrench. "Who sent you?"

"Hi." My voice sounded squeaky. I cleared my throat and tried again. "We're Clare's nephews."

"Lewis, show her the photo," Cameron said.

I took it out of my pocket with trembling fingers, smoothed the edges, then looked up at the woman who was probably our aunt, and then at the wrench in her hand, and handed the photo to Cameron.

"Really?" He snatched the photo and took another step closer to the woman and the wrench. "Can you look at this? It's a photo of our mom and her sister, Clare."

"You've got the wrong person. Clare Murray doesn't have a sister."

"Please," I said. "Can you just look?"

Rather than looking at the photo, she gripped the wrench tighter and straightened her shoulders.

"We're not going anywhere," Cameron said.

Assuming this *was* Clare, and she had the same stubborn gene as Cameron, we'd still be here next summer.

"We thought our mom's name was Jennifer," I said. "But turns out it's Katrina, which kind of suits her better, because she's kick-ass tough. She's an artist. She paints but can't sing."

Cameron glanced back at me, then said to the woman, "And she's terrible at telling jokes."

"But she's funny," I said. "She makes people laugh. And she has hay fever."

"But she pretends she doesn't because she hates being weak," Cameron said.

The woman huffed a laugh, then looked up at the ceiling. "Sodding hell in a handbasket."

She chucked the wrench onto the workbench, then strode past us, yanking her goggles off as she opened the door to another room. Her eyes were the same hazel as Mom's. This had to be Clare.

Cameron avoided meeting my eyes as he turned to follow her.

The room was an office with a small desk, a worn-out armchair and a kitchenette squeezed against the far wall. Cameron and I shuffled inside while she filled a kettle.

"Did Mom send you a photo of us?" I asked.

"Maybe she did and maybe she didn't." She dropped a tea bag into a mug. "How does your mother take her tea?"

"She isn't with us." As I said it, I realized that Mom wasn't with Clare either. We'd come all the way out here, and Mom had never been here.

"Our mom uses a teapot," Cameron said. "Because she always has at least two cups, and it's a waste of a tea bag otherwise. And the milk goes into the cup first. Our dad made her do a taste test once, and she could tell."

"That was years ago," I said.

"Yeah, well, you're not the only one who can remember useless facts."

Clare turned around and took off her baseball cap. She reminded me so much of Mom that I wanted to hug her. Cameron sank onto the arm of the chair.

"I've got a car to fix," Clare said. "The owner will be back soon. Talk fast."

"Do you know where our mom is?" Cameron said.

"No. Next question."

"She promised to meet us in Edinburgh," I said. "But she hasn't come. And we thought maybe she might've contacted you. And that you could help us."

And give us a hug and beg us to come and live with you, while you sort out everything.

"Katrina has a habit of leaving the people she's meant to love," Clare said.

My body tensed. "Mom wouldn't leave us. Something must've gone wrong."

"I haven't seen Katrina for seventeen years," she said. "She never wrote or phoned. Until we received the photo of the two of you, we thought she was dead or rotting in prison. My parents mourned her for six years, and then out of the blue, we both receive a photo of two wee boys playing dress-up. While our lives were being torn apart, Katrina was busy making a new one. So, no, I can't help you."

"But we're family," I said.

That had to count for something. Mom was always telling us family were the only people you could trust.

"Katrina gave up being my sister a long time ago."

Cameron gestured to the workshop. "Your life looks pretty good to me. You run your own business. In the town where you grew up. On an island, surrounded by water and hills and fishing."

"I wasn't meant to be here. Katrina was always the one who dreamed of coming back," she said. "But by the sound of your accents, she got to travel instead of me. Where's she been hiding all these years? America?"

"Canada," Cameron said.

She nodded. "I can see her there. She always liked wide-open spaces."

"You could've left, too," I said.

"His majesty's intelligence services requested I not leave the country." She dropped the teaspoon in the sink with a clatter.

"The king asked you not to leave?" I said.

When she smiled, she looked even more like Mom.

"Back then, it was the queen," she said. "And MI6 who interrogated me. They warned me that any travel on my part would be interpreted as fleeing the country."

Someone knocked on the open office door. "Sorry to interrupt."

The man was wearing a fishing vest, mirrored sunglasses and a floppy fishing hat that grazed the top of the doorway. This guy was tall. And he sounded mildly amused that he'd stumbled on Clare slacking off. His lips twitched as if he was trying not to grin.

"Bloody hell," Clare ran to the door.

"Not a good time?" he said.

Clare eased past him, then shut the door.

We could hear her telling him that his car was almost ready. The man replied in low tones that I couldn't make out. Family emergency, Clare said, and then they moved farther into the workshop.

"I can't believe she won't help us," I said.

"We need to change tack." Cameron stood and glanced at the door. "Stop asking her to help us find Mom and ask about other stuff."

"What other stuff is there? That's all that matters."

Cameron stuck his hands in his pockets. "I want to know why she thinks Mom's guilty."

"Why are you so desperate for Mom to be guilty?" I threw up my hands. "You actually think Mom's some murdering extremist? Are you listening to yourself right now?"

"She was meant to be here." He sunk back onto the chair arm. "I really thought Mom would be here."

I exhaled and sat on the other arm. "There are other explanations, you know. Maybe Mom's a spy and she got called away on another mission, or maybe she defected. Or maybe she was a sleeper agent, and Schenk came to wake her up."

"With a gun?"

I threw up my hands. How could he give up on Mom?

Cameron rubbed his head. "Let's just ask Clare what happened before the riots."

"… I recommend the sticky-toffee pudding," Clare said over her shoulder as she opened the door.

Then to us she said, "The next ferry leaves in twenty minutes. If you run, you'll make it."

I stood. "Why won't you help us?" My chest tightened.

"That man doesn't even live on the island, but twice a year, for the last sixteen years, he's brought his car to me. But not everyone was willing to overlook who I was related to. I've worked hard to build a business and a life here, and I won't let Katrina wreck it again." Clare turned her back on us and leaned on the kitchenette counter. "I'm sorry, but you need to leave."

"Why do you think our mom's a terrorist?" Cameron straightened his shoulders. "Did she pull the legs off spiders when she was little? Did she make bombs in her dorm room?"

Clare shook her head. "No."

"Then why do you hate her?" I asked. "Please tell us what happened."

Clare sighed and turned to face us. "Okay, but then you leave."

We both nodded.

Clare folded her arms. "Katrina was my person, and I was hers. And then she moved to London."

"And?" Cameron said.

Clare looked at the ceiling as though she was praying for strength, then continued. "I was still at university in Glasgow, but visited her whenever I ran out of food or needed boyfriend advice. She was excited about her new finance job, but avoided questions about it. She said she worked in a bank, so what was there to tell? It was spreadsheets and numbers, and, no, I couldn't meet any of her friends from work because they were older and never went out drinking. But I'd catch her checking her phone, and one weekend she ran off to deal with an emergency, which she refused to discuss."

"When was the last time you saw her?" I said.

"Two weeks before the riot, I found out my tosser of a boyfriend was cheating on me. I jumped on a train to London, cried all the way there and went straight to the bank where Katrina claimed to work."

"She wasn't there?" Cameron asked.

"They'd never heard of her. I was in a bit of a state by then and left an overly dramatic message on her voice mail. She called me back ten minutes later and told me to meet her at the Tate."

My head snapped up. "The gallery that was robbed during the riots?"

Cameron stood up straight. "What was Mom doing there?"

"She'd just started working there. Finally, a job in the arts, Katrina said, and please would I promise not to tell our parents because it was a secret. If I hadn't been in such a mess, I doubt she would've even told me." Clare's shoulders dropped. "My big sister had landed her dream job in an art gallery and wasn't going to tell me."

"What did you do?" I asked.

"I told her I'd been to the bank where she was meant to be working and that no one had heard of her. So, if she'd just landed the job in the Tate, where had she been working for the last year? Katrina laughed it off, said I must've got the wrong bank. But I'd spent my whole life with Katrina. I knew when she was lying."

"Lying to family's only acceptable in life-or-death situations," Cameron said.

Clare frowned.

"It's one of Mom and Dad's rules," I explained.

"How many life-or-death situations have you been in?" she asked.

Cameron shrugged. "One or two."

"Sit." She gestured to the chair, then rinsed out two more mugs.

Cameron perched on one arm, and I took the other.

She made tea, then handed us each a chipped mug.

I blew on the tea, then took a sip. It was milky. The way Mom drank it.

"My brother did a ton of research," Cameron said. "And there was nothing about Mom working in an art gallery."

"I told the police, but nothing came of it," Clare said.

"And that's it?" I clutched the mug. "A job in an art gallery, and you assume your sister's a criminal?" She was as bad as Cameron.

"A job Katrina wanted to keep secret. In an art gallery that happened to get robbed," Clare said. "And then she disappears, abandons our family, and the paintings are never found."

My muscles tensed. "You think Mom's an art thief?"

Was she kidding?

Cameron looked at me. "Art thief is better than a terrorist."

"No," I said. "Mom being completely innocent is better."

"But she isn't," Cameron said. "And neither is Dad."

"Will you get over it?" I said. "They were protecting us. No way Mom and Dad would've killed those people if they hadn't put a gun to your head."

"Katrina killed someone?" Fear flashed across Clare's face.

"Yeah," Cameron said. "At a barbecue."

She stared at him for a couple more seconds, then snapped into action.

"This conversation's over." She took the mugs from us and dropped them in the sink. "I answered your questions, now it's time for you to leave."

Her lips were tight, her shoulders set. The same expression Mom had at the barbecue when she'd told us to run.

A lump formed in my throat. Was she really throwing us out? I looked at Cameron, expecting him to argue, but he shook his head and made for the door.

I tried to do the same, but it was like my subconscious was mixing up Clare with Mom, and instead of leaving, I threw my arms around her. She smelled of engine oil rather than paint, but it still felt familiar.

Clare stiffened, then patted my back. "Don't waste your lives on someone who doesn't want to be found."

I stepped back. "We're going to find her."

"Come on, Lewis," Cameron said. "We can wait on the beach for the next ferry."

CHAPTER
16

CAMERON

Lewis sulked all the way back to Edinburgh, mumbling about love and loyalty and how could Clare give up on her own sister. But the way he said it, I knew he also meant me. How could *I* give up? I hadn't given up on Mom *or* Dad. But when Clare had told us not to waste our lives, instead of sharing Lewis's outrage, I'd felt relieved. Here was Mom's sister giving us permission to go home.

Back at the guesthouse, Lewis escaped to the attic to research the art gallery, leaving me with the dinner rush, which was even busier than usual because a new guest had booked in at short notice.

Maggs counted the pile of potatoes on the counter in front of me. "Do another two, would you. He sounded like a big eater."

I looked at her. "He actually told you he needs more potatoes than will fit on a normal-sized plate?"

"You can tell a lot from a person's voice." She leaned down to check the roast beef in the oven. "Shame Clare reacted as she did. Will you try your grandparents?"

I picked up another potato, peeled the length in one long slice. "One family member disowning us is enough."

I couldn't face going through another day like today. Next time I saw Aisha, I'd tell her hope *did* have an expiration date.

"Clare has reason enough to bear a grudge," she said. "Goodness knows how different her life should've been. But you're not to blame, and she'll eventually see that."

"She lives in her hometown," I said. "She never had to change her name or her friends."

"Not the life she chose though." Maggs gathered handfuls of the peeled potatoes and plopped them in a huge pot of water. "You can argue 'til the cows come home over what your mum did or didn't do, but intentional or not, her actions unraveled Clare's dreams. She was studying law. Did she tell you that?"

I shook my head.

"Probably why the injustice of it hit her as hard as it did," Maggs continued. "As far as I know, and this is secondhand information, your aunt was politely asked to leave her university."

"Why didn't she fight harder?" How long had Clare tried before she'd given up?

"I haven't seen Clare in years, but back then, she looked awfully like Katrina, and the entire nation hated her for it," Maggs said. "No one would give her a job. The car repair business was your grandfather's. He still had a few loyal customers, and Clare had friends and neighbors who felt bad about not doing more for your grandparents. Though I imagine it would've been a hard slog for her in the beginning."

I couldn't imagine Longview without Mom and Dad, but we'd have our neighbors. We'd have Molly. If Mom and Dad didn't come for us, at least we'd have everyone back home.

Maggs patted my hand. "Your aunt created a different life than the one she'd planned, and you will, too."

"I don't need a new life. I'll get my old one back." I chucked the last potato into the pot, splashing water that sizzled on the hot stove.

"And well you might, but, in the meantime, you can make a start on the carrots. Your brother, God bless him, created a vegetable shelf in the pantry. Bottom shelf on your right; bring the whole lot."

I found the bag and dumped it on the island. "Did you know Mom worked in the art gallery that was robbed during the riot?"

Maggs stopped stirring a pot of sauce. "I did not."

"Clare thinks Mom might've stolen the paintings."

"Looks like you've unpicked the jumper and knitted yourself an eight-finger glove," she said. "Your mother's as unlikely to steal paintings as she is to start a riot. She loved art. Believed it brought communities together."

It was the first recognizable thing I'd heard about Mom since we left Longview. When our elementary school needed a new playground, Mom had organized an auction and offered free art classes, so people could create pieces to donate. Most of Longview and half of Turner Valley had dribbled in and out of the gallery that spring. Molly painted a portrait of her horse. Our homeroom teacher sketched the sheriff's car turtle-up in a snowstorm, and Mrs. Baxter painted a still life of her tomato plants.

I looked at Maggs. "If Mom didn't do anything wrong, why isn't she here now?"

"Be patient. Your mother will come for you, and then you can ask her yourself."

Lewis believed that, too. But Clare had been waiting seventeen years for Mom to come home.

I peeled carrots until my fingers cramped. Mom's painting watched me from the other side of the room. Now that I'd seen the sleeping-warrior island in real life, it was easy to recognize it.

Maggs attacked lumps in the sauce with a wooden spoon. "Ruby left you a note."

"Is it about dead queens?"

"No, you strange child, it's about computers." She waved her oven mitt at the glass table. "I stuck it to the laptop."

I dropped the peeler and dove for the table.

A yellow sticky note, in scratchy handwriting: *Dark-web browser and virus protection installed. You are untraceable.*

My heart raced. At last, I could contact Molly.

"Can you manage without me?" I asked as I opened the laptop.

"Have done for the last seventy-two years."

My fingers hovered over the keyboard. The cursor blinked in the message bar. What should I say? *Sorry for being a coward and running. Why didn't a double homicide make the headlines? Does the sheriff's office have any idea who Schenk is? I miss you.*

Are you OK? I typed.

And waited.

Then added, This is Cameron.

Nothing.

Haggis laid her head on my lap. I stroked her while I watched the screen.

Someone knocked and opened the back door at the same time. "Hiya, only me."

Aisha.

She looked at Maggs, who now had three pots on the go, then at me watching an inactive laptop screen. "I hope you're not paying him."

"The boy's had a busy day," Maggs said. "Sit yourself down and tell me your news."

Aisha perched on one of the kitchen stools. "I came to see Ruby. I've a book for her."

"Is it about dead queens?" I said.

"*Tch*, pay him no notice." Maggs filled the kettle, the gush of water killing further conversation.

Aisha sat with her back to me. She was wearing her castle uniform of kilt, white shirt and tartan headscarf, which I now knew was a hijab. I shifted the laptop, so if she turned, she couldn't see the screen.

Maggs puttered around the kitchen — mugs clonked on the counter, the biscuit-tin lid popped, the fridge door sucked open. I focused on the laptop screen. Was Molly reading my messages right now? Was she figuring out a reply, biting her nails, twirling her hair?

"I bumped into your mum this morning," Maggs said.

My head snapped up, but she was talking to Aisha, not me. Of course she hadn't seen Mom.

The kettle whistled steam.

Maggs lifted it off its cradle and poured water into the pot of carrots. "She looked tired."

Aisha shrugged.

"She said you haven't been to see your brother in a while."

I tried to imagine Aisha with a brother. Was he older or younger? Did he have the same naive belief that everyone in the world was good?

Aisha rotated the biscuit tin, its metal bottom scraping against the countertop. "I've been busy with my job and swim training."

"And when school starts up, you'll have even less time." Maggs leaned across the counter and put her hand on Aisha's arm. "Those fancy cakes you bake — when they don't turn out the way you wanted, sometimes you need to blame the oven and not the cake."

"The cake should've known not to stay in the oven," Aisha said.

I had no idea what they were talking about, but it wasn't cakes and ovens.

Maggs took the tin from Aisha and handed her the book. "Ruby's in the lounge. No doubt she'll be glad to have someone her own age to talk to after spending the day in Nora's company."

Aisha stood and made for the door, then turned around. "What are you searching up?"

I slapped the laptop shut. "What's the book about?"

She narrowed her eyes. "Villains."

"Who's the villain?"

"Depends on who's telling the story," she said. "And, of course, which version you want to believe."

My mouth went dry.

She smiled mischievously. "But not even *you* could mistake Queen Mary for a villain."

I sagged against the chair back. I was getting as jumpy as Lewis.

Haggis nuzzled Aisha's leg, and she leaned down to pet her.

"Can Haggis come to the lounge with me?" she asked Maggs.

"Mind she doesn't jump on the sofas."

Haggis barked, then trotted after Aisha.

I opened the laptop. Molly still hadn't replied. What story did Molly believe about me? Was I the villain or the hero, or the coward who ran away?

I typed, Please message me. It's safe — we can't be traced, then snapped the laptop shut.

Ruby's sticky note stared back at me.

"If you don't need me, I'll go and thank Ruby for her help with the laptop," I said to Maggs.

"Away and make new friends."

When I caught up with Aisha in the hallway, she looked back at me. "Remind me never to employ you."

As we walked into the lounge, a car door clonked shut outside, and Nora and Ruby, who were sitting in the armchairs by the unlit fire playing chess, looked up.

"I brought you a book, and Will's skiving," Aisha said.

"I came to say thank you," I said. "For fixing the computer."

Ruby didn't smile as much as not frown, which I interpreted as, *you're welcome.*

"What book?" Nora rubbed her hands. "Is it a good one?"

"If you like dead people," I said.

Aisha glared at me, then held the book out for Ruby. "It's about Mary, Queen of Scots."

Ruby looked lost, like she'd never been given a gift before. Her mouth twisted, and I wasn't sure if it was the start of a smile or tears.

Someone opened the front door, tinkling the bell above it. I stepped into the doorway of the lounge to check who it was.

The man was tall and broad with hair that wasn't brown or

blond, but that muddy in-between color. He clutched a duffel bag in one hand and a phone in the other.

Ruby mumbled a question, and Aisha's reply was to ask Professor Pham because he used to lecture history and knew everything.

The man turned toward the voices and saw me.

"Hullo," he said. "Do you know how I check in?"

Nothing about him was familiar, so why was I breaking out in goosebumps?

He swung the duffel bag over his shoulder and scrolled through his phone. "I've got the confirmation email if you need to see it."

I skittered past him, behind the reception desk, and read the entry Maggs must've added this afternoon.

Thys Visser. Was that a Dutch name?

His accent wasn't like Schenk's. But he didn't have a Scottish accent either, or the clipped accent we'd heard in London. But then, Nora sounded different to the Fisbys, who sounded different to Ruby. Even Maggs and Clare had different lilts, and they only lived two hours from each other.

"You were the fifth guesthouse I called." Thys Visser put down his bag. "And that was after I tried all the big hotels. Edinburgh's full, seemingly. Not a wise time to visit, I think."

As he spoke, I searched his features for any similarity to Schenk or to Goatee Guy. Other than being white, I couldn't see any.

He looked around. "Drummond House will suit me well."

I wasn't sure how he could tell from the hallway, but I nodded anyway. "Mrs. Ross has you in Glenfinnan."

He put his phone away. "Lead the way."

As I climbed the stairs, with Visser at my heels, my neck prickled.

Glenfinnan was a front room, looking out over the street and the park. It smelled of Maggs's washing powder. The bed was tightly made, a neatly folded towel on top. I held open the door for Visser, and as he passed, I got a whiff of the ocean — seaweed and salt spray.

He set his duffel bag on the bed, then turned to me. "I didn't catch your name."

"It's Will." I thrust the key into his hand. "Dinner's at six."

"I have plans," he said. "Apologies."

I nodded and hurried back to the kitchen, where Maggs was sliding a tray of half-boiled potatoes into the oven. Glasses and plates and cutlery and water jugs were lined up on the island, waiting to be carried to the dining room.

"The new guest arrived, Thys Visser." I picked up one of the empty jugs. "Did he say where he was from?"

Maggs straightened. "He did not. Why?"

Because he gives me the creeps, even though nothing about him is familiar, and he seems like a perfectly normal guy. Even saying it in my head sounded paranoid. I held the jug under the tap, the water shushing and bubbling.

"You were right; he looks like he'll eat a lot." I switched jugs and filled the next one. "But he's not staying in for dinner."

"He'll be eating leftovers tomorrow, then." Maggs wiped her hands on her apron. "How's my girl? Is she still in the lounge?"

"Haggis?"

"Aisha," she said. "Still in that dreadful nylon kilt an hour after closing."

"Maybe she likes it."

"*Tch*," Maggs said. "That girl usually changes outfits three times a day. Lord, during term time, she's tearing off her school blazer and tie before she's in the back door."

"What happened to her brother?" I said. "Was he the cake or the oven?"

Maggs frowned, then her face cleared, and she chuckled. "Faizal's most definitely the cake. Not a bad bone in that boy's body, but if there's trouble, you can count on him finding it, or it finding him."

"You said Aisha hadn't visited him," I said. "Is he in hospital?"

She shook her head. "It's not my story to tell."

Maggs tilted her head at the jugs I'd just filled. "The tables won't lay themselves."

I turned to the glass table and flipped open the laptop for one last check before the dinner rush started.

A text from Molly.

My heart soared.

"You look like you won the lottery," Maggs said.

I laughed as I clicked on the message.

I'm living my life, don't contact me again.

My whole body went rigid.

I read it a second time and a third. She didn't want to talk to me? Not ever? Did everyone back home feel the same? People we'd known our whole lives shutting us out. Molly and the Baxters and Hunter and all our other friends, our *only* friends, desperate to be rid of us. Tossing us out like unwanted trash.

Pressure erupted from deep inside of me, ripping through my stomach and my chest and my lungs, up through my throat.

I wanted to scream. I wanted to yell at Mom and Dad, and at

the world, but mainly at Mom because she'd torn apart our lives, just like she'd torn apart Clare's, and now we'd never go home.

I snatched up one of the jugs and hurled it across the room at Mom's painting.

Glass shattered in an explosion of noise and glitter.

Shards clinked to the floor on a slosh of water.

The pressure in my chest eased.

My tunnel vision cleared.

I took in the scene.

Maggs holding back Haggis.

Jagged glass strewn across the puddled floor.

Water dripping from Mom's painting.

"Not a lottery win, then?" Maggs said.

I crouched down and hugged Haggis because I'd scared her and because I didn't want to see the pity in Maggs's eyes.

"Keep her there while I get her lead." Maggs looped Haggis's leash around the table leg, then clipped it on her collar.

"Sorry," I said, my throat dry, my voice hoarse.

Maggs held out a cloth. "Dry off your mum's painting."

I ruffled Haggis's ears, then shuffled to the painting.

The painting wasn't Mom, but it was as close as I could get. If she was standing here in front of me, would I apologize or would I yell? Or would I hug her and cry?

Glass tinkled as Maggs swept it into a pile.

I took a deep breath and wiped water from the pink clouds. Then from the stone buildings of the city and the calm blue sea with its lonely islands. And when the cloth was too damp to soak up any more, I turned to get a fresh one.

"Maggs?" My voice shook.

"Yes, dear."

I held out the cloth, so she could see the smear of green paint.

"Well, that shouldn't happen." She took the cloth off me and sniffed at it, then frowned. "How peculiar. It's not oil paint."

I looked at the smeared remains of the sleeping-warrior island. "Have I ruined it?"

Please let it not be ruined.

She stepped up to the painting and rubbed her finger over the smudge that was once an island. "Well, I never."

I squeezed my eyes shut. "Can you fix it?"

I could hear the cloth rubbing against Mom's painting. And Maggs tutting. And Haggis's paws scratching the floor as she tried to pull free of her leash.

"Well, that makes more sense," she said. "Katrina, you canny wee devil."

My eyes snapped open. "What?"

Maggs had wiped away the entire sleeping-warrior island, and underneath, floating on the sea in what looked like black ink, was an upside-down *V* with an arrow through it.

I traced the symbol with my finger. "What does it mean?"

"I haven't a clue, but Katrina wouldn't deface a painting for no good reason." She looked at me. "You don't think I was meant to find this all those years ago, do you?"

I thought maybe the answer was yes, but Maggs looked so concerned that I said, "Not unless Mom expected you to throw water over it."

CHAPTER
17

LEWIS

Maggs handed me a bowl of frog spawn that she said was rice pudding, but I had my doubts. I was to take it downstairs to Professor Pham because it was his favorite, and between the Fringe Festival and the sunny weather and the fact it was Friday night, all of the guests had headed into town and Maggs had cancelled dinner. I'd tried to persuade Cameron to deliver it, but he refused to move from the attic, where he'd spent the entire day brooding over yesterday's message from Molly.

Yes, Molly's reply was heartless. I was crushed, too, but now that going home was off the table, I'd expected him to be slightly more interested in Mom's symbol. I'd doodled it a million times and read websites on hallmarks and trademarks and mystical motifs because, unlike my brother, I wanted to find Mom and Dad.

I opened the gate in the sidewalk railing and went down Professor Pham's front steps to his basement apartment. Bees buzzed in and out of the flowerpots that crowded the door.

I rang the bell.

Don't make eye contact. Hand over the rice pudding and leave.

The door creaked open.

"What?" Ruby stood in the doorway, her blue hair in two stubby braids.

My fingers relaxed their grip on the bowl. "What are you doing here? I thought you were out."

She shrugged. "I don't like the sun."

How could she not like the sun? Was she a vampire?

Her face scrunched up. "Is that rice pudding?"

"I know, it looks gross," I said. "Do chocolate brownies not exist here?"

"We're not Neanderthals." She spun and disappeared back inside, leaving me on the doorstep.

"What about the rice pudding?"

"I'm not your servant," she called back from the gloom.

I stepped into what had once been Maggs's private apartment.

It was at least ten degrees cooler down here. I could feel my sweat evaporating, leaving my skin crusty and tight.

"In here," Ruby called.

I followed her voice into the front room, where Professor Pham was sitting at a table covered in open books. A single armchair sat next to a stone mantelpiece, framed photographs of ruined castles and churches lined up along it. The rest of the walls were taken up with bookshelves. Would he have any books on symbols? Without the arrow, Mom's upside-down *V* could've been a Greek letter or a mathematical function or just a plain old upside-down *V*, but the arrow made it none of those things, and my hours of online research had turned up nothing.

"I hope this isn't a new trend," the professor said to me. "I'm not a guesthouse."

I slid the bowl onto the table. "Maggs made you rice pudding."

He grunted a thanks and scooped up a heap.

"Don't you have emails to send?" Ruby folded her arms.

Not anymore. Molly was the one person we thought would stand by us. If she wouldn't help us find Schenk, then no one else would.

Ruby tilted her head and raised her eyebrows.

I looked from Ruby, who knew about untraceable texts, to the professor, who'd bought this apartment from Maggs right after the riots and then watched her guests from behind a newspaper for the last seventeen years. What was it that he was watching for?

"I should get back," I said.

"Stay until I've finished." The professor pointed at the bowl with his spoon. "If I hang on to it, Maggs will expect it back washed."

I took a breath. Glanced around the room. Then at the table spread with books.

"What are all the books for?" I said to fill the silence, before Ruby could fill it with another question.

"Ruby here wants to know about Mary, Queen of Scots." The professor ate another heaped spoonful, then leaned back in his chair, a contented look on his face.

"The Scottish queen from five hundred years ago," I said.

And one of the twenty paintings that had been stolen from the gallery. The exhibition had been titled *Events That Shaped Our Nation*. I'd looked at pictures of every one of the stolen paintings, holding my breath in case I recognized any. Mom had stacks of her old paintings in the shed, but the stolen paintings weren't among them. Clare's suggestion that Mom had something to do with the theft was as much a dead end as contacting Molly had turned out to be.

Professor Pham picked up two of the books and held them out for Ruby to take. "Read these first. If you get through them, I'll lend you more."

Ruby took the books, stroked the cover of the top one.

"However," the professor said, "as I used to tell my students, books are no substitute for the real thing. Have some imagination. See it for yourselves. It's all there waiting to be discovered — the castle, Greyfriars, Holyrood Palace, Arthur's Seat, the Royal Mile."

Ruby hugged the books. "Thank you. I'll bring these back."

I picked up one of the books, a picture of the castle on the front. I wanted to see all the things Professor Pham was sending Ruby to explore. Maybe we'd come back one day with Mom and Dad.

"I expect a full report." The professor held out his empty bowl for me to take. "From you too, Will. Be curious, and the mysteries of the world will reveal themselves."

I took the bowl and followed Ruby into the hall.

"And, Will," Professor Pham called.

I backed into the room.

"I don't know why you're here, but if I were you, I'd steer clear of Nora Bidwell. She'd sell her own mother if she thought she'd get a story out of it."

I scuttled after Ruby, the spoon rattling against the inside of the bowl. As we climbed up to street level, we met the Fisbys carrying their wagon of props down the front steps of the guesthouse.

"Hullo, hullo," Mr. Fisby said. "We just popped back to change for our final show."

"Are you checking out?" Ruby said.

"We'll be here another couple of days." Mr. Fisby glanced at me. "We've some unfinished business."

Mrs. Fisby laughed and elbowed him. "We've seen all the other street performers, of course, but we haven't seen any of the big shows. Got to keep an eye on the competition."

"And we've got more free tickets than we can count." Mr. Fisby touched his nose. "Once you're in the business, you're in business."

"Ignore him." Mrs. Fisby dug into the pocket of her green pants. "Take these. Tickets for Cirque Berserk, spectacular show. Six motorcycles racing around inside a metal sphere. They're for tonight, so no use to us."

Mrs. Fisby pressed two tickets into my free hand. "A gift for all your hard work."

I thanked them, then Ruby and I watched while the Fisbys bounced down the street, their wagon rolling behind them.

I slid the tickets on top of Ruby's pile of books. "You can either explore the history of the city or watch motorbikes on a spin cycle."

She looked down at the tickets. "I only need one."

"What about your grandfather?"

"He's busy with something." She held out one of the tickets, then her cheeks flushed. "I'm not asking you to go with me. Give it away if you don't want it."

As soon as I took the ticket, she spun away and ran up the front steps.

After leaving Professor Pham's bowl in the kitchen sink, I headed back to the attic.

I paused outside Ruby's bedroom door and looked at the flying motorbike on the ticket. Could I go into the city to see the show and explore the castle and the other sites the professor had recommended? I didn't know what half of them were, but wasn't that the whole point of exploring?

What was I thinking? The only things I should be investigating were Schenk and Mom's symbol.

I slid the ticket into my back pocket, then trudged up the narrow stairs to the attic, the air temperature raising with every step.

Even though our bedroom window was wide open, the air was stagnant and smelled like sweaty armpits. Cameron was finally out of bed, sitting at the writing desk, the laptop open in front of him.

"Did you find anything?" I leaned over to see if he'd found a different website on symbols. "Mrs. Baxter's Facebook page?"

I'd checked Mrs. Baxter's page about a hundred times since we got here. Mainly because she'd been at the barbecue, but also because she kept up to date with local news and liked to be the first to share it.

"A bear and her two cubs have been spotted in Highwood Pass," I read out loud. "The construction of the long-awaited cow bridge is underway. Useful stuff."

"I messaged her," Cameron said.

"And?"

"No reply."

"Researching Mom's symbol or Schenk or even the stolen paintings would be more useful." Sweat ran down my back.

"Forget the paintings. I know enough," he said.

"I bet you didn't know two of them were recovered." I waited for his look of surprise. It never came.

Cameron sighed. "One from an evil but dim South American dictator. And a second from a tech billionaire with questionable ethics. And a third painting may or may not have been bought by some distant royalty in Edinburgh, who may or may not be lying."

My skin tingled. "How do you know?"

"If they're lying?"

"About a third painting being in Edinburgh?"

"Aisha told me." He went back to reading Mrs. Baxter's news.

"Who has it?"

Cameron shrugged. "Does it matter?"

I paced. "If we could find the painting, maybe we can prove it wasn't Mom who sold it on, and maybe that would prove she never stole it in the first place."

It was a plan. Of sorts.

"That's a lot of *ifs* and *maybes*," Cameron said.

"No more than an upside-down *V* with an arrow through it drawn eighteen years ago that probably has nothing to do with anything." I reached to take the computer off him. "But it's all we've got."

He slapped it shut and plucked the ticket from my pocket. "What's this?"

"A ticket for a show," I said. "Stop being a child and give me the computer."

He read the ticket, then looked up at me. "You should go, you love motorbikes."

"I love riding them, not watching someone else ride them."

When I'm on my dirt bike, I can't think about anything else, or I'll crash. It's the only time I manage to switch off my brain.

"You've been holed up here for a week, Lewis."

"I went to Rothesay with you."

"Other than that," he said. "And you heard Clare, we have to live our lives."

"She told us not to waste our lives looking for Mom, so thanks, but I think I'll ignore her advice."

"Where did you get the ticket?"

What was his obsession with the ticket? I threw up my hands. "If I tell you, will you give me the computer and tell me who has the third painting?"

He nodded.

"The Fisbys got the tickets for free and gave them to us."

He raised his eyebrows. "Us?"

"Me and Ruby." I held out my hand for the laptop.

"The battery's about to die," he said as he handed it over. "No idea where the charger is."

"Are you kidding me?" Could he be any more annoying?

"Go to the show, Lewis."

"If it gets me away from you, maybe I will." My heart did a little jolt as I said it.

CHAPTER
18

CAMERON

I stood at the attic window and watched them leave. Lewis had a bounce in his step, and they were chatting, Ruby looking up at Lewis and Lewis smiling down. If I didn't know better, I'd think they were flirting. Luckily, I'd never have to compete with my brother on the dating front. Heck, if I was a girl I'd choose Lewis over me.

Withholding the computer charger had been the right thing to do. If Lewis had stayed, he'd have wasted another five hours obsessing, and we'd be no closer to finding a way out of this mess. I'd been ready to head home, but Longview, it turned out, wasn't going to welcome us back like Rothesay had welcomed Clare.

But if I wasn't Cameron Larsen from Longview, who was I? At the moment, I was a shadow in the attic. Only Will existed, and he was on his way to the festival with Ruby.

Once Lewis and Ruby were out of sight, I hung my head out of the window. The attic was like an oven.

I spun as the door creaked open, but it was only Haggis, her leash in her mouth.

"Sorry, girl, we're housebound," I said.

Haggis dropped the leash at my feet and looked up with pleading eyes. She looked even hotter than me.

"Okay, but backyard only."

I picked up the leash and went downstairs, Haggis bouncing at my heels. It was Friday night, and everyone was out except me. I'd never been alone on a Friday before — weekend nights were for hanging with friends or curling up at home watching movies with Mom and Dad.

As we passed through the dining room, I picked up an empty mug and a crumb-filled plate, then left them in the kitchen sink.

I stroked Haggis while I looked at Mom's painting. The symbol looked like a squiggle in the ocean from here, and maybe that's all Mom had ever intended it to be. A doodle she regretted and covered up with an island that belonged somewhere else. Whatever it was, Lewis was right: the date under her signature was eighteen years ago. Mom had painted it a year *before* the riots. Just because we were desperate for a clue didn't mean this was it.

Haggis bounded outside as soon as I opened the door. It wasn't any cooler out here, but at least there was a breeze.

"Where should Lewis and I go next, Haggis?" I asked. "I'm out of ideas, and we can't stay here forever."

We'd found Clare. We'd contacted Molly. Neither of them cared. Our family didn't want us, and neither did our friends. I wanted to be angry, but my chest ached so much all I felt like doing was curling up on the grass.

"Hiya." Aisha was leaning out of a window on the second floor of her house. "Wait there."

She disappeared, then five seconds later reappeared at her back door. Haggis sprinted up the steps to greet her.

After patting Haggis, Aisha looked at me. "Avoiding the washing up?"

"Everyone's out," I said.

She came down the steps. "I'm joking. But not really. Anyway, pleasantries aside. I got your text."

Text? I hadn't sent her a text. It must've been Lewis — what was he up to?

I nodded and hoped it was enough for her to continue.

"It's the Wallace family," she said. "Jamie Wallace, the boy we saw at the castle staring at an empty wall? The one I know from swim meets? You still look confused."

I scrambled for a reason other than the truth, which was I had no idea why we were having this conversation. "Do you wear a headscarf when you swim?"

"It's like a swim cap, but with a collar thing." She waved away any further explanation. "Anyway, the simple answer to your question is, I don't know when the Wallaces got hold of it. If they have it at all. Them having the Queen Mary painting is only a rumor, but it is a persistent one."

The paintings! Of course, Lewis was scurrying down another rabbit hole. I gave a knowledgeable nod.

Aisha continued. "Piecing together all the rumors, and what I know of the Wallaces, if you put a gun against my head and forced me to guess, then I'd say the Mary painting's been in their possession for at least a decade."

She grinned.

"It's not easy to think straight with a gun against your head."

I picked up a stick and tossed it for Haggis.

"Moving swiftly on to your other question — why they would risk harboring a stolen national treasure," Aisha said. "Mrs. Elizabeth Wallace is an MP who uses the ancientness of her family as proof she cares more about the country than her rivals. Which is rubbish. She's completely up herself. I couldn't find any link between her family and the painting. But her husband, Jamie's dad, is a descendant of …" She made a drum roll with invisible sticks.

"I have no idea."

She threw up her hands. "Mary, Queen of Scots. Which makes sense because …"

"She had her head chopped off," I said.

Haggis dropped the retrieved stick at my feet.

"You have a disturbing fascination with death," Aisha said.

"Her cousin *chopped off her head*," I said. "Not what you expect from a family member."

"She didn't want to."

"That's comforting."

Haggis looked back and forth between us as if to say, *Could one of you throw the damn stick?* I chucked it.

Aisha folded her arms. "It doesn't matter why they have it. Queen Mary belongs to the nation, and her painting belongs in the castle. And you're welcome."

"Sorry," I said. "And thank you."

Although I had no idea what Lewis wanted with the information. So what if some rich family had the painting? We could hardly waltz into their mansion and dust for fingerprints. *Crap.* That's exactly what Lewis had suggested — prove someone other than Mom had stolen the painting.

"I'm going to ask Jamie about it," she said. "His swim team always goes to the same place on a Friday night. Our team has an open invitation to join, but we never do. Rivals and all that."

"You're going to walk up to some boy you hardly know and ask him if his parents bought a stolen painting?"

"I'll be more subtle," she said. "Are you coming?"

Did I want to be involved in this crazy scheme? Probably not. Did I want to go into town on a Friday night? Absolutely.

I shrugged. "Why not."

———

L E W I S

This was the first normal thing I'd done since the barbecue. If standing in the street watching a woman in pink-feather hot pants spin a Hula-Hoop on her nose could be considered normal.

"The Fisbys' act was better than this," I said.

I'd dragged Ruby straight to the Fisbys' show because I wanted to make sure they *were* actual street performers. We'd watched them juggle flowerpots with their feet and flaming torches with their bare hands and toss knives at each other. And by the time they took a bow, and the crowd erupted, Mr. and Mrs. Fisby had convinced me they were exactly who they appeared to be — retired circus performers who loved what they did too much to give it up.

"You're biased because they gave you free tickets to a motorbike circus," Ruby said.

"They gave them to both of us." I couldn't help but smile.

I was in Edinburgh, in the middle of a festival on a wide, cobbled street, watching oddly dressed people doing ridiculous things.

Ruby gave me a *whatever* kind of look. "They had no choice. I was standing right next to you."

Ruby's blue hair was loose and kinked from the braids. Her lips were shiny. Was she wearing lip gloss? Makeup didn't seem like a Ruby thing, but what did I know?

Henrietta the Hula-Hooper tipped her head, flinging the hoop into her waiting hand. She picked up four more neon hoops and a minute later was spinning them on various parts of her body. The crowd oohed and clapped, and the ring of spectators widened as people jostled for a view.

"I feel sorry for the musician." I gestured to the performer on the other side of the street. "He's playing to himself."

"He can't sing."

"But he's painted gold," I said. "Think how long it'll take to wash off. And he's got a lot to compete with. The stilt-walking bagpipe player. The human statue with the spider hanging from his hat who raises his sword if you put a penny in his kilt bag."

"He's meant to be Robert the Bruce," she said. "And it's called a *sporran*, not a 'kilt bag.'"

"Who's Robert the Bruce?"

"I know you don't actually care," Ruby said. "You made it pretty clear at the castle you think history's boring."

I should pretend not to care, but I wasn't like Cameron. I couldn't morph to fit any social setting. I only knew how to be me.

"I like history," I said. "For example, I know this street's called the Royal Mile because it's a mile long and links the castle to the palace."

Ruby rolled her eyes. "That's geography not history. And a two-second internet search hardly counts as being interested."

I'd also looked up the castle, which was pushing one thousand years old. How could anyone not want to see that?

Hula-Hoop Henrietta was now spinning herself as well as the hoops. Ruby's interest had obviously faded though, because she was looking up at the turreted cathedral next to us. This city was amazing.

We had an hour to kill before the motorbike circus. I wanted to see the castle, but Will had already been with Ruby, and according to Ruby, it was already closed. But I might never get another chance, and seeing the outside of it was better than nothing.

I checked the phone-map of street performances for one near the castle. "Have we seen Mighty Gareth yet?"

"I saw him earlier in the week," Ruby said. "A puny bloke lifting milk cartons. I think it's meant to be ironic."

"We could get our faces painted," I said.

"I'm not eight." She turned away from the performance and edged through the crowd.

I followed. "You can access the underground city from here. And, hello, an underground city, who wouldn't want to see that?"

She turned, her eyes bright. "It's a warren of tunnels with chambers where people used to live. There were even shops down there. Thousands of people living completely underground." She caught herself. "But, as far as I remember, you weren't impressed."

Cameron wouldn't have been, but I was, and this could be my only opportunity to see any of it.

"How about we see the castle first, and then the tunnels?" I said.

"Why are you so perky? Did whatever untraceable text you sent get a reply?"

I shrugged. "Not a useful one. But thanks anyway. For helping. That was kind."

I shifted from foot to foot, waiting for her to ask why I needed to be untraceable. I was prepared this time — a rambling explanation about fooling my parents into thinking I was at math camp in Toronto. It didn't quite hang together, but I was ready to embellish. My parents were Amish and didn't condone air travel. Or I'd been offered a full scholarship to the University of Edinburgh and wanted to check it out, but my parents were set on Yale. Or ...

"My mum's dead," she said.

My brain froze.

She turned away and struggled through the circle of spectators.

What should I say? That I knew how missing your mom felt? That I was sorry?

I shuffled through the crowd and caught up as she popped out in the empty space in front of the gold musician. He was belting out a song about walking five hundred miles. Even though he was singing off-key, I recognized it as one Mom used to listen to.

"Your granddad's cool," I said.

Ruby fiddled with a leather bracelet, one of three on her wrist. "He isn't, but he's my granddad, and my dad doesn't care, so ..."

"I'm sorry. About your mom."

"Don't pretend you know how it feels."

"Like you're no longer tethered to the earth," I said. "And if you drifted away, no one would notice, or even care."

Ruby looked up from her bracelets, a crease between her white-blond eyebrows. "How do you cope with being alone?"

"I'm not alone," I said, then cringed. The whole point of pretending to be Will was to fool people into thinking I was alone.

She tilted her head.

"I have Maggs," I said.

"Your employer?" She shook her head. "You're even more of a saddo than I am."

"Being alone doesn't make you a loser," I said. "It makes you brave."

The musician's amp screeched.

Ruby looked up at the darkening sky. "I heard the castle's lit up at night."

CHAPTER
19

CAMERON

The Smugglers' Labyrinth was the ground floor of a stone building on one of the cobbled streets that wound up to the castle. Aisha and I joined the end of the sidewalk lineup.

"Does everywhere in this city have a lineup?" I said to Aisha as we waited.

Her dress tonight was made from material printed with a black-and-white map. Her headscarf was the same red as her Converse high-tops. I had on a boring white T-shirt and cargo shorts.

"If by 'lineup' you mean a queue, yes, but only in August during the festival. Except this place, which is always busy."

"Because they allow underage kids," I said.

"Until ten o'clock."

An empty soda can clattered over the cobblestones. One of the girls in front of us turned and kicked it back up the hill. It clattered again as it was kicked farther back in the lineup.

"Do *you* ever come here?" I thought of Maggs saying Aisha's parents would eventually allow her some freedom again and wondered if they knew she was out tonight.

"I used to," she said.

The line shuffled forward.

"What changed?" I asked.

"The hero became the villain, and the justice system has no honor." She straightened her shoulders. "Which is why we're here, so focus."

"That made absolutely no sense," I said.

The can clattered toward us again.

Aisha turned and walloped it back down the line. "It annoys me that the Wallaces get away with it when other people wouldn't."

"Like your brother?" It was a wild guess that I instantly regretted. "Don't answer. It's none of my business. We find Jamie Wallace, accuse him of possessing stolen goods ..."

"A national treasure worth millions," Aisha said. "And not Jamie, his parents. And you're right, my brother's none of your business."

Dad said never to ask anyone personal questions unless you were willing to answer theirs. As much as I wanted to forget all of Mom and Dad's advice, some of it was useful.

We shuffled forward.

The soda can sailed past us again.

"So, we convince Jamie to hand over the painting *and* snitch on his parents." I checked the flip phone. "In the next fifty-three minutes."

"Don't worry about the ten o'clock rule," she said. "The bar staff never check. Too many hidden corners."

"You want us to persuade Jamie to meet us in a broom closet?"

"In one of the vaults."

"Like in a bank?"

"Like in a tunnel," she said. "This place is on the tunnel system."

I'm sure my heart missed a couple of beats before I managed to say, "I thought the tunnels were a myth."

"I didn't say they were a myth. If you'd listened, what I actually said was, there are loads of myths *about* the tunnels. The tunnels are real, and this is one of them. It's brilliant. Like stepping back in time."

"You mean it's dark and damp with tiny, cramped spaces." My chest tightened.

"Which makes it difficult for the staff to identify teens from adults," she said. "It's why it's so popular."

How could I get out of this?

The lineup surged forward, and we found ourselves at the front.

"Maybe you should go in alone," I said. "You know this Jamie guy, and I don't, and you seem …"

Aisha tugged me into the bar.

Inside, the walls of the Smugglers' Labyrinth were the same worn stone as the outside. The only light came from thick, dripping candles tucked into wall crevices. But the air didn't smell of damp earth — it smelled of spilt beer and aftershave, and the ceilings were high and arched, and music thumped from hidden speakers. I wasn't trapped underground. It was only a bar.

We wove through rickety tables and shouted conversations to the back of the bar, then ducked under a low arch into another room with smaller tables also packed with people drinking and telling wild stories about their day. I expected Aisha to slow down as we approached a stone wall, but she veered at the last second and turned into another chamber. No tables here, just a mass of kids, chatting and laughing.

A girl squealed Aisha's name and threw her arms around her. A wave of recognition spread, kids close enough to hug her did, others waved and yelled hellos. Aisha's face lit up as she returned hugs. Maybe it was only me who made her irritable.

The swimmers were a bunch of kids from early to late teens all mixed in together. Longview didn't have enough kids to hang out with this many people, never mind this many people who acted as if they liked one another.

A tall white guy wove through the crowd holding one jug of beer and another of dubious orange liquid above everyone's heads. When he plonked them down onto the one and only table, jammed up against the far wall, everyone cheered.

"That's Jamie," Aisha said.

When he wasn't being dwarfed by an oversized castle fireplace, the guy was huge. "He's built like a bear."

"More like a Saint Bernard," Aisha said. "Come on."

Aisha tugged me into the throng.

"Hiya," she said to Jamie Wallace.

"Aisha." Jamie threw his long arms around her.

Aisha hugged him back.

Did everyone hug here?

"This is brilliant," Jamie said. "I keep inviting all the other teams, but no one ever shows."

"We're here to spy," Aisha said.

At least she was honest about it.

Jamie grinned. "Our secret formula is swim fast, never party on a Monday night and peeing while swimming is harder than you think and requires practice."

Gross.

Aisha laughed.

Jamie finally noticed me, stuck out his bear-paw of a hand. "Are you a swimmer?"

"Soccer player." I shook his hand, hoping he wouldn't crush my bones. "We dribble rather than pee."

Jamie thumped me on the shoulder. "I didn't think Americans had a sense of humor."

"Will's Canadian," Aisha said.

"Even better," he said. "Come on, I'll introduce you to everyone."

L E W I S

We'd just passed a couple of drag queens ballroom dancing on roller skates when the castle came into view. Purple lights shone up at the stone walls and bathed the cobblestones. There were turrets and domes, and cannons poking out of arches, and flags flying in the breeze. Excitement popped in my belly. I was in Scotland, in the outer courtyard of a castle.

The castle's iron-braced wooden doors were shut, stone knights standing guard either side. As we wandered around the courtyard, I imagined carts of grain and gunpowder clattering in to be unloaded and horses galloping off to battle.

Every time a tourist walked past, the spell of the castle broke, so I leaned my elbows on the chest-high wall that ran around the courtyard and looked out over the lights of the city to the hollow blackness of the ocean.

Ruby joined me, but faced the other way, looking across the courtyard to the city center and the hills beyond. She slouched against the wall, relaxed at last. Even though we weren't the same in the way she thought, we were similar in other ways, and for the first time since the barbecue, I felt almost happy. Was I allowed to be happy here when Cameron was so miserable?

"This castle is the most besieged place in Europe," Ruby said. "Why do people wage war, do you think?"

I shrugged. "Greed? Fear?"

"Or revenge," she said.

"Starting a war isn't going to help anyone though, is it?" I said. "If they talked it through, I bet they'd find better solutions than killing off innocent people."

"Maybe some people struggle to forgive," Ruby said.

Is that why Schenk had come after Mom and Dad, for revenge? I shook the thought away and focused instead on the domes and spires of the city, floodlit gold against the ink-black sky.

Ruby nudged me. "Some bloke's staring at you."

I glanced over my shoulder.

All the excitement, the hum in my veins from being here, evaporated.

Goatee, ponytail, squinty eyes. We'd been found!

Tourists and noise closed in, and suddenly I couldn't breathe.

"Are you okay?" Ruby searched my face with concern.

I shook my head. Tried to take a deep breath. Gasped. Tried again.

She took my hand and dragged me across the courtyard.

Was he going to shoot me? Take me away and lock me in a windowless cell? I searched for Cameron. But he was back at the guesthouse. I wanted to shout for Mom and Dad, but they weren't here. Why weren't they here?

As we hit the Royal Mile, I shot a look over my shoulder, but we'd been swallowed by the crowds. The noise closed in on me — feedback from a microphone, a crying child, and everywhere people clapping and laughing and cheering for more. I tried to slow my breathing, but there were too many people and not enough air.

"Down here." Ruby pulled me down a side street.

Only a trickle of people here. I sucked in air, but it was too thick to reach my lungs. Ruby shoved me behind a dumpster and ordered me to sit. I slumped onto the sidewalk. Found a pocket of air. Breathed in and out. In and out.

A siren wailed in the distance. A bicycle thub-thub-thubbed down the cobbled street.

Ruby peeked around the dumpster.

"Can you see him?" I said.

"If you can talk, you can move." She dragged me up, and we were off again.

Crossing the road. Running down a winding hill. Merging with a group of teenagers. Stumbling into a bar.

"You'll get to see the underground city after all," Ruby yelled in my ear.

CAMERON

As the night wore on, the music got louder and our voices hoarse. After Jamie introduced me as his new pal, the entire team wanted to hug me. I was handed drinks and pulled into conversations that, with the background noise and the accents and the speed at which jibes were fired back and forth, were difficult to understand. I didn't care. I laughed along with them. Raised my glass when they did. I was a teenager again.

When the music turned from pop to fiddles, the swim team cheered and rushed from our alcove in a wave of enthusiasm.

"Have you ever been to a *ceilidh*?" Aisha shouted in my ear.

"A what?"

"Come on." She pulled me to the dance floor.

It was like ballroom dancing, but a million times faster with lots of spinning and skipping. Aisha tugged and shoved me into position, and together we galloped around the dance floor with everyone else in synchronized chaos. By the time the fiddles stopped, my face hurt from grinning.

"The next one's easier," she said.

"Next one?"

"They always play three in a row." She laughed and clutched my hand. "Come on."

I caught onto the steps faster this time, and by the end of the dance, I was whirling Aisha around rather than her whirling me, her skirt fanning out as she spun.

Jamie asked Aisha to dance the third dance. I made it three steps when one of the girls yanked me back.

By the end of the set, everyone was red-faced and laughing and dripping in sweat.

Back in our corner, Jamie handed me a glass of the orange soda, then clinked my glass with his. "It's Irn-Bru, Scotland's national drink."

"I thought that was whisky."

He shrugged. "Only if you're over forty."

"Cheers," I said and took a gulp of the sugary drink.

Maybe one day these kids would be my friends, and I would belong. I had no idea how we'd manage it, but I'd think about that later. All I wanted to do now was laugh and dance and try to keep up with the conversation.

Someone knocked my elbow, and the drink sloshed over the top of the glass and down my shirt. I waved at Aisha and pointed to the orange splat. She grinned.

I wove through tables, back through the candlelit bar and under the washroom sign. Then pushed through the door and headed to the sink.

Three cubicle doors, one shut. A guy at the urinal. The barred window was open, feet passing by on the street outside.

I took off the shirt, held it under the tap, then scrubbed. Urinal Guy joined me at the sinks, washed his hands, shook his head as if to say, *Tough luck, buddy,* then left. I held up the shirt — still orange.

The cubicle door opened.

"Cameron?"

My heart jumped into my throat. Lewis?

I spun around to face him. "What the heck are you doing here?"

He flung his arms around me. "The guy from London, he's here. We were outside the castle, and he's here, Cameron. How did he manage to find us, and Mom and Dad can't? They're never coming for us, are they?"

I grabbed his shoulders and looked him in the eyes. "Lewis, calm down. Are you sure it was Goatee Guy?"

"One hundred percent sure."

Of course he was. "Where's Ruby now?"

"She went to the bar."

As long as the swimmers stayed in their tucked-away alcove, Lewis would be able to get to the bar, find Ruby and make it back outside without being seen.

I pulled the shirt over my head, sopping wet and still orange.

"You go first and get Ruby out of here. Find a cab. Get back to the guesthouse." I squeezed his arm. "Be careful, okay? I'll meet you there."

"Then what?"

"Just get back to the guesthouse, then we'll figure it out."

We'd have to leave Edinburgh. Just as I was imagining being able to stay.

We looked at each other for a heartbeat, then Lewis nodded and pushed through the door.

I counted to twenty, then followed and hovered in a shadowy corner watching Lewis make his way to the bar.

Someone ducked through a group of people to his left. Red headscarf. Cheeky grin. Aisha. *Crap.*

Lewis looked back at me, panic in his eyes. *Stay calm, Lewis. You can do this.*

Ruby's blue hair reflected the candlelight. She was nudging through the crowd, a glass in each hand.

Aisha's red scarf coming one way.

Ruby's blue hair coming the other.

On a collision course with Lewis in the middle.

Crap.

I leaped from the shadows and dove for Ruby before she made it past the last group of tables.

"Thanks." I took one of the glasses and took a gulp.

"What happened?" She nodded at my shirt.

"Walked into a tray of drinks," I said. "You should see the other guy."

I glanced over my shoulder long enough to see Aisha and Lewis arm in arm on their way back to the swimmers.

Ruby slid her drink onto a high-topped table, cluttered with empty glasses. "You sound like you've recovered."

"Do you mind if we go home?"

"What if he's still out there?" She hopped onto the stool. "Besides, I thought you wanted to see the tunnels."

"What's the quickest way out of here?"

"I bought drinks."

I tried to down my soda. Managed half. Slammed the glass back on the table.

Ruby shook her head. "Just when I think you're nice, you turn into a knob again."

Ruby's route to the exit took us dangerously close to the dance floor. I kept my head down, hoping all the swimmers were too exhausted to still be dancing.

When we pushed into the fresh air, the density of people didn't thin out any. The area outside the bar was jammed with kids and flashing lights. Red and blue lights.

Police.

This could not be happening.

"I'm guessing you don't have fake ID?" Ruby said.

"Not on me." My mind raced. On one side of the door was Lewis and potential exposure, on the other side was an ID check, which could lead to the same. *Crap.* I rubbed my sweat-soaked hair.

I was delusional to think we could make a life here. Tonight had proved we couldn't even go out of the house at the same time.

And what would happen when school started? Only one of us could go? Only one of us would get to play soccer, go to parties, make real friends? Date? I'd be half a person living a half-life.

The happiness of the night crashed around my feet.

I shoved through the kids in front of me and came up against a cop, his arms stretched wide to stop me from passing. "You're not going anywhere until I see some ID."

CHAPTER
20

C A M E R O N

Ruby's ID worked. Either the cop hadn't bothered checking her
date of birth, or her ID was fake.

When he held out his hand for mine, I patted down my
shorts, dug my hands in my pockets and made a show of looking
for a driver's license or student card that wasn't there.

"Must've left it at home," I said.

We were in the street, next to one of the cop cars. I'd tried to
text Lewis, but had been gruffly told to put away my phone.

The officer — yellow teeth and a patchy beard — rested his
hands on his belt, his fingers dangling over a baton. "What's your
full name, son?"

Not Cameron Larsen because there wasn't any paperwork to
prove he existed. Or Willem Murray van der Berg because all hell
would break lose.

"Daniel," I said. "Daniel Johnston."

I could still recite his date of birth. Prove it with a passport.
Problem was, he wasn't eighteen either.

Ruby didn't react to my lie. She looked at the cop rather
than me.

"Can we go now?" She sounded bored.

"I need to see some ID from your wee pal first."

He made us sound like we were ten.

"He told you — he left it at home."

The cop scratched his beard. "Would you prefer I phone your parents? Ask them to bring it down for you?"

That would be great. Go ahead. I'd love for you to do your job and find my parents. Even Lewis had finally accepted Mom and Dad were never coming for us. Either something had gone wrong, or they'd never had any intention of meeting us. I didn't know which was worse.

"They're out of town." I shrugged and tried to look as bored as Ruby.

"Then you have a problem." He unclipped the handcuffs from his belt.

He had to be bluffing. No way he'd arrest me. Would he?

"Officer Collingwood!" I blurted. "She'll vouch for me."

The cop raised his eyebrows.

"She's a friend." A woman whose stroller I carried down an escalator, but it was all I had. "She works at Scotland Yard."

When Padma said to call her if I needed anything, she probably didn't mean bail.

The cop opened the back door of the squad car. "In you get."

"I'd rather wait out here." And run as soon as you turn your back. Edinburgh wasn't safe now Goatee Guy had found us, but where would we go next?

"In the car," he said.

I told Ruby to leave me, but she said she didn't abandon people and, besides, what would she tell Maggs if I got arrested? She climbed into the back seat. The officer looked at me as if to say, *Your turn, sonny.* I took a breath, then climbed in.

I ignored Ruby's questioning look and texted Lewis a warning about the police check.

"You do know Scotland Yard's not actually *in* Scotland?" Ruby said.

Why the heck was it called Scotland Yard, then? "Where is it?"

"London. They have no jurisdiction here. And why would a police officer lie for you anyway?" Ruby glanced at the cop, now in the front seat calling it in.

"I panicked, okay?" I said. "I didn't expect him to actually call Scotland Yard. I thought he'd … I don't know …"

"Let you off because you happen to know a police officer?"

"I guess."

The police radio crackled. The cop's side of the conversation was clear, but the replies were muffled. I heard him say "Collingwood," then "Daniel Johnston," then "Smugglers' Labyrinth," and then confirm that, yes, he needed to speak to Collingwood. Said he'd wait. Yes, he'd hold me.

Maybe Padma would take pity on me and convince the cop to let me off with a warning. If she got the message.

The cop looked over his shoulder at me. "Looks like you're in luck. Detective Collingwood happens to be in the city. Must be a fan of the festival."

You have got to be kidding. The whole point of mentioning Padma was to avoid being questioned by police, and now she was about to turn up! A detective. Who loved asking questions. If Scotland Yard was in London, what was she doing here?

The cop got out of the car, then popped his head back inside. "Could be a long wait. Sounded like I woke her up."

I waited until the cop pounced on another teenager, then tried the door. Locked. The windows wouldn't open either.

I slumped against the back seat. The car stank of stale sweat. Or was that me?

Ruby kept glancing at me. Had she realized I wasn't Lewis yet? That she'd lost the nice one and been left with the — what was it she'd called me?

"When did you change your shirt?" Ruby was frowning. "Where did the moose-crossing one go?" Yup, she really thought I was Lewis.

I shrugged. "It's inside out. Thought it might hide the stain."

"It didn't work." She was looking right at me, yet couldn't tell I wasn't the same Will she'd spent the evening with.

I really was only half a person. And according to Ruby, the worse half. Maybe in the next place, Lewis should be the one to go out into the world.

"Useful, thanks. I hadn't noticed." I spun away and stared out the window.

"I should've left you when I had the chance," she said.

"Most people do," I mumbled back.

Ruby shuffled as far away from me as she could, and we sat in strained silence. I watched the door of the club. Lewis stayed safely inside, and there was no sign of Goatee Guy.

A sharp rap on my window made me jump.

Padma.

She looked more exhausted than she had at the airport after an international flight and a crying baby.

She flashed her badge at the cop, then yanked open my door. "Out. Now." She glared at me, then glanced at Ruby. "You too, Miss Blue Hair."

Padma marched down an alleyway. "Get a move on."

"She's a badass," Ruby said. "Brilliant."

I'd expected Padma to arrive with her baby strapped to her chest. Without the squirming bundle, she was fierce.

"Go along with whatever I say," I said, so only Ruby could hear. "I'll explain later."

I had no idea how I'd explain this night away. But I was back to thinking only of the next step — the problem directly in front of me.

Padma stopped at a white SUV, clicked open the locks. "Get in."

Ruby scrambled into the back seat. Two little-kid car seats blocked me from following. I lifted a sippy cup off the front passenger seat and cradled it while I buckled up.

"Four hours sleep." Padma pulled out of the alley without checking traffic. "That's it — two hours now before the baby wakes for his feed, then I have a toddler. You do remember her? Small, scared of escalators? So much for being on holiday."

"I'm sorry," I mumbled.

"Tea." She gripped the wheel. "I said call me if you needed a cup of tea. Not a big partier, you said."

"Where are your children?" I asked, trying to change the subject.

"I left milk in the mini-fridge and a note." She honked her horn at some poor taxi who hadn't noticed the lights turn green.

"Really?"

"Of course bloody not."

Ruby's head appeared between the seats. "What kind of stuff do you usually work on?" she asked. "Murders? Drug rings?"

Padma glanced at Ruby in the mirror. "I'm assuming you're underage as well?"

Ruby slinked back.

"That's what I thought."

Padma was quiet for two blocks. Her death grip on the steering wheel relaxed. She rolled her shoulders, then stretched her neck out on either side.

"Thanks for coming," I said. "And sorry, you know, for waking you up."

She let out a breath. "Where am I taking you?"

I reeled off the address of the guesthouse.

She glanced at Ruby in the mirror. "How about you?"

"Same place."

"Your parents there?"

"No," she said. Almost a whisper.

Padma turned on the radio. Country music! I had no idea you could get country music in Scotland. I waited for Padma to change the channel. Instead, she turned it up.

By the time we pulled up outside the guesthouse, my muscles had relaxed, and my eyes were heavy.

I thanked Padma and opened the door. We were back. No prison cells or police interrogation. No bumping into Lewis arm in arm with Aisha. No grand confessions to Ruby required. Had Lewis made it home? Not that the guesthouse would be home for much longer.

"Not so fast." Padma unfastened her seat belt, shifted round to face me.

Ruby froze, balanced on one of the baby seats.

"You can go," Padma said to Ruby. "This one will be along in a minute."

Ruby shot me a weak smile, fumbled with the door, which was on child-lock. I jumped out, opened the door for her, then steadied her as she stumbled onto the sidewalk.

She righted herself. "I'll watch from the window in case you need a witness."

"Thanks, I think."

I waited until Ruby was safely in the house. Until the lounge light came on. Until the curtain twitched.

"My bed is waiting for me," Padma called out.

I was back, but not safe. Padma was police. She would be able to detect a lie, but I couldn't tell her the truth. I wish I could because I didn't want to run again. Where would we go now that no one wanted us?

The car was silent when I eased back inside. She'd switched the radio off, no more deep crooning voices. I sat on my hands to stop them from shaking.

"I'm a detective," Padma said. "I solve crimes. Uncover lies. Correct wrongdoings."

I bit my lip to stop myself from begging her to help us. Clare had been told she couldn't leave the country. What if that happened to us? We'd be watched, but not protected. Whoever was after us would have a clear shot.

"There's nothing to solve," I said.

"I ran a search on your passport, Daniel Johnston," she said. "You're fifteen."

"So?"

"Fifteen-year-olds don't usually take off on holiday by themselves. They run in packs. Like wolves or hyenas." Padma settled back in her seat.

A black taxi pulled up. My heart kicked into overdrive. If Lewis stepped out of it, it was game over.

The door opened.

Mrs. Fisby hopped out, followed by Mr. Fisby struggling with their wagon of props. I tried to get my heart rate back under control while I watched them carry their wagon up the front steps and go inside. Who would turn up next? Lewis with Goatee Guy on his tail? Was Goatee Guy Schenk's man? Or did more than one person want Mom and Dad dead?

I wish I *was* a wolf or a hyena. Then I wouldn't have to hide. I'd chase rather than be chased.

Goosebumps broke out on my skin as an idea formed.

It might work.

Padma had got hold of my passport information. Could she dig out information on Schenk, too?

"I need your help." *Here goes nothing.*

"Lucky for you that's what I get paid for." Padma tilted her head, waiting for me to continue.

Stick as close to the truth as possible. Short answers. Look her in the eyes.

"I came here to look for my father," I said.

Truth.

"Okay, that's a start," she said. "Who's your father?"

"I don't know his name, his real name, that is."

Close to the truth.

"What do you know?"

"My mother met him here."

She watched my face, probably for signs of stress — a twitch, a glance to the right, a bead of sweat running down my forehead.

"They got caught up in the London riot."

It was the truth. Would she go for it?

She nodded. "Go on."

I cleared my throat. "My mother was pregnant with me. Just."

Not for another year, and with Lewis as well, but Daniel Johnston was almost sixteen, so maybe the math worked. Crap. Did it?

I kept going. "They got separated during the riots, and she never saw him again. His name wasn't on any of the victim lists. I thought if I came to Britain, I could find him, and Maggs, the lady who runs the guesthouse, is a family friend. She let me stay for free."

I was rambling. Throwing in truths with half-truths and downright lies, hoping Padma couldn't separate which was which. The desperation in my voice was real.

"What name did your father give your mother?"

"Schenk."

A blatant lie, which should stab at my heart and make me feel like crap. But it didn't because I was sick of being chased like a terrified rabbit. From now on, I was going to be a wolf.

"Do you think he'll be in any of the police databases?" I added.

"You're asking me to abuse my authority to access police records?"

That's exactly what I was asking her to do.

"You're my only hope." My biggest truth yet.

She looked out the window, tapped the steering wheel. "You're a pain in the arse, you know that? Next time I'll carry the bloody pram myself."

She was going to do it.

She pulled out her phone from the center console. "What's your phone number?"

I gave her the number of the new phone.

She typed it in. "I'll text, so you have my number. If you call me for anything other than an offer to babysit, I'll arrest you for police harassment."

"Babysitting only. Got it."

"I'll call as soon as I find anything."

"Thank you." I opened the door, then had a thought. If Padma was searching through the records anyway ... "Could you look for a guy called Thys Visser as well?"

"Would you like me to bake you a cake while I'm at it?" She leaned over and pushed my door fully open. "Scram."

I jumped out. Ruby was still standing at the window, watching out for me.

"Stay out of trouble," Padma said. "And instead of feeling sorry for yourself, why don't you help your friend with whatever she's dealing with at home."

I looked back at Padma.

Padma started the engine. "I uncover lies and correct wrong-doings. Best remember that."

CHAPTER
21

LEWIS

Cameron ripped off my quilt in the middle of the night. My head spun as I sat bolt upright. Were Mom and Dad here? Had Goatee Guy followed us home from the club? Snatches of last night flashed through my brain — the shock on Aisha's face when I'd told her about the police check, climbing out the ladies' bathroom window. Following Aisha down hidden steps, jumping on a crowded tram, hiding in the attic waiting for Cameron to come home.

Bright sunshine blinded me.

I rubbed my face. "What time is it?"

"I'll give you a clue." Cameron threw open the window. "I've served breakfast, washed the dishes and been to the supermarket because Visser ate all the bread. And the mailman's been."

I squinted. Stumbled to the bathroom. You'd think the relief that no one had arrived to shoot us would cancel out the disappointment of Mom and Dad not being here. It didn't. Even though I'd finally accepted they weren't coming, it still hadn't sunk in.

"Do you want to know how I know the mailman's been?" Cameron said through the bathroom door.

"It's a mail *woman*."

"I'm not going to ask how you know that because it's not relevant."

I knew because whenever I heard anyone outside, I leaped to the window, my heart pounding, hoping I'd see Mom and Dad. From now on, I'd be leaping to the window to check it wasn't Goatee Guy. Mom and Dad weren't coming. If I repeated it enough times, maybe I'd get to the stage where I didn't want to cry every time someone who wasn't them arrived at the guesthouse.

When I opened the bathroom door, Cameron was still there, arms folded.

"In case you're interested," my pain-in-the-ass brother said, "the mail consisted of two bills, a letter and a supermarket discount voucher for toilet paper."

Just because I'd slept until — I checked the phone — 11:37 a.m., he was torturing me with the details of everything I'd missed.

"Cameron, come on. I'm sorry I slept late, okay? I'll do dinner."

"The letter was addressed to us," he said.

"Was it from Mom and Dad?" Excitement bubbled up through my chest. "What did they say?"

Cameron's jaw was clenched, no hint of a smile.

The bubbles in my chest dropped like rocks to my belly. "Let me see it."

"I can't." Cameron rubbed his head. "The letter's gone. I hoped you had it, but unless you sleepwalked downstairs ..."

"What do you mean it's gone? Maggs probably put it some-where. Where is she?" I dove back into our bedroom to find some clothes. "I'll go and find her."

He followed me into our room, then sunk onto his bed. "I've already talked to her. While I was at the supermarket, Nora told Maggs she'd picked up the post from the doormat and propped it on the reception desk — two bills, the voucher and a letter for Mr. Cameron Lewis, which she assumed was a previous guest. By the time Maggs went to fetch them, the letter was gone."

I yanked on my sweatpants. "It fell off the table, and the dog took it."

"Why would Haggis take it?"

"She thought it was a dog treat?"

"Haggis mistook the letter for a treat, but not the bills or the supermarket voucher?"

I grabbed my *Math? Easy as pi* shirt from the drawer, pulled it on, then looked at him. "Letters don't just disappear."

"Unless someone takes them," he said.

My stomach flipped. "You think Goatee Guy came here?"

"Or Visser took it."

"Why Visser?" I still hadn't met Visser, but nothing Maggs had said rung alarm bells.

"There's something about him," Cameron said.

"What do you mean? Like what?"

He shrugged. "It's like I've seen him before."

"Where? Canada? The airport? London?"

"I don't know." He looked up at me. "Nothing about him is familiar. It's more a feeling."

I wanted to tell him to stop being vague. We needed details. Hard facts. But he looked so worried that I kept all that to myself and sat down beside him. "If Visser took our letter, then he knows who we are. And if we take it back, then he'll know that we know that he knows."

We sat side by side in silence for a few minutes, then Cameron leaped off the bed. "We'll take a photo of it, then put it back where we found it. Then Visser becomes prey."

Cameron's grand plan, which he'd outlined last night, was to chase rather than be chased. Be wolves rather than rabbits. He was sketchy on the details. I'd told him it was a solid plan until someone shot us.

"What if he has a gun?" I said. "We can't just wander into his room. What if he catches us?"

"He's out." Cameron grabbed the phone off the desk. "When I was on my way back with the bread, he ran past me and said he was headed to the beach. I saw the beach from the castle, Lewis. He'll be gone ages. I'll go get his key and meet you outside his room."

What if Visser was hiding in the park watching the house with binoculars, waiting to see how we reacted? What if his room was booby-trapped?

I made my bed, then crept out of the room. Turned back. Pulled on socks and sneakers in case we had to leave in a hurry, then tiptoed down the attic stairs, avoiding the second-last step because it creaked the loudest.

I peeked into the corridor.

Cameron stood outside Visser's door, the key is his hand. "Come on."

"Shouldn't I keep watch?" I shouty-whispered.

He waved me over, then opened the door.

"Is he in there?" I said.

"Would I be standing here answering stupid questions if he was?"

I was about to follow him inside when I heard someone coming up the stairs from the main floor.

Cameron dove into Visser's room. Instead of following, I panicked and slammed the door. What had I done? I fumbled with the handle trying desperately to get inside and hide.

"Are you all right?" Ruby asked.

I spun to face her.

Her hair was back in its stubby braids, and she looked pale again, like she had the day she'd arrived. Had I done that to her? If she hadn't been with me last night, she wouldn't have been chased by Goatee Guy, wouldn't have been picked up by the police.

"I'm sorry about dragging you into last night," I said.

Her eyebrows pulled together. "Who was that bloke?"

I wished I could tell her.

"No idea." I shrugged.

"You were terrified," she said. "And then you were rude."

It was a good summary of the difference between Cameron's and my reactions to stress. Ruby was as perceptive as she was smart. As great as she was to be with, I should probably avoid her.

"Thanks for looking out for me yesterday." I cleared my throat. "But I need to get on with the cleaning."

"What with?" she gestured at my empty hands.

I looked down as if surprised they weren't holding the bucket of cleaning supplies or the vacuum cleaner.

"I thought Maggs didn't clean occupied rooms," Ruby said. "On account of guest privacy."

"Mr. Visser requested it. He spilled tea all over his bed." I made a whoosh with my hands. "The whole teapot. Maggs said the sheets would stain if they weren't washed immediately."

She didn't look convinced, but instead of calling me out, she said, "Did the policewoman get back in touch?"

"No, why would she?"

Cameron had said Ruby was in the house when he'd had his conversation with Padma, but did she suspect something?

Ruby shrugged. "She seemed like someone who might care."

I'd never met Padma, but I nodded.

"You best get a move on," Ruby said. "Before the sheets stain."

"Right, yes."

She waited for me to make a move.

I opened Visser's door and slipped inside. Cameron was standing behind it.

He let out a breath as I closed the door, then strode to the chest of drawers and rifled through shirts in various shades of blue.

I listened at the door until I heard Ruby's door click shut, then turned and faced the room.

The bedsheets were pulled up, but wrinkled. "Did you check the bed yet?"

"Yes."

"Did it look this messy before you checked it?"

"I remade it," he said.

I smoothed out the sheets.

Cameron closed the drawer, then opened the one underneath.

I crouched and peered under the bed — dust bunnies. I pulled back the rug — a drugstore receipt dated two months ago.

Cameron unzipped Visser's duffel bag.

I headed for the bathroom. The shower was gleaming white, a bottle of shampoo and another of shower gel, same brand, stood together, labels out. Towels folded. Whatever else Visser was, he was tidy. I shook the bottles to check all they held was liquid, then ran my hands between the folds of the towels. Lifted the lid of the toilet tank and peered inside. Nothing.

Toiletries and grooming products were lined up behind the mirror above the sink. Every bottle contained what it was meant to. This was a waste of time. He must've taken the letter with him.

I slammed the mirror shut.

"Try and make more noise, would you?" Cameron said from the doorway.

Instead of turning to face him, I stared at the bottom edge of the mirrored cabinet, where the corner of what could be an envelope was now poking out.

I gripped it between my fingers and pulled, but it was lodged tight.

Cameron reached around me. "Pull on it again."

I tugged on the envelope while Cameron jiggled the cabinet. The contents rattled.

Just as I was getting worried that Cameron was going to wrench the cabinet off the wall completely, the envelope slid free.

I held it in my hands.

Mr. Cameron Lewis, 20 Glencairn Cres, Haymarket, Edin-burgh, in Mom's curly handwriting. My heart sped up.

"Open it," Cameron said.

I turned over the envelope. The seal was broken.

Cameron snatched it and pulled out a sheet of paper. "It's a bunch of numbers."

I took the paper from Cameron. The page was lined, torn holes down the side as if it had been ripped out of a notebook. It had been folded in four to fit in the envelope, the creases in a neat cross. Rows of handwritten numbers marched across it — *3-1-4-1-1-5-9-4* and on and on, covering the entire page. Purple ink.

"It means something," I said. "We just have to figure out what."

"We don't even know it's from Mom."

"It's her handwriting." I held up the page for him to see. "And look at the zero. It has a dot in the middle of it, just like Mom's. And purple's her favorite color."

"'Because what use is purple other than to make people smile?'" Cameron quoted Mom.

"Mom wrote this," I said. "What if Mom and Dad need our help? What if that's why they never showed?"

"You're the numbers guy," he said. "It can't be that difficult."

"You want to give it a try?" I held out the sheet of paper.

He huffed. "The only numbers I would recognize are GPS coordinates. Clearly, Mom wrote it for you."

I searched the numbers. "*3-1-4*. Why is that familiar?"

Cameron clutched my shoulders. "Come on, Lewis. You can do this. Did Mom ever mention a number? Think, Lewis. Did she say anything to you the day of the barbecue?"

Last week's barbecue had started off like every other neighborhood get-together. Cameron and Dad looked after the barbecue, and our neighbors kept the drinks flowing while Mom and I prepped food in the kitchen. Whenever it was just Mom and me, our conversations were always random, pinging all over the place like a pinball machine. We'd talked about the camping trip, and whether I was excited about going into senior high in the fall. I remembered she'd made a cheesy math joke because I was wearing my *Math? Easy as pi* shirt.

The same one I was wearing now.

"Pi!" I hugged Cameron.

Cameron hugged me back. "What about pies?"

"The mathematical kind, not the apple kind." Laughter bubbled up. "Pi. 3.14, and on to infinity. The last unit we did in math? The number that relates a circle's circumference to its diameter? Look at my shirt, Cameron. I was wearing this the day of the barbecue."

He snatched the paper back off me and scanned the numbers again. "You sure?"

"One hundred percent."

He gestured for me to dazzle him with my next brain wave. "*Annnd?*"

"I have no idea." But it was a message from Mom. At last.

Now we just had to figure out what she was trying to tell us.

CHAPTER
22

C A M E R O N

While Lewis scribbled the numbers from the photo, I went downstairs to tell Maggs about Mom's letter and Visser stealing it.

By the time I got back, Lewis was grinning. "It isn't pi."

"And that's good, how?"

"Mom sprinkled in fourteen extra numbers." He waved a scrap of paper.

I snatched it from him and read the numbers. "Am I meant to be seeing something? Because I'm not." I reread them; still nothing.

Lewis turned back to the desk. "I'm working on it."

I wandered to the window and watched the clouds roll in. "Maggs gave us the day off to solve Mom's code," I said.

She'd called it a riddle as if it was a game rather than our whole future.

"Mm-hmm." Lewis remained hunched over his papers.

"She's going to ask Visser to leave," I said.

Lewis kept scribbling.

"She wants him out by dinnertime because she doesn't want bloodstains on her carpets or bullet holes in her walls."

Lewis's head snapped up. "What?"

That got his attention.

I shrugged. "I think she was joking."

"Do you want me to solve this or not?"

I waved him back to his work and watched the rain pitter-patter on the window.

By the time Visser jogged up the front steps, the rain was hammering down and the street was one giant puddle.

An hour later, when the rain had eased off, Visser headed back out. He wasn't carrying anything, which meant he wasn't leaving for good.

"I'm going after Visser," I said as I darted for the stairs.

Lewis leapt from his chair and grabbed my arm. "Why would you do that?"

"We're the wolves, Lewis."

I expected him to argue, but he nodded, then released his grip on my arm. I tore down the stairs and out the front door.

At the end of our street, Visser turned left. I sprinted as far as the corner, then crouched behind a dumpster. I pulled up the hood of the *University of Edinburgh* hoodie I'd found in Maggs's junk room. It smelled of oil paint and dust.

Visser glanced up at the houses, checked his phone, crossed the road when a man stepped out of a car, then turned left when he hit the main street.

I raced to the corner, then pretended to look in the window of a store that wasn't a store at all, but a café. A little kid slammed his palms on the window. Then squished his nose against the glass. I moved on.

No sign of Visser's black jacket. Buses rumbled past, their

tires sploshing through puddles. The stoplights turned red. The traffic paused.

Visser was on the other side of the street, hunched over the ticket machine at the tram stop.

I hid in a doorway until the next tram hummed into the station. Until its bell dinged. Until the doors slid open. Until passengers stepped off. Until Visser boarded. Then I sprinted across the street through oil-slick puddles and slipped through the doors of the tram.

I found a seat next to the window, kept my hood up. The lights were on in the tram, and Visser was reflected in the window, standing even though there were seats, hands at his sides rather than holding on to the overhead rail. I dug my hands in my pockets and found the scrap of paper with Mom's fourteen numbers. It was folded, so only the first three numbers were visible — *1-4-6*. Something clicked in my brain. That string of numbers was familiar.

L E W I S

After Cameron left to "hunt" Visser, I headed to the kitchen with a pile of paper and a handful of markers in various colors that Cameron had found in the junk room. Cameron had said Maggs was kidding about the blood and the bullets, but I didn't want to be in the attic by myself. The water pipes sounded like gunfire, and every creak was Goatee Guy creeping up the stairs.

Maggs was sitting on her couch knitting what looked like a sweater for a wide child with short arms.

"There's tea in the pot," she said.

I dumped the paper and pens on the table. "Did you talk to Visser?"

"I told him I'd made a mistake and double-booked the room and he'd need to find somewhere else to stay."

"How did he take it?"

"Stoically."

"Did he seem … dangerous?" I'd watched Cameron follow him down the street. I hadn't seen his face, but he looked as tall and bulky as Dad.

"He was charming," Maggs said.

"Charming like an art thief or charming like a contract killer?"

"*Tch*, child." She put her knitting down and walked to the island. "The man's been here two days and all he's done is steal a letter. It's the one who followed you from London I'm more concerned with. So, stop wittering and get on with cracking your mum's riddle."

She poured two mugs of tea and handed me one. "Thys Visser will be packed and gone by teatime." She patted my cheek, then went back to her knitting.

I curled my hands around the warm mug and watched the rain dribble down the window. I'd written Mom's rogue numbers in reverse, removed the prime numbers, added them, divided them, reordered them lowest to highest, highest to lowest, odd then even. But no matter how I manipulated them, they remained a list of random numbers.

I took a sip of tea, then, on a blank sheet of paper, copied Mom's code exactly as it was on the photo. I circled the fourteen extra numbers and drew lines between the circles as if I were playing connect-the-dots — lowest number to highest. No map or symbol or picture leaped from the page. I stared at the circled numbers — *1-4-6-4-5-1-1-2-2-5-1-2-8-3*.

What are you trying to tell us, Mom?

———

C A M E R O N

Visser got off at the second stop, Princes Street, then darted through a gap in the traffic.

I crossed at the pedestrian crossing with the crowds. Even with the rain, downtown was packed, and by the time I'd reached the sidewalk, Visser had disappeared in a sea of umbrellas and colorful raincoats. I zigzagged through people until I reached the end of the block, then, with my back against the window of a souvenir store, checked the side street.

Visser was lining up at a hot-dog stand. He bought a bottle of water, downed it, chucked the empty bottle in the recycle bin, then carried on up the street.

I followed.

At the next intersection, he turned left. I raced to the corner and hid behind a mailbox. Visser slowed, checked his phone, looked around at the stores and restaurants lining the street, then set off at a jog.

I sprinted to the next shelter — posters for festival shows zip-tied to scaffolding.

Visser ducked into a doorway.

I counted to ten, tugged my hood to cover more of my face, then strolled past the café Visser had entered. I doubled back and pretended to read the menu taped to the window. Visser dipped into a booth. The server brought a tray with two glasses of water. Who was he meeting?

I ducked into the next doorway, a high-end clothes store with the door propped open. As I read Mom's numbers again, the spark of recognition glowed, but snuffed out just as quickly.

A sales assistant in a tailored suit cleared his throat. I lowered my hood, said hullo, said I was waiting for my father to arrive, no I didn't want to browse while I waited, thank you all the same. Then I crouched down to wait for Visser and his coffee date to finish up.

1-4-6 — the first three numbers were so familiar. But why?

The streets were quiet back here. The pedestrians looked like locals rather than tourists, walking with purpose rather than wandering. A bus stopped on the other side of the street with a hiss of brakes. A billboard for a stage show was plastered along its side, the performance dates in neon pink.

1-4-6 was a date!

Fourteenth of June, our birthday.

L E W I S

I fumbled for the burner phone as it buzzed in my pocket, my fingers shaking. The only person who phoned rather than texted was Mom.

"It's our birthday."

Scratch that. The only people who phoned rather than texted were Mom, or my brother when he wanted an instant response.

"The first three numbers are our birthday — *1-4-6*," he said.

"Fourteenth of June."

Could it be that simple? I drew a circle around *1-4-6* and tried to figure out what happened to the code if those disappeared. The next three numbers were *4-5-1.*

"Some excitement would be nice," Cameron said.

"The next three numbers don't make sense as a date."

"What if it's two numbers — fourth of May." He sounded giddy, like a five-year-old making up fart jokes. "That's the day we won the soccer championship."

I ringed *4* and *5.* But it could also be four digits — *4-5-1-1.*

"Lewis, speak to me."

"If we start messing around with the length of the numbers, there are too many combinations."

He sighed. I imagined him pulling his hand through his hair. Had Mom written the code herself, or had Dad helped? I imagined them sitting up late one night, figuring it out together.

"There has to be another clue," I said. "Or maybe it's more math. Maybe I need to factor them or create an equation."

"You're making it too complicated," Cameron said.

I looked at the paper with the entire code of sixty numbers, the rogue fourteen numbers circled. "I'm putting the phone down, don't hang up."

"Lewis," he hissed through the phone.

I found a black pen, drew lines between each column and between each row, making a grid.

The three numbers of our birthday, *1-4-6,* were all in the first row.

The second row had two numbers circled: *4* and *5.* Cameron was right — the date we won this year's soccer championship.

My pulse raced as I checked the other four rows, then I leaped off my chair as one more obvious date jumped out.

I snatched up the phone. "You're right, it looks like they're dates. Six dates, Cameron. Mom sent us six dates."

"I knew it!"

"Where are you?" I glanced at Maggs, who'd forgotten about her knitting and was watching me.

"I'm outside a café waiting for Visser," Cameron said. "He's with someone. I need to wait until they leave so I can see who it is."

A weight settled in my stomach. "What do you mean he's with someone? What if it's Goatee Guy? What if it's a trap, and they're about to kidnap you?"

Maggs came to stand beside me. "Tell him to come home."

"Is that Maggs?" he said. "Tell her I need to stay and see who Visser's meeting."

Did he really think he could fight off two men? Visser was huge, and Goatee Guy looked like a fighter. As much as my brother wanted to be the wolf, in this situation he was still the rabbit.

"We have to crack Mom's code before Visser does," I said. "Come home. I've got an idea."

CHAPTER
23

LEWIS

In addition to our bedroom and the bathroom with its hammering pipes and rust-stained tub, the attic had three other rooms. Opposite our room was a second bedroom, and next to that was the junk room, or as Maggs called it, the "bits-and-bobs room." The room next to ours was Maggs's craft room, as tidy as the junk room was messy. An easel next to the window, a table against one wall with a sewing machine on top and a bookshelf loaded with jam jars filled with beads and sequins and buttons and ribbon.

Using paper and sticky tape I'd dug out of the junk room, I set to covering the walls of the craft room to make a giant, room-sized whiteboard. Mom's code was like a math problem where you had to solve for X before you could work out Y. We'd found the dates, and now we had to figure out what message Mom had hidden in them.

Down in the street, a car sloshed through puddles. A woman shouted for her dog to come back. Rain pitter-pattered against the window.

I finished puzzle-piecing paper on one wall, shifted the table into the center of the room and started on the next.

Feet pounded on the sidewalk. I peered out the window. Cameron was back.

I snatched up a black marker and, on the wall I'd already covered, wrote *14/6 — our birthday.* The marker squeaked across the paper.

Cameron thumped upstairs.

I sidestepped to the right and wrote *4/5 — soccer championship.*

"What the heck are you doing?" Cameron stood in the doorway wearing a gray university hoodie, his face damp with sweat or rain, probably both.

I pointed to the stack of paper. "Can you finish off that wall?"

"This is your great idea? Writing on a wall?" He strode to the window, opened it and hung his head outside.

I considered the next few numbers. "*1-1-2.* Eleventh of February or first of December?"

"Pass. What are the other dates?" he said.

"25/12 — Christmas Day." It was those four numbers that had convinced me about the dates because Dad loved Christmas. He started getting excited at the beginning of December and would leave candy in our shoes and hide messages in our schoolbags.

Cameron frowned, pulled the paper from his pocket. "That only leaves two more numbers — 8 and 3. How does that work?"

"August and March? Summer vacation and spring break?" It didn't fit with the rest, but it was the only way the other dates made sense.

"Whole months rather than specific days?" He rubbed his thumb over the numbers. "Are we sure about this?"

Out on the street, someone was singing to music we couldn't hear. I squished beside Cameron and peered out the window. It was Aisha coming back from work in her tartan castle uniform. She climbed her front steps. Her door banged shut behind her.

"We've got our birthday and the soccer championship and Christmas," I said. "Let's focus on those first."

"And what if June 14 isn't our birthday? According to my passport, it's in September."

"That's Daniel Johnston's passport, and you're not Daniel Johnston."

"I'm not Cameron Larsen either."

He was like one of those annoying radio commercials that repeated over and over and over. "Come on, Cameron, you know when our birthday is."

"Do I?" He rubbed his head. "How are we meant to know what's fake and what's real anymore?"

Outside, a car door slammed shut. A dark-haired woman beeped the lock, then crossed the street. There was something familiar about her hair and the determined way she walked.

She glanced up at the guesthouse.

My whole body exploded. "Mom!"

I raced out of the room, down the stairs, Cameron crashing behind me. It didn't matter if anyone saw us together. Mom was here. She'd come for us!

I threw open the front door and launched myself at her.

Only it wasn't Mom.

But my momentum and urge to hug were unstoppable.

Clare gasped in surprise as I wrapped my arms around her, then she tentatively patted my back.

I untangled myself. Wiped my eyes with the back of my hand. Sucked snot back up my nose.

"Why are you here?" Cameron said from behind me.

"I've been asking myself the same question. As did my customers when I called to cancel tomorrow's appointments. And the ferryman who swore he couldn't remember the last time I made the crossing." She pulled an envelope from her back pocket. "This arrived in this morning's post. I wanted to throw it in the rubbish, but I kept thinking of the two of you, and I couldn't."

Cameron shoved past me, snatched the envelope and scooped out the contents.

A sticky note and a flash drive.

He read the note, then handed it to me. The sight of Mom's handwriting, written in the same purple ink as her code, sent a jolt of excitement through me — *Please take this to Maggs.*

I flipped it over, but the other side was blank. That was it?

I handed the note back to Clare. "What's on the drive?"

"I'm assuming it holds an ocean of apologies and explanations," Clare said. "But it needs a password."

Cameron laughed and fist-pumped the air.

I grinned. "It's upstairs."

Clare frowned. Not the reaction I'd expected. But she wasn't looking at us, she was looking at something or someone behind us.

Standing halfway down the staircase, his duffel bag slung over his shoulder, his black jacket in his hand, was Visser. He really was tall, and Cameron was right, there was something familiar about him.

He looked at Cameron, then at me, then back at Cameron.

And then his mouth curved into a half-grin, and suddenly I knew where I'd seen him before. He wasn't wearing sunglasses, or the floppy fishing hat, but he had that same smug look on his face as he'd had when he'd walked in on us in Clare's workshop. Visser was Clare's best customer. The one who'd had his car serviced twice a year for the last sixteen years, even though he didn't live on the island.

Cameron snatched the lamp off the reception desk and held it like a sword. "Run, both of you. I'll keep him busy."

"Thys?" Clare came forward to stand beside us. "What are you doing here?"

Cameron glanced at Clare. "You know him?"

"He's the guy from Clare's shop," I said.

"The guy who came for his car?" Cameron looked back at Visser. "Did you follow us?"

Visser held up his hands and continued to the bottom of the stairs. "I'm not here to hurt anyone."

Cameron let out a roar and ran at him, his shoulder ramming Visser's chest. Visser dropped his bag and, in one fluid movement, twisted, flipping Cameron onto his back. I watched helplessly as my brother hit the floor with a thump, the air whoomphing from his lungs, the lamp skittering out of his hand.

My brain screamed at me to run, but I couldn't leave Cameron. I grabbed the lamp and held it above my head, ready to strike if Visser attacked again.

The dining room door swung open.

"What on earth?" Maggs looked at Cameron on the floor, then at me clutching her lamp above my head, then Visser, then Clare.

"Hello, Maggs," Clare said.

Maggs composed herself, closed the door behind her. "Clare, why don't you and the boys go into the lounge, while I settle Mr. Visser's bill. I'll make sure no one disturbs you."

"I think I'll stay," Visser said. "Things just got interesting."

"We've a full house." Maggs marched behind the desk. "Will you be paying with cash or card?"

I helped Cameron get up off the floor. He rubbed his shoulder, glared at Visser.

Visser bent to pick up his bag and at the same time reached into its side pocket.

Cameron grabbed the lamp off me and whacked Visser's head like he was hitting a home run.

Visser went down.

"Sodding hell!" Clare rushed to Visser's side. "Why did you do that?"

"He's got a gun," Cameron said.

Clare reached into the bag and pulled out a wallet.

Not a gun.

"Thys?" She leaned low over his face. "He's breathing."

Visser groaned.

Cameron and I took a step back. Clare slid her hands under Visser's shoulders and helped him sit up.

He rubbed his head. "*Godverdomme*," he mumbled.

No idea what it meant, but he sounded like Schenk.

I looked at Cameron. "Should we hit him again?"

He shrugged. "Probably."

Clare glared at us. "Behave, the both of you."

She looked and sounded just like Mom.

"I'm okay." Visser straightened himself. "I just need a minute."

"You can have your minute in the lounge." Maggs herded us all through the door. "I'll keep the guests away. Stay put until I give you the all clear. There's a poker next to the fire, boys, if you need to clobber him again."

CHAPTER
24

L E W I S

As soon as Maggs closed the door on us, Clare said, "Sit. All of you. Now."

Visser sunk into one of the armchairs, reached behind his back, yanked free a patchwork cushion and placed it behind his head. Cameron sat in the matching chair, never taking his eyes off Visser. I perched on the arm of Cameron's chair.

Clare stood with her back to the fireplace, glaring at Visser.

The clock on the mantelpiece measured out the silence.

Tick. Tick. Tick.

"You're obviously not a financial advisor from Leeds," Clare said. "Or a recreational fisherman."

The red welt on Visser's temple was swelling. Cameron hadn't apologized for whacking him. I wouldn't either. He'd been spying on Clare for sixteen years. He'd followed us here. And gun or no gun, he'd sounded scarily like Schenk.

Visser shifted in his chair.

Cameron and I both jumped up. Clare went for the iron poker.

"Easy." Visser held up his hands in surrender.

Clare kept hold of the poker. "How did you know the boys

were here?"

"I overheard the conversation in your workshop, then followed them."

"You eavesdropped?" Clare said.

Of all the things Visser might've done, listening in on our conversation wasn't the one I'd be questioning.

"Who the hell are you?" Cameron said.

Visser rubbed a hand over his face. "If I tell you, you'll be in more danger than you're already in."

I didn't like the sound of that. We'd already been threatened at gunpoint, watched two people die, been chased through London and Edinburgh — how much more dangerous could it get?

"I'm trying to keep you all safe." He touched his injured head and winced. "But you're not making it easy."

"Who are you keeping us safe from?" I said.

Visser took a breath. "You have no idea what you're getting yourselves into."

"We're already in it," Clare said. "Up to our necks. And the only person I see trying to cause us harm is you."

I liked how she said "us" as if we were a unit.

"I worked for the same organization as your father," Visser said to Cameron and me. "I'm his best friend. We grew up together in Amsterdam."

So Visser was from Holland, too. And what about Schenk? Had we been looking at this all wrong, trying to uncover Mom's past when it was all about Dad?

Cameron sank against the back of the armchair. "So, our dad really is Dutch?"

Visser nodded.

"What organization did he work for?" My thoughts kept time with the clock —

Tick, spy,

Tick, undercover cop,

Tick — my stomach churned as the word *terrorist* whispered through my brain. No, Dad wasn't a terrorist. No way.

Visser finally stopped looking at Clare and turned to me. "We worked for Siebo Ryker."

"Are we meant to know who that is?" Cameron said.

"He's better known as Het Voet."

"Bloody hell." Clare sighed and shook her head. "The Dutch mafia boss. Called 'The Foot' because allegedly he shot himself in the foot to prove he feels no pain."

The information hit me like a tornado. I tried to unravel it, so I could make it into something other than the obvious. Dad couldn't be a mobster.

"I was there," Visser said. "Ryker shattered every bone and lost three toes. Believe me, he felt it. But he'd do it again. He likes theatrics."

"Our dad worked for the mafia?" Cameron leaned forward.

I stared at Cameron. "You believe him? He's obviously lying. No way Dad worked for someone who makes his money from selling drugs and killing people."

"And money laundering," Visser said.

I felt numb. If Cameron nudged me now, I'd topple off the chair arm like a bowling pin. I curled my toes into the rug, trying to find an anchor.

I looked at Cameron for support, but he kept his eyes on Visser. Why wasn't he calling out Visser?

"Dad would never kill people or sell drugs." I wanted to sound strong and convincing, but my voice cracked at the end.

"He didn't," Visser said. "Your father and I were Ryker's thieves. Robbery, nothing else."

"Well, then, glad that's all cleared up." Clare gave a dismissive wave of her hand. "Stealing so drug lords and contract killers could spend their hard-earned wages. It's almost charity."

Visser looked at her. "It's not the life we wanted."

"My heart bleeds," she said.

Cameron stood and glared down at Visser. "How did our dad end up in the mafia?"

"He didn't," I said. "Why are you listening to him?"

Cameron glared at me over his shoulder, then looked back at Visser. "In the scenario, which may or may not be a true representation of reality, where our dad worked for a Dutch mob boss, how did he end up there?"

Visser glanced at Clare. "Koen and I got into some trouble when we were young."

"The criminal kind?" Clare still had the poker, but she was holding it like a walking stick now, tapping it on the stone hearth.

Visser nodded. "It started off with pick-pocketing tourists. Amsterdam's full of them; it was too easy. Then we moved on to stealing car radios."

"What did you do with the money?" she said.

Please don't say drugs. Please don't say drugs.

"We gave most of it to our mothers. Claimed it came from a newspaper delivery job."

Thank goodness.

"And we bought cigarettes and alcohol with the rest."

"Dad smoked?" I said.

"Everyone smoked something back then." Visser shrugged. "It was Amsterdam."

"How did you make the leap from petty theft to the mafia?" Clare asked.

"We broke into the wrong car. Ryker must've had cameras on it. We were dragged in front of him. If we got out at all, we expected it would be minus a few fingers, but instead, Ryker handed us each 400 guilders. It was more cash than either of us had ever seen at once. He told us to get cleaned up and come back."

"How old were you?" Cameron asked.

"Fifteen."

Our age. When Dad was our age, he was recruited to work for the mob. If I believed Visser. Which I didn't.

"Then what?" Cameron said.

Visser glanced at Clare then back at Cameron. "We became his thieves. He'd send us to Schiphol airport to steal passports. We'd get twenty or thirty a day. If there's anything easier than robbing tourists, it's robbing stressed-out tourists. Then we moved on to houses. Sometimes Ryker wanted jewelry, other times he was after documents or computers."

"Why computers?" Cameron asked.

"Blackmail."

Oh, great, blackmail — add that to the list.

"Let me guess," Clare said. "From there, you moved on to art galleries?"

"We robbed jewelers first," Visser said. "Amsterdam's a major diamond center in terms of both cutting and selling diamonds.

Once we learned how to break into the diamond vaults, we knew we could get through any security."

Clare raised her eyebrows. "The Tate gallery's security, for instance?"

What? Clare was still hung up on the art theft?

Visser nodded. "The London art theft was complicated, but textbook. We scouted out the gallery for a few weeks — learned the security shifts, located the cameras, stole access codes."

"But our mom wasn't involved." I looked from Visser to Clare. "Just because she worked there, doesn't mean she was part of it."

"She wasn't," Visser confirmed.

Thank goodness.

"Is that where my sister met Koen?" Clare said. "At the Tate?"

Visser nodded. "The second day we were there, Koen went on a coffee run to the gallery's cafeteria and came back in love."

It was the same story Dad told round the campfire and at Christmas and anytime we were all cuddled up together. He'd bought two coffees for him and his best friend, and as he was leaving the café, Mom walked in. He'd handed her one of the coffees and said, "I thought I'd never find you."

"So, Mom had nothing to do with the mafia?" Cameron said.

"Nothing." Visser looked at Clare, who let out a long breath.

I didn't want to believe Dad did either, but Visser was convincing, and both Cameron and Clare were obviously buying it.

"What happened to the paintings?" Cameron asked.

"We split them between two vans. When Koen didn't make the ferry to Rotterdam, I assumed he'd got caught up in the riot.

The paintings in my van made it back to Ryker, who sold them on. Art is untraceable. It's like banknotes without serial numbers."

"Was the Mary, Queen of Scots painting in your van or Dad's?" Not that I believed any of it, but if it did turn out to be true, I wanted to know if Dad had sold his haul of the paintings.

"Really?" Cameron threw up his hands. "You find out Dad worked for the mafia and ran off with $15 million worth of stolen art and that's your question?"

"Why did you ask about the Mary painting?" Visser sat up straight. "Do you know where it is?"

I looked at Cameron for help.

He kept his eyes on Visser. "We've never seen any of the paintings."

Visser looked at me.

I shook my head. "We haven't. It was a lucky guess."

"The Mary painting was one of eight in your father's van," Visser said. "Now they'd probably fetch closer to $40 million. But there's never been as much as a whisper about any of them. Ryker owns a warehouse in the no-man's-land of one of the world's biggest freeports. He's either sold, stored or negotiated a deal for every player out there, and none of the paintings your father took ever surfaced."

Except the Mary, Queen of Scots, if Aisha was right.

"What about the riot?" Cameron said. "Did you and Dad start that as well?"

I jumped up. "It's not enough Dad was in the mafia? You need to pin the riots on him as well?"

Cameron shifted in the chair. "I'm making sure we cover all the bases."

Visser glanced at Clare. "Katrina and Koen didn't start the riots."

"See," I said to Cameron. "I told you."

Clare finally hung the poker back on its hook, then turned to Visser. "I sense there's a 'but' coming."

What? I looked at Clare. "There is no 'but.'"

"But," Visser said.

I spun around to face him.

No, no, no. I wanted to cover my ears. Dad was *maybe* guilty of art theft, nothing else. And Mom was innocent. She'd met Dad and convinced him to run from the mafia. The end.

"The paintings were important to Ryker," Visser said. "He'd lined up buyers, and I got the impression one of them was too dangerous to disappoint. Ryker was on edge, wanted to go over every detail again and again. He decided the refugee rally wasn't enough of a distraction. Stirring up trouble was easy. The London mob owed him."

"So Dad *didn't* start the riot." It meant something. In this whole mess, it had to mean something. And Cameron was right — art theft was more forgivable than inciting a fatal riot and clubbing a policewoman to death. If I believed any of it. Which I didn't.

"Dad *knew* that the London mob was going to start one though," Cameron said. "And he stood by and let it happen."

"Yeah, we both knew," Visser said. "But it was way bigger than we expected. The London gang stirred up trouble to the north to draw police away from the museum and leave our getaway clear. But the riot to the south was started by someone else."

"Enlighten us." Clare folded her arms.

Visser glanced at Clare, then shifted in his chair. "Katrina knew about the second riot, before it happened."

"You mean she predicted the demonstration would turn violent," Clare said.

He shook his head. "She knew the riot was going to happen. It's the reason we made the decision to switch out the lorry for two vans and split up the paintings."

Heat flushed through my body. I jumped up, pulse racing. "You're lying."

Cameron dropped his head in his hands. Clare turned away and clutched the mantlepiece.

Couldn't they see he was lying? "You're a criminal, why should we believe anything you say? Why are you even here?"

"To keep you all safe," he said.

Clare turned back around and narrowed her eyes at Visser. "How very gallant."

Visser stood and looked at Clare. "When Koen disappeared, Ryker didn't only lose out on the paintings, his reputation took a hit. No one betrays a mob boss and lives. He'll keep sending more goons like Schenk until one of them succeeds in bringing your nephews back to him. Then he'll use them to get to Koen. But I can help. I can give all three of you clean identities. Any nationality. The boys could go back to Canada. And you could join them."

Part of me wanted to shout "yes." The part that made my chest ache. But the other part, the logical half, knew Mom and Dad wouldn't be there. If even half of what Visser said was true, Mom and Dad couldn't come out of hiding. *We* had to find *them*.

"What's the catch?" Cameron said.

Visser turned to face us. "You stop searching for your parents."

"No way." Was he crazy?

"This is exactly why I hid the letter." Visser sighed. "I knew Koen's kids would be stubborn."

I wanted to ask how he knew we'd found the letter when we'd put it back exactly where we'd found it. Did he fingerprint it? Have the room wired with microphones?

"What happens if we don't agree?" Cameron asked.

There was no way we were agreeing to this.

"I can't protect you. Ryker wants your father, and if you manage to find out where he's hiding before Ryker does ..."

"He'll what?" Cameron folded his arms, daring him to continue.

"He'll do whatever it takes to get you to talk. And once he has your father, you'll be of no further use."

"And?" Cameron pushed again.

I didn't need Visser to answer. I could dream up horrible things on my own, thank you very much.

Clare took a breath. "I think we've heard enough."

Visser looked straight at me. "He might let you go. Or he could have you shot, chopped into pieces and thrown in the North Sea."

Hearing it turned out to be worse. I leaned on the coffee table. Felt a bit sick.

"I said that's enough," Clare said. "I'll discuss your proposal with my nephews and let you know their final decision."

There was nothing to discuss. If Mom and Dad couldn't come to us, we'd go to them.

Cameron slipped the flash drive into my hand. "I'll meet you in the attic."

CHAPTER
25

CAMERON

When I got to the attic, Lewis was hunched over the laptop watching the cursor blink on a blank screen. He looked like I felt — defeated.

"I typed the numbers into the flash drive," he said. "They didn't work."

I leaned against the desk. "If we take Visser's deal, it doesn't matter."

It was the end of the road. We were the sons of a criminal and a terrorist.

Lewis stared at me. "We're not giving up."

After everything we'd just heard, he really wanted to keep searching for Mom and Dad?

"Visser's trying to save us from the mafia, Lewis. You heard him — the foot guy shot himself to prove how tough he was, and he dices people into fish food. You can't reason with someone like that." I pushed off the desk and strode to the window.

Brian's car pulled up outside. I bet he wasn't grappling with whether to risk his life searching for people who didn't want to be found.

Lewis came to stand beside me. "Even if I believed Visser, which I'm not saying I do, Dad was only fifteen when he joined the mafia. He stole for them, that's all. And he left eventually. Even though he knew The Foot would kill him, he chose to walk away."

Really? Lewis was trying to make Dad out to be honorable? "He worked for the mob for almost a decade, Lewis. You really think he never hurt anyone? That he and Visser never once had a run in with a security guard?

"And what about the riots?" I said. "They *knew*, Lewis. Both Mom and Dad knew. And where are the paintings they stole? Because we know they're not back with their legal owners."

"So you're saying that Dad, who drives a twenty-year-old truck and cuts trees for a living, has $40 million squirreled away," Lewis said. "It doesn't make sense, and you know it."

I turned away from the window. "Why did Dad steal them, then? Why not run *before* the art theft and the riots?"

Lewis's hand shot into the air like he did when we were in school and he had the answer to a particularly complicated math problem. Here we go, what fantastic scenario had my brother dreamed up?

"Mom and Dad stole the paintings to stop Ryker getting hold of them." He started to pace. "They were going to return the paintings to their rightful owners, but the riot happened."

"The riot that Mom knew about," I said.

He waved away that annoying detail. "They made it as far as Edinburgh, left the Mary painting to Mrs. Wallace, by which time they'd been blamed for the riots, so they had to hide the rest and run."

Of course Lewis would dream up a heroic act to explain why our parents would steal $40 million worth of art.

"One flaw." Actually, there were a whole heap of holes in his theory, but I'd start with the most obvious. "Why didn't Mrs. Wallace hand the painting back to the castle?"

He shrugged. "That's on her. Not Mom and Dad."

"So, in this scenario of yours, Mom and Dad are the heroes, while Jamie Wallace's mom is a criminal?"

He nodded. "Looks that way."

I threw up my hands. "Why can't you accept Mom and Dad aren't who we thought they were?"

"It's better than being you," he said. "You want to go back to Longview and forget we even have parents. You'll probably take down their wedding photo. And Mom's paintings — you should sell those, make some money. Or you could leave them out for the garbage."

"Their wedding photo's probably fake," I said.

His shoulders slumped. "I can't believe you don't love them anymore."

My frustration evaporated, and I didn't know what to replace it with. Guilt for wanting us to be safe? Or anger that Lewis could think I didn't love Mom and Dad? Of course I loved them. My heart hurt with loving them. But I couldn't forgive them. I didn't even know who they were.

"Mom and Dad could be injured," Lewis said. "They could be locked in a cell. They could be dead. Did you think of that?"

They weren't dead. They couldn't be. But the idea that Mom and Dad were hurt or worse, that all this time they'd needed *us* rather than the other way around made me want to throw up.

"Okay." I pulled my hand through my hair. "We break the code and open the flash drive. And then, depending on what we find, we'll make a decision."

Lewis dove for the sewing table and grabbed a pen. "*1-1-2* — eleventh of February or first of December?"

I slumped on the floor under the window, my back against the wall. "I don't know. Both are in the winter. There would've been snow. Backcountry skiing or a snowboard trip?"

He laughed. "The blizzard."

"That narrows it down."

"Last winter," he said. "On the way back from the mountains, the pass got closed, and we had to stay in that bed and breakfast with the all the animal heads on the walls."

All of us had slept in one room, and Dad told ghost stories late into the night.

"February long weekend," I said. "Crowsnest Pass."

He wrote *stranded in Crowsnest Pass*, then wrote *moose heads, snowstorm, ghost stories*.

Lewis moved to the next number — Christmas Day. Wrote *Santa, stockings, turkey, snowboarding, presents*.

The last two dates were only one number each — August and March. If they were dates. Or this could be a complete waste of time. We only needed one password.

Lewis stretched out on the floor and closed his eyes.

"What are you doing?"

"I'm remembering." He opened one eye. "Do the same, then we'll compare notes."

Lewis was crazy, but what the heck. I lay down beside him, closed my eyes and let my mind wander. Molly wandered with me. In and out of birthdays and school trips, riding our bikes to the store with money jangling in our pockets, fireworks in the Baxters' field and trick-or-treating through the village. The year Molly taught me to ride her horse.

But the code was from Mom and Dad, so I dragged my thoughts away from Molly and thought of them. The summer Mom painted a target on the side of the barn and taught us to use a bow and arrow. The winter the snow never stopped falling, and Dad built us a snowboard jump from the roof of the shed. Camping in the mountains, cliff jumping into lakes, dirt biking in dried-up riverbeds. Hiking through the backwoods. Dad teaching us how to build traps. Mom showing us how to splint broken bones.

Lewis started writing. I jumped up and joined him, and together we wrote until our hands ached and the wall of paper held our life.

Clare arrived with bowls of stew, and the three of us ate dinner sitting on the floor, looking at the walls.

"Does this mean you're going to ignore Thys's warning and keep looking?" Clare said.

"We're opening the flash drive, then we'll decide." I scraped the last sliced carrot and potato cube from the bottom of the bowl.

"Good." Clare shifted her bowl to the side. "What have you got?"

"Hundreds of words when we only need one," I said.

Clare wandered round the room, reading what we'd written. It was our life, but also Mom's. Would Clare be mad that Mom had been happy?

"Did you move around a lot?" she said.

"No." Lewis stood and joined her. "We've always lived in Longview."

"Longview must be huge," she said. "To have mountains and lakes and dried-up rivers and forests."

"It's one street wide surrounded by farmland." I stacked the bowls and put them on the sewing table.

But Longview was more than that. It was Molly and our other friends. It was potluck dinners and barbecues and helping one another bale hay. It was knowing everyone and being known. It was belonging somewhere.

"But there's a hospital?" Clare said. "You were born there?"

"We were born at home. Mom hates hospitals," Lewis said.

Clare tapped the paper where we'd written down our birthday. "I need a pen."

I chucked her a marker, and she wrote *Longview* in massive letters.

She read the mess of words under *February 11*, then circled *Crowsnest Pass*.

"That's too easy," I said, but excitement stirred in my belly.

"It's only easy for you," she said. "No one else would know these dates were tied to locations."

I grabbed a marker and wrote *Turner Valley* next to the date our team won the soccer championship and *Castle Mountain* next to Christmas because we always drove out there to snowboard. Lewis laughed. Next to August he wrote *Old Man River*, our favorite summer dirt-biking spot, then *Widow Maker* next to March because it's where we camped every spring break.

"So many great days," I said.

Lewis smiled. "And they're all real. Mom and Dad couldn't have pretended for our whole lives."

I wasn't ready to think about it. Open the files, and then, depending on what we found, I'd think about the rest.

L E W I S

We had six locations — one of them had to be the password. Or it could be a combination of the first letter of all the locations in chronological order or alphabetical order or reverse order. Cameron and Clare wrote options on the wall, while I shouted out new ones.

Once the list was finished, Clare patted my shoulder. "I'll see if Maggs needs help with my room, and I should probably check on Thys in case he's fallen into a concussed coma. Come find me when you open the files."

Cameron followed Clare to the door.

"You're going, too?" I said. "There's over forty combinations."

"And you'll methodically work through each one." He handed me his marker. "I need some fresh air. Text me when you're done."

The door clicked shut behind them. It wasn't the password I was worried about. It was what I'd see when I opened the drive. What if my theory about Mom and Dad saving the paintings from The Foot was way off base, and the files contained a confession of their guilt? I shook the thought away. Mom and Dad were innocent. I knew it in my heart.

I shoved Maggs's sewing machine to one end of the table, opened up the laptop and typed in the first combination.

Incorrect password flashed up on the screen.

I stood and drew a line through it, then typed in the next one.

I'd got through about half of them when the door opened.

"I'm going as fast as I can." I typed the next one on the list.

Incorrect password.

"What *is* all this?"

I spun around. Ruby. Standing in the middle of the room scanning the walls.

My heart jumped to my throat.

I slammed the laptop shut and stood. "It's nothing."

She gestured to the notes that covered the walls. "I'm not blind, Will."

"It's a message from my mom." *Why did I say that?*

Because Ruby had looked after me last night. Because I liked her. Because I was leaving soon anyway and I'd never see her again.

She frowned. "It doesn't look like a message."

I had the urge to tell her everything. She'd lost her mom. She'd understand why I had to find mine. And she knew about computers. She could probably code a program to find the password, or just hack the file without one. But Cameron would be furious.

"Is it a game?" Ruby said.

"Yes. That's exactly what it is. My mom likes puzzles."

She nodded. "How far have you got?"

I pointed to the list of possible passwords scribbled on the wall, half of them now scored out.

She tilted her head and bit her lip as she tried to make sense of the jumble of letters. "What does it do?"

"It's a password that unlocks the next level of the game."

"Are you sure it's all in capital letters?" she said. "Because passwords are case-sensitive."

"You're kidding." That doubled the number of combinations. And if it was a mixture of lower and uppercase letters ... my brain hurt trying to work out how many combinations that made.

She gestured to the chair. "Do you mind if I try?"

I could hear Cameron in my head telling me to stop talking. To say no.

"Go ahead." I opened the laptop.

She sat, stretched her fingers as if she was about to play the piano. "Six-letter passwords are relatively easy, especially since you know all the letters. Passwords start to get difficult to hack at eight digits. Twelve-digit passwords are considered unbreakable."

I'd only been using the first letter of the first word of each location, like *L* for *Longview*. But *Widow Maker* was two words. *Old Man River* was three. *Turner Valley. Crowsnest Pass. Castle Mountain.*

I tore off the lid of the marker and, in the original order of Mom's rogue numbers, I wrote down the first letters of every word, then stepped back. Six locations, but twelve letters.

"All capital letters?" she asked.

I nodded. "Pretty sure."

"Read them out, then."

I read while Ruby typed: "*L-T-V-C-P-C-M-O-M-R-W-M.*"

Held my breath.

"Bingo." She raised her arms in celebration.

I whirled around to look at the screen, my pulse racing.

Ruby stood, and together we peered at two blue-folder icons — one named *Past* and the second named *Future*.

I took a deep breath, then leaned over the laptop, my fingers hovering over the trackpad. The room suddenly felt hot. I wiped my hands on my shorts and tried to get my breathing back under control.

"Stop dancing around, Will," Ruby said. "Choose one and click."

Breathe. Do it. Good news or bad, at least it was progress.

"It won't self-destruct," she said. "At least I don't think that's possible."

"Thanks, really. You're filling me with confidence."

"Do you want me to do it for you?" Ruby leaned over me, reaching for the trackpad.

This was it. Once Ruby opened the files she'd know my secret. She'd know I'd lied.

I slammed the laptop shut.

Ruby jerked back, as if she'd been burned.

"Sorry," I said. "It's kind of personal."

She shrugged, but I could see that I'd upset her.

I opened my mouth but didn't know what words to fill it with. How could I explain what was going on when I didn't understand it myself?

Ruby strode for the door and slammed it behind her, the bang vibrating through the floorboards. I started to go after her, then stopped myself. I'd agreed to Cameron's conditions. No matter what the files contained, I was leaving. Either to find Mom and Dad or to flee with Visser. I was never going to see Ruby again, and if I ran after her now all I'd do was leave her with more lies.

I flipped open the laptop. The cursor hovered over the *Past* file. *Please let Mom and Dad be innocent.*

I chickened out and double-clicked the *Future* file instead.

Then opened the only document the file held.

A single page.

A single coordinate.

56.514800N, –6.020285W.

I cut and pasted it into the search engine.

An island. Not Rothesay or Arran, but not far away from them. The Isle of Mull.

CHAPTER
26

CAMERON

I remember being small enough to ride on Dad's back. He was a rodeo horse trying to buck me or a crocodile turning and spinning in the lake, flipping me in the air. Mom would laugh, and Lewis would splash through the shallows, yelling it was his turn now, and I would shout *again, again*. Behind every laugh and every smile, every hug, every piece of advice, had Dad been thinking, *One day, my son will find out who I am, and he will hate me?*

I fell asleep hating him. After I'd seen the *Past* files.

The next morning, I woke up to the rustle of Lewis stuffing his backpack.

I groaned and snuggled deeper under the quilt.

And then I remembered we were leaving.

"What time is it?" I asked as I threw off the cover.

"Almost ten." Lewis reached for the photo Mom had sent Maggs — us in our backyard, capes flying — then he seemed to change his mind and left it propped against the bedside lamp.

I rubbed my cheeks, trying to wake myself up. "When are we leaving?"

"Whenever Visser gets back. He left about an hour ago."

"I thought he already had passports for us," I said.

Lewis shrugged. "Clare thinks he went to change his car."

"Why?" I swung my legs over the side of the bed.

Lewis's face scrunched. "In case The Foot knows what car he drives?"

"I mean why's Clare thinking anything when she's meant to be gone?" She'd said her goodbyes last night. Hugged us. Said she hoped one day she'd see us again.

Lewis slumped onto the bed. "Someone broke into her workshop."

I sat up straight. "Does she know who? Was anything taken? Or left?" *Like a note from The Foot threatening violence?*

He fiddled with one of his backpack straps. "She's on the phone to her neighbors and the Rothesay police. She's going to ask them to check her house, too."

"Does she think it was The Foot?" My body tensed. "Lewis?"

He looked up. "She doesn't know, that's why she's waiting for Visser."

I walked to the window, slid it open and breathed in the cool, damp air. The Foot would know Schenk was dead by now and that Mom and Dad had run. And now that I'd seen the files, I knew it wasn't only Dad and the paintings that he'd be after. The flash drive contained enough proof to send the entire mob to jail ten times over — photographs, blackmail letters, threats of violence, evidence of money changing hands and deals done. Clare had seen everything, too. It was why she'd decided she had to leave and put distance between us. Visser was going to whisk me and Lewis away to a new secret life, and Clare was going back to her old one in Rothesay.

But that was before someone broke into her shop.

"Maggs is leaving soon," Lewis said. "So, if you want to say goodbye …"

I spun away from the window, pulled on sweatpants and a T-shirt, then flew downstairs.

As I skidded into the kitchen, I collided with Haggis, who was lolloping to meet me.

"You saved me the trouble of climbing the stairs." Maggs stood at the island, a thermos in one hand and a cling-film-wrapped sandwich in the other.

My heart thumped. "Where are you going?"

"I've convinced Nora to join me for a meander up Arthur's Seat," she said. "I thought it best if you had the house to yourselves. Brian's dropping the Fisbys in town on his way to meet an old friend, and Ruby's going off somewhere with Aisha."

Haggis skuttled between me and Maggs as if she sensed something was wrong and she needed us to sort it out.

Maggs loosened the strings on a canvas backpack and slipped the thermos and sandwich inside. "Nora's waiting."

I nodded and followed her to the front door, Haggis at my heels.

"If anyone gets shot, mind you drag the body off the premises before you call the police," she said.

"Clare made us promise no more violence." I held her backpack while she wriggled into the straps.

"Good lad." She turned and patted my cheek. "And remember to eat something before you go. There's leftover bacon and black pudding in the fridge."

I pulled Haggis next to me, so Maggs could open the front door.

Lewis had probably given Maggs a hug.

"Thank you," I said. "Not for the black pudding, but for everything else."

"Away," she said. "I'm used to you now."

"I'll come back." Wherever we were going next, I'd find a way to see Maggs again. I wasn't like Mom. I didn't forget people.

"Of course you will." She squeezed my hand.

She smiled, then clomped down the front steps in her hiking boots.

Nora was waiting on the sidewalk, a raincoat tied around her waist and a straw hat on her head. I waved them off and watched them until they turned the corner.

I looked up at Visser's bedroom window. He hadn't been in any of the flash drive photographs, but could we absolutely trust him? I pulled out my phone and texted Padma: Did you find anything on Schenk or Visser?

Her reply was immediate: I'm having a smashing holiday, thank you.

Great, so much for Padma helping me.

My finger hovered over an unread message from Aisha. If I did make it back to visit Maggs, Aisha would be gone — she'd be a fashion designer or the prime minister, and she'd have forgotten all about me. I shoved the phone in my pocket and stomped back into the house.

"Have they left yet?" Lewis said from the staircase.

I couldn't speak past the lump in my throat, so I nodded.

Haggis trotted back through to the kitchen.

"Do you think we should pack the rest of the cash Mom gave us or leave it for Maggs?" he said. "As payment for staying here."

I needed to be away from the idea of leaving, and the look of hurt on Lewis's face. I knew he still wanted to go after Mom and Dad, and the only thing stopping him was me. It was the right thing to do. Dad was guilty as hell. The first few photographs had been easy to look at — the gallery, the paintings stacked in the back of a van, then street scenes, calm and orderly. People gathering with placards — laughing, holding children's hands, sharing food. Then a guy setting fire to a trash can. Another throwing a brick through a store window. And then one of Dad holding a baseball bat, striding toward the camera. I didn't need to see any more, I knew what happened next.

"You decide." I left Lewis standing on the stairs and went to the kitchen to find Haggis.

"Hiya." Aisha was crouched next to the island, rubbing Haggis's belly.

I strode to the fridge and stuck my head in it. Took some deep breaths to dissolve the lump in my throat and freeze the sadness off my face.

I grabbed a carton of milk, closed the fridge and turned toward Aisha.

"I was after Maggs," she said. "Is she in?"

"You just missed her. She went to Arthur's Seat with Nora."

She stood. "Can you tell her Mum and I made baklava and ask her if she wants any?"

I should thank her for showing me the castle and taking me to meet Jamie Wallace and generally taking my mind off how utterly crap my life was. I should say a proper goodbye.

Instead, I said, "What *is* Arthur's Seat? When Maggs told me they were going, I imagined them scaling a giant piece of furniture."

Aisha smiled. "It's the hill at the end of the Royal Mile that overlooks everything. You should go."

Not this time. But I would come back.

She turned to leave.

"Why's it called Arthur's Seat?"

"Why didn't you text me back?" she said.

Because I was sick of leaving people behind, and if I pretended Aisha wasn't my friend, it would hurt less.

"I'm sorry." *For lying to you and ignoring your text and leaving without saying thank you or goodbye.*

She narrowed her eyes as if she was trying to decide whether to forgive me, then she said, "Jamie invited us to a party."

"I can't go."

"I didn't say when it was, but I get the hint."

"I'm leaving Edinburgh," I said. "I can't go to Jamie's party or help you find the painting or climb Arthur's Seat. I wish I could."

Haggis trotted over to me and nuzzled my thigh.

"Oh." Aisha walked to the couch and sat. "No one knows for sure why it's called Arthur's Seat, but the legend most people want to believe is that it's where Camelot once stood, which it could be. It's the highest hill and looks out over the ocean and the city and all the roads leading in and out. It would've been the perfect site for Arthur to build his castle."

I sat on the other end of the couch. "What about the legends people don't believe?"

"My favorite is the hill is a sleeping dragon." She shrugged. "I like to think a dragon is watching over the city. Plus, the story of King Arthur is kind of sad."

"Why?"

"You know, the whole 'betrayed by his best friend and his wife' thing."

"Are there any heroes who weren't betrayed?"

"Families are complicated," she said.

Haggis laid her head on my lap.

"Why are you leaving?" Aisha said.

"Because families are complicated."

Aisha looked at her hands. "I did wonder why you were here by yourself."

It was a reminder that I'd lied to her about Lewis and about who we were and why we were here. About being the son of criminals.

"If someone you loved did something horrible, could you still love them?" Lewis would hate me if he knew I'd even thought it, never mind said it out loud, but I had a feeling Aisha understood.

She leaned forward, her elbows on her knees, her head resting on her knuckles. "I think until you understand their side of the story, you can't know. It's like Queen Mary. She trusted the people who should've been good, but her interpretation of the facts was warped."

"Villains change, depending on who tells the story?" I said.

"Exactly."

I stroked Haggis's head. "Do you think Jamie's family have the painting?"

"Only one way to find out." She leaned back. "The party's in an hour, if that makes a difference."

"Who has lunchtime parties other than little kids?"

"Rich people," she said. "It's a garden party."

"Like cucumber sandwiches and croquet?" Lewis would love that.

She grinned. "And opportunities to sneak around an empty house and find Queen Mary's painting."

If the party had been yesterday, Lewis would've jumped at the chance. He'd probably quiz Mrs. Wallace on her criminal tendencies over a game of croquet, then steal the painting and swap it for witness protection for us all. But it wasn't yesterday.

"I wish I could help you." I patted Haggis. "Breaking and entering's not the same when you don't have an accomplice."

Yesterday, I would've helped Lewis steal the painting to help Mom and Dad, but today I'd do it so Aisha could return Queen Mary to the castle. Because being the son of criminals didn't make me one, too.

"Ruby's coming with me," she said. "And I doubt we'll have to break down any doors — Mrs. Wallace probably has it on show, so she can lord it over her rich friends. If we find it, I'll take a photo and show it to the art historian at the castle. Not sure it'll achieve much. The police won't be able to enter without a warrant, which will give Mrs. Wallace plenty of time to switch it for a fake."

Not if I stole it first.

I couldn't undo everything my parents had done, but I could correct some of it — one day Aisha would find out who I was, and maybe if I did something good, it would help cancel out all the bad stuff Mom and Dad had done.

It was a nice thought, but Goatee Guy knew we were in Edinburgh. And now The Foot might be after Clare as well. We needed to leave.

I stood, wiped my palm on my pants and held it out for Aisha to shake, just as she'd done the first time we'd met. "Nice to meet you, Aisha."

"Likewise, Willem." She shook my hand, then looked over my shoulder and frowned. "What happened to the painting? Where did the phantom island go?"

I glanced at Mom's painting. "Oh, that; it got wet."

"And vandalized." She moved closer and peered at the symbol, then traced the upside-down *V* and the arrow with her thumb. "I've seen this before."

"Where?" I tried to look calm, like she hadn't just solved a puzzle Lewis and I had been obsessed with two days ago. Did it still matter?

"It's the mark of the stonemason who built these houses." She smiled. "It's carved under the window I usually climb through. And in a few other places. Next to the front door and the fireplace."

My pulse raced. It was too late to change anything, but if Mom *had* left something behind, it might explain why she'd made the choices she did.

Aisha checked her phone. "I should get going. And if you see Ruby, tell her to hurry up. She's getting ready at mine, and I'm not letting her go to a garden party in leggings and a sweatshirt."

I nodded.

She patted Haggis's head, then walked to the back door. "Goodbye, Will."

"Thank you," I said. "For everything."

"I hope your family complication works itself out."

And then she was gone.

And I was racing to the lounge in search of whatever Mom had left behind eighteen years ago.

CHAPTER
27

LEWIS

From the attic window, I watched Ruby walk down the front steps of the guesthouse, then up to Aisha's front door. I'd rehearsed how to say goodbye to Ruby, even practiced in the mirror, but the more I said the words, the more unconvincing I sounded. Ruby would see right through me. Besides, saying goodbye to Maggs had been difficult enough, and soon we'd be leaving Clare, too. My stomach was in knots. I'd woken up about fifty times during the night, going through every possible argument that could change Cameron's mind. The problem was, Clare and Maggs agreed with him — we had to walk away from Mom and Dad, and hope one day they'd find us.

My backpack was packed, it hadn't taken long, and now there was nothing to do but wait for Visser to come back. Cameron's clothes were strewn across the floor. His empty backpack poked out from under the bed. Everyone was out now, so what was he up to? I thought back to what he'd said about The Foot being the one who'd broken into Clare's shop. Was he was trying to convince her to come with us?

Cameron wasn't with Clare. The door to her room, across the hall from ours, was open, and she was pacing, the phone pressed to her ear. It sounded like she'd finished with the police and was now organizing new locks for her shop. She waved when she saw me, then was absorbed back into the call.

"Cameron?" I called as I jogged downstairs.

"In here!" he yelled.

I followed his voice to the lounge, where I found him crouched by the fireplace, his hands black with soot.

"When you're finished digging up whatever the dog buried in the fireplace, can we talk to Clare and convince her to come with us?"

Cameron strode to the window, slid it open, then the top half of his body disappeared through the opening.

"Cameron." Was he even listening?

He muttered something, then levered himself back inside. "I'm looking for a stonemason's mark. It's carved in the fireplace and under the windows, and ..."

He spun and raced to the front door. The bell jangled as he swung it open. Then he was back.

"... but it's a waste of time."

"Is this a delay tactic?" I asked. "Because if you're reconsidering ..."

"Mom's symbol's the stonemason's mark. I found similar marks carved above the windows and the front door, but there are no gaps or openings that could be a hiding place. The fireplace has a missing stone, but if Mom did hide anything there, it's long gone."

I ran to the fireplace. "Show me."

Cameron sighed, then followed.

"It's here." He ran his fingers underneath the stone mantel. "Right here in the corner."

I nudged him out of the way. "Let me try."

He stood back and gestured for me to go ahead.

I crouched. And there it was, the upside-down *V* with the arrow through it. The stone was rough behind the mantel and gritty with coal dust. I groped until I found the opening and reached inside. Farther, farther, until the tips of my fingers jammed up against stone. I swallowed hard. Took a breath. It was empty.

"Mom hasn't been here for eighteen years," Cameron said. "Maggs's probably had a thousand guests since then. Anyone could've found it."

Eighteen years!

I clutched Cameron's shoulders. "Eighteen years ago, Maggs lived downstairs. If Mom hid anything, it'll be there, in Professor Pham's flat."

Cameron's eyes went wide. He held on to my arms, and together we jumped up and down.

And then we stopped. And looked at each other, both thinking the same thing — *How can we search Professor Pham's flat with him in it?*

———

C A M E R O N

"It would be easy," Lewis had said. The professor's fireplace was directly underneath Maggs's. He had loads of books. Pretend to be interested, then ask for some tea. It would take less time to search the fireplace than to boil the kettle.

If it was that easy, why wasn't Lewis down here knocking on the door?

I heard the professor's shuffled footsteps.

The door creaked open.

"What did I say last time about this not being a guesthouse?" He was wearing a gray knitted cardigan, proper trousers and slippers.

As I stepped into the hall, the chill of the professor's apartment wrapped itself around me.

"Could I borrow a book?" I glanced into the room directly below the upstairs lounge — floor-to-ceiling bookshelves, just like Lewis said.

"If you want to exterminate an insect, use a shoe instead," the professor said. "But if you are here to embrace knowledge and claim your place in the world, then you will need to be more specific than merely 'a book.'"

"Could I look at what you have?" I stepped into the room, which smelled of dusty books and eucalyptus muscle rub.

The fireplace was identical to upstairs, but scaled down. I tried to imagine Maggs and Mom in here. Had Mom done what I was about to do — ask for tea, then reach behind the mantel?

"I don't lend my books willy-nilly," the professor said. "I am not a library."

I tore my eyes from the fireplace and strode to the bookshelves, then ran my finger along the spines — Oliver Cromwell, the Magna Carta, the Battle of Culloden.

The professor hovered in the doorway.

According to Lewis, I just needed to ask for some tea, and he'd disappear. I could imagine his reply if I did — "This is not a café."

"I'll make some tea, shall I?" the professor said.

My shoulders relaxed. "Thank you."

"No need to grin at me, lad. It's only tea."

Once the shuffle of his slippers had faded, I dove for the fireplace.

The stonemason's symbol was in the same place.

My heart raced as I ran my hand up behind the cool stone. *Please let there be a hollow. Please.*

The tap whooshed from down the hall.

China clinked.

And then my heart skipped a beat as rough stone fell away, and my fingers found smooth metal. Yes!

And then I was holding a red-tartan shortbread tin in my hands, blowing off the coal dust, opening the lid.

An envelope addressed to Maggs.

I put the tin on top of the mantel, tore open the envelope, then began to read.

Dear Maggs,

If you have stumbled across this letter and I am still in your life, please return it to me and do not tell a soul. But if I have disappeared, or worse, then you will have followed whatever clue I sent. I am still dreaming up ways to conceal the stonemason's symbol in a form only you could uncover.

I am sorry to burden you, but I know you'll keep a level head and be wise enough to choose the right time to tell Clare, and she, in turn, will know the best way to tell our parents. Next week, I leave for London and the beginning of the next chapter of my life, though for all intents and purposes, that chapter began two years ago, when my history professor took me for lunch and asked if I had any interest in joining MI6. It was as though I'd been waiting to hear those words my whole life ... "Are you ready to serve your country and claim your place in the world ...?"

My heart skipped a beat. It was almost the same words the professor had just said to me. Professor Pham, who taught history at the university. Who retired after the riots, then turned up at Maggs's front door.

"What have you got there?"

My head whipped up to find the professor looking down at me.

I leaped up, stuffing Mom's letter into my pocket. "A shopping list. I completely forgot Maggs asked me pick up a few things. Sorry, I've got to go."

I stumbled to the door, heart pounding.

"Could you add tea bags to the list?" the professor said. "I seem to be out."

I was halfway up the guesthouse stairs before I realized I'd left the soot-covered shortbread tin on the mantel.

CHAPTER
28

LEWIS

We sat on the back seat of the bus, Aisha on one side wearing a swishy dress covered in teapots and holding a platter of Middle Eastern flaky desserts, Ruby on the other wearing white, flared pants and a sleeveless shirt with tiny strawberries embroidered all over it. I kept looking down at my hands to hide my grin. Mom had been recruited by MI6 when she was a student. She was a British secret agent!

If you combined that fact with Dad escaping the mafia, the only answer that made sense was witness protection. All of Cameron's arguments had dissolved, leaving nothing but an illogical determination to help Aisha return the painting to the castle before we went to find Mom and Dad. I could've argued, but for some reason, Clare trusted Visser and wanted to wait until he got back before we raced off to the Isle of Mull.

Ruby's elbow knocked my shoulder as she tore a pink hairband off her head. "Sorry, I just can't."

She fidgeted with the shirt.

"Tell her she looks nice," Aisha said to me.

"You look great," I said, and she really did.

Her hair was curled at the ends, and she must've been wearing makeup, because her blue eyes somehow looked bluer, and her lips were glossy and pink. I, on the other hand, was dressed in cargo shorts and Cameron's freshly washed white tee, the ghost of an orange stain still visible in the right light, plus my sneakers, now splattered in Edinburgh mud.

When Ruby didn't smile, I nudged her. "I wish Aisha could've dressed me."

She finally met my eyes. "Why are you here anyway? Don't you have personal files to open?"

"Next stop's ours." Aisha reached up and yanked a string that dinged a bell next to the driver.

The bus left us at the end of a tree-lined street that curved and ducked and dived for what seemed like miles. We took turns carrying Aisha's platter.

Cyclists whizzed past, their faces covered by bullet-shaped helmets and wraparound shades. A few minutes later, a group of runners, all wearing the same yellow shirt, huffed and puffed past us. We only saw two cars. No double-decker buses or tourist coaches or taxis.

"It doesn't feel like we're still in the city," I said.

"This is the posh part," Aisha said as though that explained everything.

A car engine roared behind us, and we all turned to look. The sleek, black car slowed, then turned onto the sidewalk right in front of us. Iron gates swung open, and the car glided through.

"This is it," Aisha said.

Ruby looked up at the eight-foot stone wall. "Are you sure?"

"Only one way to find out." Aisha handed Ruby the platter, smoothed down her headscarf, then strode up to the gate.

I texted Cameron that there were security cameras mounted on the gate posts. He'd have to scale the wall from the other side.

Aisha waved at the camera, pressed the intercom button and gave her name.

The loudspeaker crackled, then buzzed us in.

Jamie Wallace's driveway was an avenue of massive bushes with giant pink-and-white flowers. If the Wallaces had neighbors, I couldn't see them. All I could hear were our feet crunching on the gravel, and birds — chirping ones in the bushes and quacking ones on the other side.

"They must be loaded," Ruby said.

"They inherited the house," Aisha said. "Plus, Jamie's mum's a politician, and his dad's a bigwig lawyer."

As the driveway curved back around, Jamie Wallace's house came into view.

"That's not a house, it's a castle," I said.

Ruby handed me the platter. "It doesn't have enough turrets to be a castle."

"It's got two turrets and a great big flagpole. How is that not a castle? Do they have staff?"

Ruby rolled her eyes.

"Please don't say anything embarrassing to Jamie," Aisha said.

"Like what?" I said.

"Like, 'Do you have a butler and get driven to school in a Rolls-Royce?'"

"Do they?" Ruby asked.

"No, and don't encourage him."

A woman in a black dress and a white apron stepped out of the double front doors to greet us. I looked at Ruby and mouthed, *servants*. She almost smiled.

The lady gestured to the platter in my hands. "Would you like me to take that?"

I declined because the baklava was our ticket inside the house.

I expected the woman to curtsy, but she pointed us in the direction of the party, then went back inside.

A brick path led us past a pond, which was the source of the quacking. Ducks waddled around it and floated across it. Beyond the pond, the path curved past a line of expensive cars parked in front of a long, low building that looked more like stables than a garage.

"Imagine growing up here." Ruby looked around.

"Bit of a trek from the bus stop," I said. "And if you dropped your keys on the driveway, it'd take hours to find them."

She laughed before she could stop herself. It was the first time I'd heard her laugh. It suited her.

We could hear the party now. The hum of a hundred conversations and clinking glasses. Two little girls in puffy dresses stormed around the side of the stables, chased by an older girl in a less puffy dress who waved at us.

Aisha waved back. "That's Caitlin, Jamie's wee sister. She swims as well."

We carried on along the path, which circled a rose garden and a fountain before depositing us at the edge of the party. Women in candy-colored dresses and men in pale suits were gathered in clusters. Serving staff weaved between them, offering champagne and finger food from silver trays. It looked like a scene from one of those movies where the colors are brighter than real life. Even the sun was shinier in Jamie Wallace's backyard.

Although calling it a backyard was like calling his mansion a house. The lawn was as big as a soccer field, bordered with blooming flower beds. Behind the flowers were towering trees. And behind them, I assumed, the boundary wall. I texted Cameron that he should scale the eastern side, otherwise he'd be spotted by a hundred guests and serving staff and whoever was in the open-sided tent tucked off to the side.

"Is that a band in the tent?" I said.

Aisha was as tall as me today, thanks to her lavender shoes.

She scanned the scene. "It's a gazebo with a string quartet. As befits a garden party."

The string quartet started playing something classical that I didn't recognize, but was probably famous.

Aisha adjusted her dress. "I should've worn something fancier."

"You look brilliant," Ruby said. "And anyway, we're here for the painting."

"But it's a garden party with a string quartet. And those outfits aren't from Marks and Spencer — they'll be Dior and Gucci and Prada." She turned her head to follow the progress of a woman with origami on her head. "And that's a Stella McCartney fascinator."

"I have no idea what any of those words mean," I said. "And this platter's getting heavy."

And Cameron was waiting for more instructions.

Aisha took a deep breath and looked longingly once more at the party. "Okay, I'm ready."

CAMERON

Clare yanked on the hand brake. "I admit it feels good to be doing something other than waiting and worrying about Katrina, but stealing a painting from a member of parliament isn't quite what I had in mind."

I peered up at Jamie's stone wall. We'd parked on the eastern side, as Lewis had advised. No cameras that I could see, but the overhanging trees were thick with leaves. If this was my house, I'd mount cameras here.

I opened the car door.

Clare put her hand on my arm. "Go with Thys. Stay safe. I'll go after Katrina."

"Why do you trust him?" I asked.

I checked my phone again. Padma still hadn't texted back.

"Because he didn't lie about working for The Foot. Because over the years he's had every opportunity to harm me but hasn't. And because he's the only person who's ever offered to help unravel this whole mess. I want my sister back. For you and Lewis, but also for me. I miss her." She sat back. "Plus he has a gun, which might come in handy."

"I told you he had a gun."

"Go with him."

"And you'll find Mom for us?"

She nodded. "I promise."

"Can I think about it?"

"Of course you can." She sighed. "Now, go and rescue that painting."

L E W I S

The back door of Jamie's mansion opened into a porch with a wooden bench, like you'd see in a church, a row of rubber boots tucked underneath. Ruby pushed open the inner door and held it for Aisha and me, and the platter of baklava.

We stepped into a long hallway with black-and-white tiles on the floor and wood-paneled walls. A clatter that sounded like a dishwasher being stacked echoed down the hall. We followed the noise to what I hoped was the kitchen, so we could ditch Aisha's platter and get on with the search.

The kitchen was huge, of course, with glass doors at one end opening onto a patio with a drinks bar. Serving staff were rushing about restocking trays from a banquet-sized table of food and drink.

I slid Aisha's platter onto the table, then unpeeled the cling wrap, balling it up and stuffing it in my pocket. As I straightened, my head whacked against a hanging pot. The pot clattered into the neighboring pot, setting off a domino of clangs.

The serving staff glanced my way, then scurried back to their tasks. Ruby laughed. Aisha shushed us both. I was about to tell her to blame the pots when the gigantic fridge doors thudded shut, and Jamie Wallace turned to face us. He looked different than when I'd seen him at the pub, but it had been dark, and I'd been distracted with being followed and swapping places with Cameron and getting back to the guesthouse without being shot.

"You made it." Jamie grinned at Aisha, then stuck out his hand for Ruby to shake. "I'm Jamie."

Ruby shook his hand and blushed. Really? He wasn't that good-looking, was he?

Okay, he was at least five inches taller than me, wearing a well-ironed shirt that fit him properly, with good skin, straight posture, wide shoulders and floppy hair the same straw-blond as the three girls who'd run past us. I glanced down at my mud-stained sneakers.

"Good to see you again, Will," Jamie said.

"Aisha brought baklava," I said, because what else do you say to someone you're about to steal from?

"Brilliant, thanks," Jamie said to Aisha.

"Your house is like a castle." Ruby gestured to the vastness of the kitchen.

"Would you like the grand tour?"

Yes, I thought, *but without you.*

He held the kitchen door for us, and we were back in the long hallway, minus the platter of baklava, but with the addition of Jamie.

I texted Cameron that we were in the house.

Jamie opened the first door on the left, and we shuffled inside a room with a slouchy couch, bright-colored beanbag chairs, a pile of stuffed animals and a TV the size of a king-sized bed.

"This is the kids' hangout room," Jamie said. "The pink unicorn isn't mine."

"You get your own living room?" Ruby asked.

"My parents like their peace and quiet." He pointed to the door across the hall. "That's a loo. Not particularly exciting unless you're interested in eighteenth-century ceramic toilet bowls."

"I think we're good." It was unlikely Mrs. Wallace would

hang a $5 million painting above any kind of toilet, antique or otherwise.

Behind the next door was a dining room — polished-wood table, silver candlesticks, a chandelier, a painting of a mountain and another of a horse. Then next door to that was Mr. Wallace's study — overlooking the duck pond, a heavy wooden desk and floor-to-ceiling bookshelves with one of those movable ladders. One painting — a sailboat.

We passed the red front doors, then Jamie waved at a sweeping staircase. "I could show you the bedrooms, but I can't vouch for their cleanliness. My littlest sister rescues frogs. And earwigs."

He bounded on down the hall, pointing at the next door. "Another loo. You can never have too many."

I kind of wanted to hate Jamie, but I couldn't. He was like an energetic puppy.

He strode straight past the next closed door. "My mother's study. She doesn't like anyone going in there."

Aisha gave me a look that mirrored my thoughts — *that sounds suspicious; we need to check there later.*

"And this used to be the smoking room," Jamie said as he opened the next door. "Where gentlemen retired to play cards, drink whisky and generally escape doing anything remotely useful. Now it's where the dog sleeps."

He stepped into the room and stroked a massive gray dog stretched out on the couch.

"What kind of dog is he?" Aisha asked.

"A Scottish Deerhound. He belongs to my gran," Jamie said.

"Your parents don't want the dog in their space either?" Ruby asked.

"Something like that," he said. "Come on, the sitting rooms are more exciting."

Aisha strode beside Jamie. I hung back with Ruby.

"Sitting rooms, plural," she said.

She was finally talking to me again.

"I told you." I grinned. "It'd be a nightmare living here. Imagine taking off your socks or putting down a book. You wouldn't find them for months. They probably have tracking devices sewn into everything."

The sitting room, which was at the end of the house, had two ornate rugs, four velvet couches, a fireplace the size of a cow and paintings. Lots of paintings, mostly of people. My heart did a little jolt. Was Queen Mary here?

Aisha scanned the paintings, a determined look on her face. Jamie strode to the far wall, which turned out to be paneled doors. He slid them open, and another room appeared, the mirror image of the one we were in.

"You could host a ball in here," Ruby said.

"We do all the time," Jamie said. "We're having a ceilidh in a few weeks. You should all come."

"Will's leaving today," Aisha said. "Ruby, will you still be here?"

Ruby looked at me. "You're leaving?"

"I ..." What had Cameron told Aisha?

"Where are you going?" Ruby's voice held a note of panic.

I wished I could give her an answer, but the scenarios ranged from living in a hut on the Isle of Mull with Mom and Dad, to clearing their names and going home, to being caught by The Foot before we could reach them, and I really didn't want to think about where we'd end up then.

"I'm not exactly sure." I pointed to a painting of a fierce man in a kilt with a dagger at his hip. "Who's that?"

Jamie, who'd been watching Ruby, looked at me. "The Earl of Stair. Complete git. My littlest sister threw strawberry ice cream at him after Gran told his story."

Aisha nodded. "So, that's him? I'd throw ice cream at him, too, if I had any."

"Why? What did he do?" I asked.

"He ordered the Glencoe Massacre," Jamie said. "It was three hundred years ago, but people still hate him. He sent in the soldiers, and the MacDonalds, who had no idea they were about to be betrayed, fed and sheltered them for two weeks. Then the order came, and the soldiers killed the MacDonalds while they slept."

"Wow." And I thought Schenk was evil, but at least he hadn't let us serve him a burger before he tried to kill us.

I tried to catch Ruby's eye, but she was looking down, fiddling with her bracelets.

"Were the paintings handed down with the house?" Aisha asked Jamie.

"Aye, but only a handful were here when my gran inherited. The rest had been sold or given away by previous generations. My mother scours the land in search of them. She's a wee bit obsessed with restoring our birthright."

"Are you obsessed, too?" Aisha asked.

"Not at all. Caitlin told our mother that when I inherit, I'll probably give them all away to charity. It didn't go down well."

As they approached the next painting — a battle scene with a horse stamping on a dead person — I checked my phone. Cameron was over the wall.

"Are all your mom's paintings in here?" I said. "Or are some too valuable?"

Aisha's eyes went wide. Too blunt?

The two little girls we'd seen earlier with Caitlin sprinted into the sitting room, their puffy dresses bouncing around their knees. The smaller one threw herself behind Jamie's legs, laughing. The taller one of the two held up her hands to show him how chocolatey her fingers were.

"Where's Caitlin?" Jamie asked her.

"She said it was your turn to play with us."

He knelt, and the younger one climbed on his back, then he told the older one to go wash her hands.

"We should get back," Jamie said. "I'm meant to be keeping these two out of trouble."

He led the way back to the kitchen, his little sister kicking his hips as if he were a horse. As we passed his mom's study, he hesitated, then continued.

I texted Cameron: Ground floor, north-facing room, fifth window from the right.

———

C A M E R O N

Dangling from the lowest branch of the tree, I jumped, landing on the grass in a crouch. No cars had arrived while I'd been hiding, and the only sign of a party was the music drifting from the other side of the house. That didn't mean that I wasn't on camera. Or that no one was looking out the windows.

I took a running leap over the driveway, my heel clipping it, sending stones skittering. *Crap.* I sprinted the rest of the way, my heart thundering, then dove into the flower bed under the fifth window. If Lewis was right, the painting was in here.

As I slid Maggs's bread knife under the edge of the window, a duck waddled past and gave me the evil eye. The window wouldn't budge. I needed a rock or a brick to hammer the end of the knife.

The front door creaked open.

Crap.

"I've just seen you inside," a small pink child said. "What are you doing?"

"Nothing."

She sunk down beside me. "Can I play?"

"It's a boring game. I was searching for a rock."

"Rocks are as big as cars." She sighed. "I think you mean a pebble or a stone. And don't feel bad. Some people aren't good at thinking up games. Or words."

I pointed at her hands. "Where did you find the chocolate?"

"At the party. Do you want me to get you some?"

I smiled. "No, that's okay, but thank you."

What was I saying, of course I should send her away.

"Actually," I said. "Chocolate sounds great."

She pursed her lips as if she was deciding whether to go or not, then she said, "There's fudge cake as well and trifle and buns."

"I'll stick with the chocolate."

"Don't go anywhere." She jumped up and skipped into the house, banging the door behind her.

That was close. Question was, could I get this window open before she came back?

A click above my head sent my heart racing. I flattened myself on the ground as the window slid open. *Please don't look down.*

"Will this do?"

I looked up at the small voice.

The little girl was holding out a glass paperweight in her chocolate-covered hands. "It's not a stone, but it might work for your game."

I sat up and took it from her. "Thank you."

"You're welcome, see you soon." She ran off, leaving the fifth window from the right wide open.

I climbed into a cramped study that held a leather armchair, a messy desk and a small, gloomy painting hanging on the wall. After quietly pulling the hallway door closed, I inspected the painting. It didn't look like a national treasure. A girl, around my age, was sitting unnaturally rigid. At first glance she looked very serious, but the longer I studied her, wondering how this simple painting could be worth $5 million, I realized that the girl was trying not to smile. If she'd trusted different people, would she have kept her throne and her son and her head?

I dug out my phone and checked the painting against the photo Aisha had sent. This was it. The painting that Dad had stolen from the Tate, the one Aisha so desperately wanted returned, the one the country had been mourning for seventeen years. Here. Right in front of me.

I felt a moment of guilt for stealing from Jamie's family, then pulled out the garbage bag from my back pocket. I had to put things right.

"Sorry," I whispered to Queen Mary as I carefully lifted her down. "You're going home now, I promise."

CHAPTER
29

C A M E R O N

It was too easy. No alarm bells. No sirens. No security guards chasing after me.

Clare's car was parked in the same spot, the driver's door open, the car ping-pinging.

"Clare?" Where the heck had she gone?

I carefully laid the painting on the passenger seat, then jogged around the corner. No sign of her.

The car was still pinging when I got back, so I wedged myself into the driver's seat and found the key in the ignition, the *Argyll & Bute Motors* key ring dangling. *Come on, Clare.*

I texted her.

Something chimed.

I fumbled for the lever, slid back the seat. Patted the gritty floormat. As my fingers closed around a phone, a horrible sinking feeling came over me. I sat up, bumping my head on the steering wheel, then turned over the phone with trembling hands.

My text stared back at me.

Keys in the ignition. Driver's door open. Cell phone left behind. Clare hadn't wandered off. She'd been taken!

I stumbled out of the car, feeling like someone had punched the air out of me. Clare couldn't be gone. I couldn't lose anyone else.

I leaned against the car, taking deep breaths. Clare had driven me here because she was worried about me being out alone, and while I'd been chatting to a small girl about chocolate cake, Clare was being dragged away.

She'd wanted us to wait for Visser. But no, I wouldn't listen. I just had to chase after the damn painting. And why? To prove I wasn't like my dad? What a joke. I was exactly like him — dragging my family into danger without caring about the consequences. This was all my fault.

I slammed the car door. Kicked the wheel.

A squirrel skittered up a tree.

Clare's phone vibrated in my hand, and Visser's name flashed up.

I have the car, where are you?

Was Visser part of this? Had he tipped off The Foot that Clare had found us? And if his goons took Clare now, after seventeen years of watching her, would he be able to reel us in, too?

Only one way to find out.

I texted Visser back as though I was Clare and told him to meet me at the guesthouse in an hour. Then I texted Lewis from my phone: I have the painting, stay at the party, I'll explain everything later.

I checked my pocket for the flash drive. I didn't want to hand it over, but if that's what it took to get Clare back, I'd do it.

I climbed back into the driver's seat, started the engine, then tested the accelerator pedal and found the brake. That just left the clutch. How difficult could driving a manual be? Lewis would tell me to call a cab, but Dad would tell me I could do this — *Focus on the road, keep the wheel steady and be ready to brake for a moose.* Or in this case, a bus. And Clare's car was tiny compared to our truck.

I pushed down the clutch and slid the gearshift into first. The car leaped forward, then stalled. *Crap.* I yanked it back into neutral and tried again. The car crawled.

I was going three miles an hour.

A cyclist zoomed toward me on my side of the road. His side of the road!

I jerked the wheel, and the car veered into the other lane. *Calm down. You can do this. Clare needs you.*

I hit the accelerator. The engine revved. The speedometer needle climbed to a whopping ten miles per hour. The car sounded like it was about to take off. Or explode.

I shoved the gearshift into second. The engine screeched. *Crap, the clutch.* I stamped on the clutch. Behind me, a car horn blasted.

Please don't stall. Don't stall. The tone of the engine changed. The revs dropped. Ha! I'd done it. Fifteen miles an hour.

The car, which was still up my ass, honked again. *Give me a break, I'm trying.* I changed gears and watched the speedometer climb to thirty. Easy. Now all I had to do was remember what route Clare had taken.

The car revved its engine, then overtook me. Good riddance.

But instead of racing off, it swerved and cut me off. What the heck!

I slammed on the brakes. Tires screeched. I blasted my horn for them to get out of the way but it was too late. I was going to crash into them!

Six feet, four feet.

I yanked on the steering wheel and mounted the sidewalk. If I'd been in our truck, the curb would've hardly registered and I would've been able to blast past the car and back onto the road. But Clare's car wasn't our truck.

A horrible scraping sound came from the undercarriage and Clare's car came to a sudden stop.

The engine hiccupped, then stalled.

No, no, no!

I turned the key, pumped the gas, threw it into reverse.

The back wheels spun. Oh crap, Clare's car had really grounded out.

This was it.

I dug the flash drive out of my pocket. If I gave them the files, would they let me go and give Clare back? Or would they shoot us both?

Tearing the keys from the ignition, I shoved open the door, then jumped out, my heart thundering in my chest.

The thrum of bicycle wheels made me turn.

"Help!" I leaped in front of a pod of cyclists.

Behind me, I could hear someone getting out of the black car.

The cyclists frantically rang their bells. One yelled at me to get off the road.

"They'll run you over if you don't move."

I spun around. "Padma?"

Padma had run me off the road? Not The Foot?

My heart rate dropped, and the sudden lightness made me want to giggle. Padma looked the same — black jeans, white shirt, canvas jacket, her dark hair in a braid.

I stepped back onto the sidewalk just as the cyclists whizzed past.

"Did you find out about Visser?" I walked to meet Padma. "Is that why you're here? Does he still work for The Foot?"

She held out her hand.

I looked down at Clare's keys. "You're here to arrest me for driving without a license? I thought you were on vacation."

"No. But I should have been. Would have been, had it not been for you."

"What did I do?" Did she know I'd stolen the painting?

"It'd be quicker to list what you haven't done." Instead of taking the keys, she plucked the flash drive out of my other hand.

"You can't take that," I said. "Wait, how did you know about it?"

"Jesus wept, Cameron, will you stop talking and get in the car?" She strode back to her vehicle.

Had she just called me Cameron?

Adrenaline kicked in.

"Why are you here?" I called after her.

She turned to face me. "I'm here to save your arse before someone mistakes it for your head and puts a bullet in it." She pulled a gun from her waistband and checked the safety catch.

I put my hands in the air. An automatic reaction after the last week.

"Put your hands down. This is not for you."

"How was I to know?" I lowered my arms. "Just give me a minute."

Back at Clare's car, I grabbed her phone and the painting from the passenger seat.

"What's in the bag?" Padma asked.

Padma already had the files. I wasn't about to hand over the only tradable asset I had left.

I clutched the painting to my chest. "Something from the party."

Padma raised her eyebrows.

"A plate … I mean, a tray. It had food on it. I promised I'd bring it back. Apparently it's an heirloom or something."

"Get in." Padma yanked open the driver's door, the gun in the waistband of her jeans.

"Where are we going?"

"To retrieve your brother before someone else beats us to it."

L E W I S

Ruby was ignoring me. I tried to make her laugh, brought her food, apologized a million times for not telling her I was leaving, but she'd reverted to fiddling with her bracelets and refusing to make eye contact. I was out of ideas.

Aisha filled the awkward silence with, "Do you think I can take photos of the guests' dresses? You probably need permission to take photos of posh people. Jamie would know. Anyone spotted him yet?"

We'd all been dragged into a game of tag with Jamie's sisters. One of them ended up in the duck pond, and Jamie had whisked her off to get changed. That was twenty minutes ago, and we hadn't seen him since. I'd convinced Aisha to wait until Jamie returned before continuing to search for the painting, which Cameron now had. The plan was that she would keep Jamie talking, while Ruby and I sneaked back into the house. But Ruby was ignoring me.

"I think if you cut off their heads, it would be fine," I said.

"Only clothes, no faces." Aisha handed me her glass. "And put on your big boy underpants while I'm gone. Tell Ruby the truth. You already told me why you're leaving, and it didn't kill you."

I watched Aisha set off on a circuit of the party, while I scrambled for what to say. I had no idea what story Cameron had given Aisha.

"Are you going back home?" Ruby said.

"Not right away." Maybe after Mom and Dad managed to clear their names. "It's complicated."

Another server pounced on us with a tray of drinks. I said no thanks and handed him Aisha's glass.

"Not too complicated to tell Aisha." Ruby slid her glass onto the server's tray.

I waited until the server moved on, then said, "I should've told you I was leaving, but it was kind of sudden."

"It doesn't matter."

Obviously, it did.

I pinched two brownies off a passing tray and held one out for Ruby. "You were right, you do have brownies here."

She took it and nibbled one corner.

"I'm sorry," I said.

She shrugged. "It's fine. I've only known you for a week, and you were a knob half the time anyway. Everyone leaves. I'm fine."

I remembered her question from the festival about how I coped with being alone, and I realized my previous answer had been wrong. Cameron and I *were* going home, because wherever Mom and Dad were was home, even if it was a hut on a tiny island.

"Can we talk somewhere quieter?" I said.

She shrugged. "The duck pond?"

"You won't shove me in?"

"I'll try not to." She marched in the direction of the pond.

I strode behind her trying to finish the brownie that I no longer wanted, the chocolate icing melting on my fingers.

The ducks looked like they'd exhausted themselves and were snuggled in the grass next to the pond, their beaks tucked under their wings. The chatter of the party faded, but I could still hear the band, which had switched to more cheery tunes.

I crouched and dipped my hands in the water while I thought of what to say. I couldn't confess who Mom and Dad were, but I could tell Ruby enough that when the truth came out, she'd know I'd told her all I could. I rubbed off the chocolate, swirled my hands, watched the ripples and tried to ignore Cameron's voice in my head telling me to keep my mouth shut.

"Forget it," Ruby said. "I'm going back to find Aisha."

I stood and caught her arm. "When my dad was young, he worked for someone who turned out to be not very nice."

———

CAMERON

Padma was driving a different car from last time, no crumb-filled baby seats or sippy cups. It smelled of upholstery and air conditioning, rather than sour milk.

After a few minutes, when Padma still hadn't made a U-turn, I said, "I thought we were going back for Lewis."

The indicator click-clocked as she slowed to take a right.

I twisted to look at her. "Padma?"

"I'm not wasting my breath answering pointless questions." She glanced in the mirror.

"Is someone following us?" I said.

"Decent attempt, so I'll let you have it. No, but I'm not taking any chances."

"So, we *are* going for Lewis, but we're taking a detour in case we're being followed?"

Padma pressed *play* on her dashboard screen. A country song about dirt roads and lost love filled the car.

Even though it was one I liked, I switched it off. "Will you tell me what's going on?"

"I'll answer three questions." She turned the music back on. "Think about them carefully."

I opened my mouth, but she held up her hand. "After this song. It's a good one."

She turned up the volume, then took another right.

I sank back in the seat.

She knew my name. Knew about Lewis. Knew we had the files. Was her vacation in Edinburgh a coincidence or had she followed us here from London? *Coincidences are like shooting stars,* Mom said in my head. I took a breath to ask if Padma knew who I was before or after she asked me to carry the stroller, but it was another coincidence — our cover must've been blown before we'd arrived in London.

The song ended.

"Did you borrow the children, or are they really yours?"

"A zookeeper traveling with an elephant in labor would've been a less-taxing cover. Of course they're my bloody children. What's your second question?"

"Wait, no, that wasn't a question."

"Your voice went up at the end. Two left."

Crap. Was she police or MI6 like Mom or did she work for The Foot? But if Padma *did* work for The Foot, she'd lie, so that would be a wasted question.

Padma checked the mirror. Took a left and merged onto a busy road.

"Why do you want the files and how did you know we had them?" I asked.

"That's two questions. I'll give you another song to think about the wording."

If Lewis was here, he'd manage to morph it into one question. Maybe I should wait until we collected him. But then, both of us would be in the car with Padma, both trapped, not knowing what was going on or who she was. *Think. Think.*

"As a goodwill gesture, and to stop you pulling your hair out, I'll accept that as one question." She reached over and knocked my hand away from my head. "If you keep that up, you'll be bald."

I sat on my hands.

"We've had you under surveillance since you boarded the plane in Calgary. And Clare's always been on our radar."

She glanced at me, then back at the road. "The files belong to the British government, in a roundabout way, but they're of value to a number of other organizations."

"Like the Dutch mafia?"

"Is that a question?"

I shook my head.

We drove in silence for two more songs. All the while, the question of why Mom and Dad had been at the riot kept niggling. I'd never get the photo of Dad holding the baseball bat out of my brain. Why had he done it? Why hadn't Mom stopped him? And if they'd been taken into witness protection, where were the paintings?

The traffic slowed as a bus bullied its way into our lane.

"Do you know why my parents were blamed for the riots?"

Padma checked the mirror, then changed lanes. "The British government wanted to flush out Katrina and thought putting her on the most-wanted list would serve that purpose. Bonkers idea. More uncontrollable variables than you could shake a slimy stick at."

"But my mom worked for MI6. Why would the government want to flush her out?"

She glanced at me. "What else did your mother tell you?"

"She told us absolutely nothing," I said. "She wrote Maggs a letter years ago."

Padma navigated a four-lane roundabout. She did a complete circle and exited on the same road we'd entered.

"Who do you work for?" I asked.

It was question number four, but what was the downside of asking? She wasn't going to shoot me. Not while she was driving. Even if she did work for The Foot.

"How did I get saddled with you?" She sighed. "I work for Interpol, and we've been trying to break up the Dutch mafia for years."

Relief whooshed through my body and escaped in a groan-like exhale. I uncurled my fingers and rubbed my hands on my thighs. Padma was police. She wasn't going to shoot me. Or Lewis.

"I'm surprised that wasn't your first question," she said.

"I thought you'd lie." My head snapped up. "You're not lying, are you?"

"I only lie to criminals and small children."

"Was it you who took Clare?" *Please let Clare be with Interpol.* Padma frowned.

My chest tightened as I dug in my pockets. I held out Clare's phone and car keys. "Someone snatched her from her car while she was waiting for me."

Padma glanced at Clare's phone. "Bollocks. How long ago?"

"Ten minutes before you ran me off the road."

She pressed a button on the dashboard, then told whoever was listening that Clare had been taken from outside the Wallace residence approximately twenty minutes ago.

Interpol would find her. And if not, I had the files, and even though I'd promised to take Queen Mary home to the castle, I'd give up the painting as well if it meant getting Clare back.

"We tailed you to the Wallaces'." Padma glanced at me. "But that road's so bloody quiet my team decided it was safer to station a car at either end. Whoever took Clare can't have gone far. My agents have photos of every vehicle that turned into that street and they'll dust her car for prints before they drop it back at the guesthouse."

I jingled the car keys. "They won't be able to move it."

Padma gave me a look, *Interpol doesn't need keys*, then said, "I'm assuming you've seen what's in the files?"

I shrugged.

"Don't mess around, Cameron."

"A bunch of photos."

"Photos of what?"

"London. The demonstrators, then the riot starting. A guy setting fire to a trash can."

I couldn't tell her about the photo of Dad. Saying it out loud made it real.

"Any documents?" She glanced at me.

"Copies of emails," I said. "Blackmailing and threatening people. And contracts for jobs."

"What kind of jobs?"

I shrugged. "The illegal kind."

She glared at me.

"They didn't include specifics," I said. "Just dates and names. Sometimes a location. Always an agreed sum of money. There were hundreds of them, and I only read a few. Why was the British government after my mom?"

Padma snorted.

"I answered your question about the files," I said. "You owe me one."

Padma tapped her wedding ring on the steering wheel.

Just when I thought she wasn't going to answer, she said, "We don't know why your mother ran. MI6 refused to share that data with us. All we know is, she's considered a traitor."

"What do you mean?" My stomach twisted as Padma's words sunk in.

Mom hadn't turned Dad good. Dad had turned her bad?

"I'm sorry," Padma said.

It was difficult to keep my head up, so I let it slump. The seat belt dug into my neck. Dad had turned Mom into a traitor. I was the son of a criminal and a traitor.

Padma lowered my window. "Don't puke. It'll take ages to get rid of the smell."

We were close to Jamie's house now — cobbled roads and ancient trees. What would Lewis say when I told him that Mom was a traitor, and Clare had been kidnapped, and that I'd let Padma take the files?

"After we get Lewis, where are we going?" My voice sounded far away, like someone else was asking the question.

"Need-to-know basis." Padma pulled up to the Wallaces' front gate, wound down her window and flashed her badge. The gates opened, and we drove down the crunchy driveway.

She parked in front of the house, punched out a text, then unclicked her seat belt. "Unless you're about to puke, stay in the car."

I reached out to stop her. "Don't tell Lewis anything."

I should be the one to tell him I'd ruined everything.

Padma nodded, then strode to the front door.

Lewis had trusted me, and I'd failed him.

———

L E W I S

A car crunched down the driveway. Instead of parking in front of the stables with the others, it stopped in front of the house. A lady with a dark braid jumped out.

"Define 'not very nice,'" Ruby said.

I glanced at the sky. Cameron would be able to spin our story into something that sounded reasonable. I wish I could've run this by him first.

I looked down at Ruby. Without Aisha's headband, her hair was defying gravity. Her blue hair, now frizzing free of the curls, combined with the borrowed strawberry-embroidered shirt made her look like an electrocuted pixie. An irritated, electrocuted pixie.

"He did deals with some shady people," I said. "My dad's boss, not my dad, but my dad was too young to figure it out, and when he did, he left."

"Did your mum know?"

"Not at first, and when she found out, they ran away. And everything was good until Dad's old boss found out where we lived."

Ruby's narrowed eyes sprung wide. "What happened?"

She touched my arm, which I think was supposed to relax me, but instead made me shiver. I glanced down at her fingers with their bitten-down nails and realized I really wanted to hold her hand.

I looked at her concerned face. "We ran away and came here."

"We?" Her fingers dug into my arm. "Your parents came, too? Actually, don't tell me. You shouldn't tell me."

"I want to." I peeled her hand off my arm, then threaded my fingers with hers.

She looked down at our joined hands, then up at me with those sky-blue eyes.

"My name's not Will. It's Lewis," I said. "Please don't hate me."

She rose on her tiptoes and put her free hand flat on my chest. She smelled like chocolate brownie and cherries, and I wondered whether it was her shampoo or her lip gloss. I had a moment of panic because my one and only kiss had been a disaster. I'd just finished chewing a pepperoni sandwich, and our teeth had clashed, and our noses kept getting in the way. But maybe kissing a girl would be different than kissing a boy. Maybe kissing Ruby would be different.

And then Ruby's lips touched mine, and my mind went blank.

CHAPTER
30

CAMERON

I hung my head and arms out the window, touched my fingers against the hot metal of the car. Lewis was going to hate me. Not only had I lost Clare, but I'd also let Padma take the files. Both The Foot and Interpol would soon know where Mom and Dad were hiding.

Music from the garden party drowned out the car radio. I was tempted to turn it up, but there were people next to the pond, and I didn't want to be noticed. I looked again.

Was that Lewis? And Ruby?

Ruby was on her tiptoes, Lewis's arms around her waist. They looked like they were sharing a secret. And then Lewis dipped his head, and there was no mistaking what they were up to.

While I was stealing paintings and letting Clare be kidnapped and finding out Mom was a traitor and feeling guilty about losing the files, my brother was kissing a girl.

A duck flapped its wings and quacked as I swung open the car door. Lewis carried on doing what he was doing. The gravel scrunched under my feet. Lewis was oblivious.

He wasn't anxious or scared or worrying about me.

LEWIS

Ruby's eyes widened as I was yanked backward.

Time slowed.

Then I was slammed to the ground. Was a bullet about to rip through my flesh? A knife?

"Run!" I shouted at Ruby.

I wanted to run, too, but what if they'd already found Cameron? I let out a war cry and lunged. My attacker toppled and thumped to the ground, air whooshing from his lungs with a grunt. Adrenaline shot through me as I scrambled on top of him. I pulled back my arm, ready to slam my fist into his face, but Ruby sprang and grabbed my wrist.

Cameron's face came into focus.

My muscles relaxed. Then I laughed. A manic isn't-the-world-wonderful kind of a laugh.

Cameron was alive. He was safe.

He shoved my chest. "Get off."

I scrambled to my feet. Cameron jumped up, hands clenched at his sides, eyes blazing. He looked like a rodeo bull readying itself to buck its way out of the chute and charge through anyone who dared stand in its way.

"What happened?" My skin prickled with dread.

"Clare's gone." Cameron shoved up in my face. "But don't worry, I'll sort it out, like I always do."

"What do you mean Clare's gone?" My head spun with worst-case scenarios. Had she abandoned us? Been kidnapped? Was she dead?

"What do you care?" His hands uncurled and began to shake. His lips quivered.

I could handle Cameron's anger. It was always brief and could be defused by going for a run or a bike ride, or me thumping him and letting him return the favor. But I didn't know how to handle tears. Cameron never cried.

I grabbed his shoulders and squeezed. "Where's Clare?"

Ruby stepped between us. Looked at me, then Cameron and back at me. Her face crumpled.

"We can explain," I said to Ruby.

"What's going on?" Aisha had arrived, and from the look on her face, we'd completely fooled her, too.

She took another few steps toward us, did the double-take thing that everyone does. It was weird, but I'd actually missed it. Maybe it wasn't a big deal that our secret was out.

"I don't know which one's Will." Ruby sounded like she might cry.

Okay, scratch that. Clearly, it was a big deal. I reached for her hand.

She jerked away. "Were you laughing at us the whole time?"

"No." Did she really think that?

Aisha folded her arms. "Which one of you is Will?"

"We both are," Cameron said.

"You can't both be Will. That's ridiculous. Which one lives at the guesthouse? Which one came to the pub?"

I raised my hand.

"We both live with Maggs." Cameron stepped toward her.

"And we were both at the pub," I said.

Cameron glared at me, then turned back to Aisha. "You

arrived with me, but left with him."

"Unbelievable. Does Maggs know?" Aisha's eyes went wide. "Did you scam her? What did you steal?"

"Maggs knows everything," Cameron said.

I looked at Ruby. "Please let us explain. No one could know who we were."

"You can't tell them," Cameron said.

Aisha stepped between me and Cameron. "Go on."

"They deserve to know the truth," I said to Cameron.

Cameron ducked around Aisha, grabbed my arm and yanked me away. "We're leaving, and the less they know, the better off they'll be."

I jerked out of his hold. "Stop telling me what to do."

Cameron leaned in until our noses were almost touching. "Just because you don't care about anyone other than yourself, doesn't mean I'm going to stand here and let you drag them into this. We got Clare involved, and now she's gone."

"I'm calling Maggs," Aisha said. "Then I'm calling the police."

Cameron spun to face her. "What happened to not jumping to conclusions? What happened to heroes and villains changing, depending on who's telling the story?"

"Tell us a version of this" — she waved her hand between Cameron and me — "that makes you out to be a hero, because I'd love to hear it."

"Forget it," Ruby said. "Can we just leave, please?"

Aisha glared at Cameron, then me. "If I find out either of you stole money from Maggs, I will hunt you down."

Ruby looked at me as if I was dog-dirt on her shoe, then tugged Aisha back to the house. I wanted to chase after her and explain everything until she forgave me, but Cameron was right: while The Foot was after us, it was too dangerous.

My hands curled into fists. "Are you happy now?"

"Get over it." Cameron started to walk away.

I grabbed his arm and twisted him around to face me. "You charge in, tackle me to the ground, ruin everything, tell me Clare's missing, then tell me to 'get over it'? Are you for real? You need to tell me what's going on."

He shoved me. "Clare's missing."

Another shove. "And Mom's a traitor."

I knocked his arm away before he could shove me again. "Use proper sentences, like a normal human being. What happened?"

"Here's a sentence for you — Interpol took the files, and when they find Mom and Dad, they'll be arrested. And The Foot's got Clare, so why don't you go back to your girlfriend, while I try to fix everything, like always."

"You sold out Mom and Dad!" I threw a punch, putting every ounce of my anger behind it. Cameron had given up. But instead of just walking away, he'd made it so I could never find them either.

He dodged, then kicked my legs out from under me. I thumped to the ground, pain shooting through my chest. Before I could catch my breath, Cameron dove on top of me.

I flailed against his weight. Kicked. Threw my arms. But he wouldn't budge.

"I hate you!" I yelled.

His fist connected with my stomach.

I cried out as the air left my lungs and the pain of it hit me. My body wanted to curl in on itself, but Cameron was still pinning me to the ground, his weight adding to the pressure. I was going to throw up.

Then he was gone. His weight lifted as if the wind had taken him. I rolled over and struggled to all fours. Coughed. Then slumped into a kneel, dripping in sweat.

I focused on the grass and the duck poop wedged among the blades, until the nausea subsided.

When I looked up, the woman with the braid had her arm around Cameron's neck, immobilizing rather than strangling. Cameron was holding his hands up in surrender.

"Good effort." The woman released him. "Maybe next time you could entertain the garden party with your antics. Have the orchestra play a tune."

I managed to stand, then brushed grass from my hands. Cameron shot me a look that said this argument wasn't over, then trudged across the driveway to the woman's car.

She turned her attention to me. "And don't expect any sympathy from me. You're as annoying as each other."

English accent, bronze skin, shiny black hair.

"Padma?"

"Give the boy a biscuit. Now get in the car." She strode after Cameron.

I caught up. "Did you find out who Schenk was? Is that what this is about?"

She held open the rear door for me.

I looked at Jamie's house. Ruby was in there. She hated me. Cameron was in the passenger seat, bolt upright. For some reason, he hated me, too.

I knocked on the window. "Cameron, will you just —"

My arm was wrenched back and pinned behind my back. Padma's other hand pressed on my head, pushed down and forced me into the back of the car.

"Cameron …" There were a hundred endings to that sentence: Help me. Or I can't believe you sold out Mom and Dad. Or where's Clare? Or I wish I'd managed to punch you. Or are we about to be shot and cut up into fish food?

"Will you turn that off?" I said. "I can't believe you listen to that crap."

The door slammed me in. I sprang up, pulled on the handle. It was locked.

"Cameron—"

He spun around. "Shut up. Just shut the hell up."

Padma got in, and in one fluid motion she buckled up and started driving. She glanced in the mirror. "Seat belt on. And no bickering."

I leaned between the seats. "I want to know what's going on."

She slammed on the brakes, the car skidded on the gravel, and I jolted forward. "And that is why seat belts were invented. Now, put on the damn seat belt."

I did as I was told. The middle belt, so I could watch both Cameron and Padma's expressions.

We started moving again, and Cameron turned up the music. I expected Padma to object, but she tapped her fingers on the steering wheel and hummed along to a song about tractors and fishing. Really? Who wrote this stuff?

Once we were through the gates, I slackened the seat belt and leaned forward. "Will someone please tell me where we're going?"

Padma looked at Cameron. "You want to fill him in?"

Cameron shook his head.

"I'm taking you to a safe house until we can arrange an extraction," she said. "Should have you out of here by teatime. And I have limited patience with questions, so you only get two more."

"Why are we going to a safe house? Did Visser send you? Do you know where Clare is? And that's all one question; they're subsets of one another."

"Good try."

I punched Cameron's shoulder. "Why are we going to a safe house?"

He shrugged out of my reach.

Padma glanced in the mirror. "I work for Interpol. And you'll be taken wherever's deemed safe."

So, Cameron was telling the truth about Interpol and about Mom and Dad being arrested? This could not be happening. We were so close to finding them.

I kicked the back of Cameron's seat. "Do you even care what happens to Mom and Dad? To Clare?"

He spun around. "Are you kidding me? I'm the one who's been holding all this together, while you've been sneaking around behind my back making friends and kissing girls. You're as big a liar as Mom."

This was unbelievable.

"Don't pretend you went crazy because of Ruby." I jerked forward until my seat belt locked. "*You* messed this up, not me. We held off going to find Mom and Dad because *you* wanted to prove something to Aisha. Clare was with you, and now she's gone. *You're* the one who made friends with an Interpol agent. This is all on you, and you know it. *That's* why you're pissed."

Padma motioned for Cameron to face the front, then glanced at me in the rearview mirror. "In answer to your third question—"

"I haven't asked it yet," I said.

"I made the assumption you'd ask a clever one," she said. "Was I wrong to assume?"

"No." I settled back in the seat.

"We made a deal with your parents. Well, to be fair, they did most of the negotiating," she said. "In return for agreeing to help us bring down the Dutch mafia, we, at some expense to the British taxpayer, have been keeping Clare and your grandparents out of Ryker's clutches."

"Where the heck's Clare, then?" Cameron asked.

I talked over him. "Why didn't you protect Mom and Dad, too?"

Cameron had had his chance, this was my turn — if Interpol had done its job, none of this would've happened.

"I don't suppose you know where your parents are?" Padma said.

I threw my hand into the front. "If you get another question, so do we."

Padma knocked it away. "Behave."

I sank back against the seat.

Padma pulled into an outdoor shopping mall and parked in front of an Italian restaurant. "Hand over your phones."

Cameron held out Clare's phone and his burner phone. The smartphone was in my pocket. It was my only connection with Will's world. With Ruby. I looked at the screen. No new messages. I placed it in Padma's waiting palm and immediately regretted it.

She locked the phones in the glove compartment. "Everyone out."

By the time I got out, Cameron was already following Padma, a square garbage bag clutched to his chest. Well, at least he hadn't lost the painting.

Padma held open the glass door of the restaurant. I'd eaten way too much food at the party to be hungry, but she didn't look like she cared what I thought.

Two of the tables were occupied. A couple sat at one, a bowl of bread between them. A broad-shouldered man hunched over a cup of coffee at another table. Padma strode through the restaurant, pushed through a door — labelled *Staff only* — and led us into the kitchen, which smelled of garlic. Two chefs in grubby aprons were chopping vegetables with sharp knives. They didn't look up. Padma hung the car keys on a hook, took another set, then pushed through another door, and we were back outside.

A white delivery van, with a pizza and a piece of spaghetti dancing on the side, beeped and flashed its lights.

She swung open the van's rear double doors. "In you get."

"There aren't any windows," I said.

"Ten points for observation."

Cameron climbed inside and settled himself on the floor, the painting resting on his lap.

As the doors slammed shut, the light disappeared. The van smelled of ripe cheese and soggy cardboard.

"I'm only playing along because you trust her," I said into the dark. "You'd better be right about this."

The garbage bag rustled, and I imagined Cameron hugging it like a two-dimensional teddy bear. He'd be hating this. Locked up in a small, dark place. Good. He deserved it.

The van rattled to life, the metal floor vibrating under my bum. I should've been scared, or worrying about Mom and Dad and Clare, but all I could think about was Ruby and the way she'd looked at me.

———

CAMERON

The van finally stopped moving. As soon as the doors opened, I shoved the painting at Lewis and stumbled out, then leaned against a concrete pillar. It was painted blue. There were three cigarette butts on the ground. And a blob of gum. I breathed in and out — deep lungfuls. The air smelled of exhaust fumes. My stomach turned over. I rested my forehead on the cool of the concrete and concentrated on counting backward from twenty.

"He's claustrophobic," Lewis said to Padma.

He sounded like he was underwater.

"I gathered that." Padma sounded similar.

"It would've helped if the van had windows," Lewis said. "And if you'd parked on ground level instead of spiraling up the ramp again and again."

"Next time I organize an emergency extraction, I'll bear that in mind."

Twelve, eleven, ten. Breathe in. Breathe out.

"Are you handing us over to someone?" Lewis again.

"Yes, and that's him now."

Car tires crunched to a stop close by.

A hand was laid against my back.

"Come on," Padma said. "You can puke in Visser's car, leather seats."

Three. Two. One. I took one more deep breath, then straightened.

A car door clicked open. Footsteps.

"I'm clear." Visser's voice.

"Clear." Padma.

I managed to turn around, but still needed the pillar to ground me. Visser was dressed the same — blue shirt and dark jeans — but he'd accessorized the outfit with a gun, holstered across his chest.

Lewis was looking at me, a concerned expression on his face, as if he gave a flying crap.

His eyes moved to Padma. "What's Visser doing here?"

Visser opened the back door of his car. "I'll explain when we get to the safe house."

"Give us a minute," Padma said.

Lewis carried the painting to Visser's car and asked where we were being extracted to.

"I really was on mat leave," Padma said to me. "We were in Brighton building sandcastles when I got the call that you were on a flight to London. Your timing was bollocks."

"Sorry." I dug my hands in my pockets. "And thanks for rescuing us from the pub and being here and telling us stuff."

"You're a pain in the arse, you know that?" She sighed. "What else do you want to know? Consider it a bonus round before you bugger off."

"Who's looking after your kids?"

"That's your burning question?"

I shrugged. I didn't want to know anything else about Mom and Dad. They were traitors and criminals. Mom had betrayed her family and her country. Dad was a thief who worked for the Dutch mafia. The gaps had been filled, and the facts fit together enough for me not to want to know more.

"My wife. She's a lawyer, and American, but I forgave her for both when our daughter was born."

"Are you really called Padma Collingwood?"

"Your school records said you had Miss Collingwood as a teacher for two years, so I assumed you'd remember the name. The local police knew to contact us if anyone called asking to speak to Collingwood."

"Yeah, she was nice. She gave out bouncy balls." I looked at her. "Wait a minute. If you knew where we lived, why didn't you protect us?"

"We hacked your school records *after* the deadly barbecue. Until then, we had no idea you were in Canada. We were following Schenk. If we'd known he was on his way to find you, we would've arrived earlier."

"The officers who turned up at the barbecue were Interpol?" No wonder Molly hadn't recognized them.

"We intercepted the 911 calls. Got the place cleaned up and searched before the emergency services arrived." She smiled. "Glad it wasn't me who had to explain that one to the Canadians."

"What about Padma? Is that your real name?"

"As much as Cameron or Daniel or Willem are yours."

"Why is there no record of us in Canada?"

"There's no record of you anywhere," she said.

"So, I don't have a name?"

"A name doesn't change who you are. When Visser gives you a new one, best remember that."

"I'll try," I said, and then I hugged her.

She stiffened, then gave me a quick squeeze.

I stepped back. "Can you check on Aisha and Ruby?"

She nodded. "Now, bugger off."

CHAPTER
31

LEWIS

The safe house was an actual house in a suburb with dingy duplexes and discount carpet stores.

Cameron disappeared upstairs, which suited me fine. Visser told me to keep the blinds closed and stay indoors — the freezer was stocked, and there was a television. Sit tight. Watch movies. Play I Spy.

I slumped against the kitchen counter, its edges swollen and split with age. "Where are you going?"

The whole place smelled moldy, like no one had lived here in years.

Visser tightened the holster of his gun. "To find Clare. No one else seems capable."

The thought of running away while Clare was in danger made my chest ache. We'd lost Mom and Dad, and now Clare.

Visser handed me two blue passports and a cell phone. "In case I'm not back before you leave. I've put my number in there. Text if there's a problem. There's a change of clothes in one of the bedrooms. The extraction team are on their way. Keep that phone on you — I'll call when they get close."

"Will The Foot torture her?"

Visser clapped me on the shoulder. "I'll find her."

"This is our fault," Cameron said from the doorway. "We'll help you look."

Visser barked out a laugh.

Cameron glared at Visser. "We can handle it."

What was he talking about? We'd never even held a gun.

"Two untrained, unarmed, underaged targets in the field. If you try to follow me, I'll save Ryker the effort and shoot you myself."

"You wouldn't shoot us." Cameron folded his arms.

"Try me." Visser started a glaring contest with Cameron.

I cleared my throat. "What happens if Clare gives The Foot the GPS coordinates before you find her?"

Visser turned to me. "Interpol's helicopters should get there first. And if they don't, then Ryker's men find your parents. He'll no longer have any reason to keep Clare or your mother alive. And after he's extracted what he wants from your father, he'll be dead, too."

My legs wobbled. Clare wouldn't give up Mom without a fight. Helicopters were fast. Interpol would get there first. *Please let Interpol get there first.*

"Thanks for sugarcoating it," Cameron said.

"It could've all been prevented had you trusted me with the files yesterday." Visser grabbed his jacket. "If you want to help, do as you're told. Wait for the new team. Then get the hell away from here, so we've got two less people to worry about."

"And what about everyone else?" Cameron said. "Does Maggs get an extraction team? Does Aisha? Ruby?"

"We have them under surveillance."

"And the others?" Cameron said. "The Fisbys. Nora. Brian."

Visser looked confused.

"They're staying at the guesthouse," I said. "But be careful of Professor Pham; we think he's the one who recruited Mom to MI6."

"The old bloke downstairs? How do you know? Forget it, I don't have time for this. I'll pass everything on to Padma." He swung open the door. "Lock up after me."

The back door clicked shut. Apart from the buzzing of the white, dented fridge, the kitchen was silent.

Cameron turned the lock on the back door, slid the deadbolt, fastened the chain.

"Visser left us passports." I held them out.

He snatched the top one.

"Australian. I guess the offer of going back to Canada's off the table." He flicked through until he found the photo page. "Ethan Martin."

I did the same. "I'm Matthew Wilson. But they'll probably give us new ones when we get settled, with the same last name."

"Hopefully not."

He was itching for a fight. He deserved to be thumped for blowing our cover, for letting Padma take the files, for making Ruby hate me. But I was done fighting. It was over. We couldn't go after Mom and Dad. And now, they'd never be able to find *us* either.

I shook my head and elbowed him out the way, then opened the freezer and pulled out a pizza. "I'll make something to eat." Even though I wasn't hungry. Even though I didn't care if Cameron was either, it gave my brain something else to think about.

He shrugged a whatever.

I unpacked the pizza and focused on brushing off ice crystals. "You know, Mom and Dad might not even be on that island. The GPS coordinates might be where they buried the paintings."

Cameron shrugged. "Keep thinking that if it makes you feel better."

I slammed the oven closed on the pizza. "Will you stop? Clare's missing, we're about to be shipped off to the other side of the world, we'll never see Mom and Dad again, and if they *are* on the island waiting for us, then they might die."

Maybe I *should* throw another punch, knock some sense into him.

He threw up his hands. "You're right, we failed Mom and Dad. But you know what — they failed us more. Dad was mafia, Lewis, a criminal. And Mom's a traitor."

This again. "Mom lied to us because she had to."

"Not a traitor to us, Lewis. Mom *betrayed* her *entire* country."

"How?" I folded my arms. "Because unless there's proof, I won't believe it."

Cameron shoved the passport into his back pocket. "I actually don't care anymore. I'm going home."

Really? That made absolutely no sense; he wouldn't make it.

"There's nothing to go back to," I said. "Molly doesn't want either of us back."

"She will when she understands what really happened."

"And what about her big life plans? How will you turning up with Interpol and a bloodthirsty mob boss on your tail help her? Are you that selfish?"

He spun around and stepped into my space. "Me, selfish? I've spent my entire life looking after you."

"It's *you* who needs babysitting." I poked his chest. "You charge into every situation without thinking through the consequences. We should've been on a ferry to the Isle of Mull by now with Clare, but you decided to steal a painting to prove you were a nice guy to a girl who doesn't even know who you are."

He got up in my face. "And whose fault is that?"

"Yours." I shoved him. "Half the time *I* don't even know who you are."

"Says the boy who suddenly likes girls."

"That's what this is about?" Was he for real? "You're mad because I kissed Ruby?"

He jutted his head forward. "You lied."

I threw up my hands. "I asked Hunter out because I liked him. I kissed Ruby for the same reason. How is that lying? How does that hurt you? I think the real reason you're mad is because Ruby likes me more than you. Well, get used to it, because everyone does."

It wasn't true, but I was angry, and Cameron needed to get over feeling sorry for himself. It was Mom and Dad and Clare we should be worrying about.

He shoved me backward. I tripped over a curled-up piece of linoleum and collided with the edge of the countertop. That was it. I was sick of him blaming me for everything. Sick of him messing everything up.

"People only like you because they think you're me." My muscles tensed, ready for a fight. After living in a continual state of fear, it felt good to be angry.

"No one will miss me, then." He unlatched the chain on the back door, slid the bolt, clicked open the lock.

"Maybe if you cared about anyone other than yourself, you'd have friends of your own," I shouted after him.

What I should've said was that he was brave and loyal and cared more about other people than he should. And I loved him. And please don't leave me. But I didn't, and when the door slammed shut behind him, I was alone. Not only alone in the house, but alone in the world.

CHAPTER
32

CAMERON

Visser would find Clare. Padma's team would check on Ruby and Aisha and Maggs. They'd all forget me and move on. And Lewis ... Lewis would panic, then follow me, and if he didn't that was fine. He could go to Australia or stay here and be Willem Murray van der Berg forever. He'd been Will all along anyway. Even though he had his own fake British birth certificate — I never had asked him what name was on it. Who the hell cared? He could have both identities. Be Clare's favorite nephew. Aisha's best friend. Ruby's boyfriend. It all came so easily to him. Kissing Ruby was typical. I couldn't believe I hadn't seen it coming. Liking everyone, everyone liking him back, speaking and acting without inhibitions; that was my brother. Why had I been surprised?

Well, he could carry on being him. I was Cameron Larsen, and I was going home.

I ran to the end of the block, then crossed the road. There were no tourists in this part of town. No tram tracks or taxi ranks, just a constant flow of cars. The sun was hidden behind a thick layer of gray cloud, so I couldn't tell east from west.

Ethan Martin's passport would get me on the plane, and when I got home, I'd figure out the rest. No matter what Lewis thought, I had friends there. And without Lewis, I'd make more. People would see me for me, rather than half of a pair. And Molly wouldn't have to choose between us, especially now Lewis liked girls. When I saw him kiss Ruby, that was the thought that hurt the most. Any girl I ever liked would like Lewis more.

It started raining. Not "drizzle," as Maggs called it, but big, fat globs hammering the sidewalk and bouncing up my legs.

A junction with an even busier street was up ahead. The stoplights changed, and a bus rumbled through the intersection. If I knew which direction Edinburgh airport was, I could catch a bus, but I didn't. If I had a phone, I could call a taxi, but I didn't. I checked the contents of my pockets — Ethan Martin's passport, a ten-pound note, Clare's keys and a dog biscuit. Not enough for a taxi, even if I could find one, never mind a flight home.

I turned right at the junction, because it saved me crossing a road, and kept trudging through the now-horizontal rain. I couldn't wait to get back to Canada. I was going home because I made decisions. I got things done. I didn't ignore consequences — I took risks, which was a whole heap more productive than sitting around worrying. And just because I didn't say every single thought that popped into my brain, didn't mean people didn't know me. Lewis was full of crap.

A dog trotted past. A small dog on a long leash. Its owner walked behind, absorbed with her phone, an umbrella sheltering her from the downpour.

"Excuse me," I said as she approached.

Rain beat down on her umbrella.

"Which part of town is this?" Raindrops rolled into my eyes, and I had to squint to see her face.

She reeled off a street name that meant nothing to me.

"Can you show me on your phone?" I took a step toward her.

She looked at me as if I was about to mug her, mumbled something about her dog, then scuttled away.

I was sick of people looking at me as if I was a horrible person. Ruby and Aisha had done the same, but magnified. Not that I blamed them — I'd lied to them and now I was running away.

Padma would check on them. Aisha had her family, and Ruby had her granddad. She was probably ranting to him now about how Lewis and I had tricked her and how much she hated us. Or maybe it was just me she hated. If Lewis was right, Ruby and Aisha had only ever liked him.

The smell of fresh, warm chips wafted from a café. My stomach grumbled. I could eat, escape the rain for ten minutes, ask the server how to get to the airport. I'd have no money left, but at least I'd have energy to keep going.

A motorbike swerved into the curb, launching a tsunami of gutter water over me. As if this day could get any worse. The driver hopped off and dove inside the café, leaving his helmet on the seat and the key in the ignition.

The key in the ignition.

It was bigger than my dirt bike back home, but a bike was a bike. But this wasn't like stealing the painting; the bike belonged to someone who legally owned it. I glanced in the café, but the window was steamed up. I'd leave it where it could be found. And if the police caught me? I had an Australian passport now — they'd probably escort me to the airport themselves. No downside.

I slung my leg over the bike and turned the key.

———

L E W I S

I clicked the lock on the back door, fastened the chain, threw the deadbolt. Cameron would walk it off, then beg me to let him back in. The first rule of survival is to never split up. Mom and Dad had drummed it into us since we were little.

Cameron would come back.

I checked on the pizza — still frozen.

The phone Visser left was a shiny new smartphone. Interpol didn't mess around. No missed calls.

The kitchen cupboards were almost empty — a stack of mismatched plates, a box of glasses still sealed and a frying pan. Not enough to organize. All that was in the fridge was a loaf of white bread, a carton of orange juice and a single prepacked sandwich. I closed the door. The fridge started to hum.

The phone was silent.

The drawers were better stocked — a collection of cutlery and paper napkins. Wooden spoons. Tongs. I snapped the tips together, thought of barbecues and sausages, of Mom and Dad. We'd been so close to finding them.

I woke up the phone — no missed calls. What if the new team arrived before Cameron came back and forced me to leave without him? Even though I'd told him he had no friends, he'd never leave without me. What insult had he thrown back?

My throat plummeted to my stomach. He hadn't fought back — he'd said no one would miss him.

He wasn't coming back.

I fumbled with the lock, the chain, the bolt, yanked open the door and barrelled outside. The yard was a square of concrete. It was empty. It was raining.

I raced through the gap between the houses, rain hammering down on me, then over the sidewalk and into the road. Car brakes squealed. A horn blasted. I jumped out of the way and ducked behind a parked car, my heart beating in my ears.

The car passed. Its engine faded. I looked both ways, darted to the other side and sprinted the length of the block in one direction, then in the other. No sign of Cameron. Butterflies erupted in my stomach.

Cameron was gone.

Clare was missing.

The Foot might be on his way to kill Mom and Dad.

I sprinted back to the house, now soaking wet and no further forward. I locked the door, slid the deadbolt, attached the chain, checked the phone. *Ring. Come on, hurry up and ring.*

As soon as the new team arrived, we'd go to the airport. Cameron would be there. I'd find him.

The living room consisted of a sagging sofa, a cup-stained coffee table with a stack of tattered magazines and a boxy television set worthy of a museum.

I turned the phone's volume to maximum. Climbed the stairs with it in my hand.

The bathroom was pink. Not only the carpet and the tiles, but also the sink and the toilet and the bath. The first bedroom had a double bed. I pulled the green bedspread straight. Plumped the pillows.

The next bedroom had a set of bunk beds, stripped bare, the mattresses thin and stained. A third bedroom was behind the final door — twin beds, a neat pile of clothes on each.

The pile on the closest bed was topped with a T-shirt with a Highland cow on it. I unfolded it, held it up against me. It smelled of the house — damp and moldy. How long had this safe house been waiting for us?

I threw the phone on the bed — it wouldn't ring if I kept looking at it.

I tilted open the blinds. Parked cars. A man rushing down the sidewalk, pushing a stroller, a little kid stomping in puddles behind him. The world continued without me.

Visser was out searching for Clare. Padma was coordinating Interpol, now racing after Mom and Dad, as well as protecting everyone at the guesthouse. And Cameron was charging through the city trying to make it home because I'd told him he had no friends. Meanwhile, I was sitting in a moldy house waiting to be whisked away from my entire family. Forever.

I had to do something.

Anything.

What would Cameron do? He'd probably race back to the guesthouse for the copy of the files we'd saved onto Maggs's laptop, then trade them along with the Mary painting for Clare.

I yanked off my wet shirt and replaced it with the Highland cow one, shoved Visser's phone in my pocket, ran down the stairs, then unlocked, unchained, unbolted and opened the back door. Raced outside. Turned around and raced back into the kitchen, grabbed the Mary painting, then ran.

CHAPTER
33

C A M E R O N

I abandoned the motorbike in the street in more or less the same spot the taxi had dropped us on our first day here, then waited for a tram to pass before sprinting across the road, my feet slapping through puddles.

Glencairn Crescent was quiet. If Padma's team were here, they were well hidden. The guesthouse was unlocked, and Haggis started barking as soon as I stepped inside. As I opened the dining room door, Haggis barged through, jumped up and licked my face.

"You didn't think I'd leave without saying goodbye, did you, girl?" I ruffled her ears, then offered her the dog biscuit from my pocket, which she gobbled up before following me to the attic.

My bed was how I'd left it, unmade with the quilt hanging off. Lewis's quilt was pulled straight. I picked up the photo of us from the bedside table — Lewis holding out his superhero cape looking back at me. He was probably telling me to do the same. He always assumed I'd be right behind him, that I'd have his back.

I stuffed the photo in my backpack along with the Australian passport and one of the bundles of cash. I left the second bundle for Lewis, in case he decided to stay. Or would he go to Australia and disappear forever? If he did, would he miss me?

I shifted Haggis off Lewis's bed, then lifted the mattress to reveal Daniel Johnston and Thomas Walker's Canadian passports, plus the envelopes that held our British birth certificates. One was Willem Murray van der Berg's. I took out Lewis's — Alexander Murray van der Berg. The birth certificates were fake, but Mom and Dad had still given us the same last name. They'd expected us to stay together. Willem and Alexander. Brothers.

I packed Daniel's passport and Willem's birth certificate.

The look on Lewis's face when I'd said I hoped we wouldn't be brothers in the next location. I didn't mean it. Well, I did at the time. But not really. He knew that, didn't he? Would I ever get the chance to tell him?

I sunk onto my bed, my stomach in knots. What had I done?

We were meant to stay together, no matter what. And Lewis had. He'd come with me to the Calgary police station, even though he knew it was a bad idea. And to Rothesay, even though he was scared. He'd gone to the garden party to help me steal the painting, even though he was desperate to set off to meet Mom and Dad. Every decision I'd made was the wrong one, but Lewis had stuck with me. Then, when it all collapsed, I'd taken it out on him because it was easier than admitting I'd failed at the one thing I was supposed to be good at, the only thing I could do better than Lewis — getting us out of trouble. Seeing him kissing Ruby had tipped me over the edge. Liking girls was the only thing I didn't have to share, and now Lewis had that too. In fact, he had more, because he also liked boys. I knew I wasn't being rational, or fair. It wasn't Lewis's fault.

And to top it all off, I'd broken my promise to Dad. It had been the last thing he'd asked me to do — *look after your brother.*

The bell above the front door jangled. Haggis barked. I rubbed at the knot in my chest, then crouched to stroke Haggis, whispered in her ear that we didn't have time to speak to anyone. I needed to get back to Lewis before he was carted off to Australia.

"Is anyone home?" Ruby's voice.

"Look after her," I said to Haggis.

She barked, then bounded downstairs to greet Ruby.

I grabbed Lewis's birth certificate and passport and cash, and shoved them into my backpack. We each had three identities now. We could go anywhere. I hitched the backpack onto my shoulder. Ruby would eventually go to her room. Then I'd go back for Lewis.

Ruby banged around downstairs. Padma's team was meant to be watching her. Where the heck were they? Did Ruby even know she was in danger?

"Will?" she called. "I know you're home. Can we talk?"

If she kept shouting, the whole city would know where to find her.

I'd warn Ruby, then go get Lewis.

I ran downstairs.

The hallway was empty.

"Which one are you?" Ruby stepped out of the dining room, making me jump.

I let out a breath. "Look, I'm sorry about everything. But you shouldn't be here alone."

"Your brother called." Her lips twitched, holding back anger or tears or some other emotion she didn't want to share. "He wanted me to give you a message."

Lewis was trying to find me? The knot in my chest loosened.

"He's waiting for you," Ruby said. "At the beach."

I frowned. "What's he doing there?"

"Town's mobbed. And with the rain, the beach will be empty."

Was he planning on stealing a boat and *sailing* to the Isle of Mull? Based on how well I'd messed everything up, whatever plan Lewis had, it was bound to be better than mine.

Haggis padded back through from the kitchen with the leash in her mouth.

I patted her head. "Not now, girl. I need to find Lewis."

Ruby gestured to Haggis. "I'll take Haggis for a walk and show you."

"You should stay here," I said. "I'll find him."

"He's at Birnie Rocks. You know where that is?"

I clipped on Haggis's leash and handed it to Ruby. "No, but I'm hoping you do."

Outside, Ruby stood on the sidewalk holding on to Haggis, while I raced the length of the block looking for where Padma's team had left Clare's car.

"The bus would be quicker," Ruby yelled. "And legal."

Maybe she was right. My luck with stealing vehicles would eventually run out, and I couldn't risk being pulled over this time.

The bus was packed. Ruby squeezed onto the last empty seat. I stood in the aisle with Haggis, her leash wound around my hand, one leg either side of her squirming body to prevent her greeting everyone onboard. Damp passengers steamed up the windows.

After six stops, the seat next to Ruby freed up. I sank down next to her, sliding my backpack off my shoulder and shuffling Haggis between my feet.

"I'm sorry." I looked at Ruby for a reaction, but she was staring out of a patch of window she'd wiped clean, her earbuds blocking any conversation.

When the bus stopped at the beach, we were the only ones to get off. I unclipped Haggis's leash, and she raced ahead of us on the wet sand. The rain had stopped but clouds still hung low. The beach was deserted.

"Where exactly did Lewis say to meet?"

She shook her head, her blue hair frizzed from the rain. "All he said was Birnie Rocks."

"What else did he say?"

She looked up at the cliffs rather than at me. "That's all he said — to find you, then meet him out here. Then he hung up. He wasn't making much sense."

"He rarely does."

The clouds were so low they touched the sea. *That would be fog,* Lewis would say. Was he bobbing in a boat off the shore searching for me?

"Lewis!" I shouted.

"Is Lewis his real name?" Ruby asked.

"It's what I call him." Did that make it real?

My backpack was damp against my back. I slipped one arm out of the strap and let it dangle at my side.

"I still can't tell you apart," she said.

"I'm Cameron."

She stuffed her hands in her pockets. "Doesn't help."

"I toured the castle with you. And it was me in Padma's car." I glanced to check her reaction. "You waited at the window for me."

She bit her lip. "The determined one."

I laughed. "Back home, I was the cool one."

"Sometimes you don't get a choice," she said. "You have to be whoever you need to be to survive."

"Not everything was a lie," I said. "And I am sorry. I know Lewis is, too."

She kicked a rock. It flew into the water with a *plop*.

We'd lied to her, and yet she was roaming the beach in search of Lewis, who was running around looking for me. The more time she spent with us, the more danger she'd be in.

"Go back, Ruby." I stopped walking. "You've done enough. I'll find Lewis. Or he'll find me. Go back to the guesthouse and stay there until your granddad gets back. Please."

I faced the ocean. "Lewis!"

"What about Clare?" Ruby stood beside me.

"Padma will find Clare. There's nothing we can do."

"What if we could?" she asked.

"We can't," I said. "I've got nothing left to bargain with."

"I know about the files. I helped Lewis open them."

I picked up a piece of driftwood and threw it for Haggis. She bounded after it into the water.

"You don't know who you're dealing with," I said. "We should've told you, but it's not too late to save yourself. Go back to the guesthouse. Pretend you never met us."

The fog swallowed Haggis. I called her back. As she bounded up the beach toward us, an engine whirred. A boat? Was it Lewis?

"Tell me again exactly what my brother said. Word for word."

"Answer my question first." She stepped in front of me, and for the first time since I'd met her, she held my gaze. "Would you hand over the files if they gave you Clare and promised to leave you and your brother alone?"

Would I swap Clare's safety for Mom and Dad's? And if we could negotiate some sort of bargain, then Lewis and I would be safe, too. We could go home.

"Would you?" she said.

"I don't know. Maybe. But it doesn't matter. That's not how these people work."

Ruby's phone rang. She switched it off. "I'm sorry."

"What if that was Lewis? Try calling back."

She was looking into the fog. Could she see him?

The whining of the motor was getting louder. And shining out from the fog were headlights.

"I'm sorry." Finally, she looked at me. "Please, give them the files, and they'll let you go."

CHAPTER
34

L E W I S

When the taxi driver asked where I was from, I mumbled "Australia" and to please drive faster. I was hurtling toward the guesthouse clutching a stolen painting and agonizing over which family member I should try to save. Visser said he'd find Clare, but he'd probably shoot his way in, whereas I had incriminating files and a valuable painting to trade. There was no way I could reach Mom and Dad before Interpol's helicopters, but if I could warn them, they could escape arrest. Cameron would've hatched a crazy plan for both rescue attempts by now, but he was either on his way to the airport or jumping on a train, and I had no way of contacting him. Accepting I had to do this alone didn't make it any less scary.

I had a clump of clammy money in my pocket. Every time the meter clicked, I recounted the notes and coins — 18 pounds and 25 pence.

The meter hit 16 pounds as the tram stop came into view.

"Stop here." I thrust all the money through the gap in the divider, wriggled out of the taxi, the painting hugged against my chest, then shouted a thank you as I slammed the door shut with my bum.

As soon as the stoplights changed, I raced across the street, dodging puddles and umbrellas, clutching the painting tighter as the garbage bag became slick with rain. The guesthouse was empty when I got there, which was good. I couldn't face Ruby right now. I left the painting on the reception desk while I retrieved the laptop from the kitchen. With the laptop under one arm, I tried to lift the painting, almost dropped both and decided it would be quicker to do two trips.

When I got to the attic, I propped the painting against the bed and tore off the garbage bag. Queen Mary was damp, but intact.

"Sorry about that." I wiped a drip off her nose.

Outside, a car door squeaked open, then rattled shut. I jumped up, expecting to see Padma or Visser. Instead, it was Jamie Wallace. Aisha emerged from the passenger door, her mom's flowery platter above her head, sheltering from the rain. Ruby would be next. She deserved a massive apology, but I had people to save.

I thundered downstairs, snatched the laptop and was three double-step lunges back up the stairs when the bell above the front door jangled.

"Will, mate," Jamie said. "I heard about the kerfuffle."

I hugged the laptop and slowly turned around. Jamie was still in his garden party outfit, his ironed shirt now crumpled, chocolate handprints on the shoulders.

"I'm in no position to take the moral high ground," he continued. "I knew the Queen Mary wasn't legally ours, no matter how many ways my mother found to justify it. I'm assuming it was you who took it."

"I didn't take anything." I said it too fast to sound genuine.

Aisha squeezed past Jamie, who was filling the doorway. "Oh, it's you."

I waited for Ruby to follow. Apologies and awkwardness aside, she needed to know she couldn't tell anyone about the existence of the files. In fact, it would be safer for her if she pretended not to know me.

Jamie turned and closed the door.

"I thought Ruby would be with you," I said.

"And I thought you were a decent human being." Aisha plonked the platter on the reception desk.

There wasn't much I could say to that, so I continued up the stairs. I'd write Ruby a note; it would be quicker and easier all around.

"Will, wait," Jamie said. "I was hoping we could help each other."

"Lewis." I turned around. "My name's Lewis. And I didn't steal your painting. My brother stole it for Aisha, so she could return it to the castle."

I looked at her. "He did it for you. And I know you hate me, but can you please look after Ruby? She might be in danger."

"Rubbish," Aisha said.

I didn't have time to ask which bit of my confession she didn't believe. I was at the top of the first flight of stairs before she said anything else.

"Why would Ruby be in danger?" Aisha yelled up.

When I didn't answer, she ran upstairs, her clunky shoes thumping against the cookie-dough carpet.

"Will," she said.

"It's Lewis." I turned to face her. "And Ruby knows that my mom sent me some files. If they find out, they'll think Ruby knows more than she does."

"That's cryptic." Jamie appeared at the top of the stairs.

"Who are *they*, precisely?" Aisha asked, her head tilted.

"Evil people who think we have something they want."

"And do you?" Aisha said. "Is that why you pretended to be one person? To hide from nasty people?"

"Yes, and when you see Ruby, can you tell her?" I had every intention of going straight back to the attic, but when I reached Ruby's room I stopped.

"Ruby?" I said as I opened her door.

Either Ruby was messier than Cameron or her room had been searched.

"What is it?" Aisha said to me. "Why do you look like you've just been stabbed?"

Jamie came up behind her. "Is Ruby meant to be here?"

"She left the party ages ago." The color drained from Aisha's face.

My heart thumped against the laptop, which I was clutching against my chest like a security blanket. If The Foot had taken Ruby, too, then it made the decision of who to save easier. Mom and Dad were about to be arrested, but Clare and now Ruby were in mortal danger.

"What are we looking for?" Aisha shifted clothes off the desk. "Will, I mean, Lewis, tell us what to look for."

"I don't know. A ransom note, maybe? Or her phone? Anything that might help us figure out if she wandered off on her own or was kidnapped."

Jamie rifled through the books and magazines and clothes strewn over the floor.

Aisha pulled out her phone. "I'll call her."

I held my breath, waiting to hear Ruby's phone ring from under a shirt or a sweater.

Silence.

"Straight to voice mail," Aisha said.

Ruby's shabby suitcase was under the window. I dodged around Jamie, who was now wriggling his way under the bed, and snapped open the suitcase. It contained a pair of socks, a hair tie and the Cirque Berserk ticket.

"Where's your room?" Aisha said. "Maybe she left you a note."

Good thinking. "Attic."

Aisha raced into the hallway. I grabbed the laptop and followed her up the attic stairs.

"Oh," she said as she walked into our room. "The painting."

"Cameron really did steal it for you," I said. "I told him not to, but he wouldn't listen."

As she crouched down to look at it, I noticed one of the dresser drawers was open. And my quilt was rumpled. Had our room been searched, too?

I strode to the dresser and looked in the open drawer.

The rolls of cash were gone. I dove for the bed, lifted my mattress — the passports and birth certificates had also been taken.

Either The Foot had been here, or Cameron had calmed down enough to come back. What if he'd calmed down enough to return to the safe house? My lungs constricted. He'd think I'd left with the extraction team and abandoned him. Cameron always expected people to love him less than he loved them.

I grabbed the laptop and ran for the door.

"What is it?" Aisha said. "Did you find something?"

"I have to go," I said. "If you see Cameron, tell him I'm looking for him and not to leave until I get back."

"What about Ruby?"

"I need my brother." I took a steadying breath. "I'm sorry, but Clare's gone and now Ruby, and if Cameron thinks I've left without him, then he'll leave, too, and I need him. I can't do any of this without Cameron. I have to find him."

"You need to see this!" Jamie shouted from downstairs.

Aisha jumped up, and we both charged back to Ruby's room.

"Chuffing hell," Aisha said as she walked inside. "Who took those?"

I stopped in my tracks. The rug was pulled back, and underneath, laid out on the carpet, were photographs of me and Cameron.

Jamie looked at me. "Did you know she was spying on you?"

I stumbled into the room and stared at the photos — me racing through Paddington station looking terrified. Cameron walking the dog. Me ringing Professor Pham's doorbell.

Aisha sat beside me. "But if Ruby knew you were two people, why was she so upset?"

"There aren't any photos of both of them together," Jamie said. "Maybe she didn't know."

"Why does she even have them?" Aisha searched my face.

I had no idea. Maybe Padma recruited Ruby without telling us, or Nora was onto us or the professor. There was another option, of course, but the thought of Ruby working for The Foot was too unlikely. And disturbing.

"We'd be more useful if we knew what was going on," Jamie said. "And no judgment. It can't be worse than owning stolen art."

It was a million times worse, but I couldn't do this on my own.

"First, I need you to promise you'll wait here in case Cameron comes back."

Aisha frowned. "Why wouldn't we?"

I looked at Jamie.

He nodded. "You have my word."

It came out in one long sentence without commas — the deadly barbecue, fleeing to Edinburgh, finding out Dad was on the run from a Dutch mobster and Mom was a British spy, that they wound up in the Tate gallery art theft and now had half the paintings, as well as evidence against The Foot, which was on the files Ruby helped us open. And that Clare was our aunt. And she was missing. And Visser wasn't really a guest. By the end, I was sweating.

"Blimey." Jamie blew out a breath. "And I thought my parents were negligent."

"You think this mobster bloke has Ruby?" Aisha said.

I looked at the photos. "I really hope not."

"I'll help you find Ruby *and* the paintings," Jamie said to me.

Ruby I could understand. "Why the paintings?"

"I want you to turn them over to the police," he said. "Along with the Queen Mary."

Aisha shot him a look. "And your parents get off?"

"Aye, they do. And, hopefully, so do Lewis's."

Aisha stood. "Being an ancient, rich family doesn't make you above the law. Justice doesn't have a sell-by date. Art theft's a crime."

"I'm not doing it for my parents. I'm doing it for my sisters." Jamie looked at me. "What's in the files?"

I glanced at the laptop. "Photos and documents."

Aisha folded her arms.

"Proof against The Foot." I cleared my throat. "And photos of the riot."

"Of the art gallery during the riot?" Jamie asked.

"The riot itself." I hugged the laptop. "The suspected terrorists."

His eyebrows pulled together. "What's the riot got to do with the art theft and the Dutch mobster and your parents?"

I took a breath. "The mob were behind the art theft. They started the riots to distract the police."

"Wow." Jamie rubbed the back of his neck.

"Oh, this gets better and better," Aisha said. "Your parents started the riots?"

"No," I said, even though Cameron was convinced they had.

The bell above the front door jangled. The dog barked, bounded upstairs, then raced into the room, skidding on the photos and smelling of seaweed. I grabbed her collar.

"You have no right!" Ruby flew into the room. "Get out!"

CHAPTER
35

LEWIS

Aisha jumped up and threw her arms around Ruby. "We thought you'd been kidnapped! I texted and phoned."

Ruby untangled herself from Aisha. "I'm fine. Can you please just leave?"

"Why do you have those?" I pointed at the photos.

Ruby darted around Jamie, dove for the photos and frantically gathered them up. "You're criminals," she said. "Both of you. And your parents."

"Who told you that? Padma? Professor Pham?" My hands curled into fists. "The Foot?"

Ruby, now kneeling, began to tear the photos into pieces.

"Where's Clare?" I said.

Aisha glared at me, then knelt beside Ruby and rubbed her back as if she was trying to settle a spooked horse.

I really wanted to yell at Ruby, and keep yelling until she told us everything, but the more I upset her, the less likely she'd want to help us, so I crouched in the doorway stroking the dog Cameron loved so much.

Eventually, Ruby stopped ripping the photos and slumped against Aisha.

Right about now is when Cameron would tell me to stop stalling and get on with it.

I continued to wait. For Ruby to stop crying. For Aisha to find tissues. For Ruby to blow her nose. Once. Twice. Three times.

"My granddad's a good person." Ruby looked at me, her eyes puffy. "He won't hurt her. He promised."

The air whooshed out of my lungs. *Brian* had Clare.

I fumbled for Interpol's phone. I had to call Visser before he started a shootout with the mafia.

"Your grandfather's the mob boss?" Jamie said.

"No!" Ruby said. "He's good."

"Other than kidnapping and spying on people," I said.

Jamie added, "Loving your grandfather doesn't make him good."

"Unfortunately, they're right." Aisha handed Ruby another tissue.

Visser's phone went to voice mail. I disconnected and texted him that Ruby's granddad had kidnapped Clare.

"He promised he wouldn't hurt them," Ruby said.

My head shot up.

I looked at Ruby, who was still clutching shreds of Cameron and me. "What did you say?"

"He won't hurt them," she said again, but with less conviction.

"Them?" Jamie asked.

I looked at Jamie. I needed him to ask the next question, too.

"Who else does your granddad have?" he said.

I glared at Ruby. *Please don't say Visser.* Who would rescue Clare if Visser was tied up, too?

"Will," Ruby said. "He has Clare *and* the other Will."

"You're lying." Cameron was on his way back to the safe house or at the airport. Or on a train to London. Wherever he was, he was safe.

But I could tell from Ruby's face. The way she wouldn't look at me. The way she bit the corner of her lip. She was telling the truth.

Aisha stood. "Why did he take them?"

I struggled for control, swallowing against the lump in my throat. *People wage war because of revenge*, that's what Ruby had said at the castle. Did Ruby's mother die in the riots? Brian thought my parents had killed his daughter, so he was going to kill their son?

My legs were too wobbly to hold me up.

Jamie slapped my back. "Lewis, big man, don't faint on us."

I looked at Ruby. "Did your mom die in the riots?"

Please don't say yes.

Ruby shook her head.

"Of course her mum didn't die in the riots," Aisha said. "That was seventeen years ago and she's *fifteen*."

Good, that was good. I needed to calm down. What would Cameron do next?

"Ruby, it's not your fault," Aisha said. "No matter what you wish you'd said or done to stop him, at the end of the day it was your grandfather's decision."

If Ruby had stood by and done nothing, then it absolutely was her fault. My stomach dropped. Did Ruby already know that Brian had kidnapped Clare when she kissed me? Would I have been their next target if Cameron hadn't charged in? And now Brian had taken Cameron instead of me.

"He told me to ask Will all these questions." Ruby wiped her nose with the back of her hand. "I kept refusing to help him. But then I was so angry at the party and my granddad's the only person I've got and ..."

Aisha squeezed Ruby's shoulder.

"So, you knew all along?" I stepped closer to Ruby.

Aisha glared at me.

"Mate." Jamie put his hand on my back. "I'd let Aisha handle this."

Aisha helped Ruby stand, then said, "You love your grandad, I understand that, believe me I do, but he's done something dreadful, and you can't let your life fall apart with his."

"What do *you* know about lives falling apart?"

Aisha crossed her arms, then uncrossed them, then smoothed down her headscarf.

"My big brother got into a fight at a football match," she finally said.

Ruby straightened. "What happened?"

I opened my mouth to say we didn't have time for stories, but Jamie squeezed my shoulder and shook his head.

"He didn't start it, but he didn't walk away either," Aisha said. "And he had a knife with him."

Jamie's hand slipped from my shoulder. Ruby took a step toward Aisha. I held my breath for what came next.

"He's in prison." Aisha unfolded her arms and looked at her hands. "Some days I'm so cross with him, I go into his room and break things."

If Cameron ended up in prison and left me, I'd be angry enough to smash his stuff, too.

Aisha came to her senses and looked up from her hands. "Stop looking at me. This isn't about me."

We all kept staring.

Aisha threw up her arms. "Stop."

"My granddad took them to the underground vaults," Ruby said.

———

CAMERON

They'd removed the blindfold, but I still couldn't see. It was just darkness, and my heartbeat, and the fear of what would come next.

Plastic cable ties cut into my wrists. My ankles were strapped to the chair legs with something else. Rope? I put pressure on the balls of my feet. The floor was hard, but uneven. Rock or compact earth. I strained my ears to hear above the hammering of my heart, but the *whoosh* of my breathing took over. *Calm down. Get a grip.* I counted to three between each breath. Then five. After I managed to reach ten, I allowed myself to think.

I had to work out what this place was, then find a way out.

I'd been thrown around for what felt like an eternity, but was probably five minutes, ten tops. There'd been no rumble of cobblestones. No stop-start of traffic. The car had bounced around, and I'd banged my head on something sharp, probably the bolt for a spare tire. And I'd vomited. The bacon sandwich I'd wolfed down before heading to Jamie's, which now felt like forever ago.

The smell of it clung to me. I dropped my head backward, and beyond my bubble of vomit grossness, the air smelled damp, like wet stone.

Darkness.

Rock.

Wet stone.

I was underground!

My heart rocketed. I sucked in a gulp of air, then breathed in again, but there wasn't enough oxygen. I inhaled, again and again, great lungfuls, faster and faster. Lewis was on his way to a new life thinking I'd abandoned him. No one knew I was here.

My breathing spiraled out of control, whooshing in my ears like the ocean. The room started to spin. I counted. It didn't help. I couldn't get enough air.

Footsteps. *Please help me.* I tried to shout.

"Calm down, Will."

Brian?

Brian had come to save me! He would get me out of here, take me outside. I would be free. I forced my eyes open and squinted against a spotlight, which was pointed square in my face.

"Good lad," he said. "All I want are the files. Tell me where they are, and I'll let you go."

What? No. It was a joke. Ruby had sold me out to The Foot or Professor Pham. Not Brian. Brian was everyone's friend. Brian would never hurt me.

I tried to ask him if he had Clare, but all that came out was a rasp.

"Get him some water," Brian said to the shadows.

Movement behind me. Cold metal clashed against my teeth. I jerked my head away.

"Take the water, Will."

Water. It was only water. It seeped into my dry mouth, ran down my burning throat. I gulped. Tilted the cup with my chin to get more.

"Easy," Brian said. "Don't want you puking again."

The cup disappeared. I hung my head and willed my churning stomach to hold on to the water. *Don't throw up. Don't throw up.* I breathed. *Twenty, nineteen, eighteen ...*

"I have some questions," Brian said.

I squinted against the light, still struggling to reconcile Brian the enthusiastic tourist with this version of him. The version who worked for a mobster. Who used his granddaughter as bait.

"Can we turn that thing down?" Brian said to the cup bearer.

I sniffed the air. Was it the same sweaty tough guy who'd clamped his hand over my mouth while I'd begged Ruby for help? Or were there three of them? More?

The light was dragged back until it was behind Brian. He looked the same as he always did: clean-shaven, chino shorts, button-down shirt, socks with sandals.

"What do you want?" My voice was thin.

"What do I want?" Brian snorted a laugh. "No one's asked me that in a very long time."

He dragged a stool until it was facing mine, then sat. "What I want, Will, is to bring your mother to justice. What I want is to take my granddaughter and leave this putrid city to the tourists. What I want is to retire gracefully with a set of gold cufflinks and a pat on the back. And you can help with all those things. The files, Will? I know you have them. Ruby told me."

Lying, traitorous Ruby. She'd led me into his trap, then held Haggis back while I tried to struggle free. I added her to the list of everyone who'd lied to me — Mom, Dad, Brian, Ruby. Visser? Probably. Padma? I sure as hell hoped not, but I convinced myself she'd sold me out, too. Better to be angry than scared; it was the trick I always used on Lewis.

I shook my head — no, I didn't know where the files were. No, I wouldn't help him. No, I didn't want to be here anymore.

The smack across my face was sharp and echoed off the rock.

Brian crouched over me. Placed his hands over mine. Pressed down. I prepared for another attack — back straight, muscles clenched, a "go-ahead" expression.

His face came close. I could feel his breath. Smell stale coffee. I struggled against the ties.

He placed his palm gently against my cheek.

It felt more menacing than the slap. Another wave of nausea gripped my stomach.

"You really thought you could hide by pretending to be one person? Did your mother teach you anything?" He laughed through his nose. "Which one are you, then, the right-handed one with not much to say, or the lefty with the nervous chitchat?"

Mom's voice floated through my brain — *Stick as close to the truth as you can. The foundation of lies is reality.* It had been her advice whenever we played the deception game on camping trips.

"My brother and I fought," I said.

"I heard."

"He was the one who opened the files. And now he's gone."

And Brian would never get his hands on him.

"Where did he go?"

On a plane to Australia. "You'll never find him."

Brian patted me on the head as if I were a dog or a small child. "Let's see if your aunt corroborates your story."

Then he turned to the shadows. "Bring out the woman."

Clare was here?

Lewis was right — I *was* selfish, because instead of being worried about Clare, all I felt was relief that someone else was with me in this underground prison.

L E W I S

Jamie's car was an old Land Rover with rusted wheel arches and hyperactive windshield wipers.

"How old *is* this car?" The seat belt sagged in my lap. A buckle adjusted the length, but the seat belt fabric had fused to the metal clasp.

Ruby was in the back with me, curled up against the door, staring at her phone, her seat belt hanging off her shoulder.

"She's way older than any of us," Jamie said.

She was the car. With bare metal doors, worn, sagging seats and old-fashioned dials on the scuffed dashboard.

"She was my gran's." He patted the dashboard. "I know you'd rather be grouse-hunting, but we need you to get us to the vaults. Matter of life and death."

"He's talking to the car," Aisha said. "You get used to it."

"Maybe we should get a taxi." My muscles were screaming at me to be in motion. Cameron and Clare were being held underground by a mobster or a madman, Ruby still hadn't explained which, and meanwhile, I was in a parked car that may or may not be capable of making it to the end of the street. If I'd been kidnapped, Cameron would've leaped into action by now.

Aisha, who was in the passenger seat next to Jamie, twisted round to look at me. "A taxi won't help if we don't know where we're going — we need to know which entrance."

I clutched the laptop. I'd wanted to bring the painting as well as the files, but Aisha had pointed out that running through the castle with the Queen Mary painting was probably a bad idea. Even if it was covered in a garbage bag.

Rain pitter-pattered on the roof.

The windows steamed up.

Jamie cranked down the window with the manual winder. It jammed halfway down.

"Can we at least start driving in the general direction?" I said.

"We'll be stumbling around in the dark for hours if we go into the wrong tunnel," Jamie said.

Hours! We didn't have hours.

I turned to Ruby, who was still staring at her phone. "Which entrance did they use?"

"Ruby," Aisha said in a gentler tone. "The sooner we find them, the less trouble your grandfather will be in."

I opened my mouth to argue with her logic. Guilt wasn't a radioactive isotope that diminished with time.

Ruby held out her phone to Aisha. "You follow the dot."

"How?" I asked.

"I slipped a tracker into your brother's backpack. You gave me the idea when you were joking about Jamie losing his socks." She continued looking at Aisha, even though she was clearly talking to me. "No one noticed. They were busy with something else."

Busy with what? Tying up Cameron? Whacking him over the head with a two-by-four? I clenched my hands. I would find him in time.

"You're amazing," Aisha said.

"She helped kidnap my brother." And kissed me while she was plotting it all.

"And now she's helping rescue him. I thought you believed in second chances." Aisha twisted back to the front, her eyes on Ruby's phone and the dot that may or may not be in the same crumbling tunnel as Cameron.

Jamie turned the keys in the ignition. It took a few tries before the engine caught and the car shuddered to life. "Where to?"

"Looks like they're under the Royal Mile," Aisha said. "The Smugglers' Labyrinth doesn't open for another couple of hours, so that entrance is out."

"We can break in," I said.

"If you want the police involved, that's a brilliant idea," Aisha said. "I'm sure they'd love to hear about the stolen paintings and all your criminal relations. Maybe we could ask them to bring their battering ram for the metal door to the vaults."

"I think there might be an entrance on the beach," Ruby said. "In the cliffs."

Jamie shook his head. "Too dangerous. That tunnel gets flooded at high tide. We'd be better using the castle entrance."

"Your information's five hundred years out of date," Aisha said. "The castle's tunnel entrance was blocked when David's Tower collapsed."

Jamie crunched gears, and finally we were moving.

"I've been in those tunnels," he said. "I've seen the castle's entrance. It exists."

"How?" Aisha said. "When all the historians and archaeologists and every single expert on the subject agree the castle entrance is buried under a zillion tonnes of rock?"

"Because I'm from an ancient, rich family." Jamie glanced at Aisha. "And we might not be above the law now, but up until the last century we were. How do you think we got rich in the first place?"

"I don't want to know," Aisha said.

He nodded. "We used the tunnels."

"And you're sure we can get to them through the castle?" I asked, because we didn't have time to wander about dungeons searching for a mythical entrance.

"Yes," Jamie said at the same time Aisha said, "No."

CHAPTER
36

CAMERON

Two sets of footsteps. A scuffle and a yelp. I squinted to try to see beyond the light.

"No!" Clare's voice was strangled. "Is he hurt? Did you hurt him? Cameron, are you all right?"

I tried to smile. To show her I was okay. To say thank you for not mixing me up with Lewis. For knowing I was me.

She was being held back by the guy who'd manhandled me into the car. His face was in shadow, but it was him — his hand was bandaged where I'd bitten it.

Clare looked up at him. "Are you going to stand there like a Muppet and let him do this to a child?"

When he didn't answer, she threw her head back against his chest. The air left his lungs with a *humph*, but he didn't let go of her. Clare groaned in pain, then growled in frustration.

"He's bluffing, Clare." I hoped he was. Hoped Brian would switch back to Ruby's helpful granddad.

Brian nodded for his mafia buddy to let go of Clare, then sauntered over to her. "Maybe now, you're ready to tell me where the files are."

Clare straightened her shoulders. "Go boil your head."

Brian kicked Clare's feet from under her. She crashed to the ground, her cry of shock morphing into one of pain. *No!*

I struggled against the plastic ties. "Ruby knows the password. She helped my brother figure it out."

That got Brian's attention.

"Whoops," I said. "Didn't she tell you?"

"Do you ever tell the truth?" Brian said.

Truth? Mom had said something about truth the day of the barbecue. I dug in my brain, trying to grasp hold of it, but it disappeared.

With her wrists bound behind her back, Clare struggled to push herself off the ground. Brian made no move to help. Nor did the dude with the bandaged hand.

Clare managed to get to her knees, then paused, breathing hard. My eyes were on Clare, willing her to stand and show these dirtbags how strong she was.

Brian grabbed my face and squeezed. "Give me the files, and I let her go."

Would I give up Mom and Dad to save Clare? To save myself? Dad always said to never risk more than what was at stake. Was Clare's life really at stake? Was mine? How dangerous could someone who wore socks with sandals actually be? *Not dangerous enough to be lethal*, I told myself.

I squared my shoulders. "Interpol has the files. They're probably on their way here right now."

Would Padma waste time saving us now that she had the files? Even if she did care enough to rescue us, she thought I was still at the safe house. The only person who might come for us was Visser, but he'd worked for The Foot once and maybe he'd switched sides again.

Brian's fist slammed into my face, snapping my head back and setting off an explosion of pain.

I blinked away tears. Sniffed the snot back up my nose. Tried to ignore the throbbing in my head and the shock settling into my bones.

This was the true version of Brian, and the socks with the sandals and the cheery banter were the lie. Did Ruby know? Of course she knew. She'd delivered me to him.

"How very brave," Clare said. "Beating up a bound child. What's your next trick? Stealing teddy bears from toddlers?"

Brian crouched down to Clare's eye level. "Katrina ruined your life like she ruined mine, so why are you protecting her? Tell me where the files are, and I'll untie your nephew, then drive you both back to the guesthouse myself."

Clare glanced at me. I met her eyes. Was she considering telling him about the GPS coordinates on the Isle of Mull? Should I let her? What would happen to Mom and Dad if I did?

"Here's the thing, Brian," she said. "May I call you Brian?"

He nodded.

"I think you're a small-minded man with an incredibly damaged idea of normal behavior, so while your offer is tempting, I'm going to need you to actually deliver us both unharmed to the guesthouse before I give you anything more than a knee in the nuts."

Brian grabbed Clare by the hair. "You're just like her. So smug. So *naive*."

"How did my mom ruin your life?" I said to distract Brian from hurting Clare.

And then I realized Brian hadn't mentioned Dad yet. Only Mom. He wanted to bring Mom to justice. It was Mom who'd ruined his life. Clare was just like Mom. But Mom didn't work for The Foot. Dad did. Or had Padma and Visser lied?

I had no idea who was bad and who was good anymore, who wanted us dead, who wanted to save us. *Trust your gut, Cameron. When something seems off, always trust your gut.* It's what Dad had said last weekend when I'd asked him why he'd swapped his shift and stayed home.

"You're MI6." I said it like it was a fact, like I knew exactly who he was.

"Don't tell me you mistook me for a mobster?" Brian clutched his chest dramatically. "You wound me."

"You're a government agent?" Clare looked from Brian to the shadow of the man behind her.

Why the heck would MI6 kidnap us rather than cooperate with Interpol?

If Lewis was here, he'd have worked it all out by now. But he was on his way to Australia, and I had to get Clare and me out of here, so I needed to figure this out. What was I missing?

"What's in the files?" There'd been hundreds of documents, and I'd only scanned a few. What had I missed?

Brian stepped away from Clare and strode toward me.

"Enough proof to put your father's boss in prison, I would imagine, and hopefully your father with him." Brian rubbed his finger over the cut on my forehead. "And, of course, the documents your mother stole from us."

"What documents?" Clare said.

Brian turned to face her. My body relaxed as he moved away

from me.

"State secrets. Your sister's a traitor." Brian stroked Clare's head just like he'd stroked mine before he'd punched me. "Poor Clare. Katrina really did a number on you, didn't she?"

I wanted to rip him apart.

"You work for the government," I said. "You're not allowed to hurt us."

"As far as I'm concerned, your mother is a threat to national security, which means I can do whatever I damn well please."

Brian wandered behind the spotlight.

A bag unzipped. Metal clinked.

The hollow, weightless feeling in my limbs started to fade, and dread settled in.

He reappeared, holding something in his hand. "I'm going to ask one last time. Where are the files?"

Brian is MI6. He isn't allowed to hurt me. I said it over and over in my head while I met his sneer.

He leaned closer. Pressed something cold and hard against my cheek. Clare gasped. As I tried to see what Brian was holding, my chin dipped, and the tip of a blade jabbed my skin. A knife! My heart jackhammered. Sweat trickled down my face. Or was it blood? Was I bleeding?

"Stop!" Clare managed to scramble to her feet.

Brian turned to Clare, and the pressure of the blade disappeared.

"I know where Katrina is," Clare said.

"I don't believe you."

"It's the truth," Clare said. "Let him go, and I'll tell you."

I closed my eyes and tried to remember what Mom had said about truth. She'd clutched our hands and made us both promise to remember because it was the most important rule of all. *A truth*, she'd said, *relies on what came before it.* I hadn't thought about it since the day of the barbecue. But now, underground, tied to a chair, on the verge of selling out my parents, I remembered it. And I knew what came before because Lewis and I had written two walls worth of what came before. Whatever Mom and Dad were meant to have done, whatever they appeared to be, I knew who they were.

And I knew who I was. I made decisions. I took risks. I looked after people. And I did the right thing even if it was hard.

"Don't tell him," I said to Clare. "No matter what happens, don't tell him."

Brian turned his attention back to me and held the knife flat against my cheek. I kept my eyes squeezed shut. Gripped the arms of the chair.

The knifepoint felt like a bee sting.

Then my skin popped.

A tiny sound that made my organs feel like they were imploding. Blood trickled. Not sweat. Blood.

———

L E W I S

Jamie's ancient, grouse-hunting Land Rover rattled through the Edinburgh streets.

It had stopped raining, but the windshield wipers continued to squeak back and forth. Jamie offered to switch them off, but he'd need to turn off the ignition and fiddle with a wire. We all said no.

I held my breath every time we stopped at lights or pedestrian crossings, but the engine continued to putter. Jamie must've been expecting it to die, too, because he kept revving the engine and wiping his forehead with the back of his hand, or maybe he was sweating because we were about to take on Ruby's mobster grandfather. Hopefully, it wasn't because he was panicking about being wrong about the castle's entrance to the tunnels.

Between the engine revving and the doors rattling and the wipers dragging over the rainless windshield, there wasn't much air space left for conversation. I rested the laptop on my knees, wiped my clammy hands on my shorts, then checked the phone. Visser still hadn't texted back.

The traffic slowed as we approached the city center. Pedestrians swarmed.

"It'd be faster to walk from here," Jamie said.

"Brilliant idea," said Aisha. "But we're neither a tourist coach nor a police car, so we can't stop in the road and all pile out."

I leaned between the front seats and pointed at a street that led straight to the castle. "Can't we drive up there?"

"That road's one way at this time of day," Jamie said.

"What happens if we drive the wrong way up a one-way street?"

Jamie gripped the steering wheel. "I could get a ticket."

"But we wouldn't crash into oncoming traffic and die a horrific death?" I said.

"No, the tourist coaches are allowed up, just not cars." He glanced at me in the mirror. "Do you think we should risk it?"

Cameron and Clare had been kidnapped by the mob, and Jamie was worried about getting fined?

"The castle closes soon," Aisha said.

"Do it," I said to Jamie.

Jamie swerved into the next lane, then made a sharp right through open metal barriers with a sign clearly stating that cars were not permitted.

"Your car kind of looks like a teeny-weeny bus," Aisha said.

Not like any of the buses that were parked along the road — glossy tourist coaches with tinted windows and pictures of mountains and castles on the side.

As we neared the top of the hill, Jamie clicked on the indicator and pulled into the curb. "We need to find a parking machine. Does anyone have change?"

"From now on," I said. "Let's assume everything we do is slightly illegal. It's like talking to cars, you get used to it."

I unclicked my seat belt. Should I leave the laptop or take it?

"My dad's a barrister, and my mum's an MP," Jamie said. "The only thing we're allowed to be noticed for is school prizes and sports medals."

Aisha looked at Jamie. "Your parents own a stolen painting and know about smugglers' tunnels."

"Fair point." Jamie yanked on the hand brake and unfastened his seat belt.

I was still staring at the laptop. Brian wouldn't let Cameron and Clare go without having the files in his hands, but if I took the laptop with me, all he'd have to do was point a gun and I'd hand it over.

"Here." Ruby held out a flash drive.

"What's that?" I asked her.

"The files. I copied them," she said, then hopped out the car.

When? How? But neither question would get Cameron and Clare safe any quicker, so I shoved the flash drive in my pocket and the laptop under the driver's seat.

I was halfway out of the car when my phone rang.

I looked at Aisha for advice. "It's Visser."

"He can't stop you through a phone."

I answered.

Visser asked where the hell we were because all the extraction team had found at the safe house was a burnt pizza.

I explained in as few words as possible.

He swore. A lot.

When he finally took a breath, I said, "We're going in."

"What do you mean you're *going in*? You're not commandos. Stay where you are. I'm tracking your phone."

"How far away are you?"

"Don't move; I'll be with you soon."

"How far?"

It sounded as if he slammed his hand on the horn and kept it there. Then swore.

I ended the call. "We're going in without him."

CHAPTER
37

LEWIS

Aisha greeted the woman at the ticket booth and flashed her staff pass, and we all sailed in behind her.

The castle looked different in the daylight, but just as impressive. The stone knights stood at ease while we passed over the drawbridge. Aisha took off at a run. She was still in her garden-party dress, but had swapped her heels for Maggs's rubber boots.

We followed her through a narrow alley, hemmed in with towering stone. Past a gift shop and under another archway.

Then the wall on our right fell away to reveal a courtyard lined with cannons pointing out to the ocean. Tourists wandered, clutching folded umbrellas and phones, taking photos of the cannons and the view of the foggy coastline beyond.

We wove round a tour group, then sprinted up a cobbled path that curled around the black rock. As we climbed, the rock morphed into the castle — turrets and arches and stained glass windows. As we ran through another archway, I realized the castle wasn't one giant building, but a village of churches and houses and grass and cobbled lanes.

Aisha stopped at a set of wooden stairs with a signpost pointing down to public toilets.

"This is it," Aisha said. "Where David's Tower used to stand. All that's left are the cellars."

"Which are now washrooms," I said.

She sighed, then set off down the stairs, her rubber boots thumping. We followed, but before we reached the twenty-first-century washroom doors, Aisha stopped at an opening in the rock.

Jamie stepped inside. I let Ruby go ahead of me. I didn't trust her at my back.

Spotlights illuminated the walls of the space. They looked solid.

"This isn't it," Jamie said. "Where are the dungeons?"

"Here." Aisha gestured around us. "And under most of the buildings in the castle. They locked up shed loads of people."

It would take hours to search under every building. Brian had had Cameron and Clare for too long already.

"Hammocks," Jamie said. "I remember hammocks."

"Prisoners of war." Aisha dashed back to the opening, then up the steps.

The rest of us followed. At the top of the stairs, we sprinted toward another arch and through that into another courtyard, surrounded by more stone buildings.

Tourists huddled in the entrance of one of them, reading wall plaques with pictures of battlefields and ships. We shuffled past them and down a narrow stone staircase.

Cloth hammocks were strung from wooden frames that ran the length of the room. This must be it. We all looked at Jamie.

"Not too shabby," he said.

He was right; this dungeon was luxury compared to the cellars. A dome-shaped ceiling and a high-up window that let in enough daylight to see the worn cobblestones of the floor. It even had a fireplace.

"Would you want to live here with fifty other blokes 24-7 and poop in a bucket in the corner?" Aisha said.

"Good point," Jamie said.

"Where's the entrance?" It was the first time Ruby had spoken since we left the car.

Did she want to help us, or was she waiting for her chance to escape or club us over the head with an ancient relic?

"We came through another dungeon before we reached this one," Jamie said. "A real dungeon. Dark, damp, low ceilings, iron bars."

"This way." Aisha marched through a group of headset-wearing tourists to the other end of the dungeon and down another set of stone steps.

The damp smell thickened as it mixed with an earthy tang. The temperature dropped. We kept going. Past a hole in the rock with bars across it.

"People were put in there?" Ruby said.

"But there's no light," I said. "Or air."

"The farther you go into the tunnels, the thinner the air gets," Jamie said.

If Cameron was being held somewhere like this, he'd be losing his mind.

Jamie held on to the bars and shook them. "Solid. Must be the next one."

"You're kidding." Cameron was this far underground?

We kept going down, stepping over a chain with a *Strictly No Entry* sign attached.

"I've never been down this far," Aisha said.

When we ran out of daylight, we switched on our phone lights and kept going down into the blackness.

"This is it." Jamie stroked the bars of another cell. "Two missing bars."

"Are you sure?" We didn't have time to get this wrong.

Jamie shone his light above the narrow opening. Gouged into the stone was a vertical line with shorter lines crossing it at an angle.

"This is it," he said. "That's the smugglers' symbol."

"How do you know?" Aisha said.

"Because it's in our coat of arms."

"You weren't joking about the origins of your family's money," she said.

"I never joke about history," he said. "It's too grim."

I squeezed through the gap first. Then Aisha, followed by Ruby. It was touch and go whether Jamie would fit, but he was determined.

Once he was through, he swapped his phone for Ruby's and took the lead, the light from our phones dancing on the rock walls. "They're not too far from here."

If Ruby's tracker was still in the backpack. If Cameron still had his backpack close.

C A M E R O N

Brian grabbed my chin and pressed the tip of the knife into my punctured skin. "My daughter died thinking her father was a failure. Did Ruby tell you that?"

I gripped the chair, every muscle, every nerve, every part of my brain focused on the cut in my cheek and the weight of the knife.

Brian tilted his head. "No, I don't suppose she did."

My heartbeat whooshed in my ears. Was I supposed to answer? What would happen to the blade if I did?

"I took a vow to serve my country." He took two breaths. "And your mother, with her naive view of the world, made a mockery of that vow. Have you any idea what it's like to be scorned and pitied by people who once looked up to you?"

"My parents weren't responsible for the riots. Were they?" My brain was too muddled to figure out the rest, but that much I knew. Lewis had always known. If I ever saw him again, I'd start listening.

"What else did you see when you opened the files — the intelligence agents Katrina threatened to expose?" Brian blew air out his nose. "Your mother was an arrogant idealist."

I hated him. We were going to get out of here, and I was going to smack his smug face before we left.

"Your granddaughter still respects you," Clare said as if she was talking to a child or a sick person.

As the pressure of the knife eased, my muscles sagged. My blood was now a steady trickle dripping onto my sweatpants — the spots bright red for a second before they soaked in. I needed Lewis to help me solve the puzzle of Brian. An MI6 agent who'd taken a vow but was happy to kidnap innocent people and torture them.

"Let us go," Clare said. "Be honorable."

Brian stiffened. The knife twitched, and pain shot up my cheek. Another spike of adrenaline fired through my veins. I thrashed to get free, but my wrists and ankles were bound too tight, and all I achieved was a pathetic rattle of the chair.

"I had to work for agents I'd trained," Brian said. "Watch buffoons take jobs that should've been mine. I pushed paper when I should've been out in the field. I'll be the one to bring Katrina Murray in. Let's see how they treat me then."

I scrambled for another argument, but Clare's brain was faster.

"What would Ruby think if you harmed her friend?" she said.

My heart skipped a beat — it might work.

"Ruby will never find out," Brian said.

How could Ruby *not* find out? And then the realization clamped around my chest — as soon as Brian had the files and the passwords, he was going to hand us over to someone else. I'd never see Lewis again. Never find Mom and Dad.

"I'll make sure Ruby knows," I said. "No matter where I end up, I'll make sure she knows what you are."

Everyone thought my parents were evil. I'd almost believed it, too. There was no way in hell I was going to let Brian swan around this world fooling everyone.

Anger flashed in Brian's eyes. But I wouldn't break. I'd keep Mom and Dad safe. I'd keep Lewis safe.

As Brian twisted the knife, I focused on Clare. The way the color was draining from her face. How her eyes were wide and fixed on me. How her mouth opened into an O as she screamed at

Brian to stop. I closed my eyes, and instead of thinking about the blade slicing my skin, I thought about fishing with Dad. Hiking in the mountains with Mom. Swimming in lakes and building snow forts and skipping stones.

Pain shot up the side of my face, then pulsed like an electric current through my skull, traveling to every nerve, rattling my teeth. I thought of Lewis riding his dirt bike, grinning at me over his shoulder. Of Molly singing in the truck beside me. I tried to hear which song, but someone was screaming. And Clare was shouting.

My throat felt like it was caving in. Was it me screaming? I opened my eyes to ask Clare. Black spots danced across my vision. The ocean crashed in my ears. The spotlight dimmed. Or was that the sun? Wherever I was, the light was disappearing.

———

L E W I S

The ground sloped one way, then the other, and each step was a surprise. Sometimes my foot met stone when my leg was still bent, then on the next step the ground fell away. And under my feet, the ground was rippled and rutted.

"What exactly are we walking on?" I said to break the silence and make sure Jamie, Aisha and Ruby hadn't been switched out for zombies.

"Volcanic rock," Jamie said. "With layers of history on top. Broken glass and rotting wood from the whisky distilleries. The barrels had to be decanted into bottles before being sold."

"There's also leather from old shoes and sword scabbards," Aisha said. "And bones."

A shiver ran down my spine. "Bones from what?"

"Rats," Jamie said.

That made sense.

"And human corpses."

"What?"

"Edinburgh was one of the first universities to use dead bodies to practice medicine," Jamie said. "But if you donated your body to science, you'd never make it to heaven, so they used freshly hung criminals. Or dug up recent graves."

"Or snatched people off the street they didn't think anyone would miss," Aisha said.

I was walking on forgotten dead people. "You're telling me medical students dug up bodies and murdered people?"

"They paid body snatchers to do it for them," Jamie said.

Oh, that made it so much better.

"The tunnels are dark and cold and out of sight," Jamie continued. "The perfect place to store dead bodies. And they also provided the means to transport them directly to the university cellars."

"Please don't tell me that's how your family got rich," Aisha said.

"We smuggled alcohol," he said. "French wine into Scotland, whisky out. The only people we smuggled were alive. Political prisoners, mainly."

The tunnel narrowed, and we ducked into the next section.

"Hold up," Aisha said from the back.

Our shuffling feet quietened.

"Do you need help?" Jamie said. "Are you hurt?"

Aisha shushed him.

I strained my ears until they buzzed.

"Do you hear that?" Aisha whispered.

And then I did.

Thuds of multiple pairs of boots coming up behind us.

My heart kicked into overdrive. "Go, go, go!"

Our lights bounced as we ran. Then Jamie stopped dead, and I piled into the back of him. Ruby bumped into me, apologized. Then crashed into me again as Aisha ran into her.

I shone my light up ahead. The tunnel split in two.

"I think we take the left one," Jamie said.

The boots got louder.

"Make a decision," Aisha said.

We couldn't get caught. Cameron and Clare needed saving.

"Aisha and I go right," Jamie said. "Lewis and Ruby go left. Keep quiet and hope they follow us, not you."

"No way," I hissed. "I'm not letting them get you."

Aisha pushed past me. "They won't do anything to us. Jamie's mum's an MP, and his dad's a barrister, remember."

"Go rescue your brother." Jamie pressed Ruby's phone into my hand, then turned to follow Aisha.

"Hurry up," Aisha said, louder than she needed to as they took off down the tunnel on the right.

Ruby tugged me into the other tunnel. We switched off our phones and crouched in the dark. Aisha and Jamie's feet thudding away from us, while the others got closer.

My breathing was too loud. I held my breath, then tried to let it out slowly. Somewhere above us Hula-Hoop Henrietta was twirling hoops, and the bagpipe guy was tottering on his stilts. People were laughing and eating ice cream and taking selfies with spray-painted musicians.

The boots stopped at the fork of the tunnel. Ruby buried her head against my arm. I held my breath again. *Panicking wastes energy,* Dad used to say. *Turn your adrenaline into action.* Everyone was relying on me now. Cameron and Clare, Mom and Dad, and now Jamie and Aisha.

Jamie shouted something. I couldn't make out what, but it was enough for the boots to start moving again.

I waited until the thud of boots faded, until I was sure they hadn't left anyone behind, then I stood. I could do this. I had to.

Ruby and I continued down the tunnel in silence, pretending like we hadn't just sacrificed Aisha and Jamie.

Not talking left me with space to think about what we might find. It included guns. And mafia bosses who liked theatrics. And the possibility that Ruby could still double-cross me, or that her presence wouldn't deter Brian from shooting us all anyway.

"I know you hate me," Ruby said.

"Yup."

I didn't hate her. All my emotion was concentrated on staying calm and following the dot on her phone so I could get Cameron and Clare out of here. If that failed ... well, then, I'd probably hate her.

"Yes, I copied the files off the laptop, but I never handed them over to my grandfather," she said.

My foot hit a bump, and I stumbled. "How?"

"Mrs. Ross gave me her password when I installed the software for you."

"Did you look at the photos? Is that why you kidnapped my brother?"

"It's why I'm helping rescue him."

How did that make sense? "What did you see?"

"The same as you. The riot and the people who fueled it. And a ton of documents with threats and demands and agreements." She took a breath. "My granddad said your parents were criminals and traitors, and it was his duty to track them down. And your dad *was* in some of the photos, but so were other people who could have been mistaken for him."

"Like who, Ruby?"

"You don't know what it's like to be alone," she said. "You have Cameron."

A scream ripped through the darkness. Every muscle went rigid. I hadn't heard Cameron scream like that since we were five years old and I crunched his fingers in the door of the truck.

I prayed Ruby was right and I still did have Cameron.

CHAPTER
38

C A M E R O N

I wanted to keep sitting in the truck with Molly, the windows wound down, the radio turned high, but my brain began thinking of Lewis. I imagined I could hear him shouting. Then Clare's panicked voice telling him to run. It would be typical of Lewis to show up after all the effort I'd put into keeping him safe. It would be good to see him though. I held on to the dream that my brother had come for me. That he'd forgiven me for leaving him. That he believed I was worth risking his life for.

I even imagined I could feel his arms around me and hear his voice in my ear insisting I wake up and look at him. Then Brian spoke, gruff and low. Why was Brian in my dream? I didn't want him there.

"I'm going to untie you," Lewis said.

In my dream I giggled. I have no idea why, because my face hurt and I could taste blood, and the cable ties chafed my wrists as they were cut away.

"Cameron, it's me."

I told him I was sorry. Maybe I'd be able to say it to the real Lewis one day.

"Don't try to speak," Lewis said.

Everything he'd said was true. People did like him more than they liked me. Why wouldn't they? He was funnier and kinder and wasn't afraid to be himself. All I was good at was making decisions without thinking, then pretending not to care about the consequences. That wasn't brave.

"You're the brave one." It hurt my throat to speak.

Why did everything have to hurt, even in a dream?

"Cameron." This time it was Clare's voice. "I'm going to give you some water. Don't choke."

Water would be nice. My throat was dry, and maybe it would wash away the coppery taste of blood.

My mouth filled with water. Real water. I spluttered it out.

"Slowly," Clare said.

Water dribbled into my mouth. I was ready for it this time.

"He's coming round," Lewis said.

As faces came into focus, the scene made no sense. Lewis was actually here.

I wanted to hug him.

"Go away," I rasped.

His face got closer, and he pressed something against my cheek. I flinched.

"We need to stop the bleeding," he said.

"You can't be here." I swiped his hand away.

"Yeah, because it looks like you have everything under control." He handed me his scrunched-up shirt. "Keep pressure on it."

Clare squeezed my shoulder, then turned to Brian. "Can we go now?"

"I'm afraid we're well past that stage." Brian turned to the huge bloke whose nose was now bleeding. I hoped Clare had done it.

"Go to the surface and call it in. Tell them we're ready for an extraction." Then he pulled a gun from the back of his shorts and pointed it at us.

———

L E W I S

It was a complete failure of a rescue attempt. I was on the ground, back-to-back with Clare, our wrists cable-tied together, my right ankle lashed to Cameron's left with rope. He was slumped in the chair, conscious but groggy. His hands were still free, and he was holding my Highland cow shirt against his bloody face.

Ruby, who was free to roam, prodded Brian's chest. "You promised you wouldn't hurt him."

"I had no choice, sweetheart," he said.

"I've seen what's in the files, Gramps."

"Good girl. Where are they?"

"Don't tell him, Ruby," I said.

Brian turned and pointed his gun at me. If it weren't for Cameron's bloody face, I wouldn't have believed Brian was capable of violence.

Ruby stepped in between the gun and us.

"Be careful," Clare said.

Brian lowered his gun. "Ruby, sweetheart, if you know where the files are, you need to tell me."

"I'm telling you nothing until you explain what happened at the riots."

Cameron's ankle pulled against mine, then he doubled over as if he was about to throw up. I tensed, waiting for warm vomit on my bare back, but none came.

Brian tucked the gun into the back of his shorts, then tugged Ruby off to the side. "As soon as backup arrives, one of them will drive you to the guesthouse. I'll explain everything later."

She pulled away from him. "You promised Will wouldn't get hurt and you cut his face. Look at his face. How could you do that to him?"

I doubted Ruby could convince Brian to let us go, but if she kept him talking long enough, maybe Visser would find us.

"You told me their parents were criminals and terrorists." Ruby balled her hands into fists. "You used me."

The rope pulled tight against my ankle, then loosened. Cameron was still doubled over, but he hadn't passed out, and in his hand was a set of keys.

"Budge up," Cameron whispered.

As I shuffled over, Clare shuffled with me.

"You know what I think?" Ruby said. "I think *you're* the criminal."

Brian snorted. "You think your own grandfather's a criminal? Is that all the respect I get for bringing you up?"

"Bringing me up?" Ruby said. "You occasionally let me stay in your house."

Brian's shoulders slumped. "I tried."

"Try harder," she said. "Tell me why you hate their mother so much."

My focus shifted from Cameron rubbing a key against the cable tie to Brian.

He smoothed down his shirt. "Katrina worked for me."

"Go on," Ruby said.

"We had intel that the Dutch mafia were targeting an exhibition at the Tate gallery. I stationed Katrina there with orders to identify the players and find out all she could about the heist. She got in too deep and went rogue."

"Why did she go rogue?" I said.

Brian looked at me, then at Cameron's limp form. "What's wrong with him?"

Cameron moaned.

"I think he's trying not to throw up," I said.

"You did torture him," Clare said. "Or had you forgotten?"

"Gramps, look at me, not them. Why did she go rogue?"

Brian began to pace.

This was good. If he was pacing, he wasn't watching us.

Cameron resumed sawing at the cable tie that held my wrists to Clare's.

"It was an election year," Brian finally said to Ruby. "Sympathy was building for refugees and illegal immigrants. Downing Street needed to sway public opinion. We were given a mission to cause trouble at the demonstration, then frame the protestors. Katrina didn't agree."

"What kind of trouble?" Ruby asked.

Cameron was breathing hard in my ear, as if cutting us free was draining him of his last drop of energy.

"A few scuffles, some smashed windows," Brian said. "We were to film them for release to the press. That was all. No one was meant to get hurt."

Brian stopped pacing and looked pleadingly at Ruby. It was probably an act — gain her sympathy, then pack her off home. I opened my mouth to warn her, but Cameron reminded me with a jab of the key that we didn't need Brian's attention.

"But people did get hurt." Ruby crossed her arms.

"Fights broke out in locations where none of our agents were stationed," Brian said. "A department store was torched, and a press crew attacked. It became clear the incidents were linked and being planned by someone other than us. The order came to stand down, but it was too late; the crowd panicked."

As the cable tie fell away, my wrists relaxed away from Clare's. We kept them behind our backs, while Cameron went to work on the rope that bound his ankle to mine. We'd soon be free, and Brian's henchman hadn't returned. But Brian had a gun, and obviously a knife. And knowing Cameron, he didn't have a plan beyond untying us.

"Keep going," Ruby said. "What happened next?"

"You know what happened."

"I want to hear you say it."

Brian dragged his hand over his face. "Protestors tried to escape the stampede, but fires had been set. Riot police fired warning shots to try to turn the crowd, but all that did was fuel the hysteria."

"And you battered a policewoman with a baseball bat," Ruby said.

"What?" Cameron and I said at the same time.

Brian killed the policewoman, not Dad? Clare squeezed my hand.

I looked at Brian and tried to imagine what he'd looked like seventeen years ago. Broader, probably. His hair blond, not silvery-gray. In person, I wouldn't mistake him for Dad, but hunched over on a grainy photograph, with his back to the camera, I had. And so had the entire nation.

I wanted to jump up and do a victory dance, tell my brother *I told you so.* But Brian had a gun, so all I did was turn and grin at Cameron.

"But I saw a photo of my dad with a baseball bat," Cameron said to Brian.

"He took that bat from *me.*" Brian jabbed his own chest. "As though he were some crusading hero when all he'll ever be is a petty thief for a mob boss."

"Why, Gramps?" Ruby said. "Why did you do it?"

As Brian paced, the spotlight cast his shadow on the rock walls. I tried to catch Ruby's eye. Was she really on our side?

"I was following orders." Brian stopped pacing and turned toward Ruby. "All uniforms were told to stand down, so we could identify the enemy. Anybody who continued fighting the protestors was to be taken out, civilian *or* police."

Ruby folded her arms. "And now you want the files so you can erase your mistake."

"The other photos matter, too," he said. "MI6 agents marching in the demonstration, and the mob setting fires. They prove that the operation was a government-sanctioned mission and that it escalated out of our control, not due to my incompetence, but because the mafia stirred up trouble."

"But my mom knew what the mafia were planning," I said. "And she told you. Didn't she?"

Ruby looked at me, then back at Brian.

Brian took a step toward Ruby, his hand reaching for her. "You've got to understand. Katrina was in too deep. I sensed she'd gotten too close to her mark, which, considering they're still playing happy family seventeen years later, proves I was right. We assumed van der Berg was feeding her fake intel. And even if it were true, we thought we could control the situation."

"And when you failed, you used my sister as your scapegoat," Clare said. "How honorable."

"She stole secrets." Brian spun to glare at Clare. "Put our agents at risk. Betrayed the British people."

"You gave her no choice!" Clare said.

"Those secrets were the only thing that kept them safe," I said. "Kept us safe."

"Don't try to make them out to be heroes," Brian said. "Your parents are cowards."

"No!" Cameron shot back.

"Where are they, then?" Brian strolled over and sneered at Cameron's ruined face. "They sent their children to answer for their sins because they're pathetic cowards."

Cameron let out a roar and lunged.

I kicked out, aiming for Brian's knees.

They both went down. The gun skittered out of Brian's hand. I reached for it, but Ruby snatched it up first. Cameron howled as Brian grabbed his injured face. Forget the gun. I piled in, drove my knee into the soft flesh of Brian's stomach, while Cameron swung a punch at his jaw.

"We need to go!" Clare yelled.

Cameron didn't hear or chose to ignore her. I couldn't leave him to fight Brian alone, so I stayed in there, too.

Then Ruby and Clare tried to drag us off Brian, shouting that we didn't have time.

Cameron shoved himself off Brian, his face bleeding again. I scrambled up beside him.

The radio crackled, but no message followed.

"Is there another way out of here?" Clare asked Brian.

Then we heard it — a faint rumble like distant thunder.

Ruby knelt beside Brian. "Please, Gramps, you need to help them."

Brian tried to get up but failed. "They had their chance."

Feet pounded in the tunnels. I pushed Cameron behind me. Clare took the gun off Ruby and pointed it into the darkness.

Cameron squeezed my arm. "Hide. I'll distract them."

"No." Not a chance. "You go, I'll stay."

"It's too late," Clare said.

A blur of bullet-proof vests and guns flowed from the tunnel. I threw myself on top of Cameron.

Military boots surrounded us.

"Do you two ever do as you're told?" a familiar voice said. "You're supposed to be on a bleeding plane."

CHAPTER
39

CAMERON

We emerged from the tunnels on the top of a hill, a helicopter thud-thud-thudding above us. My legs were shaking, and it took every last shred of willpower not to crumple on the wet grass.

Padma's team fell into position, flanking our ragtag crew. Clare was at the rear with Ruby, who wasn't coping well. Brian had tried to persuade her to leave the tunnels with him through a different exit, but she'd refused. Lewis walked next to me, his blood-soaked T-shirt back on. He looked like he'd been shot. He could've been. My brother risked his life for me.

The helicopter banked, then flew ahead of us.

"Will you stop waiting for me to keel over?" I said to Lewis.

"I'm sorry I took so long, but Jamie and Aisha couldn't agree which entrance to use and then Jamie's car — have you seen his car, it's ancient. Bicycles overtook us."

"You came for me," I said. "That's all that matters."

"You would've done the same for me, but faster." He glanced at my bloody face. "All those things I said to you. I didn't mean any of them."

"You were right."

"I know I'm annoying," he said. "And expect you to make every decision. And never thank you for looking out for me."

"I said you were right, Lewis. All of it was my fault."

He nudged me. "It worked out though, didn't it? I mean not great, obviously, but better than being on a plane to Australia."

And Clare was safe, and Lewis was here, and Aisha and Jamie had helped us.

I looked back at our group. "Where are Aisha and Jamie?"

"Padma said she left one of her team with them and told them to get out of the tunnels the same way they got in."

"Has anyone heard from them?" I said. "How do we know they made it?"

"Aisha texted to say they were going back for Jamie's car. He was worried about getting a parking ticket."

Pain shot through my cheek as I smiled.

Lewis continued to ramble about Jamie's family being smugglers, but weren't criminals anymore, well except for the painting, but Jamie wanted to return it.

The hill dipped, then climbed again, and as we reached the crest, a zigzag of hikers came into view being led down the hill by police in orange vests.

"Where are we?" I said.

Lewis checked the map on his phone. "Arthur's Seat."

"Camelot." Aisha was right, you could see the entire city from here, spreading out to meet the ocean to the east and farmland in every other direction.

"Wow!" Lewis stopped and gawped. "I suppose it explains the number of people hiking up it."

I nudged him on. "You should talk to Ruby."

"Are you kidding? She helped Brian kidnap you."

"But in the end, she chose us her over her own grandfather."

"Who's evil and demented." Lewis sighed. "I should talk to her."

He slowed to let Ruby and Clare catch up. I kept walking, breathing in air that smelled of breweries one minute and the sea the next, depending which way the wind turned.

Padma appeared at my side. "It'll scar."

"Thanks, I needed cheering up."

She took off her sunglasses and handed them to me.

I slid them on, and my eyes relaxed. "Our parents are innocent, Brian admitted it."

"No wonder you cause so much trouble. Your definition of innocent is seriously flawed."

"They tried to stop the riots, not cause them," I said.

My feet slipped on loose stones. Padma's hand flew out and grabbed my elbow.

"I've seen the files," she said. "Your mother tried to blackmail the British government. And when that failed to stop the mission, she roped your father in, and together they photographed agents in the field, then stole state secrets, including, but not limited to, the identities of every active British field agent and the location of every operational base. Plus, proof that the command to stir up the riots came directly from the prime minister's office."

"What would you have done?"

"Not fall in love with the bloke I was spying on, for a start. And no offense, but I'm assuming you two were a mistake, because getting pregnant in their situation was barmy."

I must've stopped walking because Padma was now in front of me.

She turned to face me. "Don't pout. I didn't say they regretted you, but you did make everything hellishly complicated. Your parents had started to trade some of the intel with us in return for protection while they tried to clear their names, but when you two came along, they decided that between MI6 double-crossing them and Ryker out for blood, it was too risky. They disappeared, then sent word they'd restart negotiations when you two were old enough to cope on your own."

Padma's words dropped in my stomach, and everything turned on its head again.

She started walking, and when I caught up, she continued. "We still don't know how Ryker found you in Canada, but here we are a few years earlier and a whole lot messier than your parents had no doubt planned."

We walked in silence. A million questions were flying through my brain, but there was one that wouldn't go away: "Why didn't they tell us?"

"To protect you. The less you knew, the safer you'd be," she said. "And also, I'm guessing, they wanted you to have a normal childhood. Even mobsters and runaway spies want their children to have birthday parties and learn to swim and walk to school without getting shot."

It hadn't worked though. Or maybe it had — we were still alive, and Lewis and I were together. I could feel his concern for me drifting through the air. I looked back and gave him a thumbs-up.

As the trail rounded the cliff face, the bottom of the hill came into view — a park with grass and trees and a pond and the flashing blue lights of a squadron of police cars, three ambulances, two fire trucks and what looked like an armored tank. Uniformed officers patrolled a makeshift barricade of orange cones and yellow tape, keeping back hordes of onlookers and camera crews.

And in the middle of it all was an ancient blue Land Rover, with Aisha and Jamie Wallace sitting on top of it waving at us.

A squad of paramedics spotted us and legged it up the hillside.

"God love the police force; they do overreact," Padma said. "As long as they don't send the bill to my lot."

"What do you think they're telling the media?"

"Terrorist's sister turns hero and saves children from collapsed tunnel."

"I like that." Clare deserved to have her name cleared.

"Or witless teens almost get shot by nutjob."

"The first one's better," I said.

"You would think that."

A black car roared up to the police tape, and an army of officers in bullet-proof vests raised their weapons.

The door flew open, and the driver leaped out, then strode toward the line of guns.

It was Visser and, even though he had his arms raised, he didn't look like he had any intention of stopping.

"Jesus wept. That man thinks he's Rambo." Padma waved to one of her people. "Tell them to let Visser through before he gets himself killed."

Instructions were given over a radio. Guns were lowered. Visser ducked under the tape and set out at an all-out sprint toward us.

"*Was* Visser my dad's best friend?"

"Still is, from what I know," Padma said. "They dragged each other through miserable childhoods, and when Ryker recruited them, they watched each other's backs. Visser's a cocky prat, but I trust him."

"How do you know he isn't still working for Ryker, and all of this isn't an act to get to us and the paintings and Dad?"

"He's been working with us for over a decade," Padma said. "After six years of watching Clare, he was ordered to kill her. He chose not to."

"Kill Clare? Why?" My wobbly legs felt wobblier.

"A message for your parents. Come out of hiding or your sister, mother, neighbor's hamster will be next, that sort of thing."

"Visser betrayed the mob to protect Dad?"

"Not quite as selfless as all that," Padma said. "Watch and learn."

Visser stormed past the paramedics, his hair plastered to his head, his face running in sweat.

He arrived in a cloud of dust and angst. "Where's Clare?"

"She's at the back with Lewis and Ruby," I said. "And we're fine, thanks for asking."

Visser nodded at me as if to say, *Nasty cut, mate*, then started running again.

"He fell for Clare?" I looked at Padma for confirmation.

She nodded. "He carried on the tradition your father started. The mob were complete plonkers not to see that one coming."

The paramedics stormed past us and surrounded Lewis, who lifted his shirt to prove he hadn't been shot or stabbed. Then two of them pounced on us, made me sit on a rock while they cleaned my face. They said it would sting. It did. Then told me they'd stitch me up when we got to the bottom and handed me water, much appreciated, and a tinfoil blanket that, no matter how much I was shivering, I wouldn't be seen dead in.

Padma was waiting for me, and we fell in step again.

"What now?" I asked.

"After the paramedics have finished with you, you'll be questioned. I'll stay with you to make sure they don't get over excited."

"And after that?" Could we all go home? "Padma?"

"Other than MI6 misbehaving, nothing's changed. Everyone still hates your parents. You still entered the country illegally," she said. "On the bright side, if the mob come after you now, they'll be playing right into our hands. But as we concluded earlier, they're hardly a learning organization."

"It was all for nothing?" I pulled my hand through the sweaty fuzz of my hair. "Leaving Canada. Dragging Clare into this. Breaking Mom's code. Stealing the painting. Brian kidnapping us. None of it means anything?"

"Cheer up. You did hand over documents that contain enough intel to put Ryker away. So, the Netherlands likes you."

"I didn't hand over the files, you *took* them."

"Did I? I thought you called me and offered them up for the good of King and Country." Padma tilted her head, waiting for me to catch on.

"You want us to go and live in Holland?"

"Not necessarily, but it would be nice if they offered you citizenship because you're well and truly buggered otherwise."

"But we're Canadian."

She raised her eyebrows. "A country that your parents entered illegally, and where there is no official record of you."

"British?"

"Smashing idea, if your mother can ever prove she's not a traitor."

"So, you're saying I don't have a nationality *or* a name?" I really didn't exist.

She glanced at the helicopter, still hovering above Arthur's Seat. "Over the next few days, bureaucrats with inflated egos and selfish motives are going to offer you all sorts of futures. Don't get hung up on who you *think* you want to be."

"I want to be Cameron Larsen living in Longview."

Padma fixed me with a stare. "That's just a collection of names. You need to work out what makes you happy. In the end that's all we are — the sum of what gives us joy."

As we reached the valley floor, the two paramedics from earlier ushered me to a waiting ambulance. I refused to get in the back of another vehicle, so they carried out a stretcher, and I sat on that while they stitched my face. Lewis found me and held my hand. I closed my eyes and tried to ignore the tugging sensation on my numbed skin.

When it was finally done, I opened my eyes to find the stretcher surrounded by faces. Lewis, of course, and Aisha and Jamie and Ruby.

Aisha gave me a hug. "Seeing as you're injured, I forgive you."

Jamie shook my hand, then changed his mind and gave me a hug, too.

"I'm sorry." Ruby stopped fiddling with her bracelets and finally looked at me. "I wanted my granddad to be the good guy and I know that's a pathetic excuse for what I did and … I'm just …"

Lewis put his arm around her shoulder.

Ruby took a shaky breath. "I'm really, really sorry. About tricking you, and your face and everything."

Only a few hours ago, it had been me apologizing to Ruby for deceiving *her*. We'd been on the beach, and she'd said something that at the time hadn't sunk in. But as I watched her struggle like I'd struggled this afternoon, I realized she'd been right.

I put my hand over her fingers, which were playing with her bracelets again. "A friend of mine recently told me that sometimes the only way to survive is to be whoever you need to be."

Ruby looked at me and nodded.

"Sorry to break up the reunion." Padma joined the row of faces. "Give us a minute, would you? Lewis, you stay."

Lewis sat beside me on the stretcher.

"We'll wait by the car for you," Jamie said over his shoulder as he, Ruby and Aisha walked away.

"I didn't want to tell you until we knew more." Padma nudged me over and sat down, too. "A team picked up your parents on Mull."

The last scrap of tension in my muscles snapped.

"Will they come here, or do we go to them?" Lewis asked.

They'd been so close this whole time.

"Why didn't they come for us?" I leaned against my brother.

"Ryker never found you because he was too busy hunting your parents." Padma took a breath. "Your parents escaped, but your father was shot."

Lewis stiffened. "Dad?"

I felt as if I'd been punched in the stomach. Lewis's arm shot around my shoulders.

"He's alive," Padma said. "But in bad shape. Your mother couldn't leave him."

"When can we see them?" Lewis said.

"What your parents did was noble, but courage and integrity don't earn brownie points with governments. They tend to reward blind loyalty and tech giants, and sadly, neither apply."

"Will our dad go to jail?" Lewis's arm tightened around me.

"The files contained enough dirt on Ryker to keep the lawyers busy for a few years. And if your father's clever, he'll only agree to testify if we offer him immunity."

"He's clever," Lewis said.

"And Mom?" I could barely get the words out.

"Katrina's got enough data to get half of MI6 sacked, if not charged. If she goes down, she'll take MI6 with her."

"But if she doesn't take them on, she'll never clear her name," I said.

"It's a conundrum," Padma said. "In the meantime, Interpol will continue to offer them both protection."

"We'll meet them there," Lewis said to me.

I nodded, not even knowing where *there* was.

"Your parents will be taken to a secure facility while everything dies down. Then they'll be given new identities and a new life."

"You mean we'll all be given new identities," I said.

Padma looked at Lewis, then me.

"Padma?" I'd never seen Padma lost for words.

"Your father will have to give evidence in Ryker's trial," she said.

She'd already told me that. "You said Ryker wouldn't come after us."

"Ryker did business with everyone from drug lords to CEOs to politicians," she said. "It'll all come out. Your parents will have more enemies than even they can handle. They may never have a permanent home or a normal life again. And neither will you if you choose to join them."

The urge to scream built in my chest. This was meant to be over, and now it could go on forever. New names. New nationalities. A rotation of friends we'd have to lie to. But it wasn't a choice, because I wasn't leaving Lewis again.

Lewis looked at Padma. "What did Mom say?"

"That they're proud of you. And they love you."

"Mom said we could survive on our own," Lewis said. "Didn't she?"

"That was the general gist of it."

"They don't want us to join them?" I hung my head so Lewis wouldn't see me cry, but my cheek throbbed, and he knew me better than I knew myself, so what did it matter?

"It's harder for them than for you," Padma said. "Believe it or not, it's easier for children to let go of their parents than the other way around."

I looked at Lewis. "You decide. I'll go wherever you go."

CHAPTER
40

L E W I S

Cameron strips off his coveralls and splashes into the sea. All very brave until the water reaches the top of his thighs, and he yelps.

"Any jellyfish?" I yell.

Mom always said that everyone has at least one irrational fear. Mine's jellyfish. I'm terrified of their pulsating, translucent bodies and greedy tentacles.

"Get in here!" Cameron shouts, then dives into a white-capped wave.

His phone sings from his discarded coveralls, that country song about being sixteen, wild and free. Country music is so uncool here it's almost cool. Cameron doesn't care either way. He seems to have stopped caring what people think.

I dig through the pockets of his grease-stained coveralls because it could be Padma. We check in with her twice a day, and she springs random visits on us as if she expects to find us building bombs or stealing sheep. She says if we want to make her life easier, we'll stay with her in Brighton over the school break — all we have to do is babysit her children and not get shot. She's invited Ruby as well, which will be good because we haven't seen her in months.

By the time I manage to find the right pocket, the phone's gone silent. Two missed calls from Jamie. Probably to say his car's broken. He's driving Maggs and Aisha to Rothesay tomorrow. The train would be faster. Scratch that, roller skates would be faster than Jamie's Land Rover.

I peel off my coveralls, which smell of fresh oil and stale sweat. We've been working in Clare's shop all day and stayed late to start work on a new project. She has this friend, a farmer, who donated us her old beater, and Clare's helping us rebuild it. The state it's in, it'll take until our seventeenth birthday to finish, which is when you can legally drive here. There's a ton of stuff to get used to, but it turns out secondary school in Scotland is the same as high school in Canada, but with uniforms. Cameron and I aren't in any of the same classes, even though it's easy to tell us apart now. Cameron's scar is silvery-smooth and makes him look tough without him having to pretend.

I chuck the phone on his coveralls, then race for the sea — the best way to get in is quickly, without thinking.

Cameron is swimming, short jerky movements and shuddering breaths. When the water reaches my thighs, I dive. The cold collapses my lungs. I manage two breaststroke movements, then surface to the sound of the country song, but I'm not sure if it's Cameron's phone again or its echo, frozen like an ice cube in my brain.

We're not in for long, because it really is chuffing cold, and I've lost all feeling in my legs. I stumble up the beach behind Cameron, who immediately checks his phone. "Five missed calls from Jamie."

Jamie obviously trusts Cameron's ability to answer more than he trusts mine, because when I check my phone, he's only called me twice.

Cameron dries his shaggy hair with his T-shirt while he calls Jamie back.

"No answer." He scrolls though his phone. "But he left a message."

I zip up my coveralls, still stinky, but they stop the wind stripping my wet skin. "Aisha needs to teach that boy to text."

Jamie does in fact possess the ability to text, but he prefers to talk. Once you get to know him, he never shuts up. If chatting was an Olympic sport, he'd win gold.

"Sodding hell in a handbasket," Cameron says as he listens to Jamie's message.

I don't know if he realizes that he swears like Clare now, or that he's picked up a bit of an accent. Or maybe he does and he's rolling with it.

"Don't tell me. His car broke down." I snag Cameron's shirt and use it to squeeze the water out of my dripping hair. I like having hair again.

Cameron stares at his phone, a shocked expression on his face.

Not Jamie's car, then.

It could be good news. Maybe Aisha's brother got released early, or Maggs has finally forgiven the professor for recruiting Mom to MI6 and cooked him an omelet. It can't be about Mom and Dad because it would be Padma calling, not Jamie.

"Cameron, just tell me."

He looks up. "Caitlin's missing."

Jamie's biggest little sister. She's a teenager — they tend to wander off by themselves.

"Jamie just got back from a three-day swim meet, and his parents told him. She's been missing for two days."

Oh. So, not a sleepover she failed to mention, or a detention she covered up.

"He wants us to go to Edinburgh and help find her." Cameron trudges up the beach, his coveralls tied at the waist.

I jam my wet, sandy feet into my sneakers and catch up with him. "What does Jamie think *we* can do that the police can't?"

The ferry blasts its horn, and we both turn to watch it dock.

"His parents are refusing to report it to the police because apparently the timing is awkward," Cameron says. "So, turns out there's a lot we can do, but we're going to need Ruby. And Aisha. And a favor from Padma."

ACKNOWLEDGMENTS

Writing can be a lonely pursuit and I am grateful for everyone who supported me. First, thanks go to my writing buddies Tracy Fox and Danielle Glavin. Tracy is the first to hear my story ideas and plotting conundrums, usually while we're walking. Danielle, who lives an ocean away, is the person I turn to when I need a knot unravelled or a story premise knocked into shape (I deeply suspect she has a magical brain). You are both amazing human beings and writers and I am lucky to have found you.

Thanks also to the great and generous authors Ali Bryan and Aisha Bushby, who cheered me on, and to editor Sandra McIntyre, who guided me through the very first draft.

Writing communities have been a tremendous resource as well as a place to connect with other writers. In particular, I would like to thank Jericho Writers, Write Mentor and the Alexandra Writers' Society.

Thanks also to the Canadian Society for Children's Authors, Illustrators and Performers (CANSCAIP). Winning the CANSCAIP prize for an unpublished YA novel was the portal that transported this story into the hands of Yasemin Uçar, Editorial Development Director at Kids Can Press. Thank you, Yasemin, for seeing its potential.

Patricia Ocampo, Senior Editor, is the book's fairy godmother, holding its hand through the maze of approvals and the one who suggested changing the main setting entirely. Once I'd completed the rewrite, the manuscript moved into the calm and supportive hands of editor Tanya Trafford, who must be able to recite most of the book by now! I had heard copyediting was about as fun as a trip to the dentist. This myth turned out to be false. Jennifer Foster handled the story with great care — no anesthetic required. As Lewis and Cameron's story traveled along the winding pathways of its publishing journey, many other capable hands helped it on its way. Most notably Shannon Swift, production editor; Catherine Dorton, proofreader; and Andrew Dupuis, who designed the brilliant cover and laid out the pages (sorry for all the edits).

The inspiration behind *If We Tell You* was my children, Jonah, Aurelia and Zara. Not their personalities (although people who know my son may recognize Jamie Wallace's big heart) but their staunch protection and championing of one another. *My* greatest champion is my husband, Andrew. From the moment I started writing this book, he was certain it would be published. Someone believing in you is a powerful thing.

And finally, my sister, Fiona, because where would this story be without siblings? When you were twelve and I was ten, you marched into my bedroom threatening to never speak to me ever again if I read one more book. Thank you for dragging me outside and for all the adventures we had.